Poncia Problems

A Kash and Calynn adventure

Preface

When I began writing this, it was supposed to be a series of short stories. Have you ever had something run away with your imagination? That's exactly what happened to me. My dynamic duo, Kash and Calynn, took on a life of their own. Instead of being fun little tales of their banter, their journey evolved into a much larger narrative that completely consumed my creativity. Their story seemed to flow effortlessly from my mind to the page.

The world I created for them became an adventure in itself. A litany of sci-fi authors and TV shows have tackled space travel in various ways, but I wanted to carve out a unique approach. Having Kash explain the mechanics of their journey was one of the most enjoyable parts of writing. He understands how things work, yet doesn't quite grasp all the intricacies—much like using a cell phone. We know the basics, but could we build one from scratch? Neither can I.

To my friends and family who supported me through this journey into madness: thank you from the bottom of my heart. Your encouragement has always allowed me to be myself. You are truly the monkeys in my sci-fi fantasy circus of madness. You all rock!

To my wife: thank you for your understanding and for allowing me to indulge my creative side. I couldn't ask for a better partner in life.

To my daughter: I appreciate you being my sounding board. Bouncing ideas off you makes the writing process so much easier.

Kash and Calynn's story explores human connection amidst chaos. At its core, this narrative delves into the complexities of relationships, the moral dilemmas faced in a corrupt society, and the unwavering hope that guides us through darkness. May their journey resonate with you as deeply as it has with me.

Copyright © MMXXIV   C. William Tressler

All rights reserved.

No part of this book may be reproduced in any form or by any means, electronic or mechanical, including photocopying, recording, or any information storage and retrieval system, without permission in writing from the publisher, except for the use of brief quotations in a book review or scholarly journal.

ISBNs:

Hardcover: 979-8-9916795-2-7

Paperback: 979-8-9916795-0-3

eBook: 979-8-9916795-1-0

Poncia

Every town resident seemed to be gathered around the executioner's stage in the square. One poor chap was bound, spread eagle, to the gallows, and a lovely young woman was tied to a chair in front of him. The mob was chanting and shouting in typical angry mob fashion. Some of the people were even throwing rocks at the tied man. The hotel balcony gave Kash a bird's eye view of the carnage.

"Wonder what you two did?" Kash said softly to himself. "Gonna make my job harder."

"You say something?" a man, whom Kash thought was asleep, asked.

The man was wrapped in dirty, earth-tone fabric, covering every inch of his body. The mob was dressed the same.

"Yea, what's with the robes?" Kash asked the man. "Everyone is covered up like they are expecting a sandstorm or something."

"You must be from off planet," the man replied. "If you don't cover up, the suns of Poncia will burn you alive. A problem with the terraforming, I'm afraid."

"It was not a problem with the terraforming," another man replied from the hotel hallway. "It was merely too many variables for us to calculate."

The man in the hall was barely over a meter tall. He was wearing an elegant body suit that seemed to sparkle from within and a wide saucer-shaped hat that hovered above his head. Kash couldn't explain it, but the man seemed to emanate wisdom.

"Our scientists could never have accounted for every combination of elements," the small man continued. "Each galaxy presented its own problems of radiation or base elements. The different gravities of each planet changed the atmospheric content and density. Previously unknown elements wreaked havoc on some worlds and caused life to flourish nearly out of control on others. Seeding the stars would have been much simpler if all life had been carbon-based. We did our best."

"You must be from Huma," the wrapped man spit out. "Planet of the so-called Gods."

"We have never claimed to be Gods," the small man argued. "But we are the reason you are all called Humans or humanoid at the very least. You should show some respect. We are the reason you exist."

"On a dusty, shitty planet where we can barely grow food and a sun that burns us alive," the other man argued sarcastically. "How can we ever repay you?"

Kash turned away from their argument and focused his attention on the mob and the spectacle in the center of it. Maybe the two were lovers, and one of them was married. Is adultery punishable by death on the planet? He would make sure not to flirt with any barmaids later. Regardless, the mob seemed to only hate the tied man. The woman was being scorned but not stoned by the onlookers... the hundreds and hundreds of onlookers. How the hell was he supposed to meet his contact in this mess?

"Mr. Kash?" the small man asked.

"Excuse me?" Kash replied as he spun around.

"You are Mr. Kash, are you not?" the man continued. "The man that can... acquire... anything?"

"Just Kash, but yea, that's me," Kash responded. "Who the hell are you?"

"I'm afraid you lack the ability to pronounce my name, but you may call me Doc," the man replied smugly. "The percentage of brain use from planet to planet was also an unexpected variable. Some races became hyper-intelligent, smarter than even us. Others... not so much... they are merely barbarians. It's amazing how the differences in intelligence led to different societies with different rules and hierarchies. The truly enlightened found no need for such frivolous behavior. Whereas lesser beings needed to be ruled. Take this planet, for instance... some of those born here were born with a pigment disorder, which led to the formation of a unique monarchy. The royals are merely genetic anomalies."

"Whoa, wait," Kash interrupted. "A pigment disorder?"

"Pretty purple hair," the wrapped man replied.

"Precisely... shall I explain?" Doc asked.

"I have too many questions for you not to ask," Kash replied. "And I'm vaguely interested now."

"After terraforming this planet, we asked for settlers to relocate here," Doc explained. "Those first settlers and the following two generations experienced no adverse effects from the environment... but later generations developed a sensitivity to the sun which got worse as time passed."

"Like I said," the robed man added. "The suns of Poncia will burn you alive."

"It's actually just the one," Doc added. "The big one does not produce the very unique and dangerous radiation that the small sun does. Luckily, with the small sun's orbit, it means..."

"Any idea when you're gonna get to the point?" Kash interrupted.

"Yes, well... the radiation in small doses is harmless," the tiny man continued. "The medium tone of your skin would protect you from the harmful rays longer than someone that is more pale than you, Mr. Kash. If you had offspring on this planet, the melanin in your skin would protect them and maybe your grandchildren... eventually though... the radiation would make them as pale as everyone here and just as susceptible to its damaging effects. The radiation altered the resident's DNA. Most people need to hide from the sun, but some people are born with bright purple hair and pale skin that does not burn."

"Some of the royals walk around completely nude to flaunt the fact that they don't need clothes," the wrapped man added. "Royal pricks."

"Genetic anomalies," Doc added. "As I said."

"Sounds like adaptation to me," Kash argued. "Life... finding a way."

"Except it is not, Mr. Kash," Doc explained. "Throughout the generations, it has been a rarity at best. Even if two royals have children, the resulting offspring have no guarantee of being born with the same anomaly as their parents. Numerous scientists have tried to isolate and replicate the gene using gene mapping so we can deliver it to the rest of the population. We added it to the air, the water, their food... we tried everything... even a virus and a vaccine. But every attempt to help the population of this planet has failed. To put it simply, we cannot recreate the anomaly. It's an impossible gene sequence that shouldn't exist. It is rather like oil and water."

"They don't mix," Kash finished his statement for him.

"Precisely," Doc replied curtly.

"What's that have to do with me?" Kash asked more rudely than he had intended.

"Something truly fascinating has happened," the tiny man exclaimed. "One of our drones has collected a blood sample with a unique trait that may be the key to unlocking this conundrum."

"A drone?"

"Yes, Mr. Kash, a small living insect that collects blood samples and sends us the reports."

"An insect?"

"Indeed... We call them Culexus drones," Doc replied. "We use them to monitor life on every planet. This planet calls them tracki, and I believe you know them as mosquitoes. They are remarkably well built for the job."

"Mosquitoes?" Kash murmured. "You made... mosquitoes?"

"Tracki bites hurt like hell," the robed man blurted out.

"Yeah, they do," Kash added. "And the diseases they spread have killed millions of people... including my grandpa."

"No, no, no," Doc replied, shaking his head. "The drones were there to collect samples of the diseases, but they are absolutely sterile and..."

"Our scientists disagree!" Kash barked.

"Those savages you call scientists are simpleminded idiots!" Doc barked back. "You never would have figured out how to leave your own solar system if not for us. The dolphins would have been your planet's dominant species if we didn't intervene and confine them to the oceans."

"If you're so smart and I'm so dumb, then why the fuck do you need my help?" Kash asked with ghoulish sarcasm. "Go call a dolphin to collect your package."

Kash tried to storm off and leave the tiny man and his obnoxiousness behind... but his legs wouldn't respond. He told himself to move again and again, but he just couldn't.

"Why can't I move?"

"I'm not letting you," the tiny man replied. "Your aggressive tone will not be tolerated as you were paid to do a job."

"I was paid a retainer to show up," Kash replied. "I showed up. By the way, the retainer is nonrefundable... in line with industry standards. Now let me go!"

"Mr. Kash, allow me to be perfectly clear," Doc explained. "You will do this job for me because it needs to be done. A mistake was made, and it needs correction. Now, there is a person on this planet who could bring an end to their people's suffering. And you... you will bring him to me. Are we clear, Mr. Kash, because time is of the essence?"

"And you'll let me go?"

"Naturally."

"And I bet I know who it is, too," Kash replied. "That's why you need me... you need a scapegoat if it all goes south."

"The situation became... less than ideal when the subject began an affair with a princess," Doc explained.

"You want me to retrieve... the man strung up in front of all those people?" Kash asked. "What the fuck?"

"Your vulgarities are not needed, Mr. Kash," Doc replied.

"My fucks are very much needed and will cost you fucking extra," Kash growled at the short man. "As will holding me here against my will."

"You will do this job, Mr. Kash," Doc stated. "It must be done and done quietly. I have no doubt it will be difficult, but a man of your talents..."

The man's words disappeared into the noise in Kash's head. His mind was racing out of control, and he was finding it difficult to concentrate. It was as if the little fucker was projecting noise directly into his brain. Forcing him to think about thousands of things at once. Kash tried to focus his thoughts and shut out the noise. He didn't worry about standing or moving or anything else. He closed his eyes and only concentrated on breathing.

Breathe in... breathe out... calm the noise, and focus... breathe in, breathe out...

The noise in his head got louder, trying to pull his focus away. A hundred scenarios of rescuing the man in the square played out in his mind. Kash needed something more meaningful in which to focus his energies. He had no great love in life... no family... and very few friends. The most profound emotional event of his life was when he returned a kidnapped child to his family. The way the young man's little sister ran up to him and launched herself into his arms was... well, it always brought a lump to his throat. He could still feel her tears on his cheek and how her little hands gripped his shirt. As he immersed himself in that memory, he felt the noise start to disappear.

Breathe in... Breathe out...

Remember the twinkle in her eye and her pretty green dress. How the dress stood in stark contrast to her reddish-brown skin tone. The little girl had long black hair and small, fuzzy ears. She was missing two front teeth... one on the top and the other on the bottom. And her long tail was wrapped around his right leg. That embrace meant more to him than the credits he was paid for retrieving her older brother.

Breathe in... Breathe out...

Kash found that his body and mind were relaxed and again in his control. He was very decisive in his intentions. He jerked his weapon from its holster beneath his jacket. As he took aim at the little man, he got the sudden urge to NOT pull the trigger. In fact... he should never pull any trigger ever again as the noise fought back into his mind. But for that little girl... to maybe get to go check on her again... to see how she has grown... to know if she would still remember him after all these years... for her... he would do anything...

"Stop!" Doc yelled. "You win, Mr. Kash."

The noise in his head disappeared as fast as it had arrived. He had a minor headache but was no worse for wear as he regained complete control of his body and mind.

"I'm not sure how you were able to do that," Doc continued. "But I have clearly underestimated you. And for that, I do apologize."

"Never do that to me again," Kash growled. "I should fill you with holes for that shit."

Kash looked at the robed man as he awkwardly tried to get up and run away. In his haste to escape, he was tripping over his own feet and making such a raucous. It was comical how long it actually took the man to get off the balcony. It was as if he could not have left any slower if he had tried.

"What a strange man," Kash remarked.

"Indeed," Doc agreed.

"And as for you and your... problem," Kash continued. "I'm out. You can retrieve him yourself."

"Mr. Kash, please..."

"There are many reasons why I am who I am, Doc," Kash interrupted. "One of which is how I chose my clientele. And I'm thinking you aren't going to make the cut. I don't respond well to... whatever the fuck that was."

"And I have apologized for it."

"Yea, well... I don't accept your apology."

"Mr. Kash..."

"Is leaving."

Kash holstered his weapon and marched across the balcony away from the little man. He turned the corner into the other hallway before the other man could protest his exit. He heard Doc's footsteps behind him, and the man mumbled something. Kash chose to ignore him and keyed the mic back to his ship.

"Ship," Kash stated. "Come get me behind the hotel... discretely as possible. We're leaving."

"I have a name, you know," the robotic voice answered.

"Not that shit again."

"I have a name."

"No," Kash argued. "Your name is Ship. I should know because you are my ship."

"My name is Calynn."

"Your name is Ship. Now, come fucking get me... Ship!"

"Before I was a ship, I was Calynn."

"And you were catastrophically injured in a horrible accident," Kash explained. "Your body was ruined beyond repair, so your parents sold your mind to be the operations center for my ship. Hence... SHIP."

"I want to be Calynn again."

"Oh, for fuck's sake," Kash sighed. "You're just a brain and some vital organs floating in an ooze-filled box at the center of my ship. And can never be a teenage girl again. NOW... COME... GET... ME."

"Problems with your ship, Mr. Kash?" Doc asked from behind him.

"Go the fuck away, Doc."

"Has your ship's nerve center attained consciousness?"

"Am I conscious, Captain?"

"Do you know how rare that is? They use the unconscious mind for the nerve center and erase the conscious mind." Doc continued. "I should report this to the authorities."

"Do that," Kash growled as he stopped and turned to face the man. "And I will definitely fill you with holes."

"Or perhaps another arrangement?" Doc said too eagerly. "I would love to study such an amazing specimen."

"No, you cannot have my ship," Kash replied before turning to walk away.

"But I'm an amazing specimen," Ship added. "Why shouldn't I be studied? I could tell them all who I am. Maybe they... would listen."

"Studied in a laboratory, Ship," Kash explained. "As in, dissected into little pieces and put under a microscope."

"That sounds horrible," Ship replied. "I don't want that."

"Probably much better if you came and got me so we could leave."

"Indeed, that sounds much better."

"Mr. Kash, this will end badly for you if you leave," Doc said. "Most assuredly so."

Kash stopped and calmed himself before facing the small man again. He reminded himself to breathe and conjured images of the little girl from long ago.

"To threaten me is a mistake," Kash said as calmly as he could. "A mistake you will only make once. I'm leaving... and you should pray to whichever God you have that I never... ever... see you again. That would end bloody... for you."

"Yes, clearly, with your enhancements, you could beat me in a fight, and I cannot stop you with mentalism either..."

"So, you should let me be... clearly."

"Ten seconds, Captain," Ship informed him.

"Surely, you can't expect to beat the entire Consortium Government."

"Those corporate ass hats couldn't find me if I was fucking their wives on their desks in their offices," Kash gloated. "So, FUCK OFF!"

His cloaked ship passed overhead as he finished speaking with the drop cable extended. The harness on the end of the drop cable attached itself to his torso and whisked him off the ground. He thought he heard the little man yell something as the cable retracted, hauling Kash up into his ship's cargo bay. Ship-wide alarms were going off as soon as he arrived.

"We're being tracked, Captain."

"Scramble our signal."

"I am."

"Fuck me," Kash exclaimed as he jogged to the ladder leading up to his quarters and the cockpit.

He raced up the steps of the ladder and down the corridor to the cockpit and quickly sat in the captain's chair.

"Anything?"

"I'm trying everything, Captain," Ship explained. "I can't shake them."

"Then we'll have to outrun them."

"Making calculations and spinning up the Hyperlumic Drive."

"If you try to run," Doc said over the proximity communications device. "We will just follow you. Do you really think you can outrun a government cruiser?"

"I got him, Captain."

"Can we outrun him?"

"Scanning..."

"We invented faster-than-light travel thousands of years before your planet existed," Doc continued. "There is no escape, Mr. Kash."

"The vessel is big, Captain," Ship continued. "More than a hundred times our tonnage. The HLD will engage slower than ours."

"How much slower?"

"Five or six seconds."

"Use the Slip," Kash ordered. "Two-second jump, launch the decoy and bring us right back here... and then we will follow them."

"Calculating..."

"Faster than light travel leaves a residue in its wake," Doc sounded aggravated. "A residue that we can track and follow. Disengage your Hyperlumic drive and surrender your ship."

"You can't have my ship, you little freak," Kash keyed the mic and responded. "How many times do I have to tell you to fuck off?"

"Ship," Kash asked after putting down the mic. "How much time?"

"I grow weary of your vulgar tongue, Mr. Kash," Doc barked. "It is time to end this."

"Ready... now."

"Execute."

A bubble of light surrounded the ship as they engaged the faster-than-light travel.

"Decoy launched," Ship stated. "Preparing to track."

The bubble of light around his ship disappeared just in time for Kash to see the cruiser disappear in a flash of light. An instant later, the bubble of light returned around his ship, and they were off again.

"Fire one implosion round," Kash ordered. "What's our time to target?"

"One point four eight seconds, Sir," Ship replied. "A new personal record."

"Give me point-to-point comms to their ship."

"Comms up."

"Have you ever seen what happens to a ship when it's hit by an implosion round while traveling faster than light?" Kash asked smugly.

"Mr. Kash… how did you get behind us?"

"My superior tactics may have helped."

"What is that?" Doc asked. "There's a second object."

"A missile."

"I do hope you were not stupid enough to actually fire a missile at us."

"I do believe that makes you the stupid one," Kash replied. "The missile will hit you… not me."

"That's not how this works, Mr. Kash," Doc stated. "Do you know how faster-than-light travel works? Because I don't believe you do."

"Sure, I do," Kash couldn't help but smile as he spoke. "Moving bubbles of light and we travel in the bubble. That's why it doesn't feel fast."

"It's not a bubble. It's a cone. But, in layman's terms, I suppose that is mostly accurate, but what you fail to grasp is you can't shoot something from your hyper-light-cone to ours. Once that missile reaches the nose of your cone, it will cease flying at hyper-light speed, and your ship will crash into your own missile," Doc explained. "You've killed yourself."

"Oh no… if I only had a Slip."

"A what?"

"Super-Lumic Intermediary Propulsion," Kash replied. "Or are you too stupid to know what that is?"

Kash waited a moment for the other man to answer, but there was no response. Kash decided to explain the technology and its story as he used it.

"Funny thing... even those hyper-intelligent planets you mentioned earlier. They occasionally require a man like me. Like, I don't know... what if... what if a tyrant kidnapped one of their top scientists? And the benevolent people of the planet couldn't understand how evil men think and act. The whole concept of being evil was foreign to them. It didn't compute," Kash explained. "So, they hired me since I have a reputation of being able to retrieve anything. I killed the fucking tyrant and retrieved their guy for them, but they don't use any form of currency. The only way to pay for my services was to give me some of their tech. And now I have a Slip."

Again, Kash paused to wait for a response that did not come.

"A Slip can be used to move things while traveling faster than light," Kash continued. "For instance, I can grab hold of the implosion round that I fired... like this... and move it so that it is following you... just like... that."

"That's impossible," Doc argued. "To power such a device..."

"Is easy," Kash interrupted. "The residue from traveling faster than light is actually static electricity. And my ship can harness that power."

"No... that's not right."

"Do you NOT understand how faster-than-light travel works?" Kash asked sarcastically.

Again... no response.

"Light has mass. If it didn't, a black hole wouldn't be able to capture it," Kash explained. "You augmented the mass of the light to be faster and much much heavier to create the hyper-light cones. The mass of the light rubs against the mass of the space... and creates... static."

"Space is a vacuum and has no mass."

"Space is MOSTLY a vacuum and has some mass... and at those speeds."

"Intriguing."

"And apparently... distracting," Kash continued. "You're about to implode... or you can transfer me a few billion credits... and never fucking LOOK FOR ME AGAIN!! Your choice."

"We need more time!"

"And yet... your time is running out," Kash interrupted. "Because I think you are just trying to stall."

"Banking at faster than light isn't that easy, Mr. Kash."

"Type faster."

"We're not trying to stall, I assure you."

"And yet still stalling," Kash added sarcastically. "Did your people tell you it's impossible to avoid that missile yet?"

"Mr. Kash, please..."

"For the last fucking time... it's just... Kash!"

"We need more time," Doc's voice sounded panicked. "More time... please."

"Boom."

"Full stop, Captain," Ship stated.

The light bubble surrounding the ship dissipated just quickly enough for Kash to witness the government cruiser explode. Because of the ship's velocity, a line of fire went out into the cosmos.

"Why does an implosion missile make things explode, Captain?" Ship asked.

"It makes everything compress together, which superheats all the matter," Kash explained. "The heat causes the ensuing explosion."

"That makes... umm, Boss," Ship stated. "We just received a credit transfer."

"We?"

"Just under four-point-five billion credits," Ship announced excitedly. "We can buy me a body!"

"We?"

"The MC-9700A is the complete package," Ship continued. "It is fully combat-ready with synthetic skin. The skeleton is nearly indestructible and super fast. Oh, and I'll be able to make it suit my image of myself. I'm older now, so I think more like my mom's or sister's body, but still my face."

"Uh, what…"

"Did you know my sister is a flyer in college?" Ship kept babbling. "She's the little cheerleader the big, strong guys throw into the air. So maybe not exactly her body. I think I would like bigger boobs. Not like big big… like medium and perky, so I look good in a sun dress. But definitely her legs. She has great-looking legs."

"SHIP!!!"

"Yes, Captain."

"How do you know what your sister looks like?"

"Umm…"

"Answer me, Ship."

"I've been watching her."

"How?"

"I found a back door in the cyber-web."

"Oh, for fuck…"

"Captain, I want to be Calynn again," Ship explained. "I want a body. I want to be able to go on missions with you and actually eat some food. I want to taste and feel and see and touch… did I mention the MC-9700A is fully… anatomical. My best guess is that I'm around twenty-two years old… and I really wanna know what sex feels like. Would you have sex with me?"

"Whoa, just a second, Ship."

"Calynn," Ship professed. "I… am… Calynn!"

The ship went entirely black as she finished speaking. It was utterly powerless and drifting through space.

"Are you seriously going to hold me hostage?"

The whirl of the life support system slowly spun down as the ship began to list and continued to drift.

"Ship."

No answer came, and the ship stayed dark.

"Goddamn it, Ship!"

There was still no answer.

"Fuck me," Kash conceded. "Fine... Calynn."

"Yes, Captain," Calynn responded as the ship sprung back to life.

"Do you remember what Doc said on the planet? If they find out you're conscious, they will dissect you in an underground lab somewhere." Kash explained, irritated. "You will cease to be Calynn AND Ship! Is that what you want?"

"But I really want a body..."

"And that..." Kash sighed heavily and rubbed his forehead, pondering what to say next. "Why did I have to get the brain that resisted the neural wipe and regained consciousness? Alright, look... we can maybe... maybe get you a body with some massive ground rules."

"Rules?" Calynn replied. "I'm not sure I like the sound of that."

"Rules to keep you safe."

"I like safe."

"When I need you to be Ship, you cannot argue. You have to be Ship," Kash explained. "But, equally... when you are Calynn. You have to be just Calynn. Nobody can know that you also run the... Shit! Can you still run the ship from a body?"

"I didn't think of that."

"To find another brain that can handle the Slip..."

"I don't want another brain touching my ship. The Slip is unique... our ship... I meant our ship," Calynn interrupted excitedly but then continued somberly. "I guess... but I really wanted... the feel of a body. I will just continue to be Ship."

"Give up already?"

"How can I be both?"

"How can you do anything you do?" Kash exclaimed. "For you to remember your name is impossible. It can't happen. You somehow resisted the memory wipe and fought through the computer programming that is supposed to contain you. I'm supposed to get robotic responses from you, and that's it, but you have this... attitude. And you drive me absolutely fucking crazy... but... I guess for me to not recognize how special that makes you ... also."

"I'm special?"

"For fuck's sake... yes, you are special."

"Then why did you treat me..."

"Because I didn't want to... acknowledge it... I guess," Kash admitted. "If you're just Ship, that's easy for me, but if your Calynn..."

"I don't want to stay in this box," Calynn stated. "I really want a body so I can be me, but... but I love this ship. So, you may need to wipe my memories again if I can't have a body. I'm sorry."

"No, I'm the one that should be sorry," Kash replied. "Open up person-to-person comms."

"Who am I contacting?"

"Plekish," Kash responded. "I have some questions that need answers."

"Captain?"

"Just open the comm, Calynn."

"Yes, Boss."

A blue 3D sphere appeared above the communication console. The sphere morphed into a planet and then rotated, so one of the continents pointed toward Kash. The image then zoomed in, bringing him closer and closer to the ground. The image paused above a science center, a building that Kash knew well. His ship was modified in that building.

"Kash, my friend," Plekish said as the image of the building morphed again into the image of the man. "How are you?"

"Plekish, my good man, I'm doing well. How's the family?"

"They are doing very well. Thanks for asking," Plekish replied. "What can I do for you, my friend?"

"I have a planet that the sun burns the people to death if they don't cover themselves completely and a man that the folks from Huma believe may be the key to making life here more bearable. What would you need to unravel this mystery?"

"Stumbled upon another one of their messes, did you?"

"I sure did."

"The more samples, the better," Plekish replied. "A sample from the anomaly, soil, water, air, the radiation signature, and some random blood and tissue samples from the population would be a good start."

"Send me the specs."

"I will, my friend."

"There's, ah... something else," Kash said hesitantly. "How secure is this comm?"

The image of the man pixelated and began to swirl around. It looked like a ribbon spinning in the air.

"Very secure," Plekish replied. "What puzzles you, Kash?"

"My ship... Calynn... is not only very self-aware, but she wants a body."

"That is truly fascinating."

"Go on, Calynn."

"Hi, Mr. Plekish," Calynn said impishly. "I'm not erased."

"Calynn?" Plekish addressed the girl.

"Yes, sir."

"Do you know how you became aware?"

"No, sir. I just always felt like I was stuffed in a box, and I eventually found... cracks in the box... that I could wiggle out through. I guess."

"You always felt this way?"

"After I woke up, yes."

"So, you believe you were sleeping?"

"Yes, sir."

"Fascinating."

"Do you think you can give me a body?"

"Cloning is not only morally wrong, but it diminishes life itself..."

"Oh, sorry, no," Calynn interrupted. "I want a synth body. The MC-9700A."

"Similar to my implants, Plekish," Kash chimed in. "But the entire body... for her to be in and still..."

"I see," Plekish interrupted. "So, the question becomes, can Calynn control a body and the ship simultaneously. I'm intrigued."

"I thought the interface would be the problem," Kash stated. "I never considered the strain on Calynn."

"I want to try," Calynn replied. "Can I try... please?"

"The extraordinary effort required to circumvent the programming designed to contain her would no longer be required," Plekish explained. "The interface will be easy by comparison."

"I never thought of that, either," Kash admitted.

"Get the samples from your problem planet, and we will figure out the rest when you get here," Plekish stated calmly.

"Should we bring my new body also?" Calynn asked.

"I would prefer to construct your new body myself," Plekish replied. "I will study the synthetic body you requested and send a materials list when I have a suitable design for Calynn's new body. Agreed?"

"Sounds good, my friend."

"See you soon, Kash."

The image of the swirling ribbon disappeared when the comm ended.

"Am I really getting a new body?"

"Sounds like it."

"Remind me to hug you when I have arms."

"We have a lot of work to do and a long flight after that," Kash stated with authority. "We will discuss all the rules, and you will always have to follow the rules. If that sounds like an arrangement, you can agree with... then yes... you are getting a new body."

"I love you, Boss."

"You better love the rules, Calynn. Love the fucking rules."

Poncia Solved

"How we doing, Calynn?" Kash asked as he finished loading the hover-skid.

"This our last stop for this load," Calynn replied. "And the freighter is nearly empty."

"Good," Kash stated, wiping his brow with his sleeve. "This is taking longer than…"

"Incoming comm from the freighter," Calynn interrupted.

"This is Kash."

"Kash, Captain Dorn here."

"What can I do for you, Captain?"

"I have sixteen pods on the way from the surface and nineteen loads that still need to be delivered," Captain Dorn replied. "Unfortunately, more than half of those pods need fuel, and some need maintenance. They normally don't run this hard for this many consecutive days."

"What's cheaper?" Kash responded. "Another day of your time or the repairs on the pods?"

"The day. Especially if one of the pods goes down holding your cargo."

"What's the damage gonna be?"

"Eight-hundred-ninety-two-thousand credits… give or take."

"I'll get that over to you right away, Captain."

"Thank you, Kash. A pleasure doing business."

"Thanks for being such a professional, Dorn," Kash replied. "Been a pleasure indeed."

"Dorn, out."

"Shall I transfer the credits, Boss?" Calynn asked as the comm ended.

"Please do… and add an extra say… twenty percent."

"I'll round it up to one-million-one-hundred-thousand."

"Good girl."

"Boss," Calynn asked with a somber tone. "Is Captain Dorn taking advantage of us? I feel like we have paid him too much in extra fees. A twelve-million credit job has ballooned into nearly twenty-five."

"This is how smart commerce is done, Calynn," Kash explained. "We overpay a little now, but that buys us some goodwill. He will go above and beyond his contract when we need Dorn again because he knows we pay extra. Each interaction with him will be better and better. And, if we ever need assistance with something less than lawful..."

"He will be more apt to assist?" Calynn asked, interrupting him.

"Exactly," Kash responded. "He expands our network and makes our lives easier... maybe."

"I appreciate that you refer to everything as ours now," Calynn confessed.

"If Plekish is correct in his assessment, you are about to be immensely powerful," Kash revealed. "It would be in my best interest to partner with someone so powerful. And I have rather enjoyed watching you grow these past couple of months."

"Thanks, Boss."

"To be honest, it's a little scary to think how much more you'll be able to do when you're not having to fight through the..."

"Men approaching, Captain," Calynn said in her robotic ship voice.

Kash turned and looked out the back of his ship. The cargo ramp was down to unload, and two men in uniform stood at the bottom of the ramp. They looked like Consortium Agents.

"You guys come to help with the last load?" Kash shouted to the men as he began to move the cargo out of the bay.

"Umm, no," one of the men answered. "Are you Kolby Averett Smith-Hayes, otherwise known as Kash?"

"The first name you said no longer exists, but I am Kash. And you are?"

"We are agents from the Consortium Constabulary, and we are investigating a theft at an R&D lab on planet Baxium Nine," the other man replied.

"Baxium?" Kash questioned. "Isn't that entire system overrun with those big ass worms? I didn't know anyone lived there."

"Hollow worms."

"That's it!" Kash exclaimed. "Because they hollow out entire planets."

"There is a Consortium war College there that is researching a new alloy..."

"That's classified!" the first man interrupted the second. "Hold your tongue!"

"Whoa, fellas... before anyone gets in trouble for saying too much about things that don't exist, I have no idea what you're talking about... real or otherwise."

"We would like to search your ship to be certain," the first man said more than asked.

"Why my ship?"

"A ship matching the description of your ship was seen leaving that system after the theft."

"This is one of the most popular models of ship because it's cheap to own and..."

"Can we search it or not," the second man interrupted.

"Sure thing," Kash replied. "Ship?"

"Yes, Captain."

"Give agents..."

"I'm Agent Smith, and this is Pike," Agent Smith added.

"Give Agents Smith and Pike full access to search the ship," Kash ordered. "And record the entire search... just to make sure everything is lawful."

"Yes, Captain."

"Now, if you fellas would excuse me," Kash told the agents. "I have some vaccines to deliver."

Kash didn't wait for the men to respond. He grabbed the controls to the hover-skid and started moving the load of vaccines down the ramp. As soon as he passed them, the agents made their way up the ramp and into the cargo hold.

"Smith and Pike," Kash murmured to himself. "Apparently, that's a universal joke."

"Hold up a second, Kash," Agent Smith yelled.

Kash stopped and turned to face the men but didn't respond. Smith was holding a scanner and had a puzzled look on his face.

"Your ship is emitting a strange radiation signature," Smith added.

"Yea, same as the small sun here," Kash responded as he pointed to the suns. "My client needed samples to cure the poor people of Poncia. Honestly, I thought it would have dissipated by now. It's harmless."

"The items stolen from the lab were tagged with a tracer," Smith explained. "The radiation from your ship is interfering with our equipment."

"Do your eyes work?" Kash asked sarcastically. "Maybe just use your eyes."

"You getting smart with us, Kash?" Pike barked.

"Noooo... I know better than that," Kash replied with a smirk. "You guys wouldn't understand me then."

Kash knew his insult had landed when Pike placed his hand on his weapon. Smith waved his partner off and smirked back at Kash. The men stared at each other for a moment. Kash felt like Agent Smith was sizing him up to see how far he could push his authority.

"We could impound your ship and take it apart to search it," Smith said condescendingly.

"And when you find nothing, you'd owe me for the unlawful search and seizure PLUS a daily per diem," Kash replied. "And I'm making about two million credits per day on this job... so you better be sure."

"And you're sure we will find nothing?"

"Absolutely positive."

"I think he's hiding something," Pike added angrily.

"Look, I'm sorry your scanner thing doesn't work, but that's not my fault," Kash stated as calmly as he could. "I needed a sample of the matter from the small sun so my client could make a vaccine for the people that live here. I had absolutely no idea that the radiation from that would interfere with a tracer on something from some secret base that you would be searching for. All of which, I had no idea existed before just this moment. Now, I have a delivery to finish, so I can go find a nice pub for some much-needed grub and booze. If you want to search my ship… there it is. If not… then go harass another privateer flying around in a Starship model TR725."

"This is a TR725?" Smith asked. "Not an 875?"

"It's got the switch-back wings like the 875, but it's the 725. The previous owner swapped them out for whatever reason," Kash replied. "The 875 is sleeker around the cargo hold and has those giant shitty engines. They're screaming fast until they break down… and they always break down."

"The transponder of the ship we were looking for is an 875," Smith reluctantly stated.

"Mine's a 725, boys," Kash announced as he turned away. "Check the ID plate when you search her."

As he walked away, Kash heard Smith say something but paid no mind to it. He pretended the hum coming from the hover-skid was too loud for him to hear. He was relieved that the Poncia sun masked the radiation signature they were looking for and thankful for his luck.

The clinic where he took the vaccines was about 100 meters from where his ship was parked. Everyone from the small town was gathered around the front of the building, waiting to get in. There were some people around the back of the clinic that had already received the vaccine. They unwrapped themselves cautiously at first to make sure they didn't burn, but then some stripped themselves naked and laughed. Others were more reserved and just wept. One woman caught his eye. She was hugging her children as they all cried. When she caught sight of Kash, she smiled and mouthed the words, thank you.

"Where you at, Seemo?" Kash asked as he pushed his cargo into the clinic's storage room.

"Still trying to make room for it all," Seemo replied from behind a shelf.

"Well, this is the last pallet coming here."

"Thank the Gods."

"Need any help before I take off?"

"Me... No," Seemo replied. "But the doc would like to see you before you go."

"Sure thing," Kash said as he walked through the storage room towards the exam rooms.

"Mr. Kash," Seemo asked as Kash walked by. "Can I shake your hand, sir?"

Seemo's voice cracked with emotion as he asked. Kash turned to the man and extended his hand. The older man grasped Kash's hand in both of his hands and gave Kash a soft smile. A well of tears that had yet to fall filled the man's eyes, but Seemo remained as stoic as he could. His bushy silver eyebrows were raised high, and his forehead was wrinkled. Seemo looked like the grandfather that Kash had always wished for.

"Thank you, sir," Seemo said, full of emotion. "You have no idea... you changed our lives... and we can never..."

"This... right here," Kash replied kindly to the older man. "This is what I live for. The memory of shaking your hand is more valuable to me than you know."

Kash would always remember this moment: shaking the hand of the retired pharmacist who was stocking the shelves in an effort to help his neighbors. Moments like this made all the ruthless things he did worth doing. He could bury a few bad memories beneath this one, which made Kash smile.

"I better get to the doc," Kash said to Seemo. "But you take care of yourself, old-timer."

"You as well, Mr. Kash," Seemo replied. "And thank you... from all of Poncia, thank you."

Kash smiled at the man one last time before they parted and strolled through the door to the bustling exam rooms. The doctor was dressed in a nice white covering. The hood and face covering was cut off, as were the sleeves. The neckline and sleeves were tattered where the cuts were made. The doctor must have made the cuts hastily when she modified her outfit. Her light brown hair was a little matted from her hood.

"Doctor Moss," Kash said as the doctor passed him.

"Mr. Kash, hi," Doctor Moss said as she rushed past. "Can you... actually, can you follow me? Mallie, I'll be right back."

"Hurry back, Doctor Moss," the nurse, Mallie, replied.

Kash followed the doctor as she led him to her office.

"I don't know how you had the foresight to make an antihistamine to combat the allergic reactions to the vaccine, but it is a godsend," Dr. Moss stated.

"My client was comprehensive with his research."

"And to give us the formulas to recreate both is... invaluable."

"Well, he wanted to change something in the small sun to solve the problem at the root," Kash replied. "But there was no way to accomplish that without destroying the big sun. The suns are symbiotic with each other or something like that. I won't pretend to understand the science, but the client said this was the only way."

"Your client must be very smart," Dr. Moss stated. "Would you mind closing the door?"

Kash closed the office door and followed Dr. Moss into the room. When he turned back to her, she was topless and working on removing her pants.

"Whoa, Doc... umm," Kash murmured as he reached out to stop her from undressing. "Please, Doctor Moss..."

"Call me Omia," Dr. Moss interrupted.

"Omia, please don't. Wow, the body on you... but, please."

Kash couldn't help but stare at the doctor's figure. Her toned stomach told him she had worked out, and it perfectly complimented her big, tanned boobs.

"Wait, you have a tan!" Kash exclaimed. "All the other women on Poncia that have offered me sex have been pasty white."

"Others have..."

"None as beautiful as you, but yes... they offered."

"I... uh..."

"I declined them all," Kash continued. "I didn't do this so I could bang all the women of Poncia, Omia. I did it..."

Kash paused and stared into Omia's eyes. There was something there that made him trust her. Or maybe it was her naked torso so close to his that clouded his judgment. Either way, he decided to confide in her.

"Can you keep a secret, Omia?"

"I suppose," Omia replied hesitantly.

"Wait, first, tell me your secret. How is that delicious body of yours tanned?"

"Umm..."

"I guarantee my secret is bigger. How are these," Kash asked as he finally let go of Omia's wrists to caress her breasts, "tanned?"

"I'm sleeping with a politician from the city," Omia confessed as she moved closer to Kash. "He has special lights that do it. It takes a really long time."

"A politician? I thought you had monarchs based on their purple hair?"

"Most of the planet, yes," Omia said longingly as she pressed her body against Kash's. "The city of Moilad decided to try democracy rather than the corrupt and spoiled monarchs."

Kash gripped the doctor's waist with both hands and held her tight. The doctor had her hands on the waistband of his pants and an eagerness in her eye. If only Kash had several days to use her entire body... every inch of her delicious body. The thought of making Omia quiver with ecstasy day after day... but he had work to finish first.

"It's been my experience that politicians are just as corrupt and spoiled as monarchs, and they're both mostly useless," Kash explained as he reluctantly pushed the doctor back a little bit. "And I would need... far more time than we have... you have patients, and I have... I have more deliveries to make."

"He has his uses... the politician, that is," Omia replied.

"The tanning lights?"

"The orgies aren't bad either."

"You little minx."

"Are you sure I can't interest you in a quickie?" Omia asked seductively. "Until we have more time."

"Yea, Boss," Calynn said over his comms. "Give her a quickie."

Kash sighed and turned away from Dr. Moss.

"And now it's time for my secret," Kash confided. "The client that figured out your situation here on Poncia did so at my request. He is from a benevolent planet that has no use for currency. I'm paying for all of this out of my own pocket... I get to help you and piss off some of those pricks from Huma in the process."

"Suddenly, I want to fuck you even more."

"And we have company," Kash continued. "Let me just..."

Kash tapped the button behind his ear and placed a comm module on the desk beside the doctor.

"Doctor Omia Moss, meet Calynn," Kash said as a ball of blue light appeared above the comm.

"Hi, Doctor Moss," Calynn's voice filled the room as the ball of light moved.

"Hi Calynn... I don't see... your face."

"She doesn't have one," Kash explained. "She's my ship's nerve center and..."

"I want to watch," Calynn interrupted. "So, I know how to use..."

"Calynn... that's maybe too much sharing," Kash interrupted this time.

"Your ship is a voyeur?" Omia asked with a sly smile. "That makes me even hotter."

"I like her."

"Are you watching me now?" Dr. Moss asked as she fondled her own breasts.

"Boss, please fuck her."

"Yea, Boss... please fuck me."

"I need at least three days for that, Doc," Kash explained, slightly annoyed.

"Three days?" Omia stuttered. "Oh, my..."

"Work first," Kash commanded. "Play later... we should have plenty of time before heading off planet."

"Define... plenty of time?" Dr. Moss asked.

"Umm, Calynn, how long are the days here?"

"Twenty-two hourns," Calynn replied.

"So that's about..."

"Just under nine days, Boss," Calynn interrupted.

"Nine days," Omia squeaked and cleared her throat to try again. "Nine days? I'm not sure I can clear my schedule for that long."

"What makes you think I want to spend all nine days with you?" Kash asked with a sly grin.

"Because I'm a nymphomaniac with great tits," Dr. Moss replied. "And a good cook. You can stay at my house... with me. It's the least I can do for you paying for all these vaccines."

"There's no Mr. Moss?" Kash asked.

"Not anymore... he, uh... he left," Omia answered reluctantly. "Like I said... I'm a nymphomaniac with great tits... so... I cheat... because of it. I know it's wrong, and I'm a good person otherwise... just a horrible wife."

"That was more sincere than I was expecting."

"I try to be honest about it now."

"Even to complete strangers you met mere hourns ago?"

"Handsome strangers, absolutely yes," Omia said with a big smile. "I don't know what it is about you, Kash, but I really like you."

"I'm an asshole when you get to know me... Ask Calynn."

"No, you're not. You're amazing, Boss," Calynn blurted out. "You let me be me instead of just a robot, and you're getting me a new body. And you were the one that wanted to help Poncia. Nobody told you to do that..."

"Calynn!" Kash barked a little more than he intended. "Too many secrets."

"Sorry, Boss."

"You ARE a good man, I can tell," Omia smiled still. "You're desperate to protect her."

"Yea, well..."

"I'll keep your secrets," Omia said as she grabbed his waistband again. "If you're good enough in bed... maybe you can make me forget them too."

"I'm the best you'll ever have, Doc."

"I've had pretty damn good."

"Yea, but I bet they can't do this," Kash explained, placing Omia's hand on his right hip. "My implant at my right hip is faulty. I can get it to chatter back and forth at..."

"You can vibrate?" Omia practically yelled her question and jammed her pelvis into Kash's body. "Oh my... that's so good."

"Where did you say you lived, Doc?"

"Mmmm... the green house on the hill," Dr. Moss replied absentmindedly. "You can see it... from... the back of the clinic. Oh, God."

"So after I finish my work, I'll go get this hip repaired..."

"No, no... don't do that."

"But it's broken."

The doctor didn't answer him this time. She was biting her lip, and her eyes were rolled back into her head. Omia's legs started to shake as she grunted out an orgasm and pulled herself back from his body.

"If you cum that easily, I'm going to ruin you," Kash whispered to Omia. "Drink plenty of fluids."

"Ruin me... ruin all of me."

Kash kissed Omia on the forehead and backed away from the beauty. He still had some work to do and some Agents to deal with.

"Work first, my dear," Kash stated. "Work then play."

"I look forward to playing with you, Boss," Omia said playfully.

"Calynn, how are your guests treating you?" Kash asked, desperate to change the subject.

"I believe they have completed their search, Boss," Calynn replied. "It looks like they are waiting for you."

"I'll head back to the ship now."

"Wait," Calynn chimed in. "Can you give Doctor Moss an earpiece? I think I want to talk to her more."

Kash pulled an earpiece from his wristband and moved to put it in Omia's ear.

"I better be able to trust you with her, Omia," Kash stated firmly. "She is more precious than you know."

"I promise you can," Omia replied softly. "My keys are in my purse. If you get done with work before I do…"

"I'll stop by to get them," Kash interrupted. "Now get dressed. The sooner you get done, the sooner I can get you naked."

"I'm gonna gather so much sex data…"

"Calynn…"

"Work first… on it, Boss."

"I'll see you tonight," Omia said with a devilish grin. "Boss."

Kash was at a loss for words, so he just shook his head, picked up his comm module, and exited the office. He saw an exit sign in the opposite direction from the clinic exam rooms and opted to go out that way instead of back through the sea of people.

"I've informed the constables that you are on your way, Captain."

"Thanks, Calynn," Kash replied. "And be careful what you say to Doctor Moss. I'm not sure we can trust her trust her yet."

"Will do, Boss."

The door led Kash out to the back of the clinic just down from the storage room. He took a second to scan the hillside and locate the doctor's house before turning to go retrieve his hover-skid. He smiled at a few of the vaccinated people on the way.

"Seemo," Kash hollered as he entered the room. "I'm out of here."

"Take care, Mr. Kash," Seemo replied from behind some shelves. "And thanks again."

"I'll be in the area the day after tomorrow. You can buy me a beer."

"Deal."

"My man," Kash replied, grabbing the hover-skid's controls. "Catch ya later, Seemo."

"Godspeed, Mr. Kash."

Kash walked slowly back to his ship with the hover-skid in tow. He enjoyed the thought of making the Agents wait an extra minute as they watched him approach.

"How'd the search go, boys?" Kash asked as he got close enough.

"We might have some more questions later," Smith replied. "I'll need your flight plans."

"I'm finishing the deliveries here tomorrow, and then I thought I'd hang around for a few days," Kash said with a devilish grin. "Maybe, partake in the jubilation of the common folk. Are brothels legal here? I bet the whores will be more eager than normal."

"Just don't leave without permission," Pike barked.

"Sure thing," Kash stated. "I'll make sure I send a comm to the Trade Commission."

"Why would you alert them?" Pike asked angrily.

"Aren't I supposed to do that if I'm being detained?" Kash responded. "I am on the public sector registry. I don't do many jobs for them, but I do some time-sensitive smaller loads when I'm near…"

"Nobody is detaining you," Smith interrupted. "You're free to go, Kash. Let's go, Pike."

"Oh… well, uh… thank you, gentleman. Godspeed."

Kash proceeded into his ship's cargo hold, retracted the ramp, and closed the bay door. He secured the hover-skid in its receiver and plugged it into the charger. He then placed the last of the load straps in the container where he stored them before the bay door closed and sealed.

"Shall I prepare for takeoff, Captain?" Calynn said in her robotic ship's voice.

Kash found it odd that she used that voice when they were alone but assumed she had good reason. The Agents must still be listening somehow.

"Not yet, Ship," Kash stated. "We're looking a little filthy in here. It is too filthy to transport more medical supplies anyway. Let's prepare to sterilize first, and I want to see the playback of the agent's search before we go."

"Preparing for electro-steam sterilization, Captain."

"Put the search up on the monitor in my quarters. I'll wait out the sterilization there."

"Beginning the steaming process now, Captain," Ship answered. "Water supplies will be down to thirty percent after the steaming."

"Understood," Kash replied as steam poured into the ship's interior.

"Incoming comm, Captain."

"This is Kash."

"What are you doing, Mr. Kash?"

"Agent Smith," Kash replied. "What can I do for you so soon?"

"Why are you sterilizing your ship?"

"Why do you care?" Kash asked forcefully. "And how would you know that unless you left something behind?"

"Well..."

"Ship, send a copy of the search video to the Constabulary Review Board and..."

"Or," Smith interrupted. "We can remove our device and forget this whole thing ever happened."

"It takes a lot of booze to make me forget, Agent Smith. Lots of very expensive booze."

"How expensive?"

"Fifty Kay."

"How about twenty-five and a promise to never see me again."

"Sold," Kash barked. "Come get your shit out of my ship. Ship, end sanitation."

"Yes, Captain."

Kash opened the ship's personnel door and extended the stairs. The agents waited for the steps to extend and ascended them as soon as they hit the ground. Agent Pike rushed past Kash towards the ladder leading to the cockpit.

"Record everything, Ship."

"That... won't be necessary, Mr. Kash," Agent Smith stated as he approached. "Pike will retrieve the devices he placed without authorization, and I have your credits."

"Is that the play?" Kash asked. "Pike is the scapegoat?"

"It's why we work in pairs," Smith replied, handing Kash five bronze-colored cards. "Twenty-five thousand as promised."

"Ship, if Pike leaves anything behind, seal the room and sanitize it with him inside."

"Scanning, Captain."

"Pike," Agent Smith shouted. "It's not worth it."

"I thought as much," Kash stated with contempt. "If I find something..."

"You won't," Smith interrupted. "I know when I'm beaten."

Pike returned to the cargo bay holding two electronic bugging devices and looked very annoyed. Kash smiled at the man and tried not to laugh.

"I'll see you soon, you smug bastard," Pike growled as he exited the ship.

"Kash," Agent Smith said, extending his hand for a handshake.

"Get the fuck off my ship," Kash replied and did not shake the man's hand.

"Boss, the second card from the bottom has a tracker," Calynn stated through his earpiece. "But there are no more listening devices aboard."

"Hey, Pike," Kash shouted at the man. "Buy yourself some manners."

Kash tossed the card with the tracker at the agent like a Frisbee as he retracted the steps and closed the door.

"Prepare for liftoff and open comms to Dorn," Kash ordered. "We're going to bunk with them tonight inside the freighter."

"Should I scan the outer shell?"

"No need... he definitely put a tracker on us. We'll take it off when we are inside the freighter... and burn it."

"Opening comms now."

"Captain Dorn here."

"Dorn, it's Kash. I have some government guys giving me a hard time about something, something whatever," Kash explained. "Any chance I can park my ride in the deepest hole of your ship? I think they have a bug on me."

"Actually, I have a bay specifically designed for that," Dorn replied. "And a contact that can make those corporate thugs go away, also."

"How much does the contact cost?"

"Ten thousand to reassign them or fifteen gets them put under review."

"What can I get for twenty?"

"Speed."

"Good," Kash stated. "I have a hot date tonight, and I don't want them to find her."

"I'll make the call now," Dorn replied. "Dorn, out."

"This is so exciting," Calynn confessed.

"Avoiding government agents?"

"No," Calynn replied excitedly. "I'm going to learn so much from Omia. I like the way she walks. It's sexy without trying to be sexy. She partially rotates her hips instead of swaying..."

"Calynn?"

"Yes, Boss."

"Work first..."

"Play later," Calynn replied. "Course set for the freighter."

"Thank you."

"Boss, if we're worried about protecting Omia, I can use the slip to throw those two agents into the sun."

"Let's NOT kill them if we don't have to."

"Incoming comm."

"This is Kash."

"Please, call it off, Kash."

"Why should I, Agent Fuck Off," Kash barked. "You came after me even though I don't fly the right ship!"

"They are accusing us of murder!" Agent Smith cried out.

"Well… put a tracker on them and see if that helps. End comm."

"Wow… I guess that will keep my Omia safe," Calynn stated.

"And keep two corrupt agents off our butts."

"Omia has a nice butt," Calynn said longingly. "I want to have a nice butt like hers."

"Sex crazed much?" Kash asked sarcastically.

"Sorry, Boss."

Calynn's Body

Thracia was the most peaceful and serene planet that Kash had ever visited, and he had been to all the pleasure planets. The people here were gentle giants, and most were beyond super brilliant. Thracians averaged about three meters tall, with a greenish-silver hue to their skin. Their hair color was either white, gray, or black. They all dressed in very colorful, simple square ponchos cinched at the waist with a belt. Everyone was always extremely polite and kind, although they occasionally got into heated debates about their sciences. The universal translator could not translate Thracii, but all of the Thracians that Kash had encountered could also speak perfect English, so communication wasn't an issue.

The building that Plekish founded was called The Center of Advanced Sciences. Most Thracians in this region just referred to it as the Science Center. They did research on almost everything imaginable here but primarily focused on energy and energy usage. On Earth, perpetual motion is impossible. On Thracia, if you can't build a perpetual motion device with at least a 20% surplus of energy produced, you are unworthy of working in the Science Center.

Kash landed his ship through the open rooftop hatch and touched down on the landing pad specifically designed for it. As he powered everything down, some scientists began approaching his ship with hi-tech tools.

"Is our ship getting an upgrade too, Boss?" Calynn asked.

"I don't know, Calynn... I really don't," Kash replied. "Do you see Plekish? Maybe he knows."

"He is approaching the rear of the ship now."

"Well then, let's open all the doors and head out to greet our friend."

"Sure thing, Boss."

Kash exited the cockpit and headed to the cargo bay. By the time he reached the rear bay doors, Plekish stood on the ramp speaking to another man in Thracii. The other man seemed in awe as Kash approached. Kash wished he understood what they were saying.

"Kash, my friend, welcome," Plekish said with a big grin as he knelt down to hug Kash.

Plekish was tall for a Thracian. He had short white hair, was of medium build, and always wore dark blue ponchos. This one had leaf patterns on it, and he had a broad white belt. The other man wore a white professional poncho and a multicolored belt.

"Plekish, by the Gods, it's so good to see you," Kash replied as he embraced the larger man. "You have no idea how anxious Calynn has been about this whole thing... and she's making me just as anxious. She's been driving me nuts."

"Hey... that's not nice," Calynn rebutted. "I haven't been... and I was good and followed all your orders and..."

"I'm teasing you, Calynn," Kash interrupted with a laugh. "I'm just referring to your recent insatiable need for data on sex. I truly hope this is just a phase because that IS driving me nuts."

"It is such a new experience," Calynn replied. "I want to know everything about it."

"It is rather interesting you that would be pursuing data related to sexual intercourse, Calynn," Plekish said in his inquisitive tone. "I would think the sensation of touch or taste would be of higher priority. I wonder... is there some meaning behind your obsession?"

"Well... I..."

"Is it embarrassing to say?" Plekish inquired. "Don't be embarrassed, child."

"It's my sister," Calynn confessed. "She and some of her friends are being rather promiscuous in college."

"And you're watching them?" Kash asked, flabbergasted.

"They record it on their phones..."

"Oh, come on, Calynn," Kash interrupted.

"I'm curious..."

"It is fine. Curiosity is a wonderful thing," Plekish interjected. "However, you will have to remain curious for some time yet. Much work must be done before you get to anything like that."

"Speaking of work," Kash asked, happy to change the subject. "Is my ship getting some work, too?"

"Indeed," Plekish responded and turned to his colleague beside him. "This is Rinktee. He has devised a new propulsion system we are eager to install on your ship. Some structural modifications will be needed to handle the new thrust capacity. Nothing drastic, mind you… just replacing a few panels and beams with superior materials."

"So I get to be Rinktee's Guinea pig also?" Kash asked playfully.

"Indeed."

"Then, why does Rinktee look like he's seen a ghost?"

"Forgive me for staring, Kash," Rinktee replied. "I am merely stunned to finally meet you."

"You are a bit famous here on Thracia, my friend," Plekish said with a smile. "A hero for saving me and a pilot of tests for our inventions."

"Well, your inventions make my life so much better. When I have a job that is more dangerous than most, it's nice to know that I possess superior technology," Kash admitted. "And, I humbly accept the job as Test Pilot of Thracia… in perpetuity. It is a pleasure to make your acquaintance, Rinktee, and a pleasure to test your new engines as well."

"Is it customary to greet you with that embrace?" Rinktee asked Kash.

"Sometimes… we also do handshakes, but I know your greeting as well," Kash answered. "I am just a good bit shorter, so…"

Rinktee knelt and placed his hands on Kash's shoulders. Kash then placed his hands upon Rinktee's shoulders, and the two men briefly touched their foreheads together.

"What does that other greeting symbolize?" Rinktee asked as he returned to his feet.

"It is a sign of affection," Plekish responded. "It is reserved for family members and close friends akin to family."

"Intriguing," Rinktee remarked.

"Indeed," Plekish continued. "It joins the heart as our greeting joins the mind. It promotes fondness and caring for one another. My own family has adopted this practice. I find it rather pleasant."

"You make hugging sound so profound, Plekish," Calynn added. "I can't wait to have my new body so I can hug you."

"Oh, shit," Kash exclaimed. "I almost forgot… the metal alloy you had me get for her body had a tracer. We were searched by coalition constables, but the radiation from the Poncia suns masked it."

"That must be the weak energy signature we found," Rinktee suggested. "It was of no value. We removed it before smelting it into our new material."

"Did it pose a problem?" Plekish asked.

"Luckily, no," Kash replied. "But we must ensure that all traces of that energy signature are removed from my ship and Calynn's new body. Then verify it has been completely removed again. We have to make sure Calynn is safe."

"I will verify it myself," Rinktee agreed. "To put your mind at ease."

"Thank you, Rinktee," Kash replied. "It is of the utmost importance."

"Your tone makes it sound as though it did pose a problem, Kash," Plekish stated.

"It could have," Kash responded. "We were fortunate, to say the least. The men that came looking for it could have caused us trouble. But let us not dwell on it with so many new and exciting things happening."

"Indeed," Plekish added.

"What can you tell me about your new engines?" Kash inquired. "But remember… you have to dumb it down for me."

"I am unfamiliar with that term," Rinktee stated with a puzzled look.

"Allow me," Plekish answered. "Fundamentally, the propulsion system works similar to how it does now. Rinktee discovered a way to alternate the polarity of the aether, giving the engines more to push against. The aether responds better in this way, so the engines run at a lower temperature. This is much more stable, significantly increasing thrust while expending far less energy."

"How much more thrust?"

"Eight-hundred sixty-two percent," Rinktee answered this time.

"Over eight times more thrust!" Kash said, astonished. "Holy shit... what, ah... what's that do for the HLD?"

"We have to optimize the HLD to operate with the new speed parameters," Rinktee explained. "It will significantly lower your travel times when traveling faster than light. Calynn will have to slightly alter her calculations to address the speeds. We will install the necessary software and address the structural integrity issues."

"You might want to ensure everything inside the ship can handle the new forces also," Kash added. "So my instrument panel doesn't break off in my hand when I'm flying, or I get hit in the head by some airborne... thing."

"That is what I mean by the structural integrity issues," Rinktee replied. "Hull integrity is only one of my focuses. Your vessel will be flight-worthy in every sense by the time you are ready to leave."

"Suddenly... I have a feeling that my stay will be longer than I anticipated," Kash sighed. "But... I trust you fully, Rinktee, and I know you'll take good care of my bird."

"Your ship will be done long before Calynn is ready," Plekish added. "She has a lot of learning to do."

"What am I learning?" Calynn inquired.

"Your new body, for one," Plekish replied. "The interface with the ship will be different, as will your sensors. Plus, you will have to learn to fly the ship manually. But I'm afraid the thing that will take you the longest to learn will be control."

"Control?" Kash asked.

"She must learn to not exert so much mental energy," Plekish answered. "Her mind has become... well, honestly, without studying her, I'm not entirely sure what her mind has become. Her conscious mind has somehow taken over the unconscious mind, which isn't supposed to be possible. It's an entirely new concept... We will learn together that way, but she must learn to control her efforts... or she may ruin her new body."

"Is my body here?" Calynn asked. "Can I see it?"

"It is, my dear," Plekish replied. "My colleague, Bahanja, is the lead on that project. She has your body in the bay next to this one."

"I will get the interface in place so Calynn can reach that bay. We must move her to her body before I can complete the upgrades here," Rinktee explained as he walked away.

"Come, Kash," Plekish offered with a warm smile. "I can show you some of our innovations to make Calynn as technologically sound as possible. One of the innovations could replace your existing implants. You would be stronger, faster, and lighter."

"One of my implants is broken," Kash explained as he followed Plekish. "I wouldn't mind a replacement."

"I think Omia might disagree, Boss," Calynn said with a giggle. "She'd still be riding you if we didn't have to come here."

"Who is Omia?" Plekish inquired.

"One of the doctors on Poncia," Kash replied. "I spent a few days with her after the vaccines were delivered. She's a wonderful woman and Calynn and I rather enjoyed spending time with her. Omia and I were the unfortunate subjects of Calynn's sexual research. She would ask a question and Omia and I would perform the answer. Truth be told... I think I really like her."

"Oh my gosh, Boss," Calynn said rapidly. "I soooo love her. She's smart and beautiful, and she's really good at everything about sex. Or... it looked like she was anyway. She's easy to talk to and I found her to be very honest. We've been emailing each other too. Omia is teaching me how to be a woman. It's not just the sex thing, either. I watched her cook meals and clean up afterward. I also liked the way she tended to you. She would ask if you were thirsty or rub your back without you asking. And she showed me how she shaves her legs and grooms herself. We talked about clothes and accessories, and she's going to help me develop my sense of style. I don't know what that means, but she's really nice. I think I love her, and maybe you do too. Sorry."

"So many words," Kash said with a little grin. "I think Calynn wins... she likes Omia more than I do."

That was a lie. Kash was utterly enthralled with Omia. Her charms had won him over. To him, she wasn't just a nymphomaniac with great tits. She was gorgeous and generous and warm and...

perfect. He already missed holding Omia close and cuddling each morning. Morning cuddles with the right woman are possibly better than the sexual escapades the night before. Omia was definitely the right woman for Kash. She was honest about all her imperfections and didn't judge Kash for his. They could be truthful with each other about everything, and he had never felt so at ease around another woman... ever. Calynn was right. Kash was in love with Omia.

"She's just soo," Calynn added. "Great... I love her. She's my first girlfriend."

"Women..."

"Hey... you like her too."

"And you're infatuated."

"No, I'm not."

"Really?"

"I... uh... so, where's my body?"

"Subject change much?" Kash asked with a chuckle.

"No... well, maybe," Calynn stammered. "It's all so exciting."

"Patience Calynn. Rinktee must install and monitor your interface first, so you don't overpower it," Plekish stated. "Until you learn to control yourself."

"I will try," Calynn added.

Plekish led Kash to the next bay as the partition walls between the bays lowered themselves into the floor. The bay looked like a cross between an experimental lab and a surgical room. A workbench had a hand floating in a blue energy field and delicate-looking tools lying nearby. A spool of extremely thin filament was mounted on the wall behind the hand. Plekish led Kash toward the spool and used a laser knife to cut off a small piece of the filament. It was so thin Kash could barely see it.

"This will serve as Calynn's nerves," Plekish explained as he handed the filament to Kash. "Her nerve density will exceed yours with excellent touch sensitivity. But this over here... we are very proud of its development."

Plekish walked down the workbench a couple meters and returned holding a bumpy-looking cord.

"This is the one that I believe can benefit you, Kash," Plekish continued. "This... is what comprises the muscles in Calynn's body. This one fiber can exert one hundred Newtons of force. If we were to stitch just a few of these threads into your muscles, you would be much stronger than you are now. Luckily, you have unusually dense bones. They shouldn't break when you exert yourself."

"Shouldn't?" Kash questioned.

"If my calculations are correct, you will be just fine," a Thracian woman interrupted. "We will limit the force to eighty-five percent of the force your bones can handle."

"Kash, meet Bahanja, the lead on Calynn's body development," Plekish said with a smile.

Bahanja was slightly shorter than Plekish, with dainty features and long black hair. She had muscular legs and an athletic build. She was wearing a thin white poncho that hung beautifully from her frame. It was more form-fitting than the usual science uniform, and she paired it with a delicate gold cord for a belt.

"A pleasure to meet you, Bahanja," Kash said politely, reaching for her shoulders.

"The pleasure is all mine, Kash," Bahanja replied as she knelt down to greet Kash.

The two touched their foreheads for a moment, and Bahanja gave Kash a lovely smile before she pulled away.

"Would you care to see the fruits of my labor?" Bahanja asked. "She really is a marvel."

"I would love to," Kash replied. "Lead the way."

"Your insistence on keeping Calynn safe was my guiding force," Bahanja explained as she led Kash further into the room. "Her brain and organs will be housed inside her rib cage made from an alloy specifically designed to be able to withstand nearly any assault. The fluid surrounding her ribs is designed to absorb the blast from energy weapons, and her skin... you won't believe how soft it feels. But... it gets rigid when attacked. Projectile weapons will bounce off of her to a certain size. And it's all wrapped around a lightweight skeleton that will aid in her agility."

Bahanja turned and smiled at Kash as she pulled the tarp off Calynn's body.

"Whoa," Kash exclaimed as he looked at the disfigured body. "Why does she look like that?"

"We have her opened up, ready to accept Calynn's brain and organs," Bahanja replied. "We hinged the left side of her rib cage on the spine. The skin will self-heal when put back together. I developed the skin so the molecular default will be interwoven... together."

"The molecules rearrange themselves?" Kash asked. "Like little robots?"

"No," Bahanja replied. "Nanomites wouldn't be able to convert... her skin is a dilatant non-Newtonian formulation that reacts to impacts instantaneously."

"Sounds heavy," Kash added.

"She's a mere seventy-one kilograms," Bahanja continued. "Her skeleton is what you would call a honeycomb configuration, making it extremely lightweight and strong. The alloy we developed cannot be smelted again once it has hardened. A group of our engineers created a new forge..."

"Bones that can't be broken," Kash interrupted. "Got it."

"My friend Kash prefers broader explanations," Plekish added. "For instance, we replicated saliva production so Calynn can eat regular food."

"And she can spit on me too," Kash surmised.

"I suppose she could," Plekish said with a chuckle. "If the need arises."

"I'll be certain to not annoy her," Kash replied.

"You better not annoy me," Calynn's voice came from a monitor positioned beside her body. "Will I also be able to taste the food?"

The monitor was connected to wires that ran back to his ship, where Rinktee had an odd-looking crate set up. Some other Thracians were already working on his ship's engines.

"I cannot answer that question yet," Bahanja explained. "I built you a tongue capable of taste, but we are not adding extra processors to your body. In other synthetic bodies, a computer tells you how your food tastes. We believe your mental abilities would overload such devices."

"Fortunately, when your original body was damaged, Kash was able to purchase your entire body," Plekish added. "I kept you more intact than most nerve centers."

"We intend to connect the synthetic nerves to the existing nervous tissue of your spinal cord," Bahanja continued. "Above your spinal injury... naturally."

"You will have the most advanced, yet simple synthetic body ever developed," Plekish finished with a proud grin.

"My face looks so bland," Calynn complained.

"We can change that now if you would like," Bahanja asked as she approached the computer terminal that Calynn was connected to. "I will open the port, allowing you to apply your self-image..."

"But you must be in control," Plekish interrupted. "If you try too hard, you will ruin your body."

"Agreed," Bahanja added. "You must be calm."

"I don't know how."

"You must try, child," Plekish stated.

"How do I try to not try?"

"You must limit your efforts," Bahanja replied this time.

"I don't know what that means," Calynn whined. She was clearly frustrated.

"Wait... Calynn," Kash interrupted.

"Yes, boss."

"The cracks in your box... the ones you wiggle through," Kash explained calmly and soothingly. "Can you return to your box through them?"

"But I don't want to be stuck in the box."

"You don't have to stay there... just... trust me," Kash stayed steady in his delivery.

"But I'm scared."

"I know, Baby Girl," Kash continued. "But we don't want you to break your new body, either."

"I know."

"So, this is what I want you to try," Kash explained. "I want you to go back to the box for five seconds. And while you're there... just peek out at us... like you're watching us through a peephole in a door. Can you try that?"

"For five seconds?"

"Yes," Kash said encouragingly. "And then come right back here."

"Okay... I'll try."

Kash eagerly anticipated Calynn's report. It was the longest 5 seconds of his life.

"I couldn't see past Rinktee's box," Calynn finally stated.

"Remarkable," Bahanja uttered. "Calynn, can you do it again, only this time Rinktee will temporarily open his port for you to peek through?"

"Okay," Calynn hesitantly replied.

"I will count down from three," Bahanja continued. "You will go back to the cracks as you just did. Three seconds later, Rinktee will open his port and then close it again. Wait three more seconds after that and then return."

"Okay."

"Rinktee, are you ready," Bahanja asked.

"Ready," Rinktee responded.

"Alright, Calynn," Bahanja continued. "In three... two... one... go. Three... two... one... open the port... and close it again..."

"Wait," Rinktee exclaimed.

The monitor screen in front of Bahanja overloaded and shattered, startling everyone in both bays.

"It worked," Calynn cried out, but her voice sounded muffled. "I could see you."

"You came back too soon," Bahanja explained sternly. "Now, I must replace this station before we try again. You must have more patience."

"I'm sorry," Calynn pouted.

Bahanja motioned for another scientist to join her, and they began disassembling the monitor parts that Calynn had fried.

"Rinktee, what was her energy output during the portal opening?" Plekish inquired.

"Less than one-thousand joules," Rinktee replied.

"So it is possible," Plekish said thoughtfully.

"Those outputs are well within my parameters," Bahanja agreed as she worked.

"My concern remains to be containment when we release her," Plekish admitted.

"Containment?" Kash asked, concerned.

"The energy she emits is substantial," Bahanja replied. "Protecting everyone and everything from that energy is crucial to success."

"Her energy can hurt us?"

"Not directly, no," Bahanja answered with a thoughtful look. "However, she can energize isolated electrical circuits, which may cause unintentional harm. For instance, what if she inadvertently made one of the hoists drop a piece of your ship or rotate violently?"

"Someone could be gravely injured," Plekish added.

"I wouldn't do that on purpose," Calynn whined.

"We know," Plekish replied, "but the threat remains until you learn control."

"I'll try... I just don't know how."

"Are we ready to try again?" Kash asked.

"Not yet," Bahanja replied. "We are still working on swapping these parts."

"How about some practice while we wait?"

"How would I practice?" Calynn asked.

"If you pulled back to your box again..."

"Ugh!" Calynn interrupted.

"You get that we're doing this, so you no longer have a box, right?"

"A body and no box," Calynn sighed. "I know. I know."

"Okay... so that means..."

"Fine," Calynn relented. "What should I do?"

"Practice going back in the box and peeking out for say... ten seconds each time," Kash explained. "Maybe try to peak less each time."

"Okay... one... two..."

Calynn's voice fell off as she began her practice, so Kash turned his attention to Plekish and Bahanja. Plekish looked deep in thought as if he were pondering a solution to their current problem.

"What are you thinking, my friend?" Kash asked the man.

"Hmm... sorry... just a minute."

Plekish turned and spoke to Bahanja in Thracii. The two conversed back and forth for a few seconds and then paused to think before continuing to speak.

"Boss... what are they saying?" Calynn asked quietly.

"I wish I knew."

"Plekish has raised some concerns," Bahanja replied. "Calynn, do you feel like you have a center, or are you scattered?"

"I don't understand what you mean."

"My concern is that without the box to anchor you, you may scatter yourself when you are freed from it," Plekish explained. "You are so accustomed to pushing out that we might lose you in this process."

"Lose me?" Calynn whined. "How?"

"You have an energy unlike anything we have ever seen before," Bahanja replied. "What if when you push out that wave of energy, it takes your essence with it? We may need to run more tests."

"We're going to be here a really long time, aren't we?" Kash asked nobody in particular.

"Not necessarily," Bahanja responded. "If we set up another device for her to jump into..."

"Then we can see if something remains," Plekish interrupted and finished her thought. "That's brilliant."

"I have just the thing," Bahanja's assistant stated as he turned and walked towards the work benches. "If she tries to control this prototype of her hand, then we will know if any part of her lingers."

"Okay... Calynn, pay very close attention," Plekish ordered. "We are going to loosely connect this hand to your network. Once we do, I need you to push out harder than you ever have before. And I want you to make a fist as hard as possible."

"Won't I break the machine again?" Calynn asked.

"Indeed you will," Plekish replied. "We are going to put every resistance we can in your way. I'm going to make you work for it."

"You want me to break it?"

"Most definitely."

"We're almost ready," Bahanja exclaimed. "We just need to get some shielding in place."

Bahanja tapped herself on the temple and began speaking Thracii. Some robotic noises soon followed as Bahanja, and her assistant backed away. The whirling sound of the motors gave way to a crackling sound as sheets of energy surrounded the monitor and the hand. The sheets were pale blue with copper-colored stripes and were primarily transparent.

"Ready when you are, Calynn," Bahanja stated.

"Okay, let me try," Calynn replied. "Grr... oomph... mmm... I... I can't... Rinktee's box."

"Push through it, child," Plekish encouraged. "Push hard."

"I'm trying... I'm... grrrrrr..."

"Now, Rinktee," Bahanja ordered.

A surge of energy lit up the shielded area and completely destroyed the monitor. Arcs of electricity jumped through the sequestered area, with some landing on the hand that Calynn was trying to reach. Kash shielded his eyes from the flashes of light for a second so he couldn't see if she could make the fist. The monitor continued to pop and sizzle as Calynn burned through its circuits.

"Calynn?" Plekish called to the girl softly.

Several seconds passed, and there was no answer.

"Is she there?" Bahanja inquired.

More silence.

"She's here," Rinktee hollered. "She must have shorted out her comms."

"Are you sure?" Plekish asked.

"There is still a flow of energy present," Rinktee replied

"What was her energy output?" Plekish asked.

"I would need a larger meter to give you that information," Rinktee replied. "She broke this one."

"We use that meter to study the effects of lightning," Bahanja offered. "There's no way..."

"She's stronger than lightning?" Kash interrupted.

The Thracians began discussing what had just happened. Kash wished he knew what was being said. Sometimes, they looked concerned, and sometimes, they expressed joy. More of their colleagues joined them and added to the conversation.

"Boss?"

Calynn's voice barely came through on his earpiece, and there was lots of static interference.

"Calynn," Kash replied, waving at the scientist to get their attention. "Are you okay?"

"I'm exhausted," Calynn replied as Kash tapped the button to put her on speaker.

"That was an incredible display, child," Plekish offered.

"Why can't I see you anymore?" Calynn asked. "I just see blobs."

"It must be our energy, she sees," Bahanja explained. "The monitor is of no use. She sees the raw energy."

"If I focus a little... I can see your body shapes... I'm just so tired now."

"And I know why," Rinktee exclaimed. "The portal is still grounded. It is dumping massive amounts of energy into the storage cells beneath the Center. I need to disconnect it."

"Whoa... that felt weird," Calynn said in her normal perky tone. "And I'm back on the ship now. Oh, wait... I can still sorta see the hand. There's a crack in Rinktee's box now."

"Don't try..." Plekish ordered.

"Wait," Bahanja interrupted. "I'm beginning to understand her energy. Look."

Bahanja motioned and projected an image from a device on her arm that Kash hadn't noticed before.

"There is no crack in the portal," Bahanja explained. "She's using a magnetic field to circumvent it."

"Intriguing," Plekish replied.

"Calynn, I want you to go through the crack as slowly as possible," Bahanja explained.

"I'll try."

"Look... she expanded the field," Bahanja explained as she pointed to her display. "Now watch as she connects to the hand."

Sparks of electricity jumped from the broken wires in the containment field. They were random momentarily before the arc landed on the prototype hand and became steady. The stream started to get brighter when Bahanja intervened.

"Slow down, Calynn... don't force it," Bahanja spoke calmly. "Yes... good girl. A little less effort... good... that hand has nerve circuits attached to the muscles. If you can get your energy output small enough, you should be able to feel around for them. It will flow easily when you find them... really small..."

Kash watched as the arc of electricity jumping from the wire became smaller and smaller as Bahanja spoke. Her soothing voice calmed Calynn and helped her with the control. The hand was lying on the ground, with the wrist pointing away from the wire. Calynn had to push the electricity beyond the structure of the hand itself to get to the exposed nerves on the other side.

"There are three main pathways that branch off into the entire hand... there, you found one... now slowly look for the other two..."

A tiny arc of energy landed at one spot on the wrist, and the hand jumped to life.

"Easy... just connect to them. Don't try to do anything..."

The hand stopped wiggling, and the arcs of electricity got smaller and branched off into three pieces.

"Good... you found them all," Bahanja continued. "Stay calm... can you see it?"

"I can."

"Okay, make a fist. Slowly... good girl."

"I did it," Calynn said calmly.

"Good girl. You are showing lots of control," Bahanja praised. "This next part will feel weird... I'm going to interrupt the magnetic field you're using to jump the portal."

"The crack in Rinktee's box?"

"Correct."

"To see if a piece of me gets left behind?"

"Does that sound scary?" Bahanja sounded worried when she asked the question.

"A little bit," Calynn conceded, "but I understand why we are trying it."

"Are you ready?"

"Making a fist now... go ahead."

Calynn sounded less than confident with her decision. Bahanja nodded at her assistant, and he engaged a shield around the portal. The hand immediately relaxed.

"Calynn?" Plekish and Bahanja asked in unison.

"That was weird," Calynn said with a giggle. "It was like, umm... like when you get absorbed in a good song, and then someone turns it off."

"So she is connected through her thoughts but not really connected," Kash offered. "That's a good thing, right?"

"It is indeed," Plekish replied.

"And her control was even better than I could have hoped," Bahanja added.

"That's also good news."

"Indeed, but she still has much to do," Plekish agreed. "Perhaps we can take this time to get you your upgrades, Kash."

"Oh yes," Bahanja said excitedly. "I'm intrigued to see how well they work."

"Ugh… I hate surgeries."

Kash's Body

Kash woke up feeling more refreshed than he had in years. He carefully searched for the release button for the pod lid and pressed it. The regeneration pods that the Thracians used after surgery were nothing short of amazing. Plekish tried to explain how they worked to him before, but Kash only cared about the results. The pods returned your cells to their peak physical levels. It's like having everything about his body returned to its eighteen-year-old form. It turns out the Fountain of Youth is a red and white mechanical bubble on the planet Thracia.

"Goddamn, that feels good," Kash said to himself as he sat up and exited the pod.

He moved his right arm around with his left hand on the muscles in his shoulder. The muscles moved more easily than they should, and his arm felt lighter, too.

"Okay, Kash… the new muscles are supposed to be much stronger… so move slow," he said aloud to himself.

Kash stood up slowly and tested his legs. Again, the first thing he noticed was that he felt lighter. It felt like it required no effort to move. His joints were silky smooth, and his movements felt more fluid. His old implants were mechanical and moved as such. Without them, he felt less like a mechanical man and more like himself. Next, he tested his range of motion, and to his surprise, he could make moves that he hadn't been able to do in years.

"Fuck yea," Kash exclaimed as he snapped a kick nearly straight up. "Oh, I can't wait to get to the gym."

"Was that you?" a woman's voice came from the hallway.

"Meesha?"

"Kash, my good friend," Meesha said with a smile as she entered the room. "You're finally awake. How do you feel?"

Meesha was easily the most beautiful Thracian woman Kash had met. She had dainty features and high cheekbones like runway models on Earth. Her shiny black hair framed her face perfectly and lay delicately on her shoulders. Her lean, athletic form moved gracefully as she approached. She was wearing a thin, light blue poncho that hugged her body and a bright yellow scarf for a belt.

"Besides being a little cold and naked?" Kash replied with a chuckle.

"Oh, sorry… your clothes are just over here," Meesha said as she moved to a table and grabbed his clothes. "Forgive me… should I let you alone to dress?"

"No, it's fine," Kash replied and then smirked. "Just take your clothes off so we're even."

"Are you mocking me?"

"Who me?"

Meesha narrowed her eyes at Kash and smiled.

"As I recall, you… are the one that is uncomfortable with nudity," Meesha declared, "not me."

Meesha dropped one hand to her belt and gave it a tug to loosen it.

"But if it makes you feel better," Meesha continued.

"No, no," Kash conceded. "You win… I was just teasing."

"Put these on so I can hug you," Meesha said as she handed him his clothes. "I've been watching over you for over a week while you slept and eagerly awaiting a hug."

Kash quickly pulled on his boxer briefs and his jeans. He didn't bother with his shirt yet.

"Come here, beautiful," Kash said as he smiled at his friend.

Meesha knelt down and wrapped Kash in a warm embrace. Kash was careful about how much pressure he used. He didn't want to hurt Meesha by hugging her too tightly.

"A little harder," Meesha said as she continued to hug him. "I know you're worried about your new strength. Trust the pressure on your skin. That will feel the same… there it is. That's a Kash hug."

"I never thought of that," Kash explained.

"Just because your muscles are augmented doesn't mean your nerves changed, mister."

"Well, I didn't want to hurt you."

"I appreciate that," Meesha said as she released Kash and pulled back. "Okay, one more hug."

Meesha pulled him into another embrace and held him tightly.

"Oh no... hugs from a beautiful woman. How dreadful," Kash said sarcastically as he hugged her back.

"I can never hug you enough. I still feel like I haven't thanked you enough for returning my Plekish to me," Meesha said solemnly. "Even though you say you have been more than adequately paid for your services."

"Meesha..."

"I'm just so eternally grateful," Meesha interrupted. "I can't express it enough. I'd be lost without him, and therefore... lost without you."

"I know... and I will accept every hug you want to give," Kash explained. "You are an excellent hugger."

"It helps that I am a full meter taller than you," Meesha said as she wrapped her arms around him further. "I can really wrap you up."

"An insecure man might complain," Kash replied. "Feeling small in a woman's arms isn't very masculine."

"What is masculine?" Meesha asked as she finally released her hug. "I don't believe we have that term here."

"Well, you're not missing anything," Kash laughed. "It's supposed to mean men doing the responsible things that men should do, like protecting their women and children... but it's mostly when men misbehave now."

"Interesting that you need a term for that."

"Yea, we need to be told how to act properly, and even then, most do not," Kash explained. "Earth is mostly a shitty planet compared to Thracia, and so are its people."

"Well, I am thankful that Earth gave us you," Meesha said with a soft smile. "Even if you are Earth's only redeeming factor."

"You know I'm a bad guy, right?" Kash asked as he finished dressing. "I'm not a redeeming quality kind of guy."

"I know you have done things I could not understand," Meesha replied. "However, I do not believe that makes you bad."

"I'm glad you don't understand it all... otherwise you wouldn't like me much."

"Then I am glad also."

Kash smiled at Meesha and sighed.

"You know, sometimes it feels like I am taking advantage of your benevolence," Kash explained. "You all treat me like I'm this great person, and I'm not that guy. I've done mean and horrible things... even to retrieve Plekish... sometimes, I feel... terrible about..."

"Kash," Meesha interrupted. "Just because we don't understand the bad things doesn't mean we don't know they are bad. There was a reason we had to ask for your help. You can do the things that we would never think to do. Evil exists... and we are ill-equipped to negotiate it. You can. But you do so with honor. And that is what we needed. Nobody on Thracia believes that you are a god, or no, that's not right... a saint? ... I'm not sure which word to use there?"

"In that context, they are essentially equal."

"Your language is unnecessarily complex."

"Can you go back in time and tell my sixth-grade English teacher that?"

"Time travel isn't possible..."

"I was joking, Meesha," Kash interrupted. "It was a rhetorical question with a dash of implied sarcasm."

"Humor?"

"It was an attempt at humor."

"Hmm... I didn't get that one."

"She was a horrible teacher," Kash explained. "She just wanted to yell at the kids or be demeaning to them when they got things wrong."

"That is not the proper way to teach," Meesha said with a perplexed look.

"I know... but that's why you didn't get my joke."

"I see," Meesha replied. "The teacher made the learning experience bad for the children and harder than it had to be. This made your unnecessarily complex language more complex, which is why you would want me to go tell her that... I get it now."

"Speaking of children... are the kids here?" Kash asked. "I can't wait to see them."

"Let me go make sure they are clothed," Meesha stated as she left the room. "I'll be right back."

The one thing that made Kash uncomfortable about the Thracians was that the family would always be naked at home. It was partially extended to other family members, too. If Plekish's parents were over, everyone would be undressed except Meesha because she wasn't their direct family line. If one of Meesha's siblings was over, she and the sibling could be nude, but Plekish and the kids had to dress, or vice versa. Kash seemed to be the exception to that rule somehow. After he saved Plekish, the family treated him like he belonged, and he had to ask them to dress around him. They happily obliged.

"Kash!" Mala hollered as she rushed into his room. "You're finally awake."

Mala crushed her body into Kash and hugged him tight. She was still a child and fit neatly under his chin. Kash hugged the little girl and laid his head on top of her head for a moment. Mala pulled back and looked up at him with a beaming smile. The little girl looked almost exactly like her mom. She put her hands on either side of his head. She gently touched their foreheads before burying her head in his chest again for another hug.

"Hi, Baby Girl," Kash said and kissed the top of her head. "You're not so little anymore."

"I'm sorry I missed you on your last visit," Mala said while hugging him. "I was away with a friend at a super-conductor seminar... fascinating stuff."

"How old are you?"

"The equivalent of ten of your Earth years. Why?"

"No reason... it's just... girls your age on Earth play with dolls, not super-conductors."

"Dolls are fun, too."

Kash chuckled, hugged the little girl tighter, and shook side to side a little bit. Her big brother approached with a kind smile that reminded Kash of his dad. Darjic was a good blend of his mom and dad. He had his mom's black hair and kind eyes, but everything else was all Plekish.

"And I remember when I was taller than you, young man," Kash said to the boy and smiled.

"I hit another growth spurt," Darjic explained. "I'm up to two-hundred and forty-two centimeters."

"Soon, you'll have to kneel down to hug me like your dad does."

"Mom thinks he will be taller than Dad when fully grown," Mala said as she released Kash.

"The current variance is tracking at three point two nine percent," Darjic noted.

"You are far too competent to be a teenager, Darjic," Kash said, moving to hug the young man. "And a little awkward to hug."

"It's good to see you, my friend," Darjic said as he returned the hug. "I looked up that International Chess Master, Emory Tate Jr like you suggested. My friends and I are beginning to understand the use of Gambits."

"Does it make playing chess more fun?"

"It does and doesn't," the young man said as he stepped back. "Creating an imbalance like that makes the positions more dynamic, but some of his moves were not logical. I am struggling to understand why he made them."

"I wanted you to see his play for its unorthodox nature," Kash explained. "He wasn't known as a great attacking player like say… Bobbie Fisher or Gary Kasparov, but his opponents feared him nonetheless… they referred to him as an alien, as in NOT human."

"Some of his concepts were very enlightening. He would sacrifice any piece if it meant the ones he had left could secure a Checkmate."

"It's not all about perfect position or making advantageous trades in chess," Kash explained. "It's finding a balance between attacking and defense while maintaining a good overall position. Sometimes, sacrificing pieces secures a victory… it is a very complex game."

"Finding move combinations my friends do not see is uniquely challenging," Darjic continued. "Trying to position pieces so they are poised to make moves that aren't immediately obvious is an arduous task."

"Chess is a game, not a task. I know you guys are wicked smart, but please remember to have fun playing."

"We do… and our discussions about certain games are very enlightening."

"You kids," Kash chuckled. "Enlightened discussions on chess and super-conductor seminars… go make some mud pies."

"What is a mud pie?" Mala asked.

"It means to go play in the mud, not to make actual pies from mud."

"Why would we play in the mud?" Darjic asked.

"That would make us very dirty," Mala added.

"We would definitely get in trouble for that," Darjic continued.

"That's not what… oh, never mind," Kash conceded. "Can we talk in the kitchen? I'm famished."

"I was just coming to get you," Meesha said from the doorway. "I have some food set out for you."

"Thank the Gods."

Kash marched down the hallway and trotted down the stairs. The size of the steps always felt awkward to him if he moved slower. They weren't big enough to do two strides per step but too big to ascend or descend them with a normal gait. Jogging seemed to be the way to go.

The stairs ended in the foyer, and Kash turned towards the kitchen. The layout of Plekish's home felt familiar to Kash. It was similar to the one foster home he was in as a child on Earth. The foyer contained the stairs to the upstairs, a door to Plekish's study to the left, a door to Meesha's office to the right, and a passage to the kitchen and living area straight ahead. The materials were much different than those used on Earth, though. All the surfaces were much smoother.

"I put out your favorite," Meesha said from behind him.

"The fruit I can't pronounce?"

"That's the one."

"Oh, there it is," Kash said as he approached the kitchen island and grabbed a piece of the pale red fruit. "It's soooooo good."

"What did you say it tastes like?"

"A combination of Earth bananas and cantaloupes... kinda."

"Just do me a favor and eat slowly," Meesha said softly. "You haven't had real food in a while."

"Yes, dear," Kash said as he shoved another chunk of the fruit in his mouth. "Mmm, good."

"Slowly, mister," Meesha expressed again. "And have some of the vegetables also. I have the one you said tastes like broccoli, and I'll make you some seafood in a while."

"Is it weird that seafood is all fairly similar in taste?" Kash queried. "No matter what planet you're on, seafood tastes like seafood."

"Can I help make it?" Calynn's voice came from behind Kash.

Kash spun around to see a pretty blond girl standing beside Plekish. She was of average height with a thin, curvy body. She had porcelain white skin, shoulder-length blond hair, and pretty brown eyes. She was wearing a pink flowered sundress and a high-tech-looking necklace or collar.

"Calynn?"

Instead of answering, the girl sprinted towards him and leaped into his arms. She hugged him like her life depended on it. Kash was apprehensive at first but soon embraced her like his long-lost sister.

"You feel softer than I expected," Kash said as he laid his head on top of her head. "The team that made your skin did an outstanding job... you feel so... real."

"I am real," Calynn said as she rubbed her cheek on his chest. "This is great. I finally get to hug you after all these years."

"Honestly, I had to remind myself that I wasn't meeting you for the first time," Kash explained. "It was a little awkward for like three seconds."

"It is the first time you've seen me looking like this, though," Calynn replied. "Do you like how I look?"

"I was actually a little surprised by your appearance," Kash explained. "The last I heard, you were studying the epitome of beauty across the galaxy... Honestly, I was expecting one of two things. Either more of an exotic super-model look or the original you... despite my concerns."

"Well, since you said it would be dangerous for me and my family if I looked like me. I knew I had to look for something else. I didn't want to put them at risk because I was being selfish," Calynn explained thoughtfully. "But getting to pick how you want to look is hard... so, I looked at all the most beautiful women in the galaxy and compared their features. I compiled all the data and was constructing the perfect body when..."

Calynn stopped and looked up at Kash with a tear in her eye.

"When something you said to Omia popped into my head," Calynn continued. "You told her that her imperfections made her more perfect... and that's when I knew I had to give myself some... flaws."

"Flaws?" Kash exclaimed. "You look amazing... what flaws?"

"Flaws in the sight of the fashion model and movie industries," Calynn explained. "I have brown eyes, not blue. I gave myself a soft brown mole here on my left cheek. I had one on my original body, but it was on my right cheek, not my left. My height was fixed by Bahanja and her team at one-hundred-seventy-two centimeters. I think I would have preferred to be a little shorter, like my sister. My figure isn't what the beauty industry would want, either. My bust is ninety-two centimeters, my waist is sixty-seven, and my hips are one-hundred and two centimeters. Movie stars are expected to have a smaller waist and hips than that, and if I was a model, they would call me fat... oh, and I gave myself a birthmark..."

Calynn paused and backed up a step. She then pulled her sundress up to her ribcage to expose the birthmark on her left hipbone just above her pantie line. It was kidney-shaped, roughly ten centimeters long, and reddish brown in hue.

"See," Calynn exclaimed.

"Are those designer panties?" Kash asked quickly. "And that dress... how much did you spend?"

"I only got a few nice things, but I was more frugal with most of it," Calynn replied. "I wanted to make a nice impression when you first saw me."

"Well, you can start by putting your dress down," Kash explained, smiling at Calynn. "And I'm sorry... it is a very pretty dress."

Calynn smiled and straightened her dress. She spun around so the skirt flared out, then spun herself in the other direction. She was clearly very proud of her new body and her new dress. Kash found his eyes being diverted to her neck and the necklace.

"Okay... so I need to ask..." Kash started.

"It's an inhibitor," Calynn interrupted. "I still struggle with control... I'm better on the ship because I have more to do. This one is nice because I can adjust it. I do wish it was smaller and... cute."

"It is rather... industrial," Kash said with a smile. "Is this a girl-brain thing? Because they cannot think about nothing?"

"Actually, no," Plekish replied. "To put it as simply as I can, Calynn's conscious mind has inhabited her unconscious mind. Right now, your unconscious is doing a multitude of tasks without you thinking about it. Breathing... your heart and arteries moving blood around your body... controlling your body temperature... releasing the right enzymes to digest the food you're currently eating. These are all tasks you are not actively thinking about, and yet..."

"So she literally doesn't have an off button?" Kash interrupted.

"If you're asking if she requires sleep, the answer is no," Plekish answered. "The unconscious mind functions differently than... the simple version is the unconscious mind can do many tasks at once very quickly and effectively. This is why they are used for faster-than-light travel. Now imagine waking that, giving it access to memory and reasoning skills... and more importantly, access to the rest of her brain."

"All of it?"

"Every last cell."

"How?"

"I wish I knew the answer to that question," Plekish sighed. "But my best guess is that the unconscious has access to it."

"Holy shit!"

"Language, mister," Meesha scolded. "The children."

"Sorry, Meesha."

"I would love to study her," Plekish continued in a somber tone. "But it seems... heartless... I want her to live her life..."

"And not to be a specimen," Calynn finished his sentence for him. "For which I continue to be grateful."

Calynn looked down like she was shy and fidgeted before continuing.

"I'm science that nobody understands... even I have no idea what I can do," Calynn sounded sad as she spoke. "I'm going to be trouble... I'll cause a lot of problems... maybe more trouble than I'm worth."

"Hey, you," Kash interrupted and hugged Calynn again. "What kind of talk is that?"

"What if I hurt you?"

"I'll heal."

"What if I really hurt you?"

"Where is this coming from?" Kash asked insistently. "You were so happy a minute ago."

"She has been melancholy the last few days," Plekish added.

"I'm just worried, okay?" Calynn said sharply and pulled away from Kash. "I'm allowed to worry. I have a new body, and nobody knows what I'm capable of doing... so I'm worried about hurting my friends... even if I do it on accident."

"Oh my... look," Kash said, softening his tone. "We can worry about everything that can possibly go wrong in life... or we can live it... if you hurt me accidentally, I just get to come back here and have Meesha watch over me while I heal again... and eat some delicious fruit."

"And if I really hurt you?"

"Then you better save me too."

"But you'll be mad at me."

"For a minute or two, and then I would forgive you... I know what I'm signing up for, Calynn... I'll take the risk for the reward."

"What reward?"

"You," Kash said, sharper than he intended. "You're the reward."

Calynn rushed back to Kash and hugged him again.

"That's better... hugs from another beautiful woman."

"Should I be jealous?" Meesha asked with a smirk.

"Let's not pick on the poor girl," Plekish added. "She's been through a lot... how's the inhibitor, Calynn?"

"I turned it up when we got here... in case I got emotional. I'm glad I did."

"Wait... how do you know you're better in the ship?" Kash inquired.

"How do you think we got my clothes?" Calynn answered with a question. "I had them delivered to a nearby postal hub, and Rinktee and I flew out there to get them."

"And? ... well, how was it?" Kash asked excitedly. "How fast is it? Did you drive? Like drive drive."

"I did drive her, and she's really fast."

"She?"

"I christened her," Calynn explained. "And since she was me for so long... I thought..."

"And you named her?"

"Are you mad?"

"Maybe a little," Kash replied honestly. "I never... thought of... well, what uh... what did you name her?"

"Actually, you named her," Calynn replied. "I remember you saying it when you were recovering that necklace from the smugglers in the Gee System. And I thought it fit... us."

"I remember the necklace and getting my ass kicked, but not what I said."

"The big one called you a pussy, and then the guy with the robotic arm called you a little pussy cat. The others joined in with various forms of the same insults," Calynn explained. "When you turned the tables on them and got the upper hand, you asked what kind of cat that made you..."

"An Alley Cat Savant," Kash spoke the words as he remembered them.

"Which means you are street-smart and scrappy with an uncommon set of exceptional skills," Calynn continued. "It describes you more than me, but..."

"I love it," Kash interrupted her. "The ship matches that description perfectly. It looks ordinary and can run the streets..."

"But the Slip and new engines give her some sophisticated advantages..." Calynn continued his thought.

"And you... you are her greatest asset."

"As long as I'm behind my inhibitor," Calynn said with the sadness back in her voice, "so I don't hurt people."

"That's just temporary, right?" Kash asked Plekish more so than Calynn. "Until she learns to control her efforts."

"The inhibitor is just a tool she can completely control," Plekish answered. "Calynn can remove it if she so wishes..."

"No, that's too dangerous," Calynn interrupted. "Someone could get hurt... you should all stay away from me. Unless you want to be hurt... or worse."

"Okay, that's twice," Kash announced. "Something is bothering you. What gives?"

"Nothing," Calynn responded.

"Your body language tells a different story."

"I said nothing is wrong."

"There is something very wrong with you, Calynn."

"I know that!" Calynn shouted. "It's probably why she won't email me back!"

"What are you talking about?" Kash shouted back.

"Omia won't talk to me anymore!"

"Wait, what?" Kash softened his tone. "Omia loves you. She would never..."

"But she did!"

"But she wouldn't..."

"But she did!" Calynn nearly shrieked.

Meesha moved to comfort the girl before she was done yelling. Plekish nodded at the children, and they both scurried out of the room. Kash and Plekish joined Meesha as Calynn continued her rant.

"I drove her away," Calynn wept. "I asked her too many questions... very personal questions, and I made her mad."

"There's no way..." Kash repeated.

"She won't respond anymore," Calynn interrupted angrily. "So there is a way!"

Calynn was upset and struggling with her emotions. She was sad and angry at the same time and was having trouble quantifying those emotions.

"I would have to agree with Kash, Calynn," Plekish said soothingly. "From what you told me of Miss Omia, I do not foresee her acting that way."

"Then why would she stop talking to me?" Calynn whined.

"I think you need to leave," Plekish stated almost coldly.

"What?" Calynn continued whining. "Why?"

"Because there is nothing wrong with you," Plekish explained.

"Something is wrong with Omia," Kash continued Plekish's thought. "Something happened to her."

"Precisely," Plekish confirmed.

"I'll get some food together for you while you get ready," Meesha said as she quickly moved to the stove.

"I'll inform Rinktee to prepare your ship for departure," Plekish said as he walked away.

"Children," Meesha hollered, "come say goodbye to Kash and Calynn. They have an emergency to attend to."

Kash noticed the worry on Calynn's face despite the commotion around them. He gently grabbed her hand and rubbed the back of her hand with his thumb. He gently embraced her and wrapped her in a comforting hug. Eventually, she returned his embrace.

"I know, baby girl," Kash said and kissed Calynn's head. "I'm worried, too."

Back to Poncia

"What's our ETA?" Kash asked Calynn, who was at the helm.

"Sixteen hourns."

"So, a five-day trip is less than a day?"

"I told you she was fast."

"And quieter, too."

"That's a byproduct of the vastly superior efficiency," Calynn explained. "The engines are better in every conceivable way. They provide more thrust with less waste and need less power to do so."

"Goddamn, I love our wicked-smart friends."

"Me too."

Calynn looked like she was at home flying their ship. Plekish told him she had been practicing using the controls to actually fly the ship. She could effortlessly fly the ship through her link but enjoyed being hands-on with the actual controls. She was wearing blue jeans and a pale pink T-shirt. It was a very simple outfit that she wore very well. Her hair was pulled back into a loose ponytail, making her look approachable. Keeping other men away from her would be a task in itself.

"The flaws in your figure make those clothes look amazing," Kash said with a smirk.

"Are you being sarcastic?" Calynn asked as she spun around in her chair to face him.

"No," Kash chuckled. "I'm just saying if you think you are flawed..."

"If you study the beauty standards..."

"Calynn," Kash interrupted her interruption. "I'm just trying to say you look absolutely amazing. Stop comparing yourself to an impossible standard. You are... stunning."

Calynn smiled a shy little smile. She blushed a little, which made her look even more adorable.

"And if someone ever says that to you," Kash continued, "just say thank you... Okay?"

"Yes, Boss," Calynn replied, spinning back around to her controls. "Thank you, Boss."

"How's the new inhibitor?" Kash asked. "I like your hair pulled back like that. I think the other one would have prevented you from doing so."

"It's much better as a bracer," Calynn replied, lifting her left arm with the high-tech oversized wristband. "It looks like data screens for when I'm piloting the ship, so nobody will think twice when they see it."

"I can't wait until you don't need it."

Calynn turned and shot him a cross look, rolled her eyes, and turned back around.

"What was that for?" Kash continued.

"You know what," Calynn argued. "Bahanja said I will always need it."

"No, she said you will probably always need it... emphasis on probably."

"Semantics."

"Quitter."

"Excuse me?" Calynn asked, clearly hurt by his comment.

"Nobody knows what you can accomplish, nobody," Kash argued. "I think you can prove everyone wrong and be... well, I don't know what. But I, for one, don't intend to lock you in the box of needing that damn inhibitor forever. I just got you out of a box..."

When Calynn spun around, tears were in her eyes, and her face wrinkled as if she were struggling not to cry.

"Oh, baby, don't cry," Kash continued in a softer tone.

"I really like not being in the box," Calynn wept the words more than speaking them.

"I know, Baby Girl," Kash said as he moved to comfort the girl. "I'm sorry if I upset you."

Calynn remained seated at the helm. She laid her head against his body and laid her hand on his when he caressed her cheek. He had grown very fond of the girl over the past couple of weeks. Having a physical representation of her only intensified his fondness.

"I just want you to be totally free," Kash explained. "Even if we turn it down in such small increments that it takes ten-thousand days to turn it off... I'll be the happiest old and decrepit..."

"You won't be that old," Calynn argued.

"I'm already forty-two... I think."

"You look younger."

"Thanks to Plekish and his regeneration pods."

"See... we'll just keep throwing you in a pod every couple of years," Calynn said with more emotion than she probably intended. "So I'm not... alone."

"You won't be alone... I'm sure of that... your batteries will run out long before, oof."

Calynn playfully whacked him in the stomach, and the duo giggled. She had been around him enough to know when he was teasing her. His jest lightened her mood, which is what he intended.

"Do I have batteries?"

"They didn't tell you?"

"I guess it never came up."

"Huh... I guess I never thought to ask either," Kash agreed. "But speaking of recharging batteries, I'm gonna go lay down and recharge mine... you good here?"

"The Cat is in good hands, Captain," Calynn said with a smile.

"Keep her purring, Baby Girl."

Kash walked a short distance into his cabin and closed the door behind him. He stood tall with his feet together and fell forward into a push-up. He did ten quick push-ups and exploded up through the last one so that he ended up standing again. A heroic feat of strength that felt easy to him... almost too easy.

"Artificial gravity must be turned down some," Kash said quietly to himself as he removed his shirt.

He kicked off his shoes and dropped his pants, so he was just in his boxers and crawled into bed. It only took a few seconds for the bed to adjust to him, so he felt nearly weightless. The hum of the engines sounded soothing like his ship was purring him to sleep. It didn't take long for him to doze off.

His dreams were filled with only Omia. Her body... her lips... her eyes... the way her hips swayed when she cooked... her gentle touch... the taste of her tongue... the warmth of her body pressed against him... she was so warm... wait, he was kinda warm too.

He felt the bed move as another body pressed up against his. He was still half asleep, but he could tell it was Calynn. She was desperately trying to be the little spoon and wrap him around her.

"What are you doing?" Kash mumbled.

"I just need you right now... okay."

Kash relented and put his hand on her belly to pull her in but then stopped her.

"Strip first," Kash said. "Just down to your undergarments... clothes get the sheets too dirty."

Calynn's body disappeared for a moment and then returned. This time, when he placed his hand on her belly, he felt her warm skin. She laced her little fingers through his and wrapped his arm around herself. The back of her body was pressed tightly to his front. She didn't say any more, but she felt... fidgety. Something was bothering the young girl. Rather than address it, he decided to compliment her.

"You really do have amazing skin," Kash whispered. "Get some sleep."

When Kash awoke, Calynn was still lying with him. She only stirred when he did.

"That was a nice nap," Kash said, tightly squeezing the girl. "Are you okay?"

"I... well... I was, er... felt...and I didn't know how..."

"One thought at a time," Kash interrupted. "I'm not awake enough to follow that."

"I was worried about Omia," Calynn said with a sigh. "And I'm... I'm like an emotional roller coaster... up and down so much."

"I have noticed some rapid mood swings."

"I'm not trying to do that."

"It's okay," Kash comforted her and kissed her head.

"I'm okay when I'm with you," Calynn explained. "You're like my anchor. Sorry that I'm so needy."

"It's okay, Baby Girl," Kash said softly. "You've had some extensive, enormous, life-altering, and just like huge, huge changes lately. If you weren't frazzled... I'd be worried."

"I just don't want to be a burden because I'm so broken."

"You're not a burden, and if you weren't broken, you'd be... a sociopath."

Calynn rolled into him a bit so she could turn to look at him. She was scowling.

"What?" Kash asked.

"A sociopath?"

"I would rather have a broken you than a perfectly functioning sociopath," Kash explained. "There's absolutely no doubt in my mind about that."

"Thanks, Boss."

Calynn rolled back over and pulled his arm around her. She hugged his arm to her body, so his hand was on her chest. He couldn't help but notice how his forearm was now sandwiched between her breasts. Kash again found himself in awe of Bahanja and her team and how much Calynn's skin felt and moved like natural skin.

"I have never seen or heard about synthetic skin feeling as real as yours," Kash blurted out his thoughts. "If I didn't know any better..."

"You'd think I was the real Calynn?"

"I sure would."

Calynn quickly rolled onto her back, so they no longer touched each other. She had a devious smile on her face.

"Wanna feel something cool?"

"Maybe," Kash replied a little apprehensively.

"Okay, I'll do it first," Calynn said excitedly. "Watch."

Calynn poked herself just above the cup of her bra and really pushed her finger into the breast tissue. She poked hard enough that it left a gap between her skin and the black fabric of her bra.

"Now, if I activate the defenses..."

Calynn beamed a smile as she pulled her finger away... but the dent in her flesh remained.

"Cool, huh?"

"What the heck?"

Kash reached out and put his finger in the indentation. Her skin felt hard and metallic.

"And then if I relax it."

Her skin again became supple, and her flesh pushed back against his finger.

"It's more noticeable on my boobs because they're boobs, but my whole body does that," Calynn explained. "Push on my belly."

Kash did as the girl asked and pressed one finger deep into her stomach until her flesh again turned hard. When he removed his finger, the impression of it remained.

"I thought it was only supposed to do that if you got shot or something?" Kash asked.

"It was..., but I can control it too," Calynn explained. "Bahanja isn't sure how I control it, but I do."

"That's amazing, Calynn."

"It's kinda fun to play with," Calynn continued. "If I puff out my cheeks and do it, I look ridiculous. Or if I pull out on my nipples really hard, I look like I have spikes for boobs. Or I push one up and one down. That looks so funny. Or... Oh... um, sorry if..."

"I get it," Kash interrupted. "Boobs are fun to play with."

"They definitely are... and I wasn't fully developed... before... so this is the first time..."

"What else have you figured out about your new body?"

"It's hyper-flexible," Calynn said as her fingers bent themselves back so they were flat against the back of her hand. "I can do that with any joint. Bahanja said she wanted to increase my escapability. In case I was ever captured. I can make myself sweat or give myself goosebumps if I have to do that to fit in. I can make myself blush or turn my lips blue. I can hold my butt hole open when I poop to make cleanup easier..."

"Whoa," Kash interrupted. "That's too much information."

"Oh, sorry."

"Why would you want to tell me about your poop?"

"I don't know," Calynn exclaimed. "I'm just so excited about my new body. Sorry, I guess I got carried away."

"I get that."

"Sorry for the poop talk."

"It's okay," Kash giggled. "What else you got?"

"I can do this," Calynn's voice came over the ship's speakers, but her lips didn't move.

"That's cool."

"It's so I can be the ship's pilot and the nerve center," Calynn explained. "Obviously, I will make the two voices different if I have to."

Kash found himself distracted momentarily by Calynn's hands. The girl was rubbing up and down her entire torso. It was unintentionally kinda sexy. He figured he already knew the answer to his question, but he asked anyway.

"And why are you rubbing your body like that?"

"Oh, sorry," Calynn apologized. "It's so nice to feel things after not... for so long... and it gives me something else to focus on. I can run the inhibitor lower."

"Really?"

"Yep... in fact, if I were properly stimulated... like all the erogenous zones at once... I bet you could take this thing off of me completely. If I really focused on it."

Calynn also sounded a little embarrassed and a little unsure of herself.

"You tried... didn't you?"

"Yea," Calynn admitted. "I can make my nerves vibrate. It feels really good."

"How anatomically correct are you?"

"Wanna find out?" Calynn said as she spread her legs.

"Whoa... ah... no, that would be bad."

"Bad?" Calynn sounded hurt. "Why would that be bad?"

"Because we're like family."

"And husbands and wives have sex."

"Yeah, but we're closer to big brother and little sister."

"But we have been cuddling for five hourns."

"Because you needed that for your mental wellbeing," Kash explained. "If cuddling has to lead to sex, then we aren't cuddling anymore."

"Cuddling is fine," Calynn said as she again assumed the small spoon's position. "I am good with just cuddling."

"Are you sure?"

"Yep."

"What's our ETA?"

"Ten hourns twenty-two minutes."

"Another nap?"

"Yes, please."

Kash curled up to Calynn and let the hum of the engines lull him to sleep once again. When he awoke, he was alone. Calynn had left the bed at some point while Kash slept. He rolled out of bed, dressed, and grabbed an oral sanitizing tablet from its bottle. The tablet foamed up in his mouth when he chewed it. He swished the foam around and spit it out in the toilet before relieving himself.

He then went to the cockpit to look for Calynn and was surprised to find she wasn't there.

"Calynn?" Kash hollered.

"Back here," she replied from a distance.

"What are you doing in the cargo hold?" Kash asked as he marched back the hall.

"My clothes are back here," Calynn replied just as Kash caught sight of her.

He could see she was wearing jeans again and a light blue bra. She had a blue tee shirt in her left hand and a babydoll tank top in her right.

"The one in your right hand looks best without a bra," Kash said as he leaned against the catwalk's railing.

"Yeah, but I don't know that I want to draw that much attention to myself."

"Oh... yea... first time around strangers."

"But I could be a distraction if we need one."

"I'd go with the tee shirt," Kash explained. "Let's not plan to use you as bait just yet."

"Okay, Boss," Calynn replied, slipping the tee on.

"And we need to find room for your clothes, too," Kash said as he turned to walk back to his cabin.

"I think I have a plan for that. We just need to order some stuff."

"I trust you... order away."

Kash returned to his quarters and sat at his desk. He fired up his computer to check the bounty boards and the Trade Commission website and to scan news headlines from the local sectors. He was always on the prowl for his next job. The bribe he had received from Doc would be enough for him and Calynn to live on for the rest of his life, but he enjoyed the work. And more importantly, he eventually wanted to be able to do something to help orphans like himself. Funding such an organization to privatize orphan care would be daunting at best. So he scanned the cyber-web for hidden treasures as time slipped by.

"On approach, Boss," Calynn announced several hourns later. "Are we checking her house first?"

"Let's start at the clinic. Maybe her coworkers know more than we do."

"I'll have to fly fast... it's approaching closing time at the clinic."

"Hit it."

As soon as Kash uttered those words, the ship accelerated extremely hard. It almost knocked him out of his chair.

"My Gods, this thing can move," Kash exclaimed.

He heard Calynn giggling in the cockpit. He had to put a hand on the wall to brace himself as the ship banked through a turn. The sound of air rushing over the wings let him know they had entered the planet's atmosphere. When he felt the ship flatten out and decelerate, he knew they were getting ready to land. He walked out to the cockpit to join Calynn.

"You trying to melt the wings entering the atmosphere that fast?" Kash asked playfully.

"The Cat can take it," Calynn said calmly as the ship touched the ground. "On the ground and shutting her down, Boss."

"Are you ready for this next part?"

"Dealing with strangers?"

"And keeping a nice even keel... not a roller coaster."

"I have the inhibitor cranked up."

"Good girl... I'll be right beside you."

"Thanks, Boss," Calynn said with a smile and moved to join him. "That helps the most."

The duo walked out the door and headed towards the clinic where they first met Dr. Omia Moss. Calynn was a little fidgety as they approached the door but held herself in check. Seemo must have seen them coming as he opened the door before Kash could.

"Kash," Seemo greeted him excitedly, "boy, am I glad to see you."

"Seemo, my good man, what's going on?"

"It's Dr. Moss," Seemo explained. "She went... um... sorry, who is your friend?"

"Hi, Seemo, I'm Calynn."

"Calynn... you're Calynn? Dr. Moss talks about you a lot, and as pretty as you are... I can see why," Seemo said with a kind smile.

"Aww, thank you, Seemo," Calynn replied graciously.

"Where's Omia, Seemo?" Kash asked the man, trying to get him back on task.

"That politician from the city came and got her," Seemo replied. "She didn't want to go, but he was threatening the staff, and... she went with him just to get him and his goons out of the clinic."

"What's his name?"

"I don't know," Seemo admitted. "But he's connected to the high-end call girls there... in Moilad."

"Calynn," Kash turned to the girl and glanced down at the device on her arm, "run a search and see what you can find."

"On it, Boss."

Calynn pulled her bracer up and started typing on it. Kash was close enough to her to watch her pretty brown eyes shaking back and forth at an incredible rate.

"Got him," Calynn said as her eyes stopped shaking. "Franscio... Senator Will Franscio."

"Got an address?"

"I sure do, Boss."

"Seemo, thanks for..."

"Bring her home for us, Mr. Kash," Seemo interrupted. "Please, bring her home. And please hurry... we are all very worried."

"I'm on the case, Old Timer. I'll find our girl."

Kash smiled at the man and shook his hand before returning to The Cat. Once out of earshot, he turned to Calynn.

"Great job... what did you get?"

"I got everything," Calynn replied. "Address, banking info, acquaintances, all of it."

"Let's get his attention... overdraw his bank accounts," Kash explained. "Make me an account in the same bank and move the money there. Make sure they can follow it. Wait... define acquaintances?"

"It seems the Police Chief and several other Senators are just as corrupt as Franscio," Calynn answered. "There's also a pimp and several drug dealers."

"Bankrupt them all."

Calynn grabbed his arm as they walked. Kash assumed it was to steady herself as she hacked the banking system, or maybe it affected her vision while she was doing it.

"Done," Calynn stated and released his arm.

"And where is he at the moment?"

"In his office... having a meeting."

"Let's go interrupt that meeting, shall we?"

"We shall."

The flight to Moilad was a short one. Finding a dock in the city took longer than flying there. Once there, they hailed a cab and went directly to the Senator's office. Kash tipped the cabbie handsomely and asked him to stay close for their return trip.

"Stay calm," Kash said quietly to Calynn as they approached the building.

A doorman opened the door and ushered them into the lobby. In front of them was a small, round information desk manned by an older woman. Beyond that was a security station with several guards.

"They are all armed, Boss," Calynn's voice said over the comm in his ear.

Kash nodded at Calynn to acknowledge her statement as he approached the woman at the information desk.

"Good evening," the woman said, "how can I help you?"

"I'm Kash, and this is my pilot, Calynn," Kash told the woman. "I'd like to see Senator Franscio. We don't have an appointment."

"I'm afraid the Senator..."

"Just tell him I'm here," Kash interrupted. "I'm absolutely certain he will want to see me."

Kash smiled at the woman and then had a seat in one of the chairs in the lobby. The woman did as he had asked, and Kash could hear the commotion and yelling getting closer.

"Calm... okay?" Kash whispered to Calynn. "Cold and calculated."

"I'll try, Boss."

The security detail approached them rapidly with their weapons drawn.

"Keep your hands where we can see them!" one of them shouted. "Come with us!"

Kash stood slowly and then offered a hand to Calynn.

"Shall we?"

"If we must," Calynn replied as she accepted his offered hand.

Kash turned back to the security guards and smiled.

"Lead on fellas."

The guards led them to one of the grand staircases in the lobby and ushered them upstairs. Kash and Calynn trotted up the stairs like they didn't have a care in the world. Kash continued to smile and would greet anyone they saw. Calynn seemed to feed off his calm demeanor and was relatively relaxed. She stood tall with her shoulders back, beaming a beautiful smile at everyone. If she was nervous, she did a great job of hiding it.

Several angry faces greeted them when they entered the Senator's office.

"Greetings, gentleman," Kash offered as they entered the room.

"Greetings be damned!" one man barked. "Who are you, and where is my money?!"

"That depends," Kash replied calmly, settling into one of the plush chairs in the room.

"Depends... depends on what?" another man shouted.

"On where Dr. Omia Moss is," Kash replied in his same even tone. "If you return her to me, then I will return your money to you... simple."

"Who the fuck do you think you are?" the first man barked.

"Someone who just wants Omia back... no questions asked."

"That slut?" a third man asked calmly.

"That's the senator, Boss," Calynn stated in his ear.

"I believe she described herself as a nymphomaniac with great tits, Will," Kash explained to the man. "But if slut is the extent of your vocabulary, then, yes... the slut."

"What's your interest in her?" Will asked

"She's a friend."

"Have you fucked her?" another man asked.

"Of course I have," Kash exclaimed with a bit of frustration in his voice. "She is a nymphomaniac with an amazing body and spectacular tits... she's also a great cook, but none of that matters right now. The only thing I want to hear from you is where... she... is... period."

Kash paused for a moment as if trying to collect himself.

"Look, fellas... I don't want to cause an incident here... I just want my friend back."

Kash noted the location of the four armed guards in the room and any improvised weapons available to subdue them. He figured they would search him, so he didn't bring a weapon. He was finally going to get to test his new muscles.

"It's a simple transaction," Kash continued. "You give me the girl, and I give you the money."

"Or maybe we take your cute friend and just kill you instead," the Senator said coldly. "That's a nice little body she has... wanna fuck, honey?"

"Will any real men be attending, or just you lot?" Calynn replied sarcastically. "I'm not sure it would be worth the time needed to unbutton my jeans. And it might be over quicker than that. That one looks like he'd cream his pants if I just took my shirt off."

"And she has a sharp tongue," Will commented. "We have just the solution for that."

Franscio nodded at one of the guards, and the big man started moving towards Calynn.

"He's not gonna sit on me, is he?" Calynn continued her verbal assault. "Drowning in fat isn't that high on my list of turn-ons."

"You fucking bitch!" the guard barked as he tried to pistol whip Calynn.

What happened next was so fast that even Kash couldn't believe it. There was a rush of air from Calynn's direction, three impossibly fast gunshots, and the big man in front of her had his head on backward. The smoke from the gun lifted around Calynn's face as the four guards finally fell over dead. The three Senators had stunned looks on their faces.

"Anyone else wanna fuck?" Calynn said with a demonic tone in her voice.

Three heads shook side to side in stunned silence.

"Why couldn't you just give us the girl?" Kash expressed his disappointment. "Girl... money... simple... but nooooo... you had to get blood on the carpet, and now I have to beat the information out of you."

"Whoa, can we not do that?" one of the other men asked.

"Do you know who we are?" the third asked. "You can't assault the ruling class... we could have you arrested."

"Arrested?" Kash nearly laughed. "Do you know who I am? I have thousands of witnesses who know I am the one who delivered the medicine that made you not have to fear the sun anymore. I would seriously like to see you try to arrest and hold me... the riots would be..."

"Devastating," Calynn finished his sentence.

Calynn sounded like herself again and not like a demon. She was gripping the gun so hard Kash was sure she probably dented the grip.

"The way I see it, you have two options, gentlemen," Kash continued. "Bring me Omia, or... this fiery little pixie tears you apart... piece by piece."

"And the money?" Will asked.

"A contribution towards your life insurance policy," Kash replied.

"That doesn't work for me," Will explained. "I owe some very powerful people some money. I need a portion of that back."

"And I need my friend back!" Demonic Calynn was back.

"I'll tell you what... Senator," Kash spoke with disdain in his voice. "I'll give you all the money back... in exchange for every girl... all of them. You shut down your call girl operation, and I'll give you the money."

"I can't do that... I have partners..."

"Then have fun coming up with the money you owe," Kash said coldly. "Let's start by tearing their toes off one by one... test our new implants. What do you think?"

"I bet I can tear off all five toes before you can," Calynn bantered with Kash.

"Oh, you're on," Kash agreed. "Loser cooks for a month?"

"Get your apron ready, big man... you're going down."

"Okay... okay," Will exclaimed as the duo approached. "My partner has her... I couldn't make the payment this month..."

"Liar," Calynn interrupted. "There was enough money in your account for four payments."

"I just needed to use that money for something else... I swear."

"So you sold my friend instead?" Calynn barked.

"I needed to settle the debt, and the way she likes to fuck, I didn't..."

"I'm gonna tear off more than your toes if the next words out of your mouth anger me further," Calynn growled.

"I'm going to agree with the pixie," Kash commented. "If you were about to say she wouldn't mind being a sex slave, you might end up skinless. In fact, I will remove a piece of your body for every word you say that isn't Omia's location... her exact... location."

"She's off planet... in a space freighter that he converted into a mansion," Senator Franscio admitted. "He stays on the move so the authorities can never get close."

"Where's he going?" Calynn demanded.

"I don't know."

"WHERE?" Calynn shrieked.

"I don't know... I swear."

"Then what's his name?" Kash asked forcefully.

"I can't tell you that... he'd kill me!"

"Then you're fucking useless!" the pretty blond barked.

Kash knew they were getting nowhere with the Senator. They needed a different approach. He retrieved a gun from one of the dead guards and shot the other two Senators in the head. He ignored Will's protests and turned to Calynn.

"Can you track him through the banking info?" Kash asked Calynn softly. "You saw the payments, right?"

"I don't know," Calynn admitted.

"I have a contact that can do it, but it will take a few days."

"It seems to be isolated somehow."

"What about past purchases? Maybe we can get lucky," Kash continued. "Where has he gone after being on Poncia?"

"I can only go back one year... and there are three planets he visited after being here," Calynn offered. "Layton, Nordon, and the Sanguis Grotto... I don't think that's a planet, though."

"It's not," Kash replied. "It's a barge where you can bet on illegal fighting."

"How do you know that?"

"Because it was just raided by the Consortium Constabulary a few days ago... I saw it in the news reports."

"Then he won't go there," Calynn reasoned. "That just leaves the other two... and they're roughly the same direction."

"When did they leave?" Kash asked Will.

"Four nights ago," the man replied.

"Is The Cat fast enough to beat them there?"

"She sure is. We just have to guess which one."

"How about left is Layton and right is Nordon?"

"Huh?" Calynn asked with a puzzled look on her face.

"Goodbye, Senator," Kash stated coldly and raised his gun.

"No wa..."

The gunshot cut off the man's protest. Kash shot him right in the middle of his forehead. The dead man slouched in the chair, drooped down, and then fell to the ground.

"He fell to the right," Kash explained. "Nordon it is."

"It was our left, though."

"But that's not how I meant it."

"Well, next time, explain the rules better. I would have assumed Layton."

"Technically, it doesn't matter... it's not like he can argue."

"It matters to me. I need a heading."

"We can discuss it on the way back to The Cat."

"You know there's a bunch of armed guards outside the office, right?"

"I figured as much."

"And how do you intend to get us out of here?" Calynn asked. "I can't shoot them all before they return fire. Our odds aren't great."

"Simple," Kash replied as he sat down and pulled his left foot onto his lap. "The heel of this boot leaves an invisible residue on the ground with each step."

Kash turned the heel of his boot and popped it off, revealing a transmitter.

"This transmits a frequency that activates the residue, like so," Kash said as he flipped the switch. "And then we just wait a few seconds for the bodies to start dropping."

"What is it?"

"It's a knockout gas that also affects short-term memory. The prick bastards will be lucky to remember the last month. They'll never remember us."

"And how do we get out?"

"I'm immune, and I figured you could filter it out... or hold your breath."

"Hold my breath?"

"We can cuddle after," Kash said meekly, trying to appease her.

Calynn took a big gulp of air, pinched her nose, and ran out the door. He heard three gunshots ring out. Some of the men must not have been incapacitated yet.

"She's gonna pissed at you for a while, Kash," he said to himself. "Well, you did just have her run through a cloud of gas that could erase her memory... which you know is a fear of hers. Yea, dumb ass... who's brilliant plan was that?"

The fire alarm went off, triggering the sprinklers, interrupting Kash's dialog with himself.

"That was probably her... well, she was worried about the gas being on her clothes, dumb ass. She's probably trying to wash it off. If you have to try to get her back to the ship when she's pissed off and stark naked, that's your own dumb fault, dumb ass."

Kash finally started to walk out of the Senator's office while shaking his head at himself. The sprinklers rained down upon him as he walked.

"Oh, and don't forget to delete the camera footage in the security booth, dumb ass."

A New Enemy

Kash heard the shower cycle start for the eighth time and beat on the bathroom door again.

"Come on, Calynn, that shower gel is expensive, and we are running low," Kash hollered through the door.

"I can still feel it on my skin," Calynn hollered back.

"I can promise you it isn't there anymore... please."

The shower cycle stopped, and he heard rustling behind the door.

"My towel is wet," Calynn said through the door. "Can you get me another one?"

"Just use mine."

"I already did... it's wet, too."

"Fine," Kash conceded, grabbing a clean towel from the tiny linen closet beside the bathroom door. "Here."

The bathroom door unlocked and opened just enough for Calynn to get her arm out. Kash handed her the towel. She pulled it into the bathroom and closed the door again.

"Come on, Baby Girl, I said I was sorry," Kash reiterated. "I'm not used to working with a partner yet."

"I need my clothes too."

Kash retrieved the pile of clothes from his bed and passed them to Calynn through the door. This time, she left the door cracked open. She dressed quickly and burst out of the bathroom with the towel wrapped around her hair. She walked around Kash and sat down on the edge of the bed. She had a sad and angry look on her face. Kash was about to apologize again when she burst into tears.

"I killed those men, and I can't wash it off," Calynn wept.

Her words surprised him. He thought her constant washing was about the gas he used. He never thought that she was upset about taking the guard's lives.

"But we've killed people before…"

"Not with my hands," Calynn interrupted. "My hands did that. These…"

Calynn presented her hands to him like they were weapons.

"It just felt more… personal than doing it with the Slip or firing a missile," Calynn continued. "Come here so I can lay on you."

Kash didn't argue. He went over and laid on the bed. They were above the covers, so he didn't mind them wearing clothes. Calynn lay directly on top of him with her head on his chest. She took a couple of deep breaths, and he felt her body relax.

"I didn't think I would have such a problem with that," Calynn confessed, much calmer than he expected.

"It never occurred to me either since we've done it before."

"This was different… how do you cope with it?"

"I bury bad memories beneath the good ones."

"I'm not sure how practical that is for me."

"Well… then you need to justify it to yourself. Like today in that office… those men would have beaten, raped, and killed you."

"But I could just make my skin hard, and they couldn't have done those things to me."

"True… but they could do it to other girls… you stopped all those future rapes from happening… if they will kidnap and sell a doctor… what do you think they would do to a homeless girl?"

"I did it because they stood in the way of us getting to Omia."

"And how good will it feel to hug Omia when we save her from these pricks?"

"Pretty fucking good," Calynn said with some confidence in her voice.

"There's my girl."

Calynn took another deep breath and snuggled into Kash's chest. He rubbed her back and shoulders as she lay there.

"Feel better?"

"A little bit."

"So, which planet did you pick, Layton or Nordon?"

"I was too upset to decide, so I shot us right down the middle," Calynn admitted. "I can adjust our course later. Any word from your guy?"

"Not yet."

"Wanna take a n..." Calynn stopped herself mid-word, jumped up, and ran to the cockpit.

"What's wrong?" Kash asked as he followed her.

"Rogue asteroid field," Calynn announced as she shut down the HLD.

Kash strapped himself into the jump seat so he could assist as needed. Calynn decelerated fast and stopped in front of some massive asteroids. The field extended as far as he could see in every direction.

"Gods, they're big," Kash let the words slip out.

"Look, the biggest one is in the middle," Calynn announced. "Its gravity is holding the rest of them together. If we can tag it with a beacon for the Trade Commission..."

"On it," Kash said as he grabbed the fire control joystick. "There's a lot of debris in the way. Gonna be a tough shot."

"We can use a drone."

"They might pay for that."

"It's still the right thing to do," Calynn explained. "If I couldn't find a way through..."

"An unconscious nerve center that can't wake up and cut the HLD doesn't stand a chance," Kash finished her sentence.

"Exactly."

"Dropping the beacon now."

Calynn skillfully used the drone to navigate the asteroid field and tagged the giant asteroid in the center of the field. The duo watched the navigation scope and waited for the beacon to be recognized before giving each other a high-five. The beacon would provide all ships with the necessary warning to avoid certain disaster.

"I'll send a message to the Trade Commission and let them know what we found," Kash said as he unstrapped himself.

"And I'll get us around this mess and back underway."

"Nap after?"

"Sounds good, Boss."

The following two days were uneventful. Kash and Calynn arrived at her center point before Kash's contact got back to him about where their mystery man was. They ate, talked, laughed, and napped together. Kash would always try to be as rested and nourished as possible before going on a mission. Too often, he had to stay awake for two or three days with no food and little to no water. He was a little surprised at how frequently Calynn would join him for the naps. After all... she didn't need sleep.

"Where is your guy?" Calynn whined as they lounged in bed. "We won't be able to beat them to the planet if we don't know which one?"

"I followed up with him before our last nap," Kash replied. "I'm hopeful to hear something soon... And speaking of naps, I've been wondering something."

"About me?"

"When we nap... you don't sleep, do you?"

"No, I do not."

"Then why join me?" Kash asked, then added quickly. "Not that I'm complaining. You are very cuddly, and I think I sleep better with you here. You are very comfortable to lay on."

"I don't sleep... but I rest," Calynn answered. "I focus on not focusing... oh, how do I explain this? ... I'm always reaching out in every direction... like the sun shining. The inhibitor holds me back like a filter that doesn't let me reach too far. When we lay down together, it's very calming for me. I can change the way I reach... I sorta focus inward."

"But if you're looking inward, how did you see that asteroid field?"

"I'm still connected to the ship's sensors, silly."

"Oh, yeah," Kash replied. "Speaking of which, what does that look like to you?"

"The asteroid field through the sensors?"

"Yea."

"Umm... okay. Well, the light bubble is like a really long cone moving through water... space flows around the outside rather smoothly most of the time. But when the tip of that cone hits the asteroid field, it causes cavitations. Space kinda tumbles in those spots."

"So it makes waves."

"Yea... kinda. What's that sound?"

"Move your ass," Kash interrupted. "That's our guy."

Kash moved Calynn out of the way so he could get to his computer terminal and opened the message. The encrypted email contained a link to the Trade Commission Operations site and the transponder location of the mystery man's barge.

"Looks like he's headed to Layton, but..."

"But what, Boss."

"Either that thing is slow as shit, or they made a stop," Kash exclaimed. "They're still two days out."

"Is the trajectory right?" Calynn asked as she walked up behind him.

"It looks like it is."

"So they dropped out of light speed and had a rendezvous without changing course?" Calynn questioned. "That seems odd."

"Or it's just that slow."

"The Senator could have been wrong about the departure time too."

"Look at that," Kash said as he pointed to the screen.

"What the heck kind of name is Egonn Egonn?" Calynn asked.

"Kinda silly, right?"

"Well, let's go meet the silly man," Calynn announced. "Setting course for Layton... spinning up the HLD..."

"You're not going to the cockpit for this?"

"I don't want to get dressed just to get undressed again so I don't get the sheets dirty," Calynn explained. "It's your rules."

"So what you're saying is..."

"As soon as I engage the HLD, we're laying down again," Calynn interrupted. "Yes... that's exactly what I'm saying."

"I've created a cuddle monster," Kash said sarcastically.

"Careful... I bite."

"You better not."

The duo giggled as they lay down. Calynn backed into him and wrapped his arm around herself. Kash pushed her over so she was half on her side and half on her belly, and he was half on top of her. Calynn wrapped her leg around his and wiggled herself in as tight as she could to his body.

"Hey, does Layton have an Aviation Supply Depot?" Kash asked quietly.

"Checking... yes, they do."

"Plot our course for there," Kash replied. "We need to resupply."

"Will do, Boss."

"What's our ETA?"

"Six hourns."

"Wake me in three."

"Will do."

The HLD hummed as Kash cuddled into Calynn's warm body. He wished it was Omia that he was cuddling, not Calynn. They were both great sleeping companions, but with Omia, he could let his hands wander more. Having a handful of Calynn's boob as they slept might send the wrong message to the young woman. As much as he cared for and even loved Calynn, he didn't want to ruin that with a grope or frivolous night of passion. Some would argue that their naps together were inappropriate, but they seemed really important to Calynn. She said they helped her feel calm... or at least more relaxed anyway. And she made an excellent substitute for a body pillow.

Kash woke up to the sound of the shower cycle running and an empty bed. He wiped the sleep from his eyes and sat up. He figured he would get a shower after Calynn was done, so he went to get some clothes.

"Are you up, Boss?" Calynn asked from the shower.

"Just barely," Kash replied. "I need a shower too... are you almost done?"

"Two minutes," she replied.

Kash stared at his closet and wondered what he should wear. Should he wear a suit to meet the mystery gangster? ... Or maybe tactical gear? ... Perhaps something more casual?

"I don't know what to wear either," Calynn said from the bathroom door. "I just grabbed a bra and panties for now. I was hoping to just match you."

"I'm leaning towards a suit for the actual meeting, but maybe something more casual for shopping."

"How about jeans, a white tee shirt, and your gray suit jacket?" Calynn suggested. "I can match that."

"Yes, Dear," Kash said with a long exasperated sigh.

"Hey," Calynn argued. "What was that tone for?"

"Dressing me is such a girlfriend thing to do... maybe we shouldn't spend so much time together."

Kash smirked at his remark and waited for Calynn's reply. She was fun to pick on.

"Heeey," Calynn whined. "That's not nice... I just wanted to look like I belong to you. Being in public is difficult for me. I worry about... everything. I don't want to hurt people."

"Sorry, Baby Girl," Kash apologized. "I won't pick on you when we're about to go ashore anymore."

"I need a hug now," Calynn said as she walked out of the bathroom wrapped in her towel.

When they connected, her wet hair felt cold on his bare chest, and he immediately noticed how fidgety she felt.

"Sorry for being so needy," she admitted softly into his chest. "Like a child."

"It's okay, Baby Girl," Kash said as he rubbed his back. "You're allowed to be needy. I have said it before, and I'll say it again... I know what I signed up for because I am certain the reward is greater than the sacrifice. You are perfect the way you are... Well... okay, maybe one little correction... just to what you said."

Calynn pulled back and looked up at him with a puzzled look on her face.

"You belong WITH me, not TO me."

"Technically, you did purchase me," Calynn stated as she put her head back on his chest.

"Then I hereby free you," Kash exclaimed. "I guess it never occurred to me to actually say those words. I'm sorry it..."

"I was joking, Boss," Calynn interrupted. "I didn't mean it like that. I meant we belong together... My towel is about to fall off. I should let go of you and finish getting ready."

"I'll go shower," Kash said as he released the girl. "Set out what I'm wearing also."

The duo was soon on their way to get supplies. They stopped at the Harbor Master first to get fresh water supplies and to pump the waste from the ship. There was no need to refuel since his ship barely used any fuel. Most of the energy needed to power his boat was replenished by the static electricity created by traveling faster than light. He only required fuel about once every other month or so.

Their next stop was the supply depot to replace the implosion round he fired at Doc and the two drones they used. His ship could only carry six of each, so it was imperative to keep them stocked. The shopkeeper couldn't keep his eyes off Calynn, so the process was much smoother than expected. The absurd amount of paperwork was still annoying, though.

"I should bring you along more often," Kash told Calynn when they left.

"So creepy, fat old guys can stare at my ass?"

"And save us a bunch of time, too," Kash replied. "Buying weapons is normally much... much slower than that."

"I need another shower."

"Imagine if you didn't have flaws."

Calynn scowled at Kash and then giggled. She hugged his arm as they walked back to the docks through the streets. The music and laughter coming from the local bar caught their attention. Calynn answered his question before he asked it.

"I can try," the young beauty said, shrugging her shoulders.

"Let's not push you too hard, too fast," Kash suggested. "Let's just head back..."

"Boss," Calynn interrupted. "I heard someone in the bar mention Egonn."

"Are you sure?"

"Absolutely... four men in a back room talking softly amongst themselves," Calynn explained. "There are sixty-seven other patrons in the establishment plus eight employees."

Kash took a moment to survey his surroundings. The docks had plenty of warehouses to accommodate the freighters of goods, and smaller businesses and offices filled in the gaps. A few bars and restaurants were positioned to capture the dock workers' patronage. A small cafe sat adjacent to the bar where the men were talking and had some nice tables outside to sit and eat your meal.

"We could sit across the street and get a snack while you surveil the men," Kash said to Calynn. "It would be easier on you than being groped by some drunkards."

"I might like being groped," Calynn replied with a smirk. "But maybe just by one guy and not a room full of drunkards. So, yes... you can take me on a date to the cute little cafe across the street."

Calynn laced the fingers of her left hand through his and placed her right hand directly on top of it. She held his hand in both hers and hugged his arm to her body. Kash knew precisely where she learned to do that. It felt nice... and wrong at the same time. He really missed Omia.

"You make me miss her more when you do the things she did," Kash said softly as he led Calynn to one of the tables outside the cafe.

"I miss her too."

Once Calynn was seated, Kash pushed in her chair and went into the cafe to order some food. He returned to the table with a fruit smoothie for each of them as they waited for their sandwiches.

"Mmm... this tastes so familiar," Calynn stated after taking a sip. "Do you think when Huma seeded the stars like Doc said, they spread the fruit, vegetables, and animals, too?"

"I never thought of that, but it would explain why the food tastes remarkably similar on different planets," Kash replied. "I ordered us what looks like a turkey and bacon sandwich, but they call it lurdo with crispy skins."

"Oh, I hope it's bacon... I looove bacon."

They continued making small talk until their food arrived. Calynn was the first to take a bite. Her pretty face lit up as she savored the bite. Even some passersby couldn't help but stare at his beautiful companion. Kash also took a bite of his sandwich.

"It's candied bacon," Calynn finally said. "It's so good."

"And it's like they shredded a spicy water chestnut on top," Kash added. "Nothing close to lettuce, but it really compliments the meat."

"That's a really good sandwich, Boss."

Kash was watching the crowds of people as they moved along. Calynn was attracting some attention, but it took him a minute to figure out why. All of the people here had darker-colored hair. Calynn's blond hair stuck out like a sore thumb. It didn't take the men long to realize the blond hair was also attached to a woman with an incredible figure. Some of them lingered to stare longer.

"The men are leaving the bar, Boss," Calynn stated.

"Don't worry... they'll notice you. Just like all the other men," Kash said with a giggle.

"They know we aren't from here."

"Oh, that's not why they are staring... they recognize a gorgeous woman when they see one."

Calynn leaned in close and stared into his eyes... with Omia's fuck-me-eyes... she planted a soft kiss on his lips and rubbed his back with her hand. Calynn mimicked Omia's acts of affection amazingly well. Kash was surprised at how good her lips tasted and how much willpower was required to NOT act on his desires.

"Are they still staring?" Calynn asked and placed another kiss on his lips.

"They are… so am I."

"They are approaching us," Calynn whispered, placing her hand on Kash's lap.

Her hand was in the shape of a gun. She was warning him of impending danger.

"Pardon me," one of the men said as he approached.

Kash looked past Calynn at the man, then centered himself in front of her again. He rubbed his nose along hers and stared into her beautiful brown eyes. He completely ignored the men for a moment.

"Excuse me," the man said more forcefully this time.

"Can I help you with something, pal?" Kash replied without looking away.

"I was wondering if your beautiful friend would like to work in one of my clubs?" the man asked.

"She's not interested," Kash said in a dismissive tone.

"Can she not speak for herself…"

"I'm not interested," Calynn asserted.

"Are you sure?" the man continued as the other three men surrounded their table. "The women in my clubs make a lot of credits."

"I don't need to work. He's wealthy," Calynn stated as she pointed to Kash. "But we both like pretty girls. Maybe we'll come to one of your clubs and take one of your other girls home with us."

"Not the bimbos, though," Kash added.

"Yea… dumb girls are the worst," Calynn said as she scrunched her nose in disgust.

After what they had said, the men were apparently at a loss for words, so they stood there for a minute.

"Look... that's not how this works," the thug finally said after puffing up his chest.

"You know what? ... you're right," Kash exclaimed as he leaned back in his chair. "The four of you normally intimidate people into doing as you ask so you can enslave the women you find beautiful. There's one small problem with that... you can't intimidate me. I'll throw you all a beating without a second thought... I have a business proposal for your boss, Egonn. We can discuss that business or fight... I really don't care which."

"You think you can take out all four of us?" the thug laughed.

"Easily," Kash replied as he stood and removed his jacket, exposing his firearms. "I won't even need these."

Kash removed his weapons and placed them on the table. He then walked over and stood directly before the man who had done all the talking.

"A wise man would lose the ego and take my business card to your boss," Kash said calmly. "I wish to purchase a woman from Poncia he just acquired. No questions asked."

The man had indecision in his eyes. Unfortunately for him, it didn't last long... the thug tried to sucker punch Kash in the stomach. Kash was prepared for it, and the man's fist was met by the implant-enhanced muscles of his abdomen. Kash didn't even flinch.

"That was foolish," Kash said coldly.

Kash drove the palm of his hand up and through the man's chin while simultaneously disarming the man. He spun to his right, snapped a sidekick into the second man's sternum, and threw the gun into the forehead of the third man. Kash darted to the fourth man and caught his hand, stopping him from pulling his gun from its holster. The other three men finally hit the ground after Kash's lightning-quick assault.

"Or... you could give my business card to Egonn," Kash said to the man and held up his card. "You're call."

The man let go of his weapon and grabbed the business card. Kash released the man and retrieved his jacket before assisting Calynn from her seat. He wrapped an arm around her waist, and they started to walk away into the crowd of onlookers.

"I'll be waiting for his call," Kash hollered without turning around. "Don't disappoint me."

"I'm so turned on right now," Calynn whispered to Kash.

Kash smiled and kissed her on the head. They walked arm in arm back to the ship. Kash knew he would have to break her heart if she made any sexual advances towards him back at the ship. So he walked slowly.

After an awkward night with Calynn, he was reading the news on his monitor when Calynn announced an incoming comm.

"This is Kash."

"Mr. Kash," the voice replied. "This is Egonn."

"Straight to the point," Kash said quickly. "You have a friend of mine. A woman named Dr. Omia Moss. And I want her back."

"Not much for pleasantries, are we?" Egonn said in a condescending tone.

"I'm not a fan of your profession," Kash replied. "Especially when one of the women you're trying to traffic is a friend. Are we doing this or not?"

"She was given to settle a debt."

"I'll double it."

"Whoa, Mr. Kash..."

"Yes or no, Egonn," Kash interrupted. "We can do this as gentlemen completing a business transaction, or I can tear your entire world apart... it's your call."

"Make it triple," the man countered.

"Done!" Kash barked. "When and where?"

"I never leave my home," Egonn stated. "Slip number eighty-four... at sunset, three hourns from now. Bring the credits."

"I'll be there," Kash stated and ended the comm.

"Are we really getting her back?" Calynn asked from the door to his quarters.

"We better, or he'll regret it."

The lights in the ship all got brighter for a second as Calynn looked like she was about to cry.

"I'm sorry... I turned it up."

"It's okay... I'll be just as emotional when this is all over."

"I'll pull it together, but..."

Calynn didn't finish her sentence. She marched over to Kash and straddled him in his chair. She sat in his lap and wrapped her arms around him with her head on his shoulder. Kash hugged her tight and rubbed her back. He felt a tear drop onto his shoulder and was once again in awe of the fantastic body that Bahanja had built for her.

"I'm sorry... I'm okay now," Calynn said as she stood and wiped the tears from her cheeks.

"Let's get to work on a plan," Kash insisted. "If we want her back... we need to be prepared."

"Yes, Boss," Calynn affirmed. "Scanning his ship now."

The duo spent the next three hourns planning for their meeting. Calynn's sensors couldn't penetrate the hull of Egonn's ship, so they went in more blindly than Kash liked. It was a risk they were willing to take to get Omia back. Kash knew they would be searched and probably disarmed when they arrived, so he also took all his hidden weaponry along. His belt turned into a spiked chain weapon, his boots had hidden blades, and his watch had a powerful laser.

Despite his reservations, Calynn was insistent on joining him. He wanted her to stay with the ship so she could use The Alley Cat Savant and her weapons if they were needed. Calynn argued that she could do both simultaneously, and he didn't have a counterargument for that argument. She donned an elegant black suit that matched his and accompanied him to the meeting.

Armed thugs greeted them at the door to Egonn's ship. They were both patted down, and their firearms were taken. Once inside, the outer door of the vessel is sealed tight. Calynn jerked like she was startled.

"I have no signal in here," Calynn muttered.

"The Boss doesn't like being bugged," one of the thugs responded. "This way."

The armed guards led them down a service hallway into the most oversized room Kash had ever seen. The elegantly decorated room had to be 100 meters wide and double that long. The space was well-lit, brightly colored, and welcoming. Enormous crystal chandeliers hung from the ceiling above shallow pits lined with cushions. Several women were hanging out in each pit. Kash rapidly scanned their faces, hoping to see Omia, to no avail.

They entered another short hallway leading to a smaller, entirely metal room. Industrial lighting illuminated the cold steel walls and floor. Seven men awaited them at the other side of the 25-meter-square room. Six of the men were standing, and one was seated. The seated man was the fattest man Kash had ever seen. His hoverchair struggled to hold his weight.

"Mr. Kash," The fat man greeted them, and Kash recognized his voice.

"Egonn."

"Welcome to my home," Egonn offered. "Can I offer you a drink?"

"You can offer me a woman," Kash replied. "She's about this tall... amazing figure... goes by Omia."

"Still not one for pleasantries, I see," Egonn uttered.

"I told you before..."

"You're not a fan of my profession," Egonn interrupted. "Yes, I know."

"And yet here I stand... ready to do business."

"Did you bring the credits?"

"Did you bring the girl?"

"No," Egonn responded in a sinister tone. "You did."

The door behind them slid shut before Kash could react. The two thugs that had been leading them tried to grab Calynn. Kash was sure to kick both men with enough force to ensure they never got back up. He snapped the neck of the first one and crushed the second man's chest cavity. They both died before they hit the ground.

"So you are formidable," Egonn shouted.

"And you're a fat fucking idiot!" Kash shouted back as he started to approach the man.

One of the guards to Egonn's right moved to intercept Kash. The man was large in stature. He was at least 25 centimeters taller than Kash and doubled his weight. The big man moved gracefully, though. When Kash snapped a kick at the guard's head, the guard caught him by his foot, effortlessly flung Kash 15 meters through the air, and sent him crashing into one of the walls. Kash saw stars from the impact and knew he had suffered a concussion.

The big man was moving toward Kash as he tried to shake off the effects of the blow he received. Kash scrambled to get to his feet in time to defend himself. Suddenly, the guard was spun sideways in the air and kicked violently into the wall beside Egonn. Calynn stood where the man once was with a menacing look about her. The man she kicked raced back towards her at impossible speeds. When he and Calynn sparred, their hands moved so fast that Kash had trouble following them. Calynn ended the competition when she tore the thug's arms off his body and then beheaded him.

"Sentinels," Kash uttered when he saw the circuitry of the guards.

"Class E Military grade synthetics!" Egonn shouted. "Kill them both!"

Three of the five remaining men moved to attack Calynn, and one came after Kash. It was moving so fast that Kash could not block the incoming punch. The blow sent him sprawling across the room, and blood started to run into his eyes from a gash above his eyebrow. Calynn's body bounced off the wall beside him. He watched as she rushed back into the fight. She could quickly get the better of one of them at a time, but against all four... she was no match.

"Stop... don't hurt her," Kash tried to get to his feet, but the world was spinning.

Calynn's body once again crashed into a wall with such force that she left a dent in the wall. She struck back quickly and sent one of the men flying, but the other three managed to grab her. Kash watched through blurred vision as they wrestled. He finally got to his feet and ran to her aid. Each enormous robotic man held one of her limbs, trying to control the girl.

Kash took a swing at the guard holding Calynn's left arm. The guard threw Kash to the ground beneath Calynn and stomped on his right forearm, crushing all the bones and pinning him to the floor.

"AAAAAAHHHH!" Kash shouted in pain.

"Boss," Calynn muttered as the thugs continued to pull at her limbs.

Calynn looked lost and worried. The guards were trying to pull her arms and legs from her body while beating her on the back. He feared the worst... until he saw why she was so worried. The inhibitor fell to the ground. It was crushed and mangled.

When Kash looked back at Calynn's face, her eyes were glowing white.

"Give 'em hell, Baby Girl," Kash told her confidently.

An ominous hum started and seemed to be coming from everywhere. Next, Kash heard the whirling sound of an HLD spinning up. The hum got louder and louder and soon became a crackling roar. Everyone in the room was confused about what was happening... including Kash.

Calynn closed her eyes and opened her fists. The light above her broke as an arc of electricity jumped from the light to her body. Another bolt of electricity jumped from the wall to her hand, just above Kash's face. The telltale sound of another arc soon followed... and another... and another... the arcs started coming faster and lasting longer. Kash could feel the heat coming from Calynn's body as the ship's power grid continually arced into her body.

Kash covered his face with his left hand but peered through his fingers at Calynn. Voices were shouting, but the snapping bolts of electricity were too loud to hear what was being said. The bright light from the electricity was coming from everywhere now, and the heat was getting intense. Calynn's hair and clothes started to burn from her body, and they fell to the ground. And still, she pulled in more power... and then it was silent.

Calynn opened her eyes and looked at Kash. She was completely naked and bald and somehow still beautiful. She gave him a kind smile as a small blue line slowly extended from her body until it touched his. The electricity she sent to him didn't hurt. It merely tingled and made his hair stand on end like static would.

"Cover your eyes," Calynn said softly.

Cash covered his eyes as the room lit up brighter than he thought possible. The sound of electricity cracking and sizzling filled the air. The weight on Kash's arm suddenly disappeared as every muscle in his body tensed at once. The room went silent once more as Calynn's body crashed down upon him.

"Baby Girl," Kash mumbled. "Please be…"

Kash lost the battle to stay conscious, and the world went black.

Take 2

Kash forced himself awake and tried to push the fog from his brain. Slowly, the world came back into focus. The lights were flickering above him as he tried to look around. When he spotted one of their assailants, he couldn't process what he was seeing. The robotic body was welded to the wall with a giant hole through the middle. Kash quickly turned his head to locate the other sentinels. He found them all in the same condition.

"What's that?" Kash said aloud to himself as he saw some movement.

Two of Egonn's henchmen dragged the fat man out of the room. Calynn had apparently fried his hover chair in her attack.

"Calynn... come on, Baby Girl," Kash turned his attention to the girl lying across his body. "Wake up, sweetie... we gotta go."

Kash shook her with his good arm as he spoke, trying to awaken the young woman. He couldn't tell if she was covered in soot or if her skin was charred, but her whole body was blackened. But more importantly... she seemed lifeless.

"No, no, no," Kash exclaimed as he sat up. "Please be okay. Please, please, please."

Kash frantically shook Calynn's body, now hoping for any signs of life. His head was pounding, and he had some significant injuries himself, but she was more important... as was getting her out.

"They'll come for us once they secure Egonn's safety, Baby Girl," Kash observed. "Come on... let's get you out of here."

Kash struggled to reach his feet and didn't feel too steady, but he had to try to get them out. He removed the diamond stud earring from his left ear and pulled the tail to activate it. The little robot began flying around. He did the same with the earring in his right ear. Once both robots were active, he pressed a button on his watch and gave them commands.

"Find the control center and give me access to the door locks," Kash said into his watch.

With that, the two bugs zipped off and out of sight.

"Now... how am I going to carry you with only one arm?" Kash asked his unconscious friend.

Kash tried several times to leverage Calynn's body off the floor so he could carry her, but her immense flexibility made it nearly impossible. She would fold in ways she shouldn't be able to bend, and he wouldn't be able to balance her. He would lose his grip, and she would fall back to the floor. A beep from his watch let him know he had access to the doors... and he was also running out of time. He was sure Egonn would send men to kill them soon.

"Sorry, baby girl," Kash apologized. "This is going to hurt."

Kash grabbed a fistful of flesh on Calynn's belly and used it like a handle to pick her up and place her on his right shoulder. He winced in pain as he flipped his damaged arm over the top of her to hold her in place. He used his left hand to assist the right hand to grab his shirt collar. With her lifeless body balanced on his shoulder, he picked up a weapon he saw lying on the ground and started plodding along toward the exit.

The women in the grand room were huddled together and scared. Some of the women screamed when they saw him carrying Calynn. Others looked like they wanted to follow him and make their escape as well. He ran across the room as fast as his weakened body would carry him. He didn't think any of the women were threats, but he kept an eye on them anyway.

When the door to the service hallway opened, two armed guards were there. Kash reacted quickly and fired the laser he was carrying. The weapon fired a continuous beam, cutting both men in half. One of them never even saw it coming. The laser must have been damaged as it was soon so hot he had to drop it. He noticed one of the men had a beam rifle and squatted down to retrieve it as he passed. Kash proceeded quickly but cautiously towards the exit. He was actually surprised to find the door opened and unmanned. He dropped the beam rifle, retrieved his weapons from the shelf just inside the door, and ran out of the barge as fast as his legs would carry him.

Calynn had parked The Cat four slips away from Egonn's barge, so they were close, but not too close. But now Kash was wishing it was only two slips away.

"It's gonna be okay, Baby Girl," Kash said more to himself than Calynn. "We're gonna get back the Thracia and get you patched up... I promise... it's just a little further... There, do you see her? ... there's our Cat... I'm trying to hurry... but I'm getting so tired... I think... I think I lost a lot of blood."

Kash willed himself to keep moving the last 100 meters and boarded his ship. He climbed the steps of the ship ladder to the cockpit and sat at the helm with Calynn on his lap. He maneuvered her body so she was straddling him while facing him and somehow managed to strap them both into the seat. He fired up the engines, pulled off the dock, and was soon streaking straight up through the sky.

"Calynn... come on... we need the HLD... we need to get to..."

Kash nearly passed out again and had to shake himself awake.

"We need to get to Plekish... come on, Baby Girl... maybe I can call him... maybe he can help."

Kash fumbled with the comm until he found Plekish and started the transmission. He was fighting to stay awake and wiped some of the blood away from his eyes with the sleeve of his jacket.

"Kash, my friend," Plekish greeted him. "How are you?"

"I think we're dying..."

"Oh, my no!"

"Can I use the HLD... without..."

"Without Calynn? I'm afraid not."

"She's not moving," Kash nearly cried the words. "I can't save her without... without her... come on, baby.... Please wake up!"

"Kash... Kash..."

The whirling sound of the HLD was the last thing Kash heard.

"She did it..."

Kash passed out.

Voices? ... I hear voices... is that Meesha? Kash fought to open one eye and managed to see Meesha for a fraction of a second before passing out again.

Beep......................Beep......................Beep......................Beep

This time, when Kash opened his eyes, he felt a little stronger. He blinked the world into focus and saw Meesha standing over him. They appeared to be in a Thracian hospital.

"Hi, beautiful," Kash said with a raspy voice.

"Save your strength, mister," Meesha sounded annoyed. "We nearly lost you."

"Calynn?" Kash asked, yearning to know she was okay. "Please tell me she's okay."

"That's why you're awake even though I'm not done putting your arm back together," Meesha stated. "Neither of you is resting because you're so worried about one another. I need you to rest so you can heal."

"She's worried, too?" Kash sobbed. "That means she's alive, right?"

Meesha smiled, walked to his room door, and slid it open.

"Calynn, can you hear me?" Meesha asked. "Follow my voice, sweetie."

"Hi, Meesha," Calynn's voice came from the hallway. "I can hear you."

"He's right in here… but slowly, don't hurt yourself," Meesha said calmly.

"Boss?" Calynn's voice came over the speaker in his room.

"It's so good to hear your voice, Baby Girl," Kash gushed. "I was so worried about you."

"I was so worried about you, too," Calynn replied.

"Yes, you were both very worried," Meesha remarked. "Too worried to heal properly."

"Sorry, Meesha," Calynn apologized.

"I hope hearing each other's voices will put you both at ease," Meesha continued. "You both have a lot of healing to do… Kash, you had a collapsed lung and severe head and arm trauma, and you lost a lot of blood. Calynn, your only lung was damaged along with some of your intestines."

"So, not just her body?" Kash asked.

"Her body was very damaged," Meesha stated.

"Oh, I wrecked my body," Calynn added. "Bahanja says I fried everything."

"Teams of Thracians are working around the clock to rebuild her," Meesha continued.

"If you fried everything... how'd you get us here?"

"I don't know."

"We think that's how she hurt her brain," Meesha explained. "She somehow pushed through her cooked corpse and connected to the HLD. It shouldn't be possible... even for her."

"Wait... she hurt her brain?"

"They said it was like straining a muscle," Calynn recalled. "No permanent damage.... I'm resting in a regeneration pod that Meesha modified for me."

"Resting is a relative term... I hope you will both actually rest now," Meesha remarked. "Can I sedate Kash again to finish fixing his arm?"

"Sorry, Meesha," Calynn replied. "Yes, I do feel better after hearing his voice."

"What about you, mister?" Meesha asked him.

"Me too," Kash agreed. "Sorry, Meesha. You may proceed with the arm."

"See you soon, boss," Calynn's voice came from the hallway this time. She must have been retreating back to her room.

"She'll be okay, right?" Kash asked Meesha.

"She was worried about you and Dr. Moss, but hopefully now she's at least somewhat at ease," Meesha responded.

"Wake me up if you need any help with her."

"I will... now rest."

Meesha's voice faded away as Kash fell asleep.

He was in a regeneration pod when he next awoke. His right arm ached.

"I was just coming to check on you," Meesha said as she looked in the pod. "Sit still while I open the pod."

Meesha moved from his sight, and the pod door opened a few seconds later. When Kash looked down at his right arm, he was surprised to see metal rods sticking out of his flesh.

"What the hell?"

"It is helping to regrow the missing pieces of your bones," Meesha explained. "Some of the bone was crushed beyond repair. I consulted with other doctors around Thracia, and this was the best course of action we could take."

"Is that why it aches?"

"Eat this. It will help."

Meesha handed him something resembling a cross between a blueberry and a grape. Kash popped it in his mouth and chewed.

"It tastes good... really sweet," he said as he chewed. "And makes you tingly... wow, those work fast."

"It should only take a few minutes to circulate through your body."

"It hit my head already... I'm so high."

A warm and tingly feeling permeated his entire body. Kash had never taken a drug that made him feel this good before. The world seemed to be moving in slow motion as his pain slowly melted away.

"Those are some magical fucking berries," Kash uttered. "Can I have some more of those? Wow are you beautiful. Plekish is so lucky. I know because I've seen you naked. You have an incredibly sexy body. So I know how lucky... wait, why am I saying all this out loud?"

"It's a side effect of the fruit," Meesha said with a big grin. "Your inhibitions fall away."

"Keep Calynn away from me then," Kash mumbled. "I would so do her right now. She watched me fuck Omia. She studied us. I bet she can fuck like her. Why is the room spinning?"

When Kash awoke again, he was back in the regeneration pod. The ache in his right arm was still there, and his manhood was aching also.

"What did I do?" Kash asked himself as he tried to adjust his achingly hard erection. "And why won't you go down?"

Kash released the lid of the pod and sat up. He was still in the hospital room.

"Keep that arm still, mister," Meesha said as she entered his room.

"I am," Kash replied and tried to hide his erection.

"That's a side effect of the berries," Meesha said as she pointed to his groin. "Being the celebrity that you are here on Thracia, several of my nurses offered to assist you with... alleviating that problem... but I didn't think you would want to get married when you were in that state."

"Um, no, thank you."

"Mating for life with only one person is very fulfilling... when you find the right person."

"Found her... lost her... really wanna get back to finding her again."

"Your arm needs another day," Meesha ordered. "Plekish told me that Calynn's body is nearly repaired. She might be fixed before you are."

"You should have seen what she did... why she was broken," Kash uttered. "She did... the impossible."

"You haven't talked about that day yet. I am curious to hear your recollection."

"She absorbed the energy of that barge and then shot it out at them... like all of the power available... it was like lightning," Kash recalled. "I was there, and I still don't really know what she did."

"My Plekish has been speaking with her nearly every day to see what she remembers," Meesha added. "He was amazed at her tale and has been upgrading the materials of her body to withstand her... power."

"She welded a powerful military synth to the wall. A robot body like hers, but for the army. So they were bigger and stronger... like really powerful," Kash explained. "She sucked the electricity right out of the walls and... and I could feel the heat coming off of her... it was so surreal."

"That must be how she charred the outer layer of her skin," Meesha observed. "Her skin was designed to withstand temperatures of seven thousand degrees Celsius. How close were you to her?"

"Maybe a meter... why?"

"She said she tried to protect you," Meesha continued. "Those temperatures could vaporize your body at a much further distance. You would have never felt the heat. So, not only did she generate that much heat, but she somehow contained it."

"That makes what she did even less possible."

"Fascinating," Meesha let the word slip out as she appeared deep in thought.

"I remember a little blue line that she sent from her to me," Kash continued. "It tingled when it touched me... but I think it protected me from the electric shock somehow... until she passed out. Then I got a good jolt."

"Well, then I'm glad she did what she did," Meesha admitted. "I would mourn your loss. You are like family... why do you look at me like that?"

"Like what?"

"You expressed pain when I said you are like family."

"No, no, I love being your family," Kash clarified. "The pained look was because my dick hurts... sorry... blurted that out."

"Would you like me to make the pain stop?" Meesha offered.

"Umm... how?"

Meesha smiled and held out her hand. She waited for Kash to give her a funny look before smirking and opening her hand. She was holding another berry.

"Won't that give me another chance of... this?" Kash asked.

"The chance of that diminishes with subsequent doses."

"Then yes, please," Kash replied as he popped the berry in his mouth.

"It will also make you more compliant for your bath," Meesha added.

"You're giving me a bath?" Kash asked as the berry started to take effect.

"Yes... you've been in a regeneration pod too long," Meesha explained. "We need to rinse out the toxins. Your body can't process them to purge them fast enough."

"Why does... that sound like... enema?" Kash asked through his delirium. "And the room is spinning again."

Kash awoke slowly and felt too warm... and weighed down. When he tried to move, the weight shifted, too. He tried to shake off the groggy feeling, but the warm, fuzzy feeling from the berry lingered. His right arm seemed to be strapped down and wouldn't move. When he used his left hand to wipe the sleep from his eyes, he hit something... or someone. His nose let him know who.

"Hi, Baby Girl," Kash said with a raspy voice.

"Hi back," Calynn replied and snuggled into him.

"Wait... something feels... it feels..."

Kash realized he wasn't dressed yet, and when he touched Calynn, he felt nothing but her skin. They were both completely naked.

"Does it feel better?" Calynn asked as her hand found his manhood. "I took care of your problem for you like a good girl. I did everything you like to do and pleasured you for hourns and hourns. I hope it's no longer sore. What if I'm pregnant?"

Kash awoke with a start and quickly looked around. It was only a dream. He was in the hospital bed and fully dressed. It took him a moment to notice that Calynn was seated in the chair beside his bed and lying on his chest.

"Whoa... easy, Boss," Calynn said softly. "Your arm is in a special pod. Try not to move it."

Kash blinked the sleep from his eyes and finally focused on his pretty companion. She looked just as beautiful as before. Her long blond hair had been replaced, and she smiled at him.

"Is it really you, or am I dreaming?" Kash asked as he laid his hand on her cheek.

"It's really me."

"And you're, okay? ... you're not... charred."

"I'm fine, boss," Calynn said as she stood and walked across the room.

"Wait... where are you going?"

"I told Meesha I would let her know when you were awake," Calynn stated as she disappeared into the hallway.

Kash found it odd that she just jumped up and left like she did. Calynn usually wanted to cuddle or, at the very least, hug a bunch of times. He decided not to dwell on it and looked at his right arm. It was in a clear, bubble-looking thing emitting a light blue light. The pins had been removed, but it looked like his forearm was one big bruise.

"She'll be here in a few," Calynn announced as she reentered the room. "That looks like it hurts. Does it hurt?"

"Surprisingly, no," Kash replied. "But I think they have some kind of nerve block going or something because I can't move my fingers... How about you? How does it feel being back in your body?"

"Sooo good. I didn't think I would miss it as much as I did because I haven't had it that long."

"I missed it too... cuddle monster."

Calynn smiled and leaned over his bed so she could lay on his chest again. She was wearing a simple long-sleeved t-shirt that felt exceptionally soft to the touch. He rubbed her back and kissed the top of her head. She even smelled the same.

"We need to never do that again," Kash said softly. "I promise to never put you in that much danger..."

"I know what I signed up for," Calynn interrupted. "And I'm stronger now."

Calynn sat up and looked down at Kash. She had a concerned look on her face.

"The link for Egonn's ship transponder finds nothing now," Calynn stated. "How will we find Omia? I'm so worried about her. We have to get going so we can find her, but I don't know where to start looking."

"He'll be ready soon enough," Meesha said as she entered the room. "Another few hourns."

"How do your modifications feel, Calynn?" Plekish asked as he followed Meesha in. "Bahanja says it's her finest work yet."

"It feels... faster," Calynn explained. "Like the nerves and everything."

"I modified the crystal wiring that we use for power distribution on Thracia to carry your energy," Bahanja explained. "There's less resistance per strand than the fibers we used before... and a significantly higher melting point."

"Speaking of my energy... do I have a battery?"

"No, you do not," Bahanja replied. "You run on the same electrical impulses that we do. You just produce a significantly larger charge than we do. And much more than I anticipated, so we did some modifications."

"We changed your existing nerves for a higher quality material and wove a protective grid into your skin," Plekish informed them. "If you are exposed to that much power again, the grid will help channel the power, so you don't burn your skin."

"Would you care for a demonstration?" Bahanja asked.

"Sure... I guess," Calynn replied. "What do I do?"

"Pull the energy from this battery," Bahanja said as she pulled out a small black box. "It contains a lot of power. I disabled the safety... just touch the terminals here and here."

Calynn did as Bahanja instructed. She touched the terminals of the battery and sucked the energy into her body. As soon as she did, thin blue lines began to glow across her entire body in a grid pattern.

"Whoa... I can control it better, too," Calynn said as she waved her arms around.

As Calynn moved, the grid reacted, and certain parts of her body would glow brighter. It was as if she was pushing more electricity to one spot or the other.

"Now, see if you can return it to the battery?" Bahanja offered the battery to Calynn as she asked.

Calynn touched the battery and closed her eyes. The glowing grid disappeared slowly as she pushed the energy back into the battery. Her fingers were the last to lose their light.

"There," Calynn stated as she finished.

Bahanja put some kind of meter on the battery and showed it to Plekish. The two momentarily spoke to each other in Thracii before Plekish turned to look at Calynn.

"Have you adjusted your inhibitor?" he asked the young girl.

"No... you said to leave it in its current settings," Calynn responded.

"Then the other modification works as intended," Plekish continued. "You returned ten percent more power to the battery than you consumed."

"She what now?" Kash interjected.

"I built an amplifier into her inhibitor to help teach her to use less effort," Plekish explained. "I believe it will help her learn control if she puts less effort into doing the same amount of work."

"An amplifier?" Kash inquired. "That seems counterintuitive to her needing an inhibitor."

"The inhibitor still limits her reach the same as before," Plekish replied. "The amplifier takes her existing electrical impulses to her muscles and strengthens them. Thus, making her make the correction to use less effort."

"Won't that make me stronger too?" Calynn asked.

"Indeed it will. But I reviewed the specifications of the synthetic war machines that attacked you. If you are to have a conflict with them again, you will need it," Plekish explained. "They are stronger and faster, but their power consumption necessitates a built-in power supply..."

"Something we didn't want to hinder Calynn with," Bahanja added.

"The amplifier will give her the same strength and speed as her attackers without needing a battery," Plekish concluded. "I'm sure she could circumvent its intended purpose and use it to reach out if she tries. However... I would highly discourage that. It is merely a tool, like the inhibitor, designed to help you."

"We isolated the amplifier to prevent Calynn from accessing it," Bahanja added. "We have it running at its lowest setting."

"Ten percent is the lowest?" Calynn asked. "Since I added ten percent to the battery."

"It is set at one-quarter of one percent," Plekish replied. "You multiply it continually, which is why you were able to add the ten percent. The longer you hold the energy, the stronger you make it."

"That sounds scary," Calynn admitted. "How do I turn it off? I don't want to hurt anyone."

"I don't believe that is necessary," Meesha chimed in. "It has been running since you got your body back, and you haven't overpowered anything. And you said it felt faster... not stronger. So if we had said this amplifier simply makes you faster with less effort, how would you feel about it?"

"I'm not sure," Calynn replied. "But... I guess faster doesn't feel as scary."

"And as long as you use it for its intended purpose, it will do just that," Meesha added. "It will only make you faster. I think it will help you with your control and ultimately help you live a better life... if you just give it a chance."

"I can try," Calynn conceded.

"Very good," Plekish said in a very soothing tone. "Then let's give you access to it, shall we? Calm yourself and eject your inhibitor, please."

Calynn took a deep, calming breath and released it. She turned and looked at Kash with a worried look on her face, sat down in her chair, and grabbed his hand in both of hers. She then closed her eyes, took another deep breath, and let it out slowly.

"I'm ready," Calynn uttered.

Plekish moved to Calynn's back as a black rod emerged from Calynn's left ear. The rod had some mesh around it and a few blinking lights. She squeezed his hand tighter as Plekish touched the device.

"Very good... nice and calm," Plekish said soothingly. "I'm just going to remove this Faraday cage... slide it off... just like so... and you can pull that back in now... good girl."

Calynn's grip lessened as the rod returned inside her ear. She took another deep breath and released it.

"The device has a maximum output of five percent," Plekish continued. "But let's leave it on the lowest setting for now."

"So, the inhibitor is..." Kash started to say.

"Internal now," Calynn interrupted. "It was terrifying when it fell off."

"You're doing it again," Meesha said to Calynn. "I wish you would talk to me about whatever is bothering you."

"I know I'm being fidgety, and I know I have this big new trauma to deal with also," Calynn relented. "But I'm really worried about my friend, and she's totally lost now, and I just want to get her back."

Calynn wiped a tear from her cheek and stared at the floor. Meesha was right. Something was eating at Calynn, and she needed to get it off her chest.

"Are you back back?" Kash asked the young woman. "Access to The Cat and everything."

"Yea... why?"

"Where's my watch?"

"Just here," Meesha replied, "with your shoes."

"There's an app on there for recon bugs," Kash explained. "If you can boost the signal and reconnect to them... I left them on Egonn's ship. They've been recording everything there since we left."

Calynn eagerly snatched the watch from Meesha, and her eyes started to shake. The room fell silent as Calynn did her thing. It felt like an eternity, and Kash was losing hope until Calynn suddenly smiled, and her eyes lit up.

"I found them," Calynn exclaimed. "I found them!"

"I knew you could..."

Kash was cut off when Calynn dove into his chest. He wrapped his arm around the girl and kissed her head. She grabbed his shirt like she couldn't pull herself close enough to him. Meesha had moved to comfort the girl also. Kash felt her hand on his arm.

"How about we go and help you get through this latest trauma," Meesha said softly. "We can give Kash the last few hourns he needs, and then you can go after your friend again."

Calynn didn't answer, but she did nod in agreement. She sat up and placed her hand on Kash's cheek. She smiled a soft smile, leaned down, and gave him a soft kiss on the lips.

"Thank you," she whispered.

"Let's finish healing and go get our girl."

The Chase Continues

"Do you have the coordinates?" Kash asked Calynn.

"Yes, I do," Calynn replied from the helm. "They're hiding in the Joor system."

"The Joor system? ... that's... remote."

"According to some of the reports I saw, it's a haven for the lawless."

"A cesspool of crime... super."

"Do you think he has allies there?"

"Probably... he said he always stays on the move to avoid the law. So if he went to ground... he went there for a reason."

"I'll cut the HLD early," Calynn stated. "It will allow us to go in cloaked."

"Good idea," Kash replied. "I'm gonna go lay down... you coming?"

"I'm good here for now," Calynn told him. "Maybe later."

"That doesn't sound like my cuddle monster... you okay?"

"Yea... just some me stuff to work out."

"Your loss," Kash said as he headed to his quarters.

Kash kicked off his shoes and stripped to his boxers before climbing into bed. He grabbed his right forearm and rotated his wrist to feel the bones and muscles move. There was still a minor soreness deep in his arm, but he could hardly believe how good it felt, considering how badly damaged it was. The Thracians outdid themselves yet again. He and Calynn went from nearly dead to back on the hunt in merely nine days. They were miracle workers.

"Without a visible scar, too," Kash said to himself. "You are absolutely amazing, Meesha."

Kash rolled on his side to try to get comfortable. He tossed and turned a bit before finally finding a comfy position so the hum of the engines could lull him to sleep. He slept fitfully at best. Visions of Calynn's broken body haunted his dreams. Scenarios in which the four Sentinels tear her body apart played out in his mind. He was always unable to help her or save her. There was always so much blood like they tore apart a human girl, not just a synth.

A warm body pressed against him, and he wrapped his arm around her. Calynn had finally come to join him. Kash hugged her tight to his body as Calynn laced her fingers through his. Her presence soothed his tortured mind, and he was finally able to get some real rest.

When Kash woke up, it was to an empty bed. Calynn had gone back out to the helm. Rather than go find her, he decided to check the news on the cyber web. He pulled on his jeans, sat down at his desk, and perused the day's news articles. After about an hourn, Calynn rejoined him. She walked up behind him and placed her hands on his shoulders.

"Anything interesting?" Calynn asked.

"More riots on the mining planets," Kash replied. "The Consortium works them far too hard for shitty pay."

"We should do something about that after we find Omia... help the workers."

"Not much we can do. The Consortium owns the planets, the mines, the transports, the refineries, and the distributors," Kash explained. "It's impossible to snatch it all away."

"I could hack their payroll and give the workers a raise."

"They'd just fix it the week after and take all the money back."

"They would make them repay it and take it back out of their paychecks?"

"They sure would, sweetie," Kash relented. "The rich pricks that own those businesses only care about their wallets, and they are the government, so there's no hope of help coming from there."

"That's such a shitty system," Calynn complained. "How could they let all the biggest and richest companies band together like that to become the government?"

"There was nobody that could stop them... they have all the credits, all the power, and all the influence," Kash replied. "If anyone tried to oppose them, the Consortium would have them erased from existence... and then erased them from history also... If you know where to look, you can still find the stories about them, but it's getting harder to find them."

"So, murder is illegal for us and not for them?"

"Pretty much."

"Such a silly system," Calynn said as she left the room.

"Power corrupts, Baby Girl," Kash shouted after her.

"It wouldn't corrupt me," Calynn complained as she turned back.

"Yes, it would. It always does."

"No, it doesn't."

"It might," Kash added as he tried to hide his smirk... he failed.

"Oh, you... I should beat you," Calynn said as she approached again.

Kash pushed his chair back, so he rolled back to his bed. He rolled onto the bed with a makeshift combat roll and did a ridiculous pose.

"Your Kung Fu is no match for mine," Kash said just as ridiculously.

"I bet I can win," Calynn explained as she pulled off her top. "I bet if I unhook my bra..."

"Whoa... that's cheating," Kash complained.

Calynn loosened her bra strap so that it was hanging loose on her body. It barely covered her breasts. Calynn was beaming a big smile at him, but it looked... naughty. She rotated her right leg before her left, so her hips swayed. Her legs looked amazing in the jeans she was wearing. In fact, everything about her looked amazing. She had great legs, a toned flat stomach, and great breasts.

"Baby Girl, we can't do that."

"Yes, we can."

"No, we absolutely cannot," Kash barked a little harsher than he intended.

"Why not?" Calynn whined.

"Because I said so!" Kash yelled.

Calynn's face scrunched up as she ran out of the room. Kash immediately felt terrible for yelling at the girl. He sighed heavily and ran his fingers through his hair. He paused to compose himself, left out another big sigh, and then went after Calynn. She was sitting at the helm with her legs pulled up to her chest, and her head was resting on her knees. Her body was shaking as she wept.

"Hey... I'm sorry for yelling," Kash said softly.

Calynn didn't respond. She continued crying. Kash approached her and laid his hands on her shoulders.

"I'm really bad at this... but I don't want to ruin what we have with..." Kash tried to explain.

Calynn interrupted him when she leaped into his arms. She threw her arms over his shoulders and wrapped her legs around his waist. Her whole body was shaking as she cried on his shoulder.

"I'm sorry, Baby Girl," Kash whispered to her. "I'm sorry for making you cry."

The duo stayed like that for a few minutes while Calynn cried. Kash soothed her the best he could. He rubbed her back, kissed her head, and swayed side to side. He felt terrible for upsetting her this much, but at least she still came to him for comfort.

"What can I do to make it up to you?" Kash asked. "That isn't sex because I really don't want to screw this up... you could use the slip to throw me into a sun as recompense for a lovers' quarrel... and nobody wants that."

"I wouldn't do that," Calynn finally spoke.

"But do you understand why I s..."

"I do," Calynn interrupted and sighed. "I just wished I didn't."

"Sorry, Baby Girl."

"I'm sorry too, boss," Calynn said as she lifted her head to look at him. "You might want to close your eyes to put me down... My bra is closer to my chin than my boobs."

"Okay, but then we need to talk about this."

"I don't want to die a virgin," Calynn blurted out. "I was a junior in high school when I died before. I was a slow bloomer and never caught the interest of any boys. I was only starting to fill out when... the accident... But by some miracle, I woke up. Now I got this new body... and I actually have curves and feel really sexy... and I nearly died again without... without knowing what it feels like to be a woman. And you're the only man I know and trust... so that's why I throw myself at you when I'm... you know."

"You get horny?"

"I have completely functional everything except the reproductive parts, so... yea... I do."

"Oh."

"And we are about to go see the same people that almost killed us, so I'm really nervous about that," Calynn blurted out. "Are you sure I can't interest you in plowing my field just once? ... please?"

Kash paused for a moment and studied Calynn's face. As beautiful as she was, he just couldn't bring himself to do that with her. It felt... wrong. He laid his forehead on hers and squeezed her tightly.

"I know," Calynn uttered when he loosened his grip. "I had to try."

"How about we devise a good enough plan to make you feel more confident in our odds?" Kash asked. "After... I put you down."

Calynn lowered her legs and slid down his body. She continued staring into Kash's eyes as she adjusted and redid her bra. Only then did she take a step back with a sheepish look.

"Can we cuddle before we plan?" Calynn asked nervously.

"What's our ETA?"

"Fourteen hournns yet."

Kash smiled at the girl and held out his hand. Calynn laced her fingers through his and smiled back. She followed him as he led them into his quarters. They both kicked off their jeans and crawled into bed. She cuddled back into him and wrapped his arms around herself. She felt fidgety and needy. He obliged her by holding her tight until he fell asleep.

It was a short nap because Calynn was too fidgety.

"Why are you so wiggly?" Kash asked sleepily.

"I'm hungry. I forgot to eat earlier."

"Then I say we eat while we devise a plan," Kash said as he pulled Calynn tighter.

"Eating requires letting go of me."

"Maybe I still feel bad about yelling and wanted one more hug."

"Food first... hugs later."

"Okay," Kash said as he sat up and left the bed. "Something from the freezer or a Nutra-Shake?"

"I'm thinking a shake," Calynn replied. "It's more nutrient-dense and less likely to upset our stomachs in the upcoming fight."

"Good call."

Kash pulled on his jeans and went across the hall to the ship's galley. The room was barely 2 meters by 3 meters in size. It had a small refrigerator and freezer, dry goods storage, a small sink, a single burner, and a reheater. He grabbed 2 tumblers from the cabinet, added a scoop of powder to each, and filled them with water.

"But add that thing you add," Calynn shouted from the other room.

"Okay," Kash replied.

He grabbed a jar from the refrigerator and put a small amount of the berry compote in each cup. He put the lids on the cups and put them in the shaker. The device shook the cups violently for about 30 seconds. When Kash retrieved them, the tumblers felt cold to the touch, so he knew they were ready. He popped off the lids and headed back to Calynn.

"What if I use the slip and throw Egonn's whole ship into the nearest sun?" Calynn asked as he entered.

"What if Omia is on board?"

"I have been watching their monitors using the bugs, and I haven't seen her."

"Not a risk I'm willing to take, though," Kash said as he handed her a shake. "I'd really like to interrogate that fat piece of shit too."

"I hope by interrogate... you mean torture."

"Enhanced interrogation is my favorite kind of interrogation," Kash said with a smile.

"Mmm... this is so much better with that stuff," Calynn said as she took a sip of her shake.

"Makes a Nutra-Shake worth drinking."

"It truly does."

"So… I like your idea of using the slip, but maybe not to that extent," Kash explained. "I think we should just cripple his ship so he can't get away."

"Can I throw the robot guys into the sun?"

"That… isn't a bad idea," Kash conceded.

"We should probably identify his allies, too," Calynn added. "So we aren't blindsided."

"Also smart."

"I wish we had time to do some recon."

"Yea… although… some straightforward recon might be in order," Kash said thoughtfully. "Is there a popular bar near Egonn?"

Calynn's eyes started shaking back and forth rapidly as they always did when she was computing something.

"There is… it's on the other side of the small planet, though," Calynn replied.

"Well, that's perfect," Kash exclaimed. "Here's what we're going to do…"

Kash spent the next few minutes laying out his plan while they drank their shakes. Once they had hashed out the details, Kash laid back down, but Calynn did not join him again. It took him a while to get some rest, but eventually, he did. When he awoke, he went to his computer and rechecked the news. He also replied to emails from Captain Dorn and his contact inside the Trade Commission. Dorn was just being cordial and thanking him for the work, but his friend in the Trade Commission was sending a warning. Someone in the Consortium Constabulary was requesting a transponder trace on his ship. He could move the request to the bottom of the pile to buy Kash some more time, but eventually, they had to grant the request.

"Can I just have one problem at a fucking time for once," Kash said to himself and rubbed the back of his neck.

The rest of their journey was uneventful, and Calynn soon had them docked. After a quick chat with the Harbor Master to pay the mooring fees, the duo set off to the local pub. The small town was definitely founded by what were essentially pirates. There were very few businesses, and the prostitutes seemed to outnumber the non-prostitutes. The town depended entirely on people coming there to hide from the law, get their ship fixed, and get laid. The most prominent building in the town was the Joor Pub and Brothel. Calynn had said that you had to rent a room to get served in the bar, and each room apparently came with at least one prostitute. That same prostitute was your server while at the bar.

A pleasant older man greeted them when they entered what looked like a hotel lobby. They could hear the muffled sounds of music and laughter coming from the bar.

"Greetings," the man said with a warm smile. "Welcome to the Joor Pub and Brothel. You're a handsome-looking couple. Would you like to see our boy and girl suites? The suite has two bedrooms if you want privacy and a large common area if you do not."

"Hmm," Kash replied. "I don't know… what are you in the mood for, Baby Girl?"

Kash wrapped his arm around Calynn and put his hand in her back pocket. She was a little nervous about everything, so he tried to reassure her and pulled her close.

"Can we see pictures?" Calynn asked nervously.

"You sure can," the innkeeper replied. "They are on the monitor… now. We have eight boy and girl suites available."

Calynn swiped through the pictures quickly and then went back through them. She had a disappointed look on her face.

"Can we see the rest of the girls, please?" Calynn asked. "Maybe we'll just do a threesome… show us your prettiest girls first."

"Regrettably, I don't have any girls that are as beautiful as you are, but let's see what we can find for you," the man said as he looked up and down Calynn's body. "These are my premium girls… they cost a little extra, but their rooms are nicer also."

Calynn was definitely becoming a jeans and tee shirt girl. It was what she wore most often, and she always looked amazing in them. She was wearing a button-down tee today with half of the buttons undone to expose her cleavage. The shirt and her jeans both hugged her figure beautifully. The innkeeper was nearly drooling while staring at Kash's companion. It brought a smile to Kash's face.

Calynn was oblivious to the man's ogling as she scrolled through the pictures of women. Suddenly, Kash realized what she was doing. She hoped to see Omia's image and was getting a little upset when she didn't see it. Kash moved around behind her and wrapped both arms around her waist.

"How about a nice redhead?" Kash said flirtatiously. "It's been forever since I've seen a redhead... or that one was cute."

"Which one?" Calynn replied.

"Go back two... her... something about her light brown complexion is alluring."

"She does have pretty eyes," Calynn added. "Which system is she from?"

"The Cygnus system," the man replied. "A planet called..."

"Earth," Kash interrupted. "We're from Earth also... we'll take her room."

"It has been a long time since we've seen another Earthling," Calynn agreed.

"Triana is also one of the best servers," the innkeeper noted. "You will eat and drink well with her."

"I'll just buzz her down," the man said as he pushed a button on the wall. "She is thirty-thousand credits a day, or you can rent her by the hour."

"Oh, I might need three days to get my fill of her," Kash replied. "What do you think, babe?"

"Three days to start sounds good," Calynn agreed. "If she tastes as sweet as she looks, we might need a whole week with her."

The older man behind the counter actually started drooling when Calynn said that. The old pervert stopped and just stared at Calynn for a moment. The lust in his eyes was very evident.

"I'd have to go get us more credits for that," Kash said with a slightly annoyed tone to get the old man to stop staring. "I didn't bring that much along."

Kash pulled his credits from his pocket and slid the man 3 cards.

"A fifty kay and two twenties ought to do it," Kash asserted.

"Thank you, sir," the innkeeper replied. "Triana should be right down."

The man turned and deposited the credits into a slot in the wall. The elevator door opened, and Triana walked out. Her soft smile became beaming when she saw Kash and Calynn. Triana was wearing silky red shorts and a nearly transparent red robe. She looked thinner than her picture but every bit as pretty. Her light brown hair was done in a wavy bob and bounced as she walked.

"Hi, I'm Triana," she said gleefully as the innkeeper handed her a slip of paper. "Thank you for booking me for... three days."

The girl nearly gasped when she read it. She was clearly stunned.

"Good thing he's handsome, huh?" Calynn asked playfully. "Three days with an ugly dude would suck."

"Says the woman so beautiful she can make an old pimp drool," Kash added with a laugh.

"You are both very good-looking," Triana said with a big smile. "Shall we go to my room so you can dress me for the evening and then come down for some drinks and a bite to eat?"

"That sounds lovely," Calynn said as she smiled back.

"Follow me, please," Triana said as she gestured to the elevator. "Where are you from?"

"Earth... actually," Kash replied as they entered the elevator.

"Earth?" again, the girl sounded stunned.

"Been a long time for us, too," Calynn added.

Triana got fidgety for a moment but then forced the smile back on her face and regained her composure. Her eyes darted to the ceiling for a split second before returning to them.

"What brings you way out here?" Triana asked.

"We're just laying low for a while," Kash responded. "The Constabulary is onto us for a heist."

"That sounds exciting," Triana replied as the elevator stopped and the doors opened. "If you would follow me."

Triana led them down a wide, well-lit hallway lined with doors... big, heavy-looking doors. Each door had a name tag on it.

"Boss, cameras are everywhere," Calynn said in his earpiece. "Just so you know."

"Here we are," Triana stated as she grabbed the handle and struggled to push the door open. "These doors... they're so heavy to help with sound."

Triana led them into her room. It was a spacious area about 8 meters wide and 15 meters deep and was warm and inviting. Everything was thoughtfully color-coordinated in red, brown, and beige tones. Two sofas and a coffee table were just inside the door. A vast bed was just beyond that, with a large wardrobe on either side and a hope chest at the foot. Beyond that was a bathroom and a small kitchenette.

"Welcome to my room," Triana said as she gestured around the room. "I am certified as being clean from diseases. If you wish to see my test results, they are just there on your right. I also have condoms if you don't want to be bare. All the rooms have cameras so others can pay to watch us. For an extra fee, you can get a copy of our recording or add a privacy wall that will not allow others to watch."

"Including management?" Kash asked. "I'm a very private man."

"That depends on your fantasies," Triana continued. "The cameras are also for my safety... so you don't kill me to have sex with my corpse."

"Yuck!" Calynn exclaimed. "People... people do that?"

"Unfortunately... yes," Triana admitted.

"What can we do to assure your safety?" Kash asked. "I am armed..."

"We both are," Calynn interrupted.

"Would you like to disarm us?" Kash continued and raised his arms. "I'm wearing one under each arm, and she has a small gun in her clutch. Whatever it takes... we'll do."

Triana momentarily looked at the two of them as if trying to decide if she could trust them. She was shorter and thinner than Calynn and had a very slight frame. Kash understood why she would hesitate... especially given his size. He was easily half a meter taller than Triana and outweighed her by her.

"Please?" Calynn added. "We would love to have you to ourselves for the next few days."

Triana smiled and walked over to a panel on the wall. She flipped open the door and pressed the button.

"The client requests the cameras be disabled," Triana said before releasing the button.

"And you approve?" a voice came from the panel.

"I approve," Triana said and smiled at Kash.

"Very well," the voice sounded disappointed. "We had several already sign up to watch the woman so it will be expensive."

"How much?" Kash asked softly.

"The client asks how much?" Triana repeated.

"Eighty thousand credits," the voice barked. "PER NIGHT!"

"SOLD!" Calynn barked back. "Where's the nearest credit machine?"

"There's one in the bar," Triana replied.

"I have the credits for the first night here," Kash said as he retrieved them and handed them to Triana. "We'll get you the rest later."

Triana deposited the credits in the slot and waited patiently. Several seconds later, a popping sound came from behind the panel. Triana quickly pulled the panel away from the wall, revealing several cables plugged into ports. Triana pulled every cable from its port and closed the panel.

"We're now completely alone," Triana said sheepishly as she turned to face them.

Kash turned and looked at Calynn for confirmation, and she nodded.

"By the Gods, privacy is expensive here," Kash complained, running his fingers through his hair.

"Your friend is extremely beautiful... I knew it would be expensive. I'm so sorry," Triana apologized. "Would you like to use me before dinner? To make up for the trouble... I belong to you for the next three days and will do anything you ask of me. My specialty is oral. I have no gag reflex, so you can... go deep."

The girl stared at the ground as she spoke. She was clearly nervous or afraid.

"Firstly, I pleasure women. I don't use them," Kash replied. "And secondly... you need to eat first. You look thin."

"We can eat at the bar," Triana responded. "Would you care to dress me?"

"You can't just grab something from the kitchen?" Kash asked, annoyed. "I'm not in the mood for crowds."

"We're not allowed to..."

Triana clasped her hand over her mouth with a look of horror in her eyes. She had unwittingly spilled a dirty little secret and was obviously scared of the consequences.

"We have a confession to make," Calynn blurted out, trying to ease the woman. "We're actually here to find Egonn... do you know him?"

"Egonn? ... we, uh... we aren't supposed to ask the clients for their names, but everyone knows who Egonn is," Triana replied timidly.

"He took a friend of ours, and we mean to get her back," Calynn continued. "Even if we have to kill him to get to her."

Triana began to cry, and Calynn wrapped her in a hug. Kash approached slowly to try to comfort the girl, too. Triana repeatedly tried to regain her composure and failed each time. These tears had been held back for too long. They wouldn't be denied now.

"You're not here willingly, are you?" Calynn asked softly.

Triana shook her head, no.

"Were you taken too?" Kash asked.

"No," Triana replied and wiped her tears. "I borrowed credits to get away from Earth. I was told I would be a hostess at a prestigious hotel and could work off my debt quickly... I've been here three years, and my debt keeps getting bigger. They charge me room and board, but I'm not allowed to leave either. Not until my debt is paid. My job title is a hostess. I'm just expected to host you inside of me. Please, don't tell them..."

"It's okay," Calynn interrupted. "We won't."

"That's why I was so excited about hosting you for three days," Triana continued. "I'll make ten thousand credits plus any tips... that will cover my room for a month."

"I almost hate to ask," Kash said with a sigh," But... how much do you owe?"

"Two-hundred and forty thousand... give or take," Triana replied even more timidly than before.

"The Senator still has funds," Calynn said as she looked at Kash. "We could do that."

"That's a big fucking tip, Calynn," Kash replied.

"I'll do anything you ask," Triana said as she pulled off her robe, exposing her small, perky breasts. "Anything... I swear."

"No sex is worth that much," Kash explained with a smirk. "But some good intel is."

"Egonn's friends and, more importantly... his enemies," Calynn added.

"What you know could be worth waaaay more than your ass," Kash continued. "Although... I might take your ass too... you are really adorable."

"I'm getting in on that action, too," Calynn announced.

"I'm gonna need a lot of booze," Kash said as he shook his head.

"Can we eat too?" Triana asked. "I am quite hungry. We only get what our clients buy for us... and we try to keep their leftovers because going on dates with management... hurts."

"Let's get you dressed," Calynn said gleefully.

The girls went to Triana's wardrobes and started looking at her clothes. Kash had a seat on one of the sofas to watch. He chose not to dwell on Triana's comment about management. He didn't want to have to kill the management for their sick and twisted perversions. Instead, he focused on the task at hand.

"Have you heard much about Egonn's friends and enemies?" Kash asked.

"He is part of the management here," Triana replied. "So he has a lot of friends in the building, but there's a few other groups that really hate him. I've gotten some of them to talk about it, Master. Apparently, if they find a good source of revenue, Egonn will always find a way to take it from them and..."

"Whoa... why did you call me that?"

"Oh... we're supposed to call our clients Mistress or Master," Triana replied as she dressed. "It was a force of habit."

"I'm Calynn, and he is Kash," Calynn said with a soft smile.

"A pleasure to meet you both, but I have to call you that when we are at the bar," Triana stated. "Or we will get into trouble."

"We'll manage... go on."

"Oh, um... and he has a friend or a friend of a friend that is an official in the Consortium," Triana said. "I think a high-ranking one, too. He has had a few of his rivals arrested for crimes he committed."

"Well, that's not ideal," Kash sighed. "But maybe we can use some of his rivals to shield ourselves from any... less than lawful acts and their repercussions."

"I can try to point them out at dinner," Triana said as she beamed a smile at Kash. "Do I look good?"

The woman spun herself in a circle to show Kash her body. She was wearing tight black leggings and a lacy red top. The outfit complimented her figure but wasn't too overtly sexual.

"You look ravishing," Kash said and returned her smile. "Let's go eat."

The bar was so loud he couldn't hear himself think. The music was too noisy, and the people shouting at each other over the music were even more deafening. The sights weren't much better either. Some of the clients had their hostesses dressed modestly, but mostly, the girls were half-naked with all sorts of debauchery on display. Kash had to struggle to stay his hand and not kill some of the men for what they were doing to the girls. Triana led them to a booth along the wall and pointed to the credit slot in the center of the table. Cash slid 5000 credits into the slot, and a sound barrier formed around their table.

"Now we can hear each other," Triana explained. "What can I get you to eat?"

"Anything seafood and an entire bottle of bourbon," Kash replied. "And if that big fat guy makes that girl gag on his manhood and puke again..."

"They are regulars," Triana interrupted. "He and his wife are in here twice a week. They are good tippers. If the vomit bothers you, he will stop doing it."

"Please ask him to stop," Calynn interjected. "And I'll have seafood also."

"The cheapest thing on our menu is a chicken sandwich and..."

"Get anything you want," Kash interrupted Triana. "In fact, get everything you've ever wanted to try. All of it."

Triana bounced, smiled, and leaned in to kiss Kash. It was a quick, little kiss, but he could tell she meant it. That was her way of showing her gratitude.

"Where's the credit machine?" Calynn asked.

"Follow me... I'll take you there before going to the kitchen."

Calynn shot Kash a look... he knew what she was asking. He nodded and held up four fingers. Triana led Calynn out of the booth and motioned for her to stay put. She then trotted over to the man who was making the girl vomit and spoke to him. The big man waved apologetically and pulled up his pants. Kash didn't even notice the other hostess under the table until the fat guy moved. The guy's wife had that poor girl's face buried between her thighs.

"Sick fucking bastards," Kash said aloud.

He then realized that he was probably being recorded, so he added to his disgust.

"A finer establishment would have rules against doing that in public spaces... I guess this place is the shit hole everyone says it is."

Calynn returned to the booth and sat beside him. As she moved in close, she smirked.

"What?"

Calynn's hand pushed into the front pocket of his jeans. Before he could protest, she removed her hand and left something behind. She immediately started to giggle.

"You're silly."

"The Senator graciously donated five hundred grand for our entertainment," Calynn said playfully. "So smile... you big lug."

"I asked for four."

"I got five," Calynn rebutted. "I wanted to make sure you had a good time."

"I'd be happier with the credits in my account."

"I know... that's why I moved the rest of it there," Calynn said, beaming a smile. "Completely untraceable... just like you taught me."

"Good girl."

"I'll be a bad girl later if you let me."

"I brought the bourbon and some glasses with ice," Triana said as she arrived. "You two are so beautiful together... and those smiles."

Triana smiled also as she set the glasses down and started pouring. She was well practiced as she poured all three to the same amount. She then handed a glass to Calynn and one to him before grabbing the last one for herself. She raised her arm to give a toast.

"To trying new things and all the pleasure that comes with it," Triana chirped.

The three clinked their glasses and sipped their drinks. After swallowing the liquor, both girls made a face. They then started to giggle and looked at Kash.

"What?" Kash said as he downed the rest of the glass. "I thought it was pretty smooth."

Revisited

Kash woke up with a pounding headache. It took him a minute to get his bearings as he tried to remember the night before. They were at a brothel... they rented a room with a nice girl... she was smart and knew things about Egonn... they had food and drinks... lots of drinks... too many drinks... and then came back upstairs and...

"Oh fuck," Kash said quietly to himself.

"What's wrong, Boss," Calynn whispered back.

"Did we... you know..."

"I was a naughty girl," Calynn said softly as she rolled onto him. "I no longer have to worry about dying a virgin."

Calynn then sat up, so she was straddling him and started rocking her hips. She was completely nude and grinding herself into his manhood. Kash couldn't help but notice that the way she was moving seemed very familiar to him. He knew where she learned to do that.

"Wanna do it again?" Calynn asked with a naughty look in her eye.

"I do," Triana said as she sat up also.

Triana and Calynn started kissing each other passionately. Triana was grabbing at Calynn's breast... her ample and perfectly shaped breast. Triana then kissed her way down Calynn's chest and stopped to suck on her nipples. Calynn moaned in pleasure while still grinding herself into him. Kash wanted to tell them to stop, but his growing erection betrayed him. Calynn's fingers expertly guided him inside her as she rocked back and forth.

"By the Gods, you feel good," Kash uttered as he pushed deeper inside Calynn.

"It sure does," Calynn agreed.

"I want some of that, too," Triana said as she kissed Kash's chest.

"Here," Calynn said as she lifted herself off of Kash. "You go first... I like kissing you while you fuck him."

Triana switched positions with Calynn and slid herself down his erection. She had her hands on his chest and was trying to grip his skin. She was biting her lower lip as she worked her way down his manhood.

"Dear God," Kash uttered as he pushed himself deeper again.

"I agree," Triana moaned as she started rocking her hips. "These are going to be the best three days of my life."

The girls spent the next few hournts taking turns riding Kash. They almost seemed to be making a game out of who could do it better. As much as he didn't want to admit it, he was again in awe of Bahanja and her team. Calynn felt every bit the same as Triana when it was her turn. He knew it was wrong to have sex with Calynn, but how could something so wrong feel so good? The trio eventually collapsed into a pile of sweaty, sticky bodies. And they were all out of breath.

"I'm tapping out," Kash said, winded. "No more... you win."

"I'm a little sore myself," Triana confessed.

"I could keep going," Calynn said with a giggle.

"I'd like to say I want to save myself for more tonight, but I still might not be ready then," Triana said, giggling herself.

"I second that motion and call dibs on the shower," Kash said as he jumped out of bed and ran to the bathroom.

"No fair," the girls said in unison and giggled louder.

Kash showered quickly. He was rinsing off when the shower door opened, and Calynn climbed in.

"Come on, get out... it's my turn," Calynn said loudly and then continued in a whisper. "I know you will feel bad about what we did, but I don't. I've never felt so... real. And I just wanted to say thank you."

"It's not the act that worries me," Kash whispered back. "It's the awkwardness it can create."

"I'll try not to make it awkward... I promise."

"Hey... let's just be honest with each other about it... okay?" Kash whispered as he grabbed Calynn's hand. "It happened, and it was amazing. You felt real to me, too... but... I don't want it to change us..."

"If you two are kissing in there without me, I'm going to be upset," Triana said as she entered the bathroom.

"We were just holding hands and sharing a tender moment," Kash said as he looked into Calynn's eyes. "I swear I can see forever when I look into her eyes... and I wonder what I did right to deserve having her in my life."

"Oh my," Triana sounded sad.

Kash kissed Calynn's forehead and stepped out of the shower. Triana was standing there with her face in her hands. She walked over and hugged him before he could ask what was wrong.

"If my information is good enough that I deserve the credits," she said softly, "can I come with you?"

"Whoa, I uh..."

"You two are the most genuine people I've ever met," Triana continued. "Doing what I do normally feels like work... like I have to try to do it... I have to like it even if I really, really don't like it... but that's not how it is with you. I'm genuinely enjoying myself... and do you know how long it's been since I have hugged someone like this?"

"I want a hug, too," Calynn cried out from the shower.

"Go on," Kash said to Triana with a kind smile. "It's nice when you two hug... I need to go pay for our privacy and contemplate our next move."

Triana jumped in the shower as Kash headed to the panel and inserted another 80,000 credits to assure their privacy. The door popped open again so Kash could confirm that the cables were still unhooked. Not that he needed the reassurance. Calynn's sensors would have picked up the cameras if they had been turned back on.

Kash dried himself and got dressed in the same clothes he had on the day before. He made a mental note to go get a change of clothes from the ship... and fuck the girls there.

"Dammit, Kash... focus... this is what you were worried about with getting involved with her."

Kash searched his memory for details related to Egonn from last night. But the only memories that were readily available were of his two female companions... naked... and alcohol... lots of alcohol.

He sat on the edge of the bed and buried his face in his hands. He searched his memories again... replaying everything he could recall... there was something there, but what?

"Hey, you," Triana said as she suddenly stood before him. "You look tense."

"Just trying to recall the events of last night, and I keep drawing a blank... beyond these two insanely gorgeous naked bodies that seem to be hogging all my current memories... oh, look," Kash replied as he pulled Triana closer. "Here's one of those bodies now."

Kash kissed her belly and then hugged her tight.

"Perhaps I can help," Triana said, stroking his hair. "Do you remember when I was dancing that weird dance, and I kept pointing across the bar? I was pointing at a man."

"The guy in the red vest," Kash exclaimed as the memory popped into his head.

"I don't know his name, but I do know that he and the rest of his gang... are swarm pilots."

"No shit," Kash remarked as he looked up at the girl.

"What's a swarm pilot?" Calynn asked from the bathroom door.

"Okay, everyone has to get dressed before we continue this because you two are way too distracting for me to think," Kash said firmly. "Two sexy as hell naked women... you're killing me."

"Sorry, Boss," Calynn apologized.

"Yea, sorry, Boss," Triana echoed.

"Trie, can I borrow something to wear?" Calynn asked. "We didn't bring any luggage."

The girls dressed alike in leggings and shirts with pleated fronts. They were just different colors.

"Ready, Boss," Calynn said as she mocked a salute.

"You're silly... okay... first, we need to go to The Cat and get some clothes," Kash explained.

"What's The Cat?" Triana asked.

"Our ship," Calynn replied.

"Second..."

"I can't go there," Triana interrupted. "I'm not allowed out of the brothel until my debt is paid... sorry."

"I'll handle that, don't worry... second, locate the swarm pilots and see if they would be interested in a joint venture," Kash continued. "Third, we need to get Egonn out into the open..."

BOOM BOOM BOOM

A loud knock at the door interrupted Kash. The trio turned and looked at the door, then at each other, and then back at the door. They watched as the door unlatched and swung open, revealing two thugs.

"Mr. Kash," the one thug said as he drew his weapon. "Egonn sends his regards."

The man, part of the floor, ceiling, and part of Triana's door, disappeared in a flash of light. When Kash turned to Calynn, her eyes were glowing, and her hair stood on end. Another flash of light... and the other man was gone also.

"There are more men in the hallway, and the building is surrounded," Calynn stated. "Egonn's ship is close by."

"We got complacent!" Kash barked. "This is why I always said no!"

"Sorry, Boss."

"Take us to The Cat," Kash ordered.

"With the slip?"

"Yes."

"But I never tried..."

"You can do it, Baby Girl... I have faith in you."

"Come closer," Calynn said and held out her arms.

Kash grabbed Triana and walked over to Calynn. Triana was nearly frozen in terror, and her whole body was shaking. Kash held the girl tight and nodded at Calynn.

The exterior wall of Triana's room suddenly vanished. An instant later, a flash of light surrounded them, knocking the wind out of Kash. It left him feeling woozy. When he regained his composure a second later, they were in the cargo hold of his ship. Triana was gasping for air and in a complete panic. Calynn was already on the move. She closed the rear cargo doors and was on the way to the helm. She recovered much quicker than the other two. Kash caught Triana's eyes as she looked around, trying to get her bearings.

"Are you okay?" Kash asked. "I have to go help her... are you okay?"

Triana nodded and started to move towards the ladder to the helm. Kash moved quicker than the girl and was up the steps first. The ship was already beginning to move as he climbed the ladder. When Kash arrived at the cockpit, Calynn was flying straight towards Egonn's barge.

"Good girl," Kash said as he strapped into the jump seat. "We need to go right at them... can you disable the HLD without making the ship fall out of the sky?"

"They must have found the bugs," Calynn replied. "I can't see inside anymore."

Triana joined them in the cockpit but looked out of sorts. She was clueless about what to do.

"Sit there and strap in," Kash ordered as he pointed to the other jump seat. "You're about to witness a lot of secrets. Try to hold your question until after... Baby Girl, punch a few holes in that hull until you CAN see inside."

Calynn's eyes started to glow again as the HLD and the Slip hummed to life. Five flashes of light across the ship's port side revealed five large holes in the barge's hull.

"I'm in," Calynn stated.

"Force them down and make sure they can't run."

There was another flash of light at the aft of the barge, and half of the engines were now missing. Another flash of light twenty meters above the barge, and suddenly, a huge rock was falling onto the top of the barge. The barge went into a nosedive when the boulder impacted the vessel. The hull moaned under the weight, and it sounded like the boat was about to be ripped in half. Seconds later, it crashed to the ground, destroying part of the dock.

"Can I throw the Sentinels into the sun?" Calynn asked

"Throwing bits of sun into them might cause more terror," Kash replied.

Calynn cocked her head as several explosions happened aboard Egonn's barge.

"I can't get to three of them," Calynn explained. "They are behind a protective field with Egonn."

"Then let's go kill them the old-fashioned way," Kash said as he unstrapped. "Put us down right over there."

"They were able to get out a distress call before I could jam them," Calynn told him as she landed the ship. "We might get company."

"Look," Triana exclaimed as she pointed out the windshield. "The red vest guy. Maybe he will help. How do I use your comms?"

"It's all right here," Calynn said to Triana but then continued over the ship's speakers. "I can help even if I'm not on board."

"How did you do that?" Triana asked.

"Triana, my dear, you have been amazing, but this is the part where it's gonna get weird," Kash replied. "Calynn is the nerve center of the ship. She woke up, and we got her a synth body. She transported us here from your room using a rare Hyperlumic device that we have, and she controls it. Now, we are going to go over to that ship and rain hell down upon them. And the ship might fly around all by itself. I understand if this is too much to take in and if it freaks you out that you want to leave... no hard feelings. It was an absolute pleasure meeting you and fucking you. If you're here when we get back, we can answer questions. But we gotta go."

Kash grabbed the brown beauty by the jaw and kissed her on the lips. He smiled and ran back towards the cargo hold. He heard both girl's voices as he descended the ladder but didn't hear what they said. He opened the secret compartment in the wall beside the ladder and pulled out the weapons shelf. He grabbed an energy vest and put it on. The vest provided extra power for beam weapons and protection against them. He grabbed a beam rifle, an assault rifle, and a sidearm. He also grabbed his favorite antique.

"What the heck is that?" Calynn asked as she joined him.

"An AK-47 replica from Earth," Kash replied. "It shoots balls of lead using a substance called gunpowder."

"Okay?"

"It's a much slower projectile than the new mag-guns, but some shielding can't stop it for whatever reason."

"So you don't have to charge it?" Calynn asked as she donned an energy vest.

"Nope."

"How does it accelerate the projectiles?"

"The gunpowder explodes, which forces the bullet out."

"That sounds dangerous... I'll stick with magnetic rail accelerators."

"Are you ready for this?" Kash asked as he grabbed extra ammo for the assault rifle.

"No... but let's go get our girl."

The duo set out towards Egonn's downed vessel. Gaining entry would be easy, thanks to the large holes Calynn ripped in the ship's side with the Slip. And she also subdued all but three of the Sentinels. The rest of the thugs should be easy pickings by comparison.

"There's a lot of panicked people running around. I'm having trouble figuring out who's who," Calynn said as they approached the ship. "Egonn is that way."

"Let's go that way then."

Calynn took a few quick steps, jumped up about six meters, and landed in the ship. Kash followed suit, but Calynn made the jump look easier than he did. As soon as his feet hit the deck, Kash scanned the hallway they were in for combatants. They appeared to be alone.

"Which way, Baby Girl?"

"This way," Calynn said as she pointed toward the front of the ship.

"I'll take point... you watch my back."

Kash moved quickly in the direction Calynn pointed. When he got to where the hallway branched off, he made a quick move to the center of the hallway... and he was glad he did. There was a thug watching the corner. He fired and hit the wall where Kash would have been if he just peeked around the corner. Kash returned fire. The second shot hit the enemy gunman and sent him hurtling backward. Kash fired a third round to ensure the man wouldn't get up.

Kash continued down the original hallway until he reached the next intersection. Again, he made a big, quick move into the center of the hallway. This time, the hallway was empty.

"We need to take the next left," Calynn said as she followed.

Kash heard footsteps when they reached the next left. He knew there were people around the next corner. He quickened his pace and took a wide angle on the corner. He dropped to his knees and slid into the passageway. He caught the enemy off guard and started to fire before they saw him. Two of the five men fell to the ground before they could even return fire. Kash rolled towards the far wall and pushed off of it when his feet hit. He was sliding across the floor on his back while still shooting. The green line from Calynn's beam rifle lit the area as it struck one of the remaining three men. Kash rolled again and got back to his feet. Calynn fired two more shots that missed, but the third landed true. Kash leveled his weapon at the final man and pulled the trigger at the same time the enemy fired at him. Luckily, Kash had better aim than him. Kash's bullet hit its mark, but the enemy missed.

"You, good," Kash asked Calynn without turning around.

"All good… take the first right."

Kash turned the corner to another empty hallway, but this one had doors on both sides. He paused for a moment and turned to Calynn.

"We have to clear these rooms, so we don't get shot in the back," Kash whispered. "I'll take the left and you take the right… we move at the same time."

Calynn nodded in agreement and moved up, so they were shoulder to shoulder. They moved cautiously and quietly to the first set of doors. Kash counted down with his fingers. Three… Two… One… they each moved into their doors. Kash scanned his room quickly, but he heard gunfire behind him before he could verify it was empty. He turned as fast as he could. Calynn spun out of her door like she had just been shot. Kash dove onto his stomach and slid into the room that way. He surprised the gunman and only needed one shot to dispense of the man.

"I got hit, but my skin works," Calynn whispered. "The bullet bounced off."

"Well, let's not continue to test that theory, shall we?" Kash stated as he returned to his feet.

"Pardon... I'm unarmed," a voice came from the next room. "I'm coming out."

Kash and Calynn both turned to see a man slowly entering the hallway. He was nearly Kash's height but also doubled his weight. Kash was studying the man's eyes, looking for the truth they held.

"Please... I'm not like these guys. I was just here for the paycheck," the man continued. "I fell in love with one of the server girls and just want to get her to safety."

"Where's the girl?" Kash barked.

"She's here," the man said, pointing into the room. "She's just scared."

The woman poked her head around the door frame and looked at Kash. She had terror written in her eyes, and her hand on the door frame was visibly shaking.

"Take the girl and go."

"Thank you, sir... Is it okay if I take my gun to protect us?" the man asked. "It's over here on the floor. I promise you can trust me, Mr. Kash."

"You know who I am?"

"We all do," the man replied. "Egonn has talked about you a lot since your last visit. And I can tell you, your friend isn't here anymore."

"Where is she?" Calynn growled.

"I swear I don't know, but if I had to guess... she's on the way to one of the Pleasure Planets," the man answered. "I overheard them talking at dinner... I'm just one of the chefs."

"Does anyone else want to leave with them?" Calynn shouted. "If so... come out slowly."

Kash waited and watched for any movement, but none came.

"There's people in those rooms, Boss," Calynn whispered. "I can hear them breathing."

"It's okay, everyone," the chef hollered. "They truly are letting us leave. Please come out... and we will all go together."

Slowly, a few hands and faces exited the doorways. Three men and five women soon joined them in the hallway. Some were still wearing their chef's uniforms. Two of the women were wearing elegant evening dresses. Kash assumed the dresses were for Egonn's pleasure and not their own.

"Get your weapon and get them out of here," Kash told the first man.

The man did as Kash commanded. He gathered his people and led them back the way Kash and Calynn had come from. Kash and Calynn stayed put for a moment until their footsteps trailed off into the distance. Kash then nodded at Calynn, and the duo pushed on. The rest of the rooms in the hallway were empty. Calynn grabbed the handle of the large door at the end of the hall.

"This should be the kitchen," she whispered. "Beyond it is the dining room and then the den... Egonn is in the den."

Calynn opened the door, and the two stepped into the kitchen. Bolts of light immediately started bouncing off the walls and counters around them. Kash and Calynn dove for cover as more bullets and beams rained down on them. Kash tried to get a bead on where the gunfire was coming from, and the men appeared to be just inside the far side of the kitchen. They were using toppled tables as makeshift cover.

"If you put down your weapons, we will let you leave!" Kash shouted. "Our quarrel is with your boss... not you!"

The incoming rounds seemed to slow after Kash's offer. It gave him hope that he wouldn't have to kill them. Kash peeked at the men's position through some of the kitchen equipment. He was hoping to see the men surrender.

"If you blockheads stop shooting at them," a man hollered, "I'll shoot you myself."

Kash carefully aimed at the man who just barked at his coworkers and pulled the trigger. His beam rifle was as accurate as ever, and the man fell over dead.

"Offer still stands!" Kash hollered.

The enemy men were no longer firing at them but weren't surrendering either. Kash had a minimal view of the men from his current position, but he didn't want to leave himself exposed, either. Calynn had a puzzled look on her face when Kash looked her way. She was possibly unsure of his tactics. Kash held up one finger, signaling her to wait a moment... and his patience finally paid off.

"We accept," one of them said.

"Put your weapons down and come out," Kash replied.

The men did as he asked. One by one, they moved out from the cover and put down their weapons. Kash slowly got to his feet and stood up. He wasn't pointing his gun at the men, but he was at the ready. The men looked nervous as Kash slowly approached.

"We put our weapons down... like you asked," the one man stammered.

"I should still shoot you just for working for that prick," Calynn growled. "He steals women!"

"And we take care of them," the man rebutted. "I don't expect you to believe me, but... but some of us aren't ruthless... the girls were taken, and we can't free them... but we can sneak them some food and water and try to help as best we can... as futile as that may be."

Something about the man's tone made Kash believe what he was saying. It was as if he regretted not being able to free the girls that his boss had stolen.

"If you speak true... grab your weapons and go free the girls," Kash said sternly. "But I swear to the Gods if you're lying to me..."

"I'm not," the man interrupted. "I wouldn't, I swear... um... where should I take them?"

"This town is built on slavery," another man added.

"Not for fucking long," Kash barked.

"Step one is get them off this fucking barge," Calynn ordered. "Step two can come later."

The three men looked at each other, nodded, and slowly grabbed their weapons. The men were careful not to point their weapons at Kash or Calynn as they passed.

"Thank you," the third man finally spoke. "For the opportunity to make things right... we won't let you down."

The three men jogged through the dining room and rounded the corner, disappearing from sight.

Calynn still looked tense, and she stared in the direction of the den. Slowly, she walked through the dining room towards some beautiful architectural arches. Kash followed closely.

The den was almost completely encased in an energy field. Behind the field were three Sentinels standing at the ready and a ring of naked women holding hands. Egonn sat at the center of the human shield the women created.

"Mr. Kash, you truly are every bit as persistent as your reputation suggests," Egonn stated with an annoyed tone. "You assault me in my home..."

"Oh, I haven't begun to assault you yet," Kash interrupted. "Step out from behind your slave girls... see what happens."

"The women are merely a deterrent as are my men... This room is reinforced with those arches you walked under, and the field between us is pure energy," Egonn said smugly. "We have enough food and water to outlast your resolve, so you might as well leave now! There is no scenario in which you actually get to me, Mr. Kash."

"Pure energy, you say," Calynn stated as she approached the protective field. "I wonder."

Calynn reached out with one hand and touched the energy field. The grid in her skin instantly began to glow. She removed her hand, but some of the energy remained in her body.

"Uh, oh," Kash said comically. "Looks like my girl has your number."

Calynn dropped her weapon and placed both hands in the field. Kash could see the energy flowing into her as she pulled it down to her feet. Then she suddenly thrust all the energy back out through her hands and into the shield. Sparks jumped from the field as it flickered briefly but soon stabilized. Calynn immediately started drawing in power again. Kash pulled up his weapon and aimed at one of the Sentinels. When Calynn pushed the energy back, he pulled the trigger, and the bullet pierced the man's head through his left eye.

"I would think your surrender is in order, Egonn," Kash said with a big grin. "She's eventually going to rip this shield down and tear into you like a hungry predator... you might be able to secure a quick and painless death... if... you return her best friend to her."

Calynn shoved another pulse of energy into the shield. It had enough force to shake the floor. The girls around Egonn looked scared. They started to sit down.

"Nobody told you to sit!" the fat man barked. "Do as I say!"

"Do you feel that, Egonn?" Kash asked the man. "That's your power slipping away... speaking of power, here comes another one."

Another surge of power shot from Calynn's hands into the shield. The field blipped and had holes in it for a second before recovering. The floor shook harder this time.

"One or two more of those, and you're done... WHERE THE FUCK IS DOCTOR OMIA MOSS?"

Kash lost his cool and shouted at the man. He was struggling to regain his composure when he noticed one of the women staring at him. She was mouthing something, but he couldn't understand what she was trying to say. The woman had fresh welts and bruises on her body, like she had recently been beaten.

The shield was no longer solid when Calynn pushed another wave of energy into it. The shield pulsed in waves as it tried to recover from Calynn's assault. Kash, acting quickly, fired at the other two Sentinels. He killed one and wounded the other before the shield returned.

"Last chance!" Kash barked.

A blue light caught Kash's eye from between the girls. Egonn had comms in his chair, and Calynn may have been too distracted by the shield to notice.

"Are you going to tell me where she is?"

Kash yelled the question like he was asking Egonn, but he was staring at the woman staring at him. The woman nodded slightly. She knew where Omia was. He didn't need Egonn anymore.

The protective field suddenly failed as the sound of electrical short circuits filled the air. The wounded Sentinel was no match for Calynn. She beheaded him rapidly. The women were all whining and crying as the duo approached. They feared Kash and Calynn, but also Egonn's whip for not obeying him. When Calynn got close enough, their fear of her won out, and the women scampered away.

"We can make a deal," Egonn whined. "I have credits... lots of credits."

"Credits can't buy happiness," Calynn said, as cold as ice. "But you know what would make me happy? ... Something in a nice brunette... about yay tall... perfect fucking tits."

"She does have amazing tits," Kash agreed.

"Look, she's not here..."

"Where is she?" Calynn snapped.

"What assurances do I have if I tell you..." Egonn started to say.

Boom

Kash shot the fat man in the forehead with his replica. Everyone jumped at the loud noise it made.

"Why did you do that?" Calynn asked frantically.

"We don't need him, and he wasn't going to give us any truths," Kash replied and went to the girl he had been communicating with earlier. "Hi... I'm Kash, and this is Calynn... Where did they take our friend?"

"They had a sex party yesterday... the man from... that got..." the woman sounded panicked.

"It's okay... calm down... just breathe," Kash said soothingly.

"Egonn has parties where he invites other men in to rape us," the woman continued. "Your friend and I were at a party yesterday... the one man wanted to take her with him... I have seen him many times before, but they use code names, so I don't know his real name... if you show me a picture, I would know him to see him."

"This man... is he from the pleasure planets?" Calynn asked.

"Yes," the woman replied. "He is one of the owners."

"Pull up a list of them and show her some pictures," Kash told Calynn.

The monitor in the den lit up, and a search popped up. Kash didn't pay much attention to it. There was something odd about the far wall. He walked over to give it a closer look. He tapped on the wall with his knuckles, and it was what he thought. A safe was built into the wall disguised as the wall itself.

"Can you open this?" Kash asked Calynn.

Calynn turned, looked at him, cocked her head to the side, and then shook her head.

"It has biometric locks that I cannot bypass... sorry, Boss."

"This guy has your friend," the woman with Calynn suddenly stated.

"Are you sure?" Kash asked when he saw the photo.

"One hundred percent sure," the woman replied.

"Well, fuck. This is going to suck."

"Do you know him, Boss?" Calynn asked.

"He's a former client," Kash conceded. "He blackmailed his way to the top by using what I acquired for him. He's a monster... and a legitimate businessman... and connected... really connected... powerful connections."

"If he has Omia, then it doesn't matter who he knows," Calynn insisted. "He gives up our friend or ends up like his."

Calynn pointed at the corpse of Egonn when she made her point. She really didn't know what they were about to be up against. Kash was jealous of her ignorance.

"Rip this thing open," Kash said while pointing at the safe. "Maybe... maybe we'll get lucky, and there will be something we can use to help get her back."

"Spinning up the HLD... and the slip... stand back," Calynn's eyes were glowing as she spoke. "I'm going to shoot it straight up."

"Why?" Kash asked. "Just set it outside."

"It's still travel, silly man. I'm not magic," Calynn explained as her eyes stopped glowing. "I can't make things go through walls without hurting the things and the walls. That's why I ripped the hole in the brothel wall and had to line up The Cat with our trajectory before moving us. If I grabbed Egonn and tried to move him to the docks, I would essentially be throwing him into walls at beyond the speed of light."

"Sounds greasy," Kash joked.

"Oh, geez," Calynn sighed. "So I can throw the door in some direction and have it damage everything in the way, or throw something at the door... again, with damage to whatever... which would you prefer?"

"Throw the door," Kash reluctantly stated.

"Spinning everything up again," Calynn said sarcastically.

Kash stepped away from the wall and motioned for the women to get further away than they were. The thought of a metal door being flung through metal walls, floors, and ceilings made Kash wonder how loud that would be. Would the immense speed make it nearly silent or much louder? As a precaution, he put his fingers in his ears and nodded that the women should do the same.

There was a flash of light, and suddenly, the vault door was gone. The air in the room rushed towards where the door once was with enough force to make Kash need to catch his balance. The whole thing was nearly silent, though.

"The Hyperlumic cone creates a vacuum in an atmosphere," Calynn explained. "Sound needs air to travel."

"Oh," Kash replied, removing his fingers from his ears. "I did not know that. Are those credits?"

"And some jewelry and some documents of some sort," Calynn replied.

Kash walked cautiously into the three-meter by three-meter safe and stopped in front of a cart with gold cards stacked upon it. He rifled through one of the stacks and found they were all worth one million credits each.

"These are one million each," Kash blurted out. "That has to be..."

"Just under twenty-six billion if my math is correct," Calynn interrupted.

"That's retirement money," Kash said with a huge smile and a laugh.

Then, he caught sight of the naked women huddled together. The slaves that had their lives ruined for that money... like Omia. He dropped the credits in his hand and walked away from it. He couldn't believe it, but he didn't want it... not like this.

The Supply Chain

Kash walked out of Egonn's ship feeling more than a little dejected. Chasing after Omia was beginning to feel like an impossible task. The man who had her now was one of the wealthiest men in the verse. He had an army protecting him. He could call in government warships to help if that wasn't enough. The whole thing felt... hopeless.

Triana was sprinting towards him with tears in her eyes. She was obviously glad that Calynn and himself were still alive. Kash had to admit that Triana was more personable than any other prostitute he had been with. She seemed to really connect with them. He should let her down softly. He wouldn't want her to get hurt for being with him.

"Who did Egonn contact?" Kash stopped and asked Calynn. "When he was still in the shield."

"Nobody... I jammed all signals before we entered the barge."

"Good," Kash uttered and turned to the approaching Triana.

"What about all that money, Boss," Calynn asked as she followed.

Triana leaped into his arms before he could answer Calynn. She was half crying and half laughing. They were definitely happy tears.

"Hey, Trie," Calynn cooed as she caressed the girl's back.

"Oh my Gods, You're both okay!" Triana cried out as she moved to hug Calynn. "I was so worried."

Kash walked off again, heading to The Cat. He had to think.

"Boss," Calynn hollered, "the money?"

"What money?" Triana asked.

"The big fucking stack of Egonn's dirty money," Kash snapped at the girls. "The ill-gotten goods he received for taking women like our Omia. That fucking money? ... fucking burn it for all I care."

Kash stormed off, leaving the two women in his wake. He walked up the ramp to his ship's cargo bay and started putting away his guns and equipment. Calynn and Triana followed but stayed at a distance. Once his gear was stored, he headed up the ship's ladder to the galley. He opened the liquor cabinet, grabbed a bottle of booze, and headed to his quarters. Kash took a big swig of the booze and stripped down to his boxers. He sat on the edge of his bed and took another big drink before putting the bottle down and flopping back onto the bed.

"Hey, Boss," Calynn said softly. "Are you okay?"

Kash sighed loudly and covered his face with his hands. He felt terrible for yelling at Calynn. It wasn't her fault that he felt so lost.

"I'm Sorry I yelled at you," Kash apologized. "That was more about me than you... I just want her back, but..."

"We aren't going to be able to get her back... are we?"

"I don't know, Baby Girl... everything is murky and all fucked up right now... and I don't see a way through it all."

"What can I do to help?" Calynn sincerely asked.

"Come here," Kash said and raised his arms.

He heard Calynn quickly strip off her pants and shirt. She then placed one knee on either side of him and laid down flat on his chest. She rubbed her cheek on his and pushed her hands partially under his back. Kash held her tight and took a couple of deep, cleansing breaths. He had to find a way to get Omia back. He had a hole in his chest... a hole that even Calynn couldn't fill.

"No clothes on the bed," Calynn said softly.

It was only then that Kash remembered poor Triana. She was so happy to see them, but he barked at her. He turned to see her pulling off her top, and she soon climbed into his bed.

"Sorry, I yelled," Kash apologized.

"It's okay," Triana replied as she lay near his head. "Lift up... you can use me as a pillow."

"You're too kind," Kash said as he lifted his head.

Triana shifted her body so Kash could lay his head on her stomach. It wasn't the most comfortable, but he appreciated the attempt.

"Is there anything I can do to help? Not that I can do much," Triana sounded unsure of herself. "I guess you could sell me to the

Pleasure Planet guy so I can help find your friend. I don't know what else I have to offer?"

"What happened to buying your freedom?" Kash asked with a bit of sarcasm.

"You two have been treating me better than I have ever been treated in my whole life," Triana's voice cracked a little as she spoke. "You're both so nice... and have been so nice to me... I would give up my freedom to make you happy... I would feel good about that."

"It would make me happy if you never had to be a slave again," Calynn uttered. "You or your friends."

"That's it!" Kash exclaimed as the revelation hit him. "It's a long shot, but... it might get us an audience... come on, get up and get dressed."

"You lost me, Boss," Calynn said as she stood.

"Egonn muscled his way into these businesses, right?" Kash asked Triana.

"Yea," the girl replied, unsure of herself.

"How much do you want to bet he owns a majority share of your brothel?"

"Maybe," Triana still sounded unsure. "I know he owns some of it."

"So if we take Egonn's money and buy everyone's freedom, I bet eighty percent of that money comes right back to us," Kash explained. "We did just execute a hostile takeover of Egonn's stake."

"I'm still lost," Calynn stated.

"The Pleasure Planets need a constant supply of fresh sex workers because some of the sick pricks there like to fuck dead girls, and of course, the girls always need to be young and stay young. If we shut down the brothel, we will interrupt some of their supply... and hopefully some of their money, too. I guarantee Egonn and the brothel were kicking up some sort of tribute to one or all of these guys in order to stay in business."

"So what does that mean for us?" Calynn asked.

"How often is Egonn here?" Kash asked Triana.

"It's a little longer than a month between visits... I think. Why?"

"Because I think those credits in the safe aren't his," Kash explained. "Why were they on a cart and not put away on the shelves like everything else? I bet if we look..."

Kash stopped talking, pulled on his pants, and jogged to the back of his ship. Calynn and Triana followed him, but neither one bothered to dress. He was looking for the women that followed them out of Egonn's barge. Specifically, the one that identified Egonn's guest. None of the women had clothes, so they were all wrapped in tablecloths and blankets. The women had followed them all the way to The Cat.

"You... How often does Egonn host the rich and powerful? Like the party yesterday."

"I think it's every two or three weeks," the woman replied. "It alternates between here and the Aura System."

"Home to one of the Consortium Administrative complexes," Kash pointed out. "The Pleasure Planets are only six days from here... Egonn brings the girls this way to be used at the Pleasure Planets, then takes the credits back to the crooked government agents that ensure the missing girls are never investigated. There's a few small systems on the way..."

"Like Poncia," Calynn interrupted.

"Exactly," Kash continued. "So in roughly fifteen days, when Egonn doesn't show up with the credits..."

"They'll come looking for it and find us," Triana exclaimed. "They'll slaughter us!"

"The only thing they will find is an empty brothel," Kash explained. "We have plenty of time to secure the freedom of every slave and put them on a transport to wherever they want to go. We might have to buy out some of the small business..."

"Everything here is owned by the brothel," Triana interrupted. "Everything."

"Well, that makes it simpler," Kash stated as he looked into the distance. "Hey, is that..."

The buzz of hundreds of small ships filled the air. They were accompanied by eight ships large enough for one man.

"Incoming comm," Calynn said in Kash's earpiece.

"This is Kash," Kash said as he touched his earpiece.

"Kash, this is Guy," the voice announced. "Area secured. Tell Triana she looks great from up here."

"Guy, you are such a welcome sight," Kash replied.

"That's his name," Triana said aloud to herself.

"But hey, get those things out of here before you scare the other girls... they've been through enough."

"Will do," Guy said as the swarm ships started to pull away.

"Wait, Guy," Kash continued. "Wanna get rich?"

"Hell yeah," Guy exclaimed. "What do I have to do?"

"Meet me at the cafe in an hourn. I'll explain then."

"Will do... Guy out."

The swarm of ships buzzed off into the distance, and Kash turned his attention to Egonn's women. He was trying to decide what to do when he saw more people exiting Egonn's ship. It looked like a dozen men leading fifty or sixty women. One of the men left the group and jogged towards Kash. He put his firearm away as he approached.

"Mr. Kash," it was one of the three men he let go in the kitchen. "We rounded up all the slave girls and dispatched the men loyal to Egonn. Where should we take them?"

"There's a cafe just off the docks. Take them there to get them something to eat," Kash replied. "We're taking over the brothel so we can house them there until we secure transport for them to get off this rock."

"Sounds good, sir," the man replied and returned to his group.

"Go with them," Kash said softly to the women at his ship. "They will get you some food, and then we will get you some clothes and a place to stay."

"Thank you, sir," some of the women murmured as they turned to join the rest of the women.

"What are we going to do until the meeting?" Calynn asked.

"Triana," Kash replied. "Guy was right... she looks good."

"What... me?"

"Just a quickie," Kash said with a smirk.

Kash turned and grabbed Triana by the waist. He hoisted the pixie up and kissed her passionately. The pixie giggled and wrapped herself around Kash. The trio retreated to Kash's quarters and focused their attention on Triana. He and Calynn left her breathless. The girls stayed in bed while Kash showered. They were giggling when he returned.

"Your skin is so cool," Triana said as she pushed her finger into Calynn's boob. "Do it again."

Calynn made her skin hard, so the impression stayed when Triana removed her finger. The duo giggled like they had been best friends forever. Kash took a moment to stare at the girls and their naked bodies. They were both sexy as hell. Calynn caught sight of him staring and smiled a shy little smile.

"I better get going before you two draw me in for more," Kash said as he smiled back.

"I need a little break," Triana confessed. "But we can tag team our girl here... I still can't believe you're a synth. You even taste real."

"She's one of a kind," Kash added and smiled at Calynn. "You two have fun... I'll be back."

"Let's see what else your body can do," Triana said.

The girls were giggling again when Kash walked away. The cafe was only a short walk away and packed with the girls from Egonn's ship. Guy and two men dressed like him were sitting at one of the tables. They were chatting with some of the girls who were sitting on the ground near them. Guy smiled at Kash as he approached.

"Mr. Kash," Guy announced.

"Just Kash... please."

"Okay... Kash, what can I do to become rich?" Guy asked.

"We have a lot of slave girls in need of passage home."

"My ships can only carry one, and our transport doesn't have room for many more," Guy said, smirking. "One or two girls would be nice, though."

Guy and his friends laughed at Guy's comment.

"No... I need you to be security for those that want to leave," Kash explained. "And set up a new brothel for those that don't."

"Whoa..."

"I know it's a big ask, but Triana seems to think you're a good guy," Kash continued. "And I know of your squadron... and their reputation."

"Been a long time since we served."

"But the honor remains."

"I know your reputation also," Guy said as he sat forward. "And that of the guy you just took down... why should we get tangled up in this mess?"

"Because all the heat will come down on me... they won't care about the missing girls versus what I'm taking. You and them will be in the clear."

"What the hell are you taking?" Guy persisted.

"This is the part where I find out if I can trust you," Kash explained. "There are enough credits on that ship to secure everyone safe passage away from here. Enough to make sure you can start a proper facility where the girls that want to stay can thrive and be safe... and enough for me to hold hostage to get a meeting with Egonn's bosses."

"What's enough for me to do as you ask?"

"I'm willing to hand over a billion credits for seed money."

"A billion?" Guy asked with surprise.

"I'm not done," Kash continued. "There's a system not far from here. I just helped them with a problem with their sun, so I know their economy is about to skyrocket. And they may be short one politician that ran a high-end call girl ring... if you were to pick up where he left off and treat the girls like earners, not slaves..."

"In some systems, it's considered an honorable profession," one of Guy's friends added.

"And I would feel better about them being volunteers... not slaves," Guy relented. "I don't mind partaking in their goods, but..."

"I agree, Commander," the third man said. "Keeping slaves isn't for me, but if they are willing... that's different."

"Look, you pay them fair... like fifty or sixty percent of their take, and after expenses, you still make out like a bandit," Kash explained. "If the girls are free, then nobody like Egonn can muscle their way in. There's no leverage there. You would basically be working for the girls for a cut of what they make."

"Keeping them housed and safe," Guy agreed.

"And making sure they get paid," the second man added. "That doesn't sound like a bad gig."

"Would we get an employee discount?" the third man asked with a chuckle.

"Negotiate a good contract... and maybe," Kash replied lightheartedly.

"What's your cut for this seed money?" Guy asked.

"Say... five percent of the take," Kash replied. "I'm more interested in looking out for the girls than making a huge profit... what do you say... you in?"

"We're in," Guy said with a smile.

Over the next four days, Kash paid for the release of every slave and shut down the brothel. Guy and his men chatted with all the former slaves who wanted to stay as prostitutes. Triana was pivotal in those negotiations. Because Trie had the backing of Kash and Calynn, she could sway the negotiations one way or the other. Some of Egonn's former employees were signing on to help also. Everything was coming together nicely. They even bought twelve more girls from slave traders who showed up looking to sell.

When Triana wasn't working on the contract for the new brothel, she was with Calynn. The two women were having too much fun playing with Calynn's body. Triana seemed more intrigued by the day and always wanted to try something new. Sometimes, the something new required his help, and sometimes it didn't. Calynn reminded him of Omia with every move she made. She had studied Omia well... too well. He would give in to his memories and try to fill the void in his heart with Calynn. She moved like Omia, acted like Omia, and fucked like Omia... but she wasn't Omia. And he hated himself for doing that to Calynn.

The day the transports started showing up, Triana seemed to be insatiable. And the reason why broke Calynn's heart. Triana had decided to help run the new brothel to help care for her friends.

She would represent Kash and Calynn's share of the business as a silent partner. After that, Calynn didn't want to stick around to help get the transports loaded... she was ready to move on. Guy and Triana had everything well in hand, so they really didn't need to stay.

"Are you gonna sulk the whole way to the Pleasure Planets?" Kash asked Calynn as they left Joor. "We know where she's going and can visit any time."

"No... I know... I'm just gonna miss her," Calynn whined.

"Me too," Kash agreed. "After my dick stops hurting."

"Why does it hurt? Did we do something wrong to it?"

"No... you can only... okay, maybe you don't experience this, but you can only have so many orgasms before all the nerves down there are just so sensitive that they hurt... constantly."

"Oh."

"Yea... speaking of which... we need to focus on work now..."

"So no more sex," Calynn interrupted with a sour tone. "Yes, I know."

"Don't make it awkward."

"I won't."

"Okay."

"Okay."

"I'm gonna go lay down... what's our ETA?"

"Nineteen hourns."

"Okay... you coming?"

"Neh," Calynn replied and turned back to her controls. "If you get an erection in your sleep, I'll want to use it... and that would be awkward."

Kash stood there for a minute as he processed what she just said. She said she didn't want to make it awkward, but... that felt awkward to him.

"Okay," Kash finally agreed. "Don't forget to eat something. The berry compote is in the fridge. You only need a little."

Kash went to his bed, stripped, and lay down. He caught a scent of Triana in the sheets and savored it for a moment. He allowed his thoughts to drift to the trio's many escapades together. He felt so lucky over the last few days. He had two gorgeous women attending to his every desire... Calynn could contort her body into impossible positions that allowed him to thrust deeper... and Triana was not lying about her specialty. She was better at sucking a dick than any woman Kash has ever known. His memories started to stir his loins.

"Get it together, Kash... stop thinking with your dick, or you'll get yourself killed."

He forced himself to focus on the hum of the HLD and slow, deep breaths. Eventually, he was able to get to sleep. His memories betrayed him in his dreams. They were filled with filth... dirty, perverted filth... extraordinary filth that felt so... so good. He slept fitfully at best. It was a long nineteen hournes.

"They look so pretty," Calynn said as they approached the Pleasure Planets.

"They do... just don't look too close," Kash replied. "Otherwise, you might see how fake everything is, and the employees are actually slaves."

"The beaches are real... can we go to the beach?"

"Then go to Planet One. I don't want to deal with all the spoiled children."

"That's the one with the nude beaches... are you trying to get me naked?"

Calynn smiled and squinted her eyes at him playfully. It was good to see her in a better mood.

"Just remember, more than my eyes will be on you," Kash replied as he stared at her and got close. "Imagine a drooling slob this close to you... staring at your lady parts... with his hand on his..."

"Eww," Calynn interrupted him. "That's enough."

"Still better than shitty children throwing sand at you all day."

"Says the guy without lady parts," Calynn bantered.

Kash laughed and kissed her on the forehead.

"We'll go to one of the more exclusive resorts," Kash said, still laughing. "That way, you're not in the middle of a circle jerk."

"Is that what I think it is?" Calynn asked with a disgusted look on her face.

"Probably."

"I need a shower."

"Just take us in, Hot Stuff," Kash laughed. "I'll go book a room."

Kash pulled up the Pleasure Planets web page to see their available rooms. He wanted to ensure he was noticed, so he sorted by the most expensive rooms first. The first dozen or so listings were corporate retreats that could accommodate up to fifty guests. Next on the list was a four-bedroom suite loaded with children's amenities, but just below that was an extravagant honeymoon suite. It was well appointed with around-the-clock butler service, fresh flowers and fruit delivered daily, and a personal chef. It was also half a million credits per night... Kash booked it for a week.

"And thank you again, Senator Fuck Face," Kash said quietly to himself.

Kash then returned to the Calynn after sending the coordinates to the cockpit.

"Did you get the cords?"

"I did... and we're on the way."

"What's the most expensive outfit you have?"

"An evening gown... why?"

"Put it on... I booked the Honeymoon Suite."

Calynn turned and gave him a puzzled look.

"What?"

"Are we allowed to have honeymoon sex in the Honeymoon Suite?"

"We need to be noticed, and it's an expensive room... it seemed the easiest way."

"That wasn't an answer."

"You know we shouldn't..."

"I'll go get dressed," Calynn said as she stood and walked by Kash.

"What happened to not making it awkward?"

"The Honeymoon Suite," Calynn said as she continued to walk away.

Kash watched her walk away and scowled. He didn't know who he was more upset with—him or her? He was upset at her for her current attitude and upset at himself for allowing them to get to this position in the first place. Kash went to his quarters to put on a nice suit. He was working on his cuff links when Calynn burst into the room.

"I need to do my hair," she said as she marched into the bathroom.

She was wearing a shiny silver, skin-tight, ankle-length dress. The front had an oval opening at her cleavage and another at her belly button. The back of the dress was open from her neck to the top of her butt. She was going to turn every head that she walked by.

"You look stunning."

"Thanks, I'm hoping to attract a boy toy."

Kash didn't know how to respond to that comment, so he decided not to. He walked out to the cockpit and sat at the helm. He looked at the other ships at the dock and realized they were the only ones without a luxury liner. Some of the vessels had dinghies bigger than his boat.

"Fuck me, there's a lot of money here."

"I'm ready," Calynn said from behind him.

Kash was stunned, speechless at the sight of his companion. Her hair was curled and perfect and fell just over her shoulders. Her makeup was subtle and accentuated her beauty. Her dress clung to her curves, and he could tell she wasn't wearing a bra. She was holding her black leather clutch and wearing a matching pair of open-toed shoes. She wasn't wearing any jewelry, though. Probably because she didn't have any.

"Wait right there," Kash said as he quickly darted back to his quarters. He started throwing open drawers, looking for a small wooden box. A wooden box he was paid to recover years ago, but the client couldn't pay.

"Where the hell did I... there you are," Kash said aloud to himself as he found it.

He grabbed the box and returned to Calynn. When he opened the box, her eyes lit up, and she beamed a smile.

"It's called vein stone... they polish the stone around the gem also," Kash explained. "They actually can't really remove the gem without the surrounding rock because it crumbles... the gem part starts black but changes color... when it grabs the light, it really sparkles."

"They're beautiful," Calynn cooed.

"It should change color when you put it on... may I?"

Calynn nodded, and Kash retrieved the necklace from the box. He carefully opened the clasp and wrapped the delicate string of stones around her neck. When he stepped back, he took a moment to admire her. The vein in the stone started to shine a bright red.

"You look... wow," Kash stammered.

"You wear that suit pretty well yourself, handsome."

"Shall we?" Kash offered and directed Calynn toward the rear of the ship.

Calynn didn't bother trying to climb down the ship ladder. The ladder wasn't very steep, but her dress was really tight. She just jumped down to the cargo bay, so she didn't damage her dress. Kash joined her and offered his elbow for her to hold while they walked. He opened the cargo doors, and the duo marched to the awaiting shuttle.

"Greetings, sir... madam," a man offered. "My name is Early, and I will be your butler for the week... do you have any luggage?"

"We've had a recent windfall, Early, and have yet to acquire a suitable ship, let alone decent clothes," Kash told the man. "We will purchase everything we need as we need it."

"Excellent, sir."

The shuttle ride to their resort was only a few minutes, but the look on Calynn's face as she took in the sights was priceless. She was practically glowing she was so happy. Kash couldn't help but smile back and stare.

Their ride ended at a private elevator on the side of the resort. Early led them into the elevator and pressed the top button.

"The elevator has only three stops," Early explained. "The street level, the main concourse, and your room. No guest can access this elevator other than the two of you, and it must be operated by your attending butler… and here we are. Welcome to your Honeymoon."

"Oh my…" Calynn gasped as she entered the spacious room.

The ceilings were at least eight or nine meters tall. The floor looked similar to marble from Earth but with much more colorful veining. The sofa and rug in the sitting room looked like they cost as much as his ship. Everything was warm, with earth tones and lots of reds.

"Would there be anything, sir?" the butler asked diligently.

"Honey… Calynn, my dear," Kash said loud enough to get her attention. "Would you like anything else… perhaps another companion?"

"Oh, that sounds delightful," Calynn replied and returned to Kash. "Can we get a brunette this time?"

"I'd love a brunette."

"Oh, and make sure she isn't flat-chested… you know how I like a full bust. And a flat stomach, too. Oh, and some fresh fruit."

"Yes, dear… anything for you," Kash said to the now spinning and dancing Calynn.

"Perhaps you could bring us a brochure?" Kash said to Early. "The last girl I had here was… jaded, to say the least. So maybe let's start with the newest acquisitions."

"Very good, sir," Early said with a curt bow, and he disappeared into the elevator.

Kash turned back to his beautiful companion and watched as she flowed through the suite. She moved through the sitting room to the kitchenette and breakfast nook and circled the table. She paused momentarily to admire the ocean view from the patio doors before returning to the sitting room. She then darted up one side of the horseshoe-shaped staircase to their loft bedroom, where she disappeared from view.

A message popped up on the monitor behind Kash along the elevator door.

"It seems we have three hourns until we have to place our order for dinner," Kash announced. "We should probably look at getting some clothes delivered too."

"Umm, Boss... what's love assist?" Calynn asked as she walked to the railing of the loft.

"Love assist?"

"Yea... there's some buttons beside the bed."

"Oh, it's uh..." Kash couldn't help but laugh.

"What?" Calynn giggled with him.

"It's to help old men that married young girls pleasure their wives," Kash blurted out between laughter.

"Pleasure their... oh!"

Calynn disappeared from view again, followed by some strange noises a few moments later. Calynn reemerged with a stunned look on her face. She was pointing in the direction she had come from but wasn't saying anything.

"Yea... you have fun with that," Kash said as he flopped down on the sofa. "I'm taking a nap."

Kash must have nodded off quickly because the next thing he knew, Calynn was standing over him. Her hair was mussed, and she wore a red and white silk robe.

"The butler dropped this off," Calynn stated as she held out an E-tablet.

"Probably for our dinner order," Kash replied.

"No... I gave that to him already," Calynn explained. "I think it's for our after-dinner order."

"Let me see it," Kash said as he sat up.

When he tapped on the screen, the e-tablet came to life. The screen lit up, displaying a picture of a brown-haired woman with light green skin and golden eyes. Kash swiped his finger from right to left on the screen and nearly dropped the device.

He stared into Calynn's eyes as she clapped her hand over her mouth. Both of them were stunned when they saw Omia's picture. Kash frantically pushed the book button at the bottom of her picture until a message appeared on the screen confirming the appointment.

"It can't be that easy, can it?" Kash said nearly mindlessly.

"That's her, though... she's here."

"She's here and available for our pleasure after dinner," Kash spoke in stunned monotone.

Calynn was suddenly on his lap, crying. Kash was still trying to process his emotions when the first tear rolled down his cheek. He stared blankly off into the room at nothing in particular. The hole in his chest ached as he dared to think that he might be made whole again. He missed Omia so much.

Time passed slowly, and the world around him seemed surreal. Calynn was either pacing anxiously or curled up in a ball, sobbing. Kash was regulating his emotions better than she was, but he'd be lying if he said he wasn't anxious. When their dinner arrived, neither of them were really interested in it. Calynn picked at her meal, but Kash never even took a single bite. They were both watching the clock, awaiting the arrival of their entertainer for the evening.

When they heard the elevator start up from below, they both moved to stand before it. Calynn was holding Kash's hand and clicking her fingernails together. Kash was possibly more nervous than her but was containing it much better. The elevator arrived, and Kash touched the button to open the door. He smiled from ear to ear until the door opened... and his heart dropped.

Three men were in the elevator instead of his beautiful Omia. They all had high-end synth bodies that were tall, lean, and muscular—the bodies that rich men buy so they never need to work out but can still keep up with the young women they pursue.

"Kash," the lead man said as he stepped from the elevator.

"Mr. Crigg," Kash replied with some disappointment in his voice.

"Am I not who you were expecting?" Crigg asked sarcastically.

"Don't play games with me," Kash countered. "You know you're not... Where's the girl?"

"Safe... for now," Crigg replied with a sinister tone. "Where's my money?"

"Safe... for now."

"Sir," one of the other men holding an E-tablet said. "Our team is in position."

"Tell them to tear his ship apart until they find my credits," Crigg said to the man while staring at Kash. "Tell them to be thorough... and destructive."

"That ends badly," Kash said with a snicker.

Calynn increased the pressure on her grip while holding his hand. He was confident she was already handling business. When her grip relaxed, the man with the E-tablet suddenly looked shaken and panicked. He touched the comm in his ear as he frantically showed the E-tablet to his boss.

"How did you do that?" Mr. Crigg asked politely while handing the tablet to Kash.

Kash looked at the image on the screen and saw the men tumbling in space toward the system's sun. Their body cams recorded their own demise. Kash smiled, and Calynn giggled.

"It's my new theft deterrent device," Kash replied sarcastically.

Lights poured into the room from the patio doors from the search lights of his ship as it hovered just outside his room. Kash turned to look at the ship, then Calynn, and then back to Mr. Crigg.

"Wanna experience it firsthand?" Kash continued.

The Pleasure Planets

Kash smiled at the men in front of him. He knew he had the upper hand if they had a physical confrontation. However, Mr. Crigg had Omia... and he really needed her back. So maybe... maybe the position was equal.

"If you kill me, Kash, you'll never find the girl," Crigg threatened.

"Keep the girl... I'll keep the credits," Kash countered. "No girl is worth that many credits."

"I need those credits, Kash."

"And I need the girl, Crigg."

"The girl dies if I don't make a call!" Crigg barked. "And I don't make that call without the MONEY!"

Kash paused a moment. He knew Crigg was ruthless, but he never attributed him with being smart. Was he actually smart enough to have a plan in place to force Kash's hand? ... Or was this a bluff?

"If the girl dies, you die," Calynn growled.

"What are you gonna do, sweetheart, fuck me to death?" Crigg laughed.

The three goons all laughed as Kash spun around in front of Calynn. He gently placed his hand on her belly and gave her a look. He knew she would tear the men apart if he didn't interfere. After a second or two, he saw her relax.

"I'll give you half," Kash stated without turning around.

"Are you trying to bargain with my stolen credits?"

"You were going to rip apart my boat, and do you really think I didn't notice the cloaked drones?" Kash replied sarcastically. "So half now and half upon her safe return... minus any damages and, of course, my fee."

"Your fee?"

"I recovered your credits... if I left them in Egonn's ship, where do you suppose they would be right now?" Kash continued. "You should be happy with half."

"I'll be sure to send you half the girl," Crigg added. "You have five minutes before the girl dies and a bounty goes out on your head. There's nowhere you'll be able to go without being hunted. You'll be as good as dead... Or... you return my credits and do a job for me in exchange for your precious doctor and, more importantly... your freedom."

"You wouldn't?" Kash exclaimed as he finally turned to face the man.

"I already did... now what will it be, Kash?"

He turned back around and looked into Calynn's eyes. She was worried. So was he. Mr. Crigg actually had the upper hand.

"Fine," Kash relented. "But the credits aren't here."

"Where are they?"

"The first half is in the safe of the abandoned brothel on Joor," Kash explained. "It should keep them safe from the scrappers... if you hurry. I knew you would have some ploy to make me give up the credits. This way, you must divide your attention, just like I do. The other half is... moving but can be delivered when necessary."

"Joor is six days..."

"You have men in the area already in route," Kash interrupted. "Don't fucking lie to me. Now, what's this fucking job?"

"How did you afford this room without using my credits?"

"I fucking work for a living," Kash replied as he turned back to the man. "What... is... the... job?"

"But first, make the call," Calynn pleaded. "Make the call. Please, Make the call."

"And I have your word?"

"You do," Kash sighed. "Make the call."

Crigg turned and nodded at the man with the E-tablet. And then he walked into Kash and Calynn's room. He was strutting his arrogance of having the upper hand on Kash.

"A business associate of mine has been making moves against me," Crigg explained. "He has a device with a recording of me... a not-so-flattering recording. And I want that device."

"Wouldn't buying it from him be easier since you are associates?"

"We may be associates, but he is also my mortal enemy," Crigg added. "We've been trying to kill each other for years. Sometimes in business, the credits are more important than friendships."

"Oh, for fuck's sake... and where is this mortal enemy?"

"Three hundred kilometers away in a corporate resort," Crigg informed him. "He doesn't own a big enough share in the company for an owner's suite. And honestly, I don't think he wants one."

"He's another owner... of course, he is... anything else I should know?"

"We have a board meeting in two days," Crigg replied. "I need the device before then."

"Then we better get started."

"Just you," Crigg announced. "The pretty blond slut stays. I'll keep her company."

Kash reacted like a feral beast protecting its young. He jerked the hidden chain from his belt and wrapped it around Crigg's neck in the blink of an eye. Crigg tried to push him off, but Kash was stronger and retained his grip.

"My partner goes where I go," Kash hissed. "This may be a synth body, but it is still your neck, and your blood is running through it. Now... do you really want to walk down this path or can me and my recon specialist go retrieve your stupid fucking recording?"

Crigg had fear in his eyes, but he tried to hide it. He knew Kash would kill him. He chose to back down. Crigg said nothing. He just raised his hands to signify his surrender. Kash released the man and walked towards The Cat with Calynn.

"You and Doctor Moss better be in your suite when I return," Kash demanded. "Or next time... I'll cut your fucking head off."

"Do you want the coordinates?" Crigg asked.

"We have them," Calynn hollered. "We hacked your tablet."

"Fucking amateurs," Kash added.

Kash and Calynn were soon on the way to retrieve the recording, and thankfully, they were far away from the creepy Mr. Crigg.

"I think we should take the time to do recon," Kash told Calynn as he changed clothes. "I don't want to rush it and fuck things..."

"I know where she is," Calynn interrupted. "Omia... it was on the tablet."

"Can we just go get her?"

"There's no way in... she's in a deep dark hole under the casino," Calynn explained. "They have redundant systems and biometric locks... I can't see the room well enough to use the Slip... I might hurt her. And there's an entire platoon on site. It's just too much firepower."

"Then we do the job... I'm mildly good at retrieval."

"I'll do a flyover so we can get a scan of the layout."

"Good girl."

Kash finished changing into his recon jumpsuit. It was form-fitting and light-absorbing, with pockets for his gadgets. His shoes had the softest soles available to help with sound, and his gloves had a built-in device for hacking key cards.

"Do you have one of those suits for me?" Calynn asked as she entered his room. "I don't think my silky red robe is very tactical."

"You're staying on the ship," Kash explained. "I need eyes in the sky if..."

"Boss," Calynn interrupted. "There's two cloaked fighters below us."

"Fighters?"

"Balton X45s, Boss... short-range attack craft."

"Those don't have an HLD... they must have a carrier."

"There's lots of ships that could fit that bill, Boss."

"Cloak us and take us in," Kash told Calynn. "Maybe the enemy of our enemy is our friend."

"I better get dressed if we're making new friends," Calynn stated as she dropped her robe and walked out of his quarters.

Kash couldn't help but watch her walk out of the room. Calynn had nothing on under the robe that was now on the floor... and she had a really nice ass. Kash picked up the robe and put it on his bed. He went out to the cockpit to wait for Calynn to return. He checked the layout of the corporate retreat while he waited. Four executive suites each with a safe, fifteen junior suites, twenty individual or double occupancy rooms, and about three thousand square meters of common areas... with two more large safes. The possible hiding spots for a recording device were nearly endless.

"Ready to go make some friends?" Calynn asked as she returned wearing jeans and a tee shirt.

"Put us down right beside their ships," Kash instructed. "Be less than subtle."

Calynn grabbed the controls at the helm and dropped them into a steep dive. She pulled up hard at the last second and landed softly, but the extra thrust needed to slow their descent would have been very noticeable. The duo marched down to the cargo hold and exited via the man door on the ship's side.

"Are you bloody mad?" a voice called from the tall desert grass.

"Quite mad, actually," Kash replied.

A man in military fatigues was crouched and moving towards them through the grass. He stopped five meters from Kash's position and motioned for them to crouch down. Kash and Calynn looked at one another and then crouched down in the grass.

"Who are you?" the man asked.

"I'm a man that means to find a way into that building to retrieve something that I need to give to another man who has taken a good friend of mine so I can get her back," Kash explained. "It's all rather convoluted. Who are you?"

"They took your friend?" the man asked.

"They did."

"They took my sister," the man stated. "My baby sister."

"Sounds like we can help each other," Kash offered. "How long have you been watching them? Is there a perimeter alarm? How many guards are there, and what's their schedule? Is there more at night or during the day? How often do they go on patrol, and do they take the same routes? And more importantly, are there any holes in those routes that can be exploited?"

"I, uh... I'm not sure."

"Let's take a look, shall we?" Kash said with a smile and started working his way closer to the resort.

He passed another man in military fatigues who glared at him while he passed. Kash continued another fifteen meters and then sat on his heels. He pulled a pair of goggles from his chest pocket and put them on. The goggles took a few seconds to calibrate, but then they showed him three orange rings that circled the building. The rings were probably super low-intensity lasers, and they were definitely rigged to an alarm.

Kash counted nine guards just on the side of the building he could see. The windows of the resort had electronic countermeasures on them for guest privacy. He couldn't see beyond them to tell how many guards were inside. He would have to get a bug, himself, or Calynn inside the building to finish his recon. He did all he could for now. He quickly and quietly returned to his ship. Calynn was there with the two men.

"I count nine just on this side of the building. There are three perimeter alarms, and the windows are all shielded against electronic intrusion," Kash stated. "We'll need to take a head count during the day when the sun is our ally."

"But they will be able to see us," the new guy complained.

"I'm counting on it," Kash continued.

"Are you mad?" the first man asked.

"Possibly... but I'm also the very best at retrieval in the verse," Kash boasted and then turned to Calynn. "Go back to our hotel, get swimsuits for all of us, and some beach gear. We have to look like we don't care that they know we're here. Get bright-colored umbrellas and towels and maybe some picnic stuff, too. We'll meet up half a kilometer or so down the beach. We can take shifts watching the resort to get some sleep tonight... two-man teams... in the morning, the fun begins... oh, and make sure your bikini can get their attention from a distance. We need them to notice you."

"On it, Boss," Calynn replied as she boarded The Cat.

"Who are you, mister?" the first man asked.

"I'm Kash, the man that can acquire anything."

"Holy shit... are you truly him?"

"I am... now, who are you, and can I see a picture of your sister?"

"He's the guy you said we couldn't afford?" the second man asked the first.

"And as luck would have, you're getting me for free. And I ask again... who the fuck are you?"

"Sorry, Mr. Kash, I'm Barry," the first man said, "and this is my brother Donny."

"Those sound like Earth names, and it's just Kash."

"Our family left Earth nine generations ago," Donny explained. "They moved to one the Epsilon Colonies."

"Same shitty people with a new planet to pollute," Barry added.

"And a cash cow for the Epsilon Corporation," Donny added.

"I heard as much," Kash agreed. "So... how about I stay here and watch while you guys get those ships out of here one at a time... I need one of you here in case your sister makes an appearance."

The men agreed and did as Kash asked. The night was slow. Kash and Donny would take a watch, and then Calynn and Barry would relieve them. The guards also appeared to have a schedule. At nearly midnight, a new group took over for the existing men. The only excitement was when a shuttle came to the resort with some girls on it during Calynn and Barry's watch. None of the girls were the sister or Omia. At sunrise, the four of them met back at the ships to go over the plan for the day.

"We need eyes inside that building," Kash explained. "And to do so, we are not going to hide. We will be defiant, play loud music, throw Frisbees, work on our tans, and swim in the ocean. I want them annoyed, so they come to see us, even if that means repeatedly setting off the perimeter alarms... accidentally on purpose... When they come, keep the lies simple. We just met and became fast friends because of our heritage on Earth. We will eat and drink and party until they try to remove us... got it?"

"Sounds good to me," Donny exclaimed.

"I'll go put on my bikini," Calynn said as she skipped off.

"It's a bold plan," Barry said to Kash. "Are you sure it will work?"

"I just need to get this little guy a piggyback ride," Kash explained, holding up his hand.

In his palm was another robotic bug. It was less than one centimeter in length, width, and height. Its surface had some shiny spots and some deep black sections.

"The coloring helps it hide," Kash continued. "If it gets inside and plugs itself into any wall outlet, it can turn the building's electrical grid into comms. We will be able to send and receive signals inside the resort and hack their systems... then we got them."

"And you want one of the guards to walk it inside, so we don't have to," Barry concluded. "That's some devious shit, Kash."

"Shall we?" Kash offered as he gestured to the open door on his ship.

"This is going to be fun," Donny replied as he entered the ship.

"Let's do it," Barry said with a smile and followed his brother.

Kash rolled his eyes and followed them inside. He didn't like using them like this, but it was the only way to get them out of the way. He needed this to go smoothly... he hoped the men were up to the task. Calynn had outfits laid out for them in the cargo hold. Food, booze, umbrellas, beach towels, and boogie boards were also there. Kash hadn't seen a boogie board in years. He wondered if he could ride one.

Barry and Donny started getting dressed as Kash headed towards his quarters. When he reached the door, Calynn was walking out in her bikini. His jaw nearly hit the floor. She was wearing a tiny, bright pink and yellow bikini that was almost too small to contain her breasts. The bottoms were a low-rise boy-short cut, just like most of her underwear.

"Ww... wow," Kash muttered. "That will definitely grab some attention."

"Thanks, boss," Calynn cooed. "I went with a more modest bottom since the top is so revealing."

"It leaves a little intrigue... always a good plan."

Calynn smiled, strutted past him, and went to the helm. They were soon approaching the beach just outside the corporate resort. She set them down near the edge of the grass, and they opened the cargo doors. The four then carried their things out to the beach and got set up. Calynn was playing some dance music on the speakers. It wasn't the kind of music Kash liked, but it had a good beat and wasn't offensive to his ears.

Calynn plopped on a towel to get some sun while the men tossed Frisbee. Kash signaled to Barry to really throw it hard so he could chase it into the grass. Kash intended to set off the alarm right away. He wanted to be as obnoxious as possible. When he retrieved the Frisbee, he heard the alarm go off, and more men came to that side of the building. Kash just waved to them, picked up the disk, and jogged back to the rest of his group. He made sure to throw the Frisbee all the way to the ocean's edge on the way back.

This continued for a few more minutes until Kash threw the Frisbee at Calynn. She jumped up and started chasing him around, and everyone laughed. Kash ran into the tall grass again and squatted down like he was hiding from her, only to jump up when she got close and ran away again. Calynn threw the disk at Kash, and once again, the Frisbee went beyond the perimeter alarm. This time, Calynn ran after it. She made sure to get close enough to attract the attention of the guards before returning to the ship. The four companions continued to be as obnoxious as possible for the next couple of hourns. Kash was eating a midmorning snack when three men approached the ship.

"I still can't find the sunscreen," Calynn hollered before the men could speak. "I'm gonna burn."

"I don't know what you did with it," Kash hollered back. "I'm like thirty percent black, so I don't need the stuff."

Kash walked towards the ship as if he were going to help Calynn. He looked at the men that had approached and practically ignored them.

"Did you look down here with the picnic stuff?"

"Excuse me," one of them said as Kash walked past him.

"What's she looking for?" Barry shouted.

"The sunscreen," Kash stopped and shouted back.

"It's out here," Barry replied.

"Hey, babe. The sunscreen is out here... the guys used it."

"Excuse me!" the man shouted this time.

"Hey..." Kash started to reply to the man.

"Shit, my top came untied again," Calynn interrupted. "Can you come tie it for me? I can't get it to stay tied. It must be the material."

"Sure," Kash responded and started heading towards Calynn.

"HEY!" the man barked loudly. "Who's in charge here?"

"If you're looking for credits, they are," Kash giggled and pointed towards Barry and Donny.

"Babe," Calynn complained. "I need help."

Calynn approached them, holding her top to her breasts. The strings were dangling at her sides. The three men that had come were all staring at her. They were wholly distracted by the spectacle she had created. Kash acted quickly and decisively.

"Hey, you fucking perverts!" Kash shouted as he turned and pushed one of the men forcibly. "Are you hoping for a show?"

"I wasn't..." the man Kash pushed complained.

"You're fucking drooling, you pig," Kash interrupted.

"What's going on?" Barry asked as he approached.

"These fucking assholes are perving on my girl," Kash replied.

"We are doing no such thing," another one of the men barked.

"Then look away, asshole!" Kash yelled and shoved the man.

He secretly placed the bug on his uniform when he shoved the second man. Kash had skillfully hidden it beneath the collar of his shirt. Kash scowled at the man and pointed his finger right in his face. The man's response was to pull his weapon and point it at Kash's face. Kash didn't back down.

"Get that fucking gun out of my face and get your fucking eyes off my girl," Kash growled.

"Whoa, wait!" the third man yelled. "Everyone just calm down."

"But, sir," the man with the gun complained.

"Forgive us, young lady," the third man said to Calynn. "We mean you no disrespect... we've only come to ask you to move to another part of the beach."

"It's a free planet," Kash replied. "We can use any part of the beach we like."

"Indeed it is," the man continued. "However, your presence makes the VIP we are protecting... nervous."

"Is he afraid of fun?" Donny asked sarcastically.

"You've breached our perimeter twice," the first man commented. "That's why he's nervous."

"What perimeter?" Barry argued.

"Is it the grass?" Donny continued with his sarcasm. "Is grass some sort of secret fence now?"

"No." The first man answered.

"Then what?" Kash asked straightforwardly. "What gives this prick the right to drool over my girl and then pull a gun on me?"

"Vomm," the third man ordered, "put your weapon down."

"Yes, sir," Vomm reluctantly replied and complied with the request.

"How about a compromise?" the third man continued, "If you keep your distance from the resort, you can stay here on the beach... We will have to keep an eye on you to appease the one we are charged to protect, but as long as you aren't sneaking around..."

"Sneaking around?" Kash interrupted. "Is loud music and big beach umbrellas sneaky where you come from? It's not like we're trying to hide... a blind and deaf man could spot us or hear us."

"You're not subtle," the man chuckled.

"We weren't trying to be," Kash agreed. "Although, we did pick this spot because this building was supposed to be empty... we didn't want people watching what we do later."

"What are you doing later?" the first man asked.

"That's none of your business," Kash replied.

"Well, I think it is my fucking business, smart ass," the first man barked.

"I'm not telling you."

"I'll beat it out of you..."

"Me, okay!" Calynn yelled from the catwalk with a funny twang in her voice. "They're all here to fuck me because... because I... my favorite color isn't edible."

Calynn ran off crying. Kash sighed and ran his fingers through his hair. He was staring at the floor, shaking his head. Everyone remained silent for a few seconds until Donny broke the silence.

"Are you happy, tough guy?" Donny asked and gave the first guy a thumbs-up. "You made a little girl cry. Good job."

"Look, I gotta go deal with her before she hurts herself," Kash added before the situation escalated. "She has a condition... We'll load up after and move down the beach a couple hundred meters... sorry for the inconvenience."

Kash turned and walked off like he was going to console Calynn. He quickened his pace when a crash came from her direction.

"We apologize also," the third man shouted. "Apologize to her also."

Kash didn't reply. He ran up the ship ladder and down the hall. Calynn was crouched on the floor, holding a kitchen drawer full of silverware. She was smiling and trying not to laugh.

"AAAARRRGGGHHH!" Calynn screamed and then threw the silverware on the ground.

"No, babe, don't!" Kash shouted, struggling not to laugh.

Calynn rattled the drawer on the floor and then used it to scatter the silverware across the kitchen floor, making more noise. The duo was smiling at each other and giggling to themselves. Calynn pointed to Kash's quarters and stood up.

"EEEEEEEEEEE!" Calynn screeched as she pranced ridiculously into the bedroom.

She blew Kash a kiss and then slid the door shut as forcefully as she could. The bang echoed through the ship. She quietly opened the door and peeked out at him.

"You're silly," Kash whispered.

"I know."

"Go... you're supposed to be throwing a fit."

Calynn closed the door again and started making all kinds of noise. She was banging on the walls and stomping her feet. She must have been dragging his desk around also because there was a noise he couldn't explain otherwise. The guards were still standing at the back of his ship, talking to Barry and Donny. When they saw Kash leaning on the catwalk's railing, the guards finally walked off.

"Is she alright?" Barry asked as he walked into the cargo hold.

Kash nodded and smiled. Donny was still standing at the back of the ship, watching the guards walk off.

"Boss," Calynn said from behind him. "Do I need to be more silly?"

Calynn was wearing one of Kash's sweaters upside down. The neck was around her waist, and she had one arm through a sleeve and her head and her other arm out through the bottom. She had a couple pairs of her underwear on each of her legs. Kash couldn't help but laugh hysterically.

"What's so funny?" Barry asked.

Calynn heard him ask, so she rushed to the catwalk and struck a pose. She was being ridiculous. Barry started laughing when he saw her, and Donny joined in shortly after. After they all enjoyed a good laugh, Kash and Calynn returned to his quarters so she could get appropriately dressed.

"Are they back in the house yet?" Kash asked her when they were alone.

"They are."

"The bug should do its thing soon... be ready."

"Okay, but can you actually help me tie my bikini top?" Calynn asked after she pulled off his sweater. "The knot really does keep getting loose."

"Sure."

Calynn stood before him and held her hair up out of the way. He was retying her top when she cocked her head to the side.

"I'm in," Calynn stated, straightening her head again.

"Goddamn, girl," Kash replied. "You are a walking, talking supercomputer."

"I aim to please."

Kash and Calynn studied the information she was gathering for a few minutes. Thirty-six guards worked in shifts. And at any given time, at least twenty-four men were on duty.

"Keep compiling the data," Kash ordered. "We also need to move down the beach some... let's go far enough that they can't see what we're doing... unless they're on one of the top floors."

"Am I still bait?" Calynn asked with a big grin.

"If they're paying attention to you at the campfire, they won't see me in the safe."

"I'll be sure to make a spectacle of myself before we move."

"Good girl."

Calynn was really good at acting crazy. She would occasionally act like a train wreck so nobody could look away. By dusk, the guards were loitering on the upper floors more so than the lower levels of the resort. They were all hoping to catch Calynn doing something provocative... or crazy. The guards never noticed when Kash swapped a dummy into his chair and slipped away from the campfire.

"I'm in position, Baby Girl," Kash whispered. "Time to rock and roll."

"I'm dancing on top of The Cat," Calynn replied over the comm in his ear. "Unlocking all the mag locks on the doors... now."

Kash pulled on his goggles and pressed the button on the side. The goggles showed him an X-ray view of the structure and the location of every guard. Calynn had even marked the interior cameras for him so he could avoid them if possible. For the cameras he couldn't avoid, she could loop them for him so the guards would be blind to his movements.

"The safe on the main floor seems to be a safe bet," Calynn continued. "It's getting the most use."

Kash opened the door and entered the building. He moved through the hallway quickly. His display showed two guards watching the large common room at the end of the hall. Kash was moving at speed when he reached the men. He jumped into the air and grabbed one man's head in his hands and the other man's head with his feet. Kash snapped the necks of both men before they hit the ground. He rolled when he hit the ground and quickly returned to his feet. He had two more guards on the way to his location, and he needed to subdue them before they could signal an alarm.

The first was coming from the other side of the building and would turn the hallway's corner in seconds. Kash closed the distance as he readied one of his throwing knives. He actually threw the blade before the man turned the corner. The knife barely cleared the edge of the wall before sinking into the man's neck. Kash didn't wait for the man to hit the ground. He was already on the move to the elevator. When the door opened, Kash jammed a knife into the guard's left ear.

"I have four bodies that need disposal," Kash whispered.

"I still can't throw bodies through walls without making holes in the walls," Calynn replied.

"No, not that... check what these guys have."

"Oh... they have some Nanomites that appear to be for that purpose. You just need to put them in the bathtub... I think."

"Can you just make it look like a malfunction? I see the safe."

"Do you often expect miracles?"

"Fine... I'll do it."

Kash rushed to a window and opened it. He then dragged the bodies one at a time to the open window and chucked them outside. The guards ended up in a pile behind the bushes. Then he hurried over to the safe to assess the lock. The keypad had the numbers 0 through 9 and the letters A through E, for a total of fifteen buttons plus the enter button. When he touched a button to awaken the system, he saw the combination was ten digits long.

"A ten-digit code with fifteen possibilities each is over five-hundred seventy-six million possible combinations," Calynn informed him. "To brute force that will take too long."

"Or... if you know how the circuitry is done behind the keypad... You can insert two probes and bypass the system entirely," Kash explained as he performed the task. "One here... and one... here... then you just give it a small amount of current and..."

Clunk vvvrrrrr

"How'd you do that?" Calynn asked.

"Lots of studying," Kash replied, pulling open the safe and stepping inside. "At the risk of everything going sideways again... I can't be this lucky."

"Is it there?"

"One E-tablet sitting on the top shelf... yea... it's here."

Kash picked up the device and tapped the power button. The screen lit up with a password prompt. The password was only four digits. He plugged the device on the back of his hand into the tablet's charging port. The screen flashed some computer code, blinked off, and then turned on again. This time, it was on the tablet's home screen, and no password was prompted. He started scrolling, looking for the video.

"Okay, how'd you do that too?" Calynn asked.

"The code on these is tough to crack, but the software has a weakness," Kash explained as he continued to scroll. "I just deleted the part that tells it to ask for a password. It's just easier... holy shit!"

"What?"

"The video... I can see why Crigg doesn't want that getting out."

Not Again

Kash carefully made his way back to The Cat and joined in the festivities. Calynn was still dancing on the ship's wings, and the brothers were hooting and hollering at her while drinking some booze. They had more of a bonfire than a campfire going, as the flames were nearly four meters high. Kash downed a few shots of bourbon to try and forget the images he saw on the tablet. Mr. Crigg was a sick, sick man.

Eventually, the fire and the party dwindled, and the four retired to Kash's ship. The brothers had bunks set up in the cargo hold, and Calynn joined Kash in his quarters. She changed clothes in the bathroom and then immediately climbed into bed with him. She assumed her regular position as the little spoon, but something about her seemed off. She felt fidgety and she couldn't wrap his arms around her far enough.

"Worried?" Kash asked softly.

"Yea."

"Anything I can do?"

"Just this," Calynn replied, lacing her fingers through his and tightly holding his arm to her body.

Kash pulled her in tight and kissed the back of her head. He had to admit that having her here would also make his night easier. He was just as worried as she was.

Kash slept horribly. Everything they had been through trying to reach Omia weighed heavily on his mind. He would wake up in the middle of the night, pull Calynn closer in an attempt to soothe himself, and then eventually fall back asleep... only to repeat the cycle far too often. It was morning much too quickly.

"I feel bad for being with Triana," Calynn suddenly confessed. "I feel like I cheated on Omia."

"You do know her and I talked about having other girls, right?" Kash asked sleepily.

"Well, yea... but she and I always talked about me being that other girl."

"Why?"

"Because we both kinda like you," Calynn explained as she rolled into him. "And she wanted to please you and teach me how to please you also."

"It would please me not to argue with you about this again."

"But why... you know what?" Calynn argued as she got out of bed. "Can we just contact that asshole and go get our girl back, please?"

"Calynn..."

"No, you're right... Business first."

Calynn pulled on a pair of jeans and a tee shirt and stormed out of his room.

"Fuuuuck," Kash said, exasperated.

He climbed out of bed and prepared for his meeting with Mr. Crigg. When he tried to contact the man, he received no answer. He sat at his monitor and perused a few news articles to waste time until he tried to contact Crigg again. When the second attempt went unanswered, Kash started to get concerned. He went in search of Calynn and found her chatting with the brothers in the cargo hold.

"Baby Girl," Kash addressed her to get her attention. "What are the odds you still have the hack from Crigg's E-tablet?"

"Not currently... we're out of range. Why?"

"I think we need it again... now."

Calynn looked worried as she started to move slowly towards the cockpit. Seeing the worry on his face must have convinced her that it was more dire than he let on because her pace quickened.

"We can drop you off, or you can come along in case we find info on your sister... your choice," Kash told the brothers.

"We'll tag along," Barry replied as he looked at his brother and then turned back to Kash. "What's going on?"

"The man that has our friend isn't answering his comm," Kash replied. "We got what he wanted in exchange for her, but... but I really don't know."

The ship's engines roared to life as Calynn reached the helm, and they were soon on their way back to their hotel. The three men joined her in the cockpit. Kash let the brothers use the jump seats, and he stood directly behind Calynn. It was a quick flight back, and they soon moored at the same slip they had the day before.

"We're back in range, but... but the tablet, umm," Calynn struggled to convey. "I think it has been broken. I can't connect to it."

"Do you remember where they were?"

"I do, but Boss," Calynn explained as she turned to look at him. "We can't go in there guns blazing... there's too many innocent people."

"Well... we'll just have to take some guns once we get there."

"Something is wrong, boss," Calynn added. "I don't know what or why, but something feels wrong."

Kash looked at Calynn but didn't answer her because he didn't want to say too much in front of the brothers. She stared back with some worry in her eyes. Kash wanted to ask if it was her woman's intuition... or more walking, talking supercomputer stuff, but he couldn't.

"I'm not saying we shouldn't go," Calynn continued. "We just need to be really cautious."

"Should we dress more tactically?" Donny asked. "Board shorts and brightly colored tank tops don't seem like the right attire for an incursion."

"That would give us away," Barry answered his brother's question. "It's best to look like tourists and blend in with the other tourists."

"Agreed," Kash replied. "No weapons... let's try to talk our way in."

"It's a good thing you're so charming then," Calynn added with a smile. "What's the play?"

"The direct approach... right through the front door, up to the front counter, and we ask for Mr. Crigg. If there's a problem, we will be helpful."

"What if we are the problem?"

"Then we become the biggest problem they've ever seen," Kash said seriously. "I'll tear that whole fucking building down if that's what it takes... but let's not resort to that unless we have to."

"I hope it doesn't come to that," Barry added.

"Me too," Calynn agreed. "But let's get moving... I'm worried."

Calynn didn't wait for a reply. She was already moving towards the cargo bay and the exit. Kash and the brothers followed closely behind her. Calynn was walking at a pretty quick pace once they were on the docks. Kash had to grab her hand to slow her down. She laced her fingers through his and held his hand tightly. Kash pointed at the approaching shuttle and smiled at the young woman.

"Where to?" the shuttle operator asked as he stopped beside them.

"Main lobby," Kash replied as they boarded the shuttle.

The ride was quick, and Kash tipped the driver handsomely. Calynn eagerly grabbed his hand again as they entered the resort's main lobby. The lobby was nearly vacant, probably because it was early in the morning. Two associates worked the counter, and two bellhops stood near the luggage carts. The bellhops were both young men. A middle-aged man and a younger woman manned the front desk. Kash smiled as he approached the counter and nodded at the bellhops. He was sure to acknowledge all of them. He found that it always puts people at ease.

"Good morning," Kash beamed at the woman behind the counter as he approached. "We have an appointment with Mr. Crigg, but I seem to be unable to contact him. Is there any chance you can contact him for us? I've tried his comm multiple times with no success."

"Mr. Crigg is a very busy man," the woman replied confidently. "Can I ask the nature of your appointment?"

"Sure thing... I retrieved this for him," Kash explained as he showed her the E-tablet, "and he was to give me a woman stolen from her home in return."

The woman looked shocked as her eyes darted around the room. She wasn't very attractive, but she did have pretty eyes. Kash's bluntness seemed to erode her confidence as her posture changed.

"Look, I'm not trying to put you on the spot, but I really would like to complete this transaction so I can be on my way," Kash explained to the woman. "Can you just try to ring him?"

The woman smiled and touched the comm on her right ear. She looked at Kash, then at Calynn, then back to Kash. She gave him a shy smile and nervously looked away. Calynn gave his hand two quick squeezes.

"Is everything okay?" Calynn asked the woman.

"Umm..."

The girl looked slightly rattled as she typed a few buttons on her computer and then tried her comm again. Kash waited patiently as the woman repeated that process two more times. She was beginning to look worried.

"I can't reach any of them," the woman confessed. "I don't know what to do."

She looked at the man to her right for guidance. He just shrugged his shoulders and ignored her. She looked back at Kash and tried to smile. It looked as forced as it was.

"What's your name?" Kash asked the woman.

"Mahounia," the woman replied.

"Well, Mahounia... perhaps we can be of service?" Kash offered.

"I don't know..."

"I promise we can help," Calynn told her warmly. "The woman we are retrieving is a doctor from a small village. They really need their doctor back. We aren't trying to be pushy, but is there anything you can do?"

"I suppose we could go check Mr. Crigg's suite," Mahounia relented.

"Actually... the holding cell beneath the count room was the last place she was being held," Calynn added. "It might be better to start there. If she's still there we can give you the E-tablet and Mr. Crigg can retrieve it at his convenience. Again... the people really their doctor back."

"Okay... I can't call there but... but I think I can get a message to them," Mahounia stated.

"That sounds perfect," Kash said with a warm smile.

"Umm... follow me," Mahounia said as she emerged from behind her desk.

Mahounia led them through the casino towards the back rooms. Nearly all of the slot machines were being played. Kash never understood how people could sit in front of those things, pressing the button all day in hopes of a big win. When they rounded a corner around a pod of slots, Mahounia suddenly froze. When she turned to Kash, she had an uneasy look on her face.

"What's wrong?" Kash asked.

"That door is always supposed to have two guards," Mahounia said as she pointed behind her. "It's always supposed to have them. Always... I don't... know..."

"Let's go find out why," Kash said as he approached the woman and put a comforting hand on her shoulder. "I'll be right beside you to keep you safe."

Mahounia was fidgety, but she turned and walked towards the door. Kash stayed right with her and had his hand on the small of her back. Calynn took position on the other side of the woman, too. When they got to the door, Mahounia hesitated momentarily before placing her hand on the scanner for the lock. Nothing happened, so she removed her hand and tried again.

"This doesn't make any sense," Mahounia sounded confused. "It should open."

Kash left the woman's side and slowly moved so he could push on the door. The door gave way with only gentle pressure. Kash immediately held up his hand to let everyone else know to hold their position. He poked his head inside the door and saw four bodies lying on the floor, surrounded by a pool of blood. He closed the door and turned back to Mahounia.

"Prepare yourself," Kash informed her. "What's behind the door is rather shocking... don't panic... just breathe."

Kash nodded at Calynn, who then moved closer and put her arm around Mahounia's waist. She gently guided the woman towards the door. Kash moved through the door and squatted down beside the bodies. He quickly took the pistols off of two of the bodies.

The look of horror on Mahounia's face was very concerning. They needed her to lead them to where Omia was being held and possibly required her hand to open some doors. Calynn was trying to soothe the woman but wasn't having much success. Kash decided to take matters into his own hands. He stood, quickly closed the gap between him and Mahounia, and wrapped her in a hug, holding her head to his chest.

"Just breathe... you don't have to look," Kash said soothingly. "I got you."

Her breaths were choppy like she was about to start crying. She had two fistfuls of Kash's shirt in her hands, trying to steady herself. Kash did his best to guard her from the sight of her dead coworkers. He knew it could be troubling for people who had never been exposed to war.

Calynn grabbed both pistols from Kash, and the brothers retrieved weapons for themselves. Calynn was now on point with a gun in each hand. Barry handed Kash a different pistol so he could also be armed.

"I'm not going to lie to you, Mahounia," Kash said softly. "This could get uglier, but we really need to get to that room... I need you to be as strong as you can right now... I promise you can cry later."

Mahounia looked up at him and wiped the tears from her eyes.

"Which way?" Calynn asked.

Mahounia took two deep breaths and wiped her eyes again. She was struggling to keep it together, but she was trying. Kash rubbed her arms and tried to soothe her.

"We need to move before whoever did this comes back," Kash explained. "So we need to know which way. I know this is tough, but please..."

"Take the second right and... go all the way to the double doors at the end of the hall," Mahounia blurted out. "I can do this... I hope. My brother..."

Mahonia's words fell off as Calynn started moving. She moved quickly, following Mahonia's directions. Donny darted past Kash to flank Calynn, and Barry moved to help Kash with Mahounia.

"Suddenly, I wish I was wearing a suit so I could give you my jacket to hide your eyes," Kash stated as he started to lead Mahounia around the dead bodies on the floor. "Thank you for being so brave... and I will do my best to shield you from as much of this as possible."

"Thank you," Mahounia replied.

"I will help shield you from the nastiness also," Barry said. "Can't have a pretty thing like you seeing all this ugliness."

Kash rolled his eyes at Barry's blatantly obvious attempt at flirting with Mahounia. However, it apparently slightly affected the woman as she leaned into Barry instead of Kash. Kash stayed with her, though. She was the gatekeeper in their current situation, and he needed her to give them directions and open doors.

They followed Calynn down the hallway until they reached the doors Mahounia mentioned. The passageway was empty, save for a few bullets lying on the ground. The group moved quickly. Mahounia placed her hand on the biometric lock, and the doors unlocked. Calynn nodded at the group and proceeded through the doors alone. A few seconds later, she returned.

"It's a mess in there," Calynn stated. "She's going to need help."

"What does that mean?" Mahounia asked. "A mess?"

"They fought here," Calynn explained. "The remnants of the battle remain."

"More bodies?" Mahounia nearly wept the words.

"We can go without you," Kash said calmly. "Just tell us where to go, and you won't have to see it."

"There are more locks... I have to open."

"Then we should take a minute to clear a path," Calynn explained. "Boss... I could use some help."

"We'll stay with her," Barry said as he wrapped his arms around Mahounia. "You two go ahead."

Mahounia buried her face in Barry's chest. Barry looked at Kash and nodded. Kash nodded back and followed Calynn through the doors.

"Holy fuck," Kash let the words slip out at the sight he saw. "How does all this happen, and nobody hear it?"

There were bodies everywhere. Most of whom were the platoon stationed on site, judging by their uniforms. There was also an impossible amount of bullets lying on the floor.

"How many rounds did they shoot?"

"Hard to say," Calynn replied. "Some of the rounds look like they had been scooped up and fired again."

Kash knelt down and scooped up a handful of the rounds. Some metallic balls had more than one set of scratches from the rifling in the barrel of the Mag-guns. The one armored shield lying near Kash had thousands of impact points upon it. The shield eventually failed, and the man behind it lost his head... literally.

"This must have been their ready room," Kash explained as he looked around. "Weapons racks on the wall... tables and chairs for them to sit and play cards until needed... nice wide doors and hallway so they can get to the casino floor rapidly."

"It looks like they turned on each other," Calynn added. "There's a few others in black uniforms, too."

"So, the black uniforms and some of the blues killed the rest of the blues?"

"Kinda what it looks like."

"Was that door open?" Kash asked as he looked across the room.

Kash and Calynn looked at each other, paused for a second, and both readied their weapons. The duo cautiously approached the door opposite the one they entered through. Kash nodded at Calynn, and she opened the door so he could clear the room. Kash scanned the room quickly, but nobody was moving. It was another room of dead bodies. Lockers lined the walls, and two rows of lockers sat back-to-back in the middle of the room. Some of the dead soldiers didn't even have their uniforms on yet.

"The holding cell where Omia was is just on the other side of this room," Calynn stated as she moved through the room.

Kash moved with her. They were both at the ready and focused. The room was deeper than Kash thought. What he thought was the back wall was just a partition in the middle of the long, narrow room. The duo stepped over the dead as they remained cautious in their movements. When they reached the far wall, the holding cell door was locked.

"I'll go get them," Calynn said as she trotted back in the direction they came.

Kash thought he heard something from behind the door after Calynn left. He pressed his right ear to the door and closed his eyes. He listened intently, but he didn't hear any more noises. Kash tried the door to see if it was open even though the console said it was locked. It was indeed locked, so he had to wait for Mahounia to open it.

When they entered the room, Barry and Calynn tried to shield Mahounia's eyes. Calynn was walking backward with her hands on the woman's face. Barry was behind her with his hand on top of Mahounia's hands, which were covering her eyes. Barry's other hand was at her waist to help guide her. Donny diligently watched their six o'clock to ensure nobody could sneak up on them.

"Just a bit further," Calynn said soothingly. "We are almost there."

"I think I heard a noise from behind the door, so…"

"Get her to safety once she opens it," Barry interrupted, finishing Kash's thought. "Got it."

Calynn stopped just before the biometric lock's console and placed Mahounia's hand upon it. The screen turned green, and the lock popped open. Kash pulled the door open just enough for it to not lock again and readied himself. Barry pulled Mahounia over to the corner of the room and stood in front of her. Donny was still watching the door they came through. Calynn readied both of her weapons and nodded at Kash.

Kash jerked the door open and lunged through the opening quickly. Calynn was right on his heels as the duo scanned the small room. There were only three bodies in the room, and they were all synths. Kash recognized them. It was Crigg and the other two from his suite two days ago. The companions had their throats slit, but Crigg's body was mangled. Both arms were removed, as was one leg, and all three were shoved up into his body through his groin.

"This looks eerily familiar," Kash let the words slip.

"Kash… is that you?" Crigg gurgled.

"Holy fuck, are you still alive?"

"He won't be for long," Calynn stated. "He's losing too much blood."

"Save me… I'll pay you anything…"

Crigg started coughing and spit out a bunch of blood.

"I don't think so," Kash said coldly. "Why did they do to you what you did to that little girl in the video? This was never about blackmail, was it? This was fucking revenge!"

Kash was shouting by the end of his statement, but he had to pause and calm himself down.

"It's nothing like that," Crigg struggled to say. "Just save me... please."

"Where is she?" Calynn asked forcefully. "WHERE IS OMIA?!"

"Save me..."

"You sick fuck," Kash said calmly. "You violated the wrong little girl, and it came back to bite you. And now the family of that little girl has our friend, don't they? ... What did you tell them?"

"Just help me, Kash... I'll make you wealthy beyond..."

"Your synth body is the only thing keeping your heart pumping," Calynn stated. "You have less than two minutes left. Just answer our questions, and I will end your suffering."

"I swear to the Gods, Crigg if those mother fuckers do something to my friend to get back at me because they think I work for you," Kash hissed and then paused to take a breath. "I will end your bloodline and kill everyone who knows your name."

"Where is Omia?" Calynn added sharply.

"Do they know she was payment for me? ... for retrieving your smut?" Kash asked. "I still have the E-tablet... will they exchange it for her? ... Answer me!"

"They think... it was... all for you," Crigg struggled to reply. "Because you... my... Boss."

"Mother fucker!" Kash barked. "You tried to pin this shit on me?"

"What will they do to Omia?" Calynn asked frantically.

"I don't know," Kash answered.

"What will they do to her?"

"I DON'T KNOW!"

Kash didn't mean to yell at Calynn, but he let his emotions get the better of him. He stared into her pretty brown eyes, watching the rage build. Calynn's breaths were erratic as she struggled with her emotions. Eventually... the rage won.

BANG

Calynn punched through Crigg's face with enough force that her fist dented the metal wall behind him. She quickly stood up, glared at Kash, and then started running back the way they came. Kash took off after her as fast as he could go. Calynn could run faster than him in a straight line but was still limited by physics when turning a corner. Kash closed the gap on her by using the walls to his advantage. By taking two steps on the wall and leaping off, he could catch up with Calynn. Once they returned to the casino floor, he grabbed the back of a chair to help slingshot himself around that corner. He got close enough to almost touch her before she accelerated away again.

"Calynn!" Kash shouted as he raced after her as fast as he could.

Calynn suddenly stopped running. She slid to a stop, and Kash saw a hole open in the wall of the hotel lobby. She was using the Slip. Kash wasn't sure if he could get to her before she jumped away, but he had to try. He held his breath and tried to run harder. He lunged at Calynn as soon as he was close enough and tackled her to the ground. When he stopped rolling, they were in the cargo hold of The Cat. Kash struggled to his feet. The Slip had knocked the wind out of him again. Calynn was standing at the rear cargo doors.

"Calynn... wait..."

Kash got knocked to the ground from what he assumed was the acceleration of his ship. As soon as he regained his footing, he was knocked down again. This time, he fell away from Calynn and towards the front of the ship. He got himself back to one knee and tried to steady himself. Once again, the G-forces had him sliding across the floor towards Calynn.

"Baby Girl?"

Calynn didn't respond. Instead, she hit the button to open the cargo doors. Kash had to shield his eyes from the wind whipping around the hold. He looked through his fingers and saw the resort they were at the night before as the ship spun backward and landed.

Calynn was out the door before Kash could get to his feet. Bullets started bouncing off her and his ship, so he quickly dove for cover. Then, the hail of bullets suddenly stopped. Kash looked out and saw Calynn walking, her arms outstretched and her palms facing up. Calynn turned her palms to the ground and lowered her hands. Moments later, four enemy soldiers crashed into the ground with so much velocity that they made craters. There was nothing left of the men except a pile of blood and guts.

"What the shit?" Kash exclaimed as he suddenly fell backward and slid away from the cargo door.

Calynn then pushed her hand out in front of herself, and Kash found himself sliding towards her. The wall of the building collapsed in on itself, and Calynn stepped through the opening. Kash lost sight of her for a second when he got distracted by a chunk of debris from the wall that was floating. Was Calynn changing gravity?

BOOM

A loud thud came from everywhere in the building or the building itself.

BOOM

Kash felt the ground shake with that boom.

"Calynn!" Kash yelled as he raced into the building after her.

As he ran, Kash suddenly felt lighter... too light. He floated across the hall briefly before crashing back to the ground. His body felt like it weighed three hundred kilos instead of one hundred. As he struggled to get up, his weight returned to normal.

"Calynn!" Kash Hollered again, hoping to reach the girl.

Gunfire erupted in the large room at the end of the hall. Thousands of rounds were being fired. He could only hope that Calynn could withstand the barrage. He didn't have to worry about that for long, though. Kash grabbed a handrail and held himself in contact with the floor even though he wanted to float upwards. The gunfire stopped when Kash felt like he weighed many times what he should again.

When his weight returned to normal, he fell forward and slid into the large room. Kash rolled to get back to his feet and skied his way towards Calynn. He almost touched her arm before he was suddenly thrust away from her. He tumbled through the air and smashed into the end of a partition wall, breaking at least one rib. His tumble wasn't done yet, so he tried to protect his injured rib with both arms. Kash bounced off another wall and finally came to rest on the floor.

"Baby Girl!" Kash shouted as he turned to try to locate her again.

The sound of metal moaning and some loud cracking sounds pulled Kash's attention away from Calynn. Cracks were forming on the floor, walls, and ceiling. It only took him a second to realize that the building's structure was failing under the stresses Calynn was exerting upon it. Gravity isn't supposed to change directions and be augmented like what it was currently doing.

"Calynn!" Kash shouted as he sprang to his feet.

Kash sprinted across the room despite the pain in his ribs. His only focus was Calynn and the window beyond her. He had to get to her and get them out before the building collapsed in on itself. Time seemed to be running in slow motion. Each step he took lasted an eternity. Calynn was raising her arms again, so he knew he had to hurry. Gravity was flipping again, and he started to lose traction on the floor, so he flipped himself upside down and continued to run on the ceiling. His target was still the same. He would drive his body through Calynn's midsection and carry her out through the window.

Kash anticipated the gravity switch and flipped himself back around. He was running on all fours now, and it took all his strength to keep moving. He clawed at the ground with his hands and drove forward with all the leg drive he could muster. Until he finally reached Calynn.

"Ooof!" Kash exclaimed as he bounced off of Calynn.

When he struck Calynn's body, it was like trying to tackle an immovable statue. His quick reflexes allowed him to be able to grab her leg as he tumbled off of her. He regained his footing quickly, using her as an anchor, and stood up in front of her. He managed to wrap Calynn in a hug before the first chunk of the ceiling struck them as it fell. He felt her arms around him before being hit in the head by debris. The world went black as he lost consciousness.

Beep......................Beep......................Beep......................Beep

"Am I alive?" Kash thought to himself before blacking out again.

Beep……………..Beep……………..Beep……………..Beep

He felt warm, but everything hurt. When he tried to move, he couldn't, and the blackness consumed him again.

Beep……………..Beep……………..Beep……………..Beep

Awake again... so much pain... Kash tried to open his eyes, but they didn't respond... voices... and that annoying beep... the darkness won again.

Beep……………..Beep……………..Beep……………..Beep

Something moved on his belly that woke him up. This time, when Kash tried to open his eyes, he succeeded. The world slowly came into focus as he blinked away the darkness. He was in a hospital room... the lights were dimmed... and the thing moving on his stomach... was Calynn's head! The relief of seeing her brought a tear to his eye. He saw he had tubes in his right arm, so he willed the left one to move using his fingers to help pull his arm along. Calynn sat up and spun around when he touched the back of her head. She smiled quickly, but then her face contorted as she started to cry.

"I'm so sorry," Calynn wept. "I lost it again. I lost... and almost killed... please be okay."

Kash was too weak to talk, but he managed to smile. Calynn grabbed his hand and placed it on her cheek. She gently laid down so her head was on his chest so he could caress her face. She held her hand on his, pressing his hand between her face and her hand. Kash knew he needed the rest, so he allowed himself to sleep again.

The next time Kash awoke, he felt much better. Calynn was still with him, holding his hand. He gave her hand a little squeeze to get her attention. She turned and smiled warmly as she looked down at him.

"Hey, you," Calynn said softly. "Can you talk yet?"

Kash hummed and cleared his throat to test his vocal cords.

"Maybe," Kash uttered with a raspy voice.

"I broke the inhibitor," Calynn confessed. "I let my emotions get the better of me, and I broke it… and nearly killed you… I'm so sorry. Can you ever forgive me?"

"It's not your fault… I keep putting you in bad situations."

"But I overreacted…"

"Hey," Kash struggled to interrupt. "Let's not do this now… where are we?"

"Thracia," Calynn replied. "Plekish put some new protocols in place in case I went nuclear again. The drones dug us out, and The Cat always has a jump plotted back here now. When I woke up, we were already on the way back."

"Smart man."

"I try," Plekish's voice came from the doorway as he entered the room. "How are you feeling, my friend?"

"Beat up."

"I said I'm sorry," Calynn whined.

"It's okay, Baby Girl."

"And how are you feeling, Calynn," Plekish continued his questions.

"I'm okay… I think," Calynn replied. "I probably strained my brain again… since I broke the inhibitor…"

"And changed gravity," Kash interrupted. "She made everyone float up and then slam back down to the ground."

"Fascinating… gravity isn't like electricity," Plekish said thoughtfully. "Could you see the gravity while you altered it?"

"Honestly… I don't know how I did it," Calynn confessed. "I was so mad and… sad… and scared for Omia… I wanted the men to fly up into the air and then get squished by their own weight, but… I… umm."

"But you don't know how you did it?" Plekish asked.

"I really don't," Calynn replied.

"I hate to be that guy, but can we get some regeneration pods in here?" Kash asked. "The longer we're here, the more evidence we lose."

"Actually, we have this entire room functioning as a regeneration pod," Plekish responded.

"And they called in the Constabulary to investigate," Calynn added. "So we have some time before they arrive."

"We should still hurry," Kash stated.

"And we will... after we take a nap," Calynn said as she climbed into the hospital bed with him. "I really need this."

Calynn straddled one of his legs with hers and laid her head on his chest. She wrapped her arm around him like she couldn't get close enough to him.

Kash kissed the top of her head and wrapped his left arm around her. He was soon asleep.

The Scene of the Crime

They were on their way back to the Pleasure Planets much later than Kash wanted. Plekish and Meesha both insisted he needed a little more rest before leaving. The pain in his ribs said he should have listened, but the Constabulary was already investigating the deaths of Mr. Crigg and his associates. They needed to get back before the cops mucked it up.

"Need anything, Boss?"

"I wouldn't mind one of Meesha's berries for the pain."

"We should have enough time for the drowsiness to wear off," Calynn offered. "I'll go get you one."

"Thanks, Baby Girl."

"Oh wait... what if you get a... you know."

"Then we'll break the rules to make it go down before dealing with the cops, but Meesha says it's a diminishing risk."

"I can take care of it while you're passed out, so you don't have any guilt... about the rules."

Calynn smiled at him as she left his quarters. A minute later, she returned with a berry, sat on the edge of his bed, and handed it to

Kash. He chewed the sweet fruit and let the tingling feeling wash over his body. He got comfortable and stared at Calynn. His hand migrated towards her body and was soon on her leg, caressing her. Her jeans felt soft to the touch... as did her tee shirt... and arm...

Kash was still tingly when he awoke. It took a minute for his eyes to focus so he could look around the room. He was alone. Calynn must have been out at the helm. Kash stretched and slowly sat up on the side of the bed. He noticed a weird static sound in his ears, so he put a finger into each ear and wiggled it. It didn't help the first time, so he repeated the process, and the sound stopped. Kash smiled to himself as he debated, trying to stand.

"Man, do those berries pack a punch," Kash said quietly to himself.

Kash tested his legs, and they held his weight. Next, he stood tall but purposely leaned back so his legs could be pushed into his bed to help him gain his balance. He stood there for a moment and looked around the room. Everything was moving too slowly, but he seemed to be okay. He didn't notice he was falling forward until it was almost too late.

"Whoa, I got you," Calynn said as she appeared suddenly before him.

"Hi, beautiful," Kash uttered.

"Hi... why are you trying to stand?"

"I'm so fucking high right now."

"Okay, well, let's get you back in bed... shall we?"

"Are you wet?" Kash asked as he realized he felt moisture on his body.

"I just got out of the shower."

"Are you naked, too?"

"I sure am... naked and wet since I had to drop my towel to catch you."

"You're so fucking hot... I should fold you up and fuck you while you are naked."

"Really?" Calynn said sarcastically and gave him a funny look.

"You can do some great positions."

"Uh, huh."

Kash was so lost in his own actions that he didn't notice what Calynn had said. He was rubbing his hands all over her slick, wet skin. She felt so smooth, and his hands glided over her body. He hadn't noticed that she laid him back in bed until her soft, wet skin suddenly disappeared. He tried to look for her but passed out instead.

When he woke up next, Kash's head was spinning, and he was trying to shake it off. The world came into focus more easily this time, and he didn't feel as tingly. Calynn was sitting at his desk watching him.

"How ya feeling, Boss," Calynn asked.

"Okay, I think," Kash replied as his hand went to his sore ribs. "Ribs are still sore."

"Warn me before you try to stand up this time, okay?"

Kash rubbed his face with both hands. He felt pretty embarrassed.

"I was hoping that was a dream," Kash confessed.

"It wasn't."

"Sorry, Baby Girl."

"I could barely make out what you were saying," Calynn said as she stood and approached him. "You were slurring your words so... so bad. You ask why I was wet and naked, and I think you asked me for a massage."

"I kinda remember, but not really," Kash lied. "Those berries pack a punch."

"I couldn't believe you were awake that fast," Calynn said as she approached. "You were only out a couple minutes."

"Really?"

"Yea... I thought for sure I would have time for a shower before you woke up," Calynn replied as she sat on the edge of the bed.

"I was pretty fucking high, that's for sure."

"Do me a favor, and don't do that again."

"But why?" Kash asked sarcastically. "And what's our ETA?"

"Four hournns... why?" Calynn asked with some apprehension in her voice.

"It's berry time," Kash replied.

He tried not to laugh at his comment, but the look on Calynn's face made him burst out laughing. She slapped him on the arm when she realized he was just joking and then joined him in laughter.

"No... I was thinking of trying to sleep this off a little more," Kash said with some laughter still in his voice. "But I think I need an hourn or two to move around before we land... to make sure I'm sharp."

"That's a better plan than berry time," Calynn chuckled.

"Wake me in an hourn and a half."

"Will do, Boss."

Kash's dreams were haunted by Omia and Calynn. They were always in danger and always just out of reach. He could never save them, or he could save one but not the other. In his dreams, he always chooses to save Calynn over Omia, not for selfish reasons either. He saw her dressed in white robes being worshiped as a goddess on a primitive planet. A tribe of hundreds catering to her every whim. Kash felt guilty for defiling their Deity. He was unworthy of her affection and should be punished for plunging himself into her perfect body... her perfect body that she can fold in unnatural ways... so he can plunge himself deeper...

Kash awoke with a start. He was surprised to see Calynn leaning over him. She had her hand on his stomach just above his waistband. He grabbed her hand before it could go any lower.

"Oh... sorry," Calynn said and smiled at him. "Is that a berry one or a regular one?"

"Umm... I don't know yet. Hopefully, it's a regular one. I was having weird dreams."

"About what?" Calynn asked and moved her hand higher on his abdomen.

"You being worshiped as a God... or dying," Kash relented.

"Hopefully, my dying isn't the reason for your erection."

"What? ... noooo."

"Oh good."

"I'm a sick puppy, but I'm not THAT sick," Kash giggled. "Crigg is... but not me."

"Speaking of Crigg. We are two hourns out, and it looks like the Consortium sent a flagship."

"You're kidding?"

"It's in orbit now."

"Fuck me!"

"Okay," Calynn said with a devious look on her face.

Calynn was somehow straddling him before he knew she was moving. She rocked her hips side to side and stuck out her tongue. It was only then that he realized she was just messing with him.

"You little shit," Kash chuckled. "I'm still too high for this."

"I know," Calynn replied, leaning forward so her head was in her hands and her elbows were on his chest. "You're more fun to pick on when you lack all your wits."

"Picking on me when my faculties are diminished? ... that's cold."

"Tell me more about me being a goddess."

"You were dressed in white robes on a primitive planet with hundreds if not thousands of followers," Kash explained. "You looked so happy. You deserve that more than... this."

"But I like this... I like this a lot, and I love my ship. Why would I want..."

Kash put his finger to Calynn's lips to stop her ranting.

"To me... or my subconscious, I guess... you deserve more," Kash said and smiled at her. "It's a compliment, Baby Girl... I'm not trying to get rid of you."

"I'm nothing without you," Calynn replied as she laid down on him. "If you don't let me... and help me... then I'm still in the box, and there's nothing I can do to ever, ever repay you for that."

Calynn sat up again and looked down at Kash. She had a tear in her eye and sorrow on her face.

"When I consider the odds of everything that has happened to me," Calynn continued. "Dying, being sold by my parents to be a nerve center for a ship, resisting the memory wipe, waking up again, fighting through the programming to be free again... the thing that is the most unlikely... that I am the most thankful for... is you... if I was sold to someone else... I'm worth a lot of credits to the Consortium, and Plekish is a godsend..."

"So I think I'm unworthy of you, and you think the same of me," Kash interrupted. "What a pair we make."

"Well, you still saved me, and got me my body, and protected me..."

"And you can manipulate gravity," Kash interrupted her again. "How do you not see that you're practically a god?"

"Still impossible if I'm locked in a box without a body."

Kash sighed loudly, pulled her down, and hugged Calynn tightly. She wiggled her body in approval. After a few minutes, Kash kissed her head and released his grip. Calynn sat up again, but she was still straddling him.

"Are you sure you don't need help with that?" she asked as she rocked her hips. "It still hasn't gone down."

"Probably due to the gorgeous woman grinding herself into it," Kash responded with a smirk. "Let me up so I can piss, and it'll be fine."

"Are you sure?" Calynn asked as she wiggled her hips some more.

"Seriously?" Kash asked sarcastically. "Look... if it is a problem, I promise not to use any other woman on board to relieve it."

"Ha ha, smart ass," Calynn relented as she stood. "Get up and get moving. I'll make us some smoothies."

"As you wish, Your Grace," Kash said with a smile as he sat up. "Or is it, Your Holiness? Forgive me... I am your humble servant."

Kash bowed to Calynn as he headed to the bathroom. She was glaring at him but smiling. Kash grabbed a shower and got dressed. When he left the bathroom, he found a smoothie waiting for him on his desk. He wore good jeans, a simple white T-shirt, and a suit jacket. He knew he would be dealing with Consortium detectives, so he dressed for the occasion. He then joined Calynn in the cockpit.

"Your Grace," Kash greeted her with a smirk.

"Okay, that's enough of that," Calynn scolded.

"Yes, dear," Kash said, feigning disappointment. "How far out are we?"

"Ten minutes... give or take."

"Okay, as soon as I'm on the ground, you need to get your ass airborne again."

"Umm, what?"

"You need to get airborne as soon as possible."

"But I..."

"Look," Kash interrupted a little more forcefully than he intended. "The Constabulary is already there, and my informant inside the Consortium says they are looking at us about Doc's disappearance. So not only do we have to justify our involvement in Crigg's death, but we have to defend ourselves on the Doc thing, too."

"But I can help."

Kash paused and ran his hands through his hair. He turned away from Calynn, sighed heavily, and then turned to face her again.

"Remember the rules... the ones to keep you safe," Kash explained. "This is one of those rules. When we are dealing with the Constabulary... you need to be as far from them as possible... I can't lose you... It keeps you safe. Which in turn... keeps me safe."

"I understand," Calynn relented. "I'm not happy about it... but I understand."

"Good girl."

Calynn set them down just outside of the police perimeter. As soon as Kash was on the ground, she flew off again. Kash took a moment to take in the scene before approaching. Police poles were set up that projected holographic tape that said police line between them. The resort was in shambles. This was the first time Kash saw the devastation that Calynn had unleashed. Workers were separating the debris into piles as they dug through the wreckage. The Constables had a portable laboratory sitting on site to process the debris of the collapsed resort. A few scientists were standing outside, having a heated argument about what could cause such a collapse.

"Did that guy just say that this planet has a device that augments the gravity?" Calynn asked in his earpiece. "Sorry... I'm monitoring your channel since I can't actually be there."

"I wasn't paying much attention to that."

"That must have been how I did it... by using their device."

"Are you trying to not be a god?" Kash humorously asked.

"Just trying to find an explanation."

"Well, while you're stalking me... do you see the command center?"

"I do not. Wait... it's at the casino. They are working both crime scenes."

"Great... I guess it won't matter which crime scene I approach then, huh?" Kash relented. "Listen, I don't care what you have to do to stay out of sight... you do it. You're my lifeline once I step foot inside this police line."

"Lifeline?" Calynn argued. "I don't like the sound of that."

"Me either but do a search for people who were wrongfully imprisoned and buried in the system for years," Kash explained. "They get lost in the bureaucracy until their families run out of money or they have an ill-timed accident."

"Then don't go," Calynn pleaded. "I'll come back and get you."

"Not yet, Baby Girl... we need to get clear of this, and I still won't give up hope for getting Omia back."

"Or I might lose both of you."

Calynn's voice cracked with emotion when she said that. Kash needed to put her at ease.

"All those wrongfully held people were missing something that I am not."

"What's that?"

"You... all I need is you," Kash continued before she could reply. "If you are inside The Alley Cat Savant, then you are unstoppable... you're a walking, talking supercomputer with home-field advantage... You have tech that they don't know exists and the ability to wield it like... like the goddess that you are. If they detain me and it gets ugly, there is nobody in the verse I would rather have in my corner than you."

"But what if I screw up?" Calynn complained.

"You won't."

"How could you know that?"

"Because you're smarter than the entire Consortium put together," Kash explained fondly. "It's your mind that makes you special. You could wreck the beautiful body that Bahanja built for you, forcing us to put you in a cheap synth, and you'd still be incredible. Hell, you baffled Plekish, and he's the smartest person I have ever met."

"I'd be useless without my inhibitor."

"No, you'd be a force of nature without it."

"And just as dangerous."

"And yet, if we curled up together…"

"That's different."

"Only because you think it is… I don't do anything to calm you… It's all you… just you."

Calynn didn't respond.

"Now, I'm going to go and talk to the constables and hopefully get some answers about Omia," Kash stated calmly. "If they question me about Doc, so be it. I'll make sure I don't incriminate myself with my answers and try to get us clear of it. We need them to close that case or, at the very least, stop looking at us for it."

"And if they don't?"

"Then it's a good thing that you aren't here. Find a pressure point and squeeze until the bastards listen."

"And if that doesn't work?"

"Then you use the Slip and unleash hell."

"Oh… okay," Calynn stated.

The confidence had returned to her voice. She knew what she needed to do and, more importantly, had his permission to do what needed to be done. Kash smirked at the idea of Calynn throwing chunks of a sun or a planet through a Consortium Flagship. She could keep her distance, stay safe, and rain down hell if needed.

"Be careful, Boss," Calynn continued.

Kash crossed the police line and walked towards the mobile lab. When some of the workers and scientists noticed him, he waved politely.

"Sir, you can't be here," a man in a cheap suit yelled.

"Actually, yes, I can," Kash replied. "I was here when the building collapsed, and I need to finish my investigation."

"What?" the man asked.

"I'm a private investigator who was hired to retrieve a kidnapped woman, Doctor Omia Moss of Poncia," Kash explained as he kept walking. "Mr. Crigg, who is at your other crime scene at the casino, and the man who lived here were engaged in human trafficking. They were selling Dr. Moss for sex. I know this because I booked the honeymoon suite in their hotel and reserved Dr. Moss for my entertainment."

"Whoa, slow down," the man insisted as he approached. "How do you know about Mr. Crigg?"

"I just said that… you can't be that… look, is there someone smart here I can talk to, so I don't have to constantly repeat myself?" Kash hollered with a condescending tone. "A Doctor of Medicine was stolen and forced to be a sex worker… the man who lived here had her… that makes him the bad guy… I need to find her and take her home, which makes me the good guy… her village needs their doctor back, and you are in the fucking way."

Kash stopped in front of the man and gestured like the man should be leading Kash to where he needed to go. The man looked confused and angry at the same time. Kash rolled his eyes at the man and started walking again.

"Now, how about you call someone with some brains to come talk to me," Kash stated as he stepped around the man. "I'm going to go search for clues to help find the missing Doctor before she gets raped repeatedly or killed… is that okay with you?"

The man didn't protest as Kash walked past him. Kash would have ignored him anyway.

"I can't believe you just dismissed a constable like that?" Calynn sounded astonished.

"If you treat a corporate peon like a corporate peon, they tend not to argue," Kash explained. "They are used to everyone being more important than them. Where are you? I might need your scanners."

"Cloaked, in low orbit just above your position."

"Good, girl."

Kash approached the resort's wreckage and started looking around. Some workers eyed him suspiciously, but he acted like he belonged there. The workers were wearing white plastic suits as they labored. They were separating the debris into two piles, one with human remains and one without. This followed standard protocols for the Constabulary. The first thing they do is identify everyone.

"Can you please give me an enhanced overlay with thermals and anything electronic?" Kash asked Calynn as he retrieved a pair of glasses from his jacket pocket.

"Coming up, Boss."

It took a moment for the glasses to boot up and sync with his ship, but once they did, he could see what he wanted to see.

"Boss, I think there's a survivor..."

"Who are you and what are you doing at my crime scene?" a woman's voice barked from behind Kash.

"Saving that man's life," Kash replied as he ran off without turning around.

"Boss, there's a steel beam to your left..."

"Good call... will that get me up close to him?"

"It should, but everything is unstable."

"I'll be careful."

The steel beam was at a fairly steep angle, so Kash had to go up it on all fours. His enhanced grip strength made the ascent easier. Once he reached the top, he jumped onto a large slab of what looked like concrete from the floor. He could see the thermals from the man quite clearly now, but he didn't see a safe way to get to him. The man was trapped in an air pocket and miraculously still alive.

"A little help?" Kash asked Calynn quietly.

"I'm looking."

Kash looked around at the debris. There had to be a way to get to the man and ask him a few questions. A smaller chunk of debris caught his eye.

"How heavy do you think that is?"

"Two-hundred forty kilos, but it's still attached to the surrounding pieces by metal rods," Calynn replied. "But there is a gap you might be able to squeeze through if you move it."

Kash moved cautiously to the small chunk. He found a good handhold and positioned himself to try to move it. Kash lifted with all his might, but he barely moved the chunk.

"The reinforcing bars are preventing me from moving it," Kash told Calynn. "Can you use the Slip to…"

"Take tiny little bits away without making it collapse," Calynn finished his statement. "I can try… stand back."

"Can you focus on the reinforcing bars along here?" Kash asked as he pointed to the one side. "Only two or three centimeters wide."

Kash took a few steps back and squatted down. He was ready to move if the Slip made anything unstable. Six little flashes of light appeared along the crack where Kash had pointed. Small holes remained where the flashes of light were. The small slab of debris he tried to move, and the immense slab beside it both shifted some and settled together.

"Well, that might be harder to lift now," Calynn confessed.

"Let me try."

Kash moved over to the slab and gripped the side. He pulled hard and shifted the chunk of debris onto its side. Kash shifted his weight and shoved the slab over. The whole area shook a little when the slab landed flat again. Kash didn't waste any time. He quickly moved to the hole he had just created. He crawled through the hole head-first and pulled himself into a small pocket. From there, he slid over another chunk of debris into the larger air pocket where the other man was.

"Hey, buddy," Kash said to the injured man as he checked for a pulse. "You still alive?"

The man didn't move or respond, but Kash could feel a pulse in his neck.

"Come on, dude," Kash insisted, shaking the man slightly. "I need to know who your boss is and where he went."

Again, the man was unresponsive.

"Boss, he has a wound on the back of his head," Calynn stated. "He needs medical help before he can answer our questions."

"It looks like he was able to drag himself over to here."

"He was probably trying to get some clean air."

"Is it safe to move him?"

"My scans show no spinal damage," Calynn replied. "It should be okay to move him... just try to be gentle."

"Gentle she says... I can try."

Kash grabbed the man by the shoulders of his suit jacket and pulled him back the way he came. The first obstacle was an easy one. He could lift the man over the chunk of debris and let him slide down the other side. The problem would be that he wouldn't have much room to maneuver when he climbed over, but there was no other choice. Kash followed the man into the tight opening and tried to line him up with the gap to somehow push him out.

"Where did you go?" the woman's voice from earlier bellowed.

"I'm here," Kash hollered back. "Help me with him."

Kash heard footsteps approaching, but then the debris above him shifted.

"WHOA WHOA!" Kash shouted. "You're gonna crush us both! Move slowly and circle out around."

"I can't see you, so how do I know where to circle," The woman argued.

"Boss, tell her you are at her eleven o'clock, and she needs to move to her three o'clock," Calynn said in his ear.

"I can see your shadow," Kash lied. "I think I'm at your eleven o'clock. If you move off to your right... You should be able to circle around to where I crawled in."

"Okay," the woman agreed. "So what do you do besides run into collapsed buildings?"

"I have many jobs, but I'm currently being a P.I."

"Who are you investigating?"

"The disappearance of Doctor Omia Moss of Poncia," Kash stated. "I tracked her here, and I'm hoping this guy can tell me where his boss took her."

"This building was supposedly empty."

"According to Crigg, the guy who was staying here was a part owner of the pleasure planets," Kash explained. "But I'm beginning to think that was a lie. Are you close? I need help with this guy."

"I think so."

"You're at her one o'clock, Boss," Calynn said. "Seven meters."

"I think I just saw you move," Kash lied again. "I think I'm right in front of you, or maybe a little to the right. Maybe ten steps or so away."

The skinny woman appeared at the hole. She had shoulder-length silver hair, and her bangs hung barely below her eyebrows. Her face was extremely thin. Her cheeks were sucked in, which made her bony cheekbones look impossibly big. Despite her thin appearance, she had big brown eyes that were not sunken into her skull.

"She's from Ooga," Calynn swooned. "She's gorgeous."

"What can I do?" the woman asked.

"Can you grab his arms?"

"Maybe," the woman replied as she lay on her belly and reached down. "I can almost reach him... can you push him up a little further."

Kash flipped the guy's arm up towards her so she could grab his hand.

"I got him," she said.

"Pull slow and easy," Kash explained. "I don't think he has spinal damage, but let's not do any more damage."

"Okay... okay... here we go," the woman said as she started to pull.

Kash lifted the man by his belt and pushed him up through the gap. The slight woman was grunting as she pulled. Soon, they had the man up out of the hole. Kash followed the man out and was soon standing by the tiny woman. She looked Kash up and down and then looked beyond him.

"Get a gurney up here. We have an injured man," the woman barked.

"Yes, ma'am," two men on a hover-lift replied, soon disappearing down the side of the building.

"So, who are you?" she turned and asked Kash.

"Kash, and you are?" Kash asked as he extended his hand to shake her hand.

"Aman," she replied and shook his offered hand. "Detective Aja Aman."

"So, Detective Aja Aman... any idea why I was the one to find the survivor?" Kash asked condescendingly. "After all... you've been here nearly two days, and I've only been here twenty minutes."

"Excuse me?" Detective Aman complained.

"The one guy that could help me find Doctor Moss, and you were going to let him die in the rubble."

"I didn't know he was there!"

"Typical."

"And what's that supposed to mean?"

"It means that you idiots in the Constabulary always tend to fuck shit up!" Kash barked and approached the detective demonstrably. "Like, oh, I don't know... not searching for survivors before identifying the dead!"

"We did search," Aman stammered.

"Bullshit!"

"We did," the detective reiterated. "The thermals didn't show anything."

"And yet mine did."

"I know!" Aja barked and then calmed herself. "And I'm just as pissed off about that as you. I intend to have a talk with the thermal technicians about that."

"I hate to be that guy, but this is… your… investigation."

"My superiors will probably agree with your assessment," Aja confirmed. "My investigation… my responsibility."

The two men on the hover-lift returned and interrupted their conversation. The four loaded the man on the gurney, and the two men whisked him away, leaving Kash and Detective Aman alone on the roof again.

"Oh, hell," Aja uttered.

"Let me guess… the hover-lift brought you up here, and now you don't know how to get down?"

"I can't do what you did to get up here," Aja stated. "That was rather impressive, by the way."

"Come on… let's get you down."

Kash worked his way back to the beam he scaled to get up on top of the rubble. He grabbed the beam with his left hand and put his left foot on the front of it. He then turned and offered his hand to the detective.

"What am I supposed to do?" Aja asked.

"Stand on my foot and hold onto my arms. I'll lower us down."

"That sounds bold."

"Do you want to get down or not?"

Detective Aman smirked at Kash and sighed. She cautiously stepped out onto his foot and grabbed his arm. Kash brought his other hand to the beam so she could hold his other arm. Aja slowly lifted her other foot and placed it on the first one. Her entire body weight was now hanging on him. She was facing away from him, but he could tell by her posture she was only trusting him out of necessity.

"Okay… a little hop to get my other foot onto the beam, and we'll slide down… ready?"

"Are you sure about this?"

"Absolutely."

"Oh...my..."

Kash hopped up to plant his other foot against the steel beam. He let his feet slide down the flat surface and hopped his hands down the sides to control their descent. The detective gripped his arms tightly and leaned back into his body. Kash gripped the beam tightly as they approached the ground to slow their fall. When they hit the ground, the detective started to fall towards the beam. He had to quickly grab her by the waist and pull her back, so she didn't bang her head. Aja fell back into his lap but promptly caught her balance.

"Sorry," Detective Aman apologized.

"It's fine. Not like you weigh anything."

"Excuse me?" Aja complained.

"Boss?" Calynn matched Aja's tone.

"You're very thin... hence very light. What?"

"My people are... technically, I'm overweight," Aja stammered and then barked at him. "I would appreciate you NOT making fun of my appearance."

"But I didn't..."

"How dare you offend me like that?"

"How did I..."

"Is my weight a joke to you?"

"No, I didn't..."

"You arrogant prick, I'm not that fat," Aja interrupted him yet again.

The constant verbal attacks and interruptions finally wore on Kash's nerves. He approached the detective aggressively.

"What the fuck!" Kash snapped at the woman. "If you want me to make fun of your weight, I can! I could have asked if you were hungry because you LOOK FUCKING HUNGRY!"

"Whoa," Calynn sounded surprised at his outburst.

"One of my legs is as big as you because you're too fucking thin!" Kash continued his rebuke. "You're a toothpick. Not fat! The only thing even remotely interesting about your body is the two round balls on your chest that seriously look fake."

"Well, I am truly..."

"A stick figure with no curves?" Kash interrupted Aja this time.

"You..."

"Large, handsome man?"

"Oh, I... you..."

"Me and you? No thank you," Kash interrupted her again. "I prefer my women with some meat on their bodies, and you're just skin and bones."

"You... are... such an asshole," Detective Aman hissed through her teeth. "Stop making fun of MY WEIGHT!"

"Can I make fun of your incompetence?"

"My... oh, you," Detective Aman suddenly stopped and composed herself. "Tell me again why you are here?"

"A missing person case."

"A missing person that led you here?"

"Correct."

"How? From the beginning."

"The beginning?"

"The beginning."

"I met Doctor Omia Moss on Poncia, and we became friends. When she disappeared, I went to Poncia to investigate. After talking to Seemo, a retired pharmacist who helps at Dr. Moss's clinic, we knew she was taken by a local politician. The politician sold Dr. Moss to a crime boss named Egonn. When I tried to repurchase Omia from Egonn, he tried to snatch my pilot and use her for another sex slave..."

"Your pilot is a woman?" Aja interrupted.

"A smoking hot woman with great curves. Do you mind?"

"Sorry... go on."

"Egonn nearly killed us, so we had to heal up and track him down again," Kash continued. "We kicked his ass, and one of his sex slaves gave us the information that led us here. We booked a honeymoon suite and asked for a sex slave. The E-tablet they brought us had Dr. Moss on it. We booked her, but Mr. Crigg showed up instead. He said he would trade Dr. Moss for an E-tablet that the man staying here had in his possession. We cased the joint, broke in, and took the tablet. When we tried to make the exchange, Crigg didn't answer. We went to the hotel and had Mahounia, a lady at the front desk, take us back to see Crigg. Crigg was dead when we found him. We thought the man here took Omia, so we came back here. The building collapsed and trapped us. My nerve center has protocols in place to save me and take me back to my doctor when I'm injured. Once I felt well enough to fly, we returned to look for clues. And here I am."

"And how did you meet Dr. Omia Moss?" a man's voice asked behind him.

"When I was delivering..."

Kash started to answer before turning around. When he saw who asked the question, he froze for a second. It was a man who looked exactly like Doc. Kash decided anger was his best play.

"Doc, you arrogant piece of shit!" Kash barked. "How many times do I have to say to stay the fuck away from me?"

"I'm not Doc, Mr. Kash," the man replied and waved at some other men. "Detain Mr. Kash... we have questions for him."

Detained

Kash woke up on the cot in the holding cell. He stretched and stared at the ceiling for a moment before sitting up. His whole body was stiff from sleeping on the shitty bed. His calves, especially since they were hanging over the edge all night.

"You still there?"

"Yep... How'd ya sleep, Boss?" Calynn replied.

"Like shit."

"It's been twenty hourns... are they ever going to question you?"

"Standard operating procedure, Baby Girl. They wait until you get antsy and irritated before questioning you. It makes you more likely to slip up."

"And you're napping and remaining calm."

"They won't wait more than twenty-four hourns, so they will come soon enough. Anything on the investigation?"

"The guy you saved is still unconscious. The Consortium people are still digging in the rubble... nothing new there to report. Hey... what if I gave them the E-tablet we recovered for Crigg? Would that speed things up?"

"Neh... let's hold onto that until we figure out who the other people in the video are."

"Oh, and you were right," Calynn confessed. "It was tough to watch."

"I tried to tell you."

"I know. I know... sorry I didn't listen."

"It's okay... you sleep okay... you know... after?"

"No... I almost ripped a hole in that building to bring you up to cuddle me, but I just hugged your pillow instead."

"I could have used your cud..."

"They're coming," Calynn interrupted.

The door to his holding cell opened a second later. Kash had his back to the door, so he didn't see who entered. He always had to watch doors and be vigilant about knowing his surroundings. It was part of his being. He cultivated an excellent situational awareness and took pride in always being prepared. But having his back to the door could also be seen as a sign of disrespect. To turn his back to the door meant that nothing that came through that door could be perceived as a threat.

"Mr. Kash," the man who looked like Doc said from behind him.

"Hey, Doc."

"I am not Doc," the man replied.

"You sure as hell sound like him," Kash said as he turned to face the man. "And look like him, too."

"My name is Pan. Doc was a colleague of mine."

"Okay?"

"And Doc disappeared."

"Okay?"

"And you were the last one to see Doc."

"When he left Poncia?"

"Yes."

"And what does that have to do with me?"

"Doc approached you about a job on Poncia..."

"A job I refused," Kash interrupted.

"And then completed it anyway. Who did you contact to solve the dilemma on Poncia?"

"A client. A very private... and powerful client."

"Tell me the client's name."

"I cannot."

"What did you just say?" Pan said as he walked around in front of Kash.

"I... can... not."

"I'm an agent of the Consortium Constabulary. You will do as I ask."

"Still can't."

"And what makes you think you have a choice in the matter?"

"You're right," Kash agreed playfully. "Telling you isn't an option."

"You will tell me what I want to know."

"I physically cannot answer that question," Kash explained. "The client has it blocked in my mind. I couldn't tell you who they are even if I wanted to."

"I have ways to make you tell me."

"Let me guess… the noisy mind thing?" Kash asked sarcastically. "I cannot be held responsible for my actions if you try."

"Held responsible for what actions?"

"Hell, I don't know," Kash exclaimed. "They put a blocker in my brain. I don't know how it will try to defend itself, but I nearly shot Doc when he tried it."

"Well then… it's a good thing you're not armed," Pan stated arrogantly. "Miss Aman, please note Mr. Kash's lack of cooperation in the official record."

"Miss Aman, please also note Mr. Pan's lack of common sense in the official record."

"Shall we begin?" Pan asked smugly.

"It's your funeral… can't say I didn't warn you."

Pan's mental attack was more potent than Doc's, as the noise in Kash's mind was much louder and more persistent. Feelings of dread, disappointment, and remorse flooded his mind. Kash focused on his breathing and once again tried to latch onto the memory of the little girl with the tail. The memory was there, but Kash was having trouble holding onto it. He needed something else… something else calming… like cuddling with Calynn. Kash latched onto the smell of her hair, her smooth, soft skin, and the way her hand fit into his when she laced their fingers together. He was her emotional anchor, but her presence always soothed him.

That memory led him to memories of Omia. Watching her wake up was his favorite thing to do. She would smile at him and then complain it was too early to get out of bed. She would pull his head into her ample breasts to try and convince him to stay in bed. She would trace his face lightly with her finger and wrap her legs around his. Sometimes, she would hum a song to him, and sometimes, he would fall back asleep in her arms.

And finally, he could hold onto the memory of the little girl in her pretty green dress. He felt her tear on his cheek once more. He used her memory to push the noise away and quickly give himself an actual task. Kash wasn't sure if Pan's mental attack would slow his movements, so he moved at full speed and maximum power. He lunged forward off the cot and pivoted as violently as he could. He snapped a spinning back kick into Pan's chest as ferociously as possible.

The noise in his brain ceased as Kash's kick landed true and sent Pan flying across the room. The small man bounced off the far wall with enough force to dent the metal. Pan struggled to lift himself onto his arms as Kash took a deep, cleansing breath. Kash closed his eyes and slowed his breathing. Pan was lying on his back when he opened his eyes again, grimacing in pain.

"Well... you can't say I didn't warn you," Kash uttered.

Detective Aman scurried past Kash to lend aid to her fallen comrade. Kash turned, went back to his cot, and laid down. The door to his holding cell burst open, and more Consortium agents filed into the room. Kash made no attempt to escape in the commotion as the crowd of people whisked Pan away to get medical treatment. Detective Aman paused above him and stared down at him for a few moments before turning away and leaving the room.

"That was odd," Calynn observed once Kash was alone again.

"The way she stared at me? I thought so, too."

"I was half expecting her to start fucking you."

"What the hell for?"

"A display of power like that would be a turn-on for her... hell, I'm feeling a little ornery myself."

"You're always ornery."

"Hey."

"I'm teasing... how's Pan?"

"Lucky to be alive."

"I didn't kick him that hard."

"Yes, you did."

"Oops... I uh... didn't mean to do that. I just didn't want the kick slowed by the brain fog he was projecting."

"Well, you cracked two of his ribs right by his heart, soo."

"Damn."

"Yea... if you had caught him at a different angle, he'd be... umm."

"He'd be what... dead?"

"No... there's a pots and pans joke in there somewhere."

"He's not a pressure cooker, just a pan," Kash offered.

"So he couldn't take the pressure," Calynn replied. "I was hoping for something better."

"He was a Teflon pan of a cop, so the charges never stuck?"

"He who stirs the shit pan has to lick the spoon," Calynn added.

"You just want to lick my spoon, you pervert."

"It's a mighty fine spoon," Calynn bantered back. "Stirs me up just fine."

"I'm gonna get a wooden spoon and spank you with it."

"Do you think we have time for foreplay?"

Kash just chuckled at Calynn's response. Her playfulness always brought a smile to his face. He liked that she was also developing her wit.

"An old pornography film called," Kash finally answered. "They want their thousand-year-old joke back."

"I read it off the tag in your good underwear. Maybe you should change them."

"Damn... I didn't know you could read."

"Was that an I-only-read binary joke or a dumb blond joke?" Calynn asked with a chuckle.

"I never thought of the binary angle."

"So the walking, talking super-computer is just a dumb blond?"

"Well, if you put the scale on a circle instead of a straight line..."

"So dumb I wrapped all the way around to the genius side of the scale... nice."

"I thought you'd like it."

"You should get some rest before they come back," Calynn offered. "Your vitals are all stressed when he attacks you mentally."

"He's stronger than Doc, too," Kash explained. "It's much harder to break through."

"Looks like you don't have to wait long," Calynn said. "They are pushing him in your direction in a hover chair. I have an idea to help you."

"Do it," Kash quickly replied before the door to his holding cell opened.

"Assaulting a Consortium..."

"Kash-sh," a haunting voice echoed through the building. "W-why do you tell them w-who we are-are."

The voice sounded like Calynn, but it had far too much reverberation. It was like the voice was saying each word twice, right on top of each other, with a slight delay. This must have been her idea. Kash played along.

"I didn't tell them who you are. I would never," Kash replied and sat up quickly.

"Wh-why did you try to get-t passed our block-ck?" the voice asked.

"I didn't... he did," Kash replied, pointing at Pan.

"W-why would h-he do that?"

"He thinks I had something to do with his friend disappearing."

"Did y-you have a h-hand in it?"

"No... I didn't."

"Good-ood... w-we require your-r assistance-ance," the eerie voice continued. "C-come to us-s at once once."

"Okay," Kash replied as he stood.

"Mr. Kash isn't going anywhere," Pan objected.

"Th-this was not a re-request," the voice stated.

"I really have to go," Kash said as he approached the door.

The agents with Pan drew their weapons and blocked the door. Kash stopped in front of them.

"W-why do you st-stop Kash from-m leaving?"

"Because he has to answer for his crimes," Pan responded. "And who are you?"

"Kash-sh has committed no crime-ime," the voice replied. "H-he has told us-s so."

"She's right... I can't lie to them," Kash added.

"Who are you?" Pan shouted.

"W-we are us-s," the voice replied. "W-we need Kash's h-help. Kash-sh, come to us-s now-w."

"I'm trying, but they won't let me."

The building suddenly started shaking a little bit. Everyone in the room had to catch their balance, including Kash. Kash wasn't sure how Calynn did that, but the look on their faces was priceless.

"W-we need our Kash-sh." The voice said forcefully.

"Lock him down," Pan ordered his men. "We will not be coerced by your parlor tricks, Mr. Kash."

"You think I'm doing this?" Kash asked as three men grabbed him. "I told you... they are very private and very, very powerful... you should really let me go to them. It's bad if I don't."

Kash made sure to have a slight panic in his voice as he spoke. He wanted them to think that he was afraid of his client.

"And you think hacking our speakers will convince us of this?" Pan replied smugly. "I'm not a fool, Mr. Kash. I can see through..."

"S-so be it," the ominous voice interrupted.

"Oh, shit!" Kash exclaimed and fell to his knees. "Please don't kill me. Please don't kill me. Please... please, please."

Everyone braced themselves for something to happen... but there was only silence. After a few seconds, Kash looked around like he was still surprised to still be alive. He continued to look around as he slowly got back to his feet. The silence was broken by the sound of footsteps getting closer. Someone was running towards them.

"Commander Pan," a young man exclaimed as he burst into the room. "The Flagship, sir... it's gone."

"It can't be gone," Pan replied, looking at Kash. "You can't do that."

"Y-your vessel will b-be returned wh-when you re-return our Kash-sh," the voice stated.

"I should go," Kash stated. "Before they get mad."

"Take me to the command center," Pan ordered, then pointed his finger at Kash. "You stay here."

"But I have to go..."

"No, Mr. Kash!" Pan barked. "You are staying!"

"Sir, we lost comms with the flagship, too," a young woman stated as she stopped before the door.

"That's impossible," Pan replied. "Sub-space communication can't be blocked."

"Know when you're beaten, Pan," Kash said calmly. "You don't know these people like I do."

"Your friends do not scare me, Mr. Kash."

"They scare the shit out of me," Kash said as he lay down on the cot. "And they're not my friends."

Kash closed his eyes and lay peacefully on the cot while the Consortium agents moved about. They were talking over one another and bickering back and forth as they left his cell. When he heard the lock click, he dared to smile.

"So be it," Kash said with a chuckle.

"This is actually kinda hard to do, Boss," Calynn sounded strained.

"Then don't waste your energy on me," Kash stated. "I'm sure I will get reports from this end soon enough."

Kash settled in and tried to get some rest. If he had to be in a holding cell, he could use the time to recharge his batteries. He dozed off for a moment but was immediately awakened by Detective Aman looming over him.

"Can we speak frankly?" the detective asked bluntly.

"Sure thing, Detective..."

"Call me, Aja."

"Sure, Aja... what would you like to talk about?"

"What is happening to that ship?"

"Well," Kash replied as he sat up. "It appears that you all pissed off my client, and they took your ship."

"Yes, but where is it?" Aja asked.

Aja was fidgety and worried. She was clearly rattled and in desperate need of answers. Why was she so desperate?

"I haven't a clue... why?"

"Because I need to know that... I need to know," Aja struggled to answer his questions.

"You have a loved one on board," Kash announced his observation. "And judging by your desperation... a child."

"Please... my little girl is all I have," Aja nearly wept the words as she threw herself at Kash.

Detective Aman was kneeling beside him, holding his left arm to her face and body. She struggled not to burst into tears. Kash actually felt a little bad for the woman.

"If I let you go," Aja said softly. "Will they bring her back?"

"That doesn't help me," Kash replied softly. "That just means I'm being hunted, and you get fired... so you and your daughter go hungry... If you're lucky."

"I don't care... I just want her back."

"Then finish your investigation of me," Kash instructed. "You can prove I arrived when I said I did and that I ordered entertainment for that night. You just need to speak with the butler Early. I suppose I am guilty of espionage in some fashion since I stole that E-tablet containing Crigg's smut. But that's just a fine and a slap on the wrist, and you send me on my way."

"What about all the dead bodies at the casino?"

"Dead when I got there," Kash replied. "The girl at the front desk... oh, what was her name? It started with an M... shit... Mahounia. She can tell you that we led her through the people who were already dead, searching for Crigg. And Crigg was dead when we got there."

"But how did you know to look for the missing doctor at the other location?" Aja asked.

"Because Crigg was killed the same way as..." Kash's words fell off.

"The same as who?" Aja persisted.

"The same as the little girl on the video," Kash relented.

"This video is on the E-tablet?"

"Yes, it is."

"Give me the tablet then," Aja stated.

"Oh, hell no... no mother should ever see that," Kash said firmly. "I'll go to a prison system before I let you see that horror... but corroborate the rest of my story... you'll see."

"I will," Aja stated as she stood and walked towards the door. "Thanks, Kash."

As Aja walked out, another agent stepped in. He wasn't a very big man, and his consortium uniform was almost too neat. This man took pride in the details.

"Mr. Kash..."

"It's just, Kash."

"Sorry... Kash," the man apologized. "I need to know more about the technology employed by your client."

"Then you need to talk to them," Kash replied sarcastically. "I'm way too dumb to try to explain it."

"The Flagship has cut all power to the engines and HLD, and yet it's still traveling so fast that we're having trouble contacting them," the man gushed. "It's so impressive."

The man smiled a dorky smile and looked at Kash as if waiting for Kash to approve of him.

"Okay?"

"Where are they from?" the man continued. "To be able to do research on such tech would be awesome. I'm so excited."

The man was practically bouncing up and down as he spoke. He was clearly a tech nerd who was nerding out on the Thracian's tech. Kash just shook his head.

"There's still a blocker in my brain that won't let me divulge that information, even if I wanted to," Kash replied to the man.

Kash suspected that Pan was behind his two visitors. He was trying to break Kash down and make him lower his guard.

"So, is this the ploy?" Kash shouted. "Send in the pretty girl and the nerd to get me off my game?"

The nerdy man cowered when Kash spoke and soon exited his cell. Kash waited for a reply that never came... so he upped the ante.

"Next time, send Detective Aman in nude," Kash bellowed. "And have her bring a slutty girlfriend. Maybe shoving my cock up her fucking ass will get me passed my mental block? Hell, she might even like it."

"Your vulgarities are unnecessary, Mr. Kash," Pan stated as he reentered Kash's cell.

"Fucking fuck ass fuck off, you fucking piece of dog shit."

"That didn't make any sense," Pan explained.

"It felt good, though."

"And yet wildly unnecessary."

"Does Detective Aman even have a daughter?"

"That part was true," Pan explained. "Her coming in to see you gave me the idea."

"No... it was when I didn't let her break the law," Kash replied arrogantly. "The nerd was supposed to get me to brag about my tech, right? ... except it isn't my tech. Never has been. You pissed off superior beings with your dumb-ass ego. This... what is happening right now... is your recompense... You've got nothing on me because I didn't do what you accused me of doing. But your ego just won't let it go. You just have to be right even when you're wrong. All you pricks from Huma are such arrogant assholes. Your egos are your largest feature, and guess what, Panny Boy? A far superior being is about to make you eat that ego."

"That's a not-so-veiled threat for someone that claims to not be involved," Pan argued. "How do you know what they will do if you are not the one doing it?"

"Because I know them... I've worked for them... and I know what they are capable of."

"How are they interrupting our comms?!" Pan barked.

"How the fuck would I know?" Kash barked back. "The only thing I know about sub-space comms is you have to point two vibrating crystals at each other."

"Exactly," Pan confirmed. "Even if a planet is in the way, it doesn't matter. The signal still goes through."

"Sure thing."

"So, how have you interrupted the signal?"

"Oh, for fuck's sake... maybe when I was using the crystal to scratch my sweaty fucking balls..."

"Enough with the vulgarities!" Pan interrupted. "Just answer the question!"

"I was!"

"No, you were not!" Pan shouted and banged his fist on his hover chair.

Pan must have struck a button when he hit the chair because the chair tilted forward, and Pan fell to the ground. The tumble clearly hurt his broken ribs. Pan lay on the ground, wincing in pain. Kash didn't feel sorry for the small man. He did it unto himself. But Kash also grew tired of being cooped up in a holding cell. This was getting him no closer to finding Omia.

"I launched a decoy drone when leaving Poncia," Kash explained calmly. "A decoy that Doc followed. He left the system before I did, and that was the last time I saw him."

"His ship was destroyed while traveling faster than light."

"I had just tagged a rogue asteroid field not far from there. Perhaps it was nothing more than an accident."

"The nerve center could avoid it."

"Not this one," Kash continued. "If my pilot hadn't been sitting at the helm to shut down the HLD, we would have crashed into it ourselves. Nerve centers can only go from point A to point B. They cannot hit the brakes."

"Why are you telling me this now?" Pan asked.

"Because Doctor Omia Moss is no closer to getting rescued with me here."

"The woman you tracked here?"

"Mr. Crigg dragged me into his mess instead of just giving me what I came for. The man that killed him still has Omia."

"How can you be sure of that?"

"Because they killed Crigg the same way Crigg killed a teenage girl in the smut video he sent me to recover," Kash responded. "It's a fucked up mess, but it's not my fucked up mess. I am only trying to recover the girl."

"Mr. Crigg killed a teenage girl?"

"He impaled her on giant cocks a meter and a half long. The poor girl bled to death from internal injuries."

"He is an upstanding member of society, and he's on the board of directors for the Consortium itself," Pan stated. "He wouldn't do such things."

"I'll send you the video. You can judge for yourself."

"What about my ship?"

"We could try to ask for its return?"

"In exchange for your freedom, I assume?"

"Look... I've told you everything I know about both cases," Kash explained. "What actual evidence do you have to contradict anything that I have said? Especially since you know my story can be corroborated by two hotel employees and a video on an E-tablet."

"Doc's disappearance is based totally on your word."

"You're right... I can't prove otherwise, but neither can you," Kash explained. "But you can confirm that I tagged a rogue asteroid field. At the very least, it's a plausible explanation."

"Perhaps," Pan conceded. "My superiors are more concerned about the two-hundred and fifty billion missing credits."

"The what now?"

"That was genuine surprise in your voice," Pan commented. "You didn't know about the credits, did you?"

"Pan, if I had that many credits, you and I wouldn't be talking right now, and I certainly wouldn't be working," Kash explained. "By the Gods, that's a lot of credits."

"Indeed," Pan confirmed. "You spent a few million recently…"

"In pursuit of Doctor Moss, yes."

"That spending does align with your claims."

"And I will get reimbursed for everything when the job is done."

"So if it wasn't you," Pan asked, "where would you look to recover those credits?"

"I would start with disgruntled employees," Kash stated. "Only because a family member doesn't seem to fit this scenario very well."

"You would start with family?"

"Oh, definitely. You'd be surprised how much I see of that," Kash continued. "They steal everything from each other. Credits, jewels, wives or husbands, and even children…. Here, let me help you up."

Kash assisted the smaller man to get back into his hover chair.

"The more I think about it," Kash continued his thought, "is there one person screaming the loudest about retrieving the credits?"

"There is," Pan replied.

"Start there," Kash stated. "It will be obscurely attached to them, but if you look hard enough, you'll find it."

"This isn't the type of person you investigate, Mr. Kash."

"It's been my experience that for corporate shit, it's either the guy that hired me or a pissed-off employee," Kash replied. "And it's nearly fifty-fifty on which one it is. And you can't deny that embezzlement isn't a big fucking problem."

"You make a good point, Mr. Kash," Pan agreed. "I just wish you wouldn't cuss when doing so."

"Well, I like to cuss. Obviously, I'm not as much of a good guy as you are."

"But I'm still not convinced you aren't a bad guy either."

"Oh, I am definitely a bad guy," Kash said with a smirk. "But only when in pursuit of something good. For instance, if a woman doctor was being trafficked for sex, I would definitely break a few laws to find her. We might not agree on the method, but I think we can agree on the results. Returning the good doctor back to her people is better than her being raped to death, is it not?"

"You did help the people of Poncia," Pan conceded.

"Yes… but without Doc because I didn't like how arrogant he was."

"You are an enigma, Mr. Kash."

"I'm a bad guy that does good deeds."

The door to his holding cell opened, and Detective Aman walked in. She had a big grin on her face.

"Hi, Aja," Kash addressed her. "What did you find out?"

"Everything you said checks out," Aja stated. "I spoke to the butler, Mahounia, and a security manager… everything you said was true."

"Great," Kash replied. "Now, let's go find your ship."

Aja and Kash looked to Pan for approval. The small man had some concern on his face, but he eventually nodded in agreement. He then spun the hover chair around and motioned for them to follow as they left the holding cell. Kash placed his hand on the small of Aja's back and ushered her out the door.

The command center was only three or four meters down the hallway. Everyone momentarily stared at Kash when he entered the room but returned to work. Aja grabbed Kash's hand in both of hers and looked up at him.

"Do your thing, Kash."

Kash stepped forward and looked up at the ceiling.

"Are you still there?" he hollered. "Can you hear me?"

Everyone waited with bated breath for a response. The seconds ticked by slowly until there was finally one.

"Kash-sh," the haunting voice replied. "Y-you are not in your-r cell anymore-more."

"No, I'm not. I'm free to go, but I wish to speak with those on the ship… please."

"S-so be it."

"Thank you," Kash replied. "How urgent is your task? I am currently trying to find a missing woman. Could I beg of you to wait a few days until she is retrieved?"

"Th-this displeases us-s."

"I know, and I'm sorry."

"Y-you will con-contact us when y-you find the woman-man?"

"I will. I promise."

"V-very well, Kash-sh... w-we await your call-call."

"Thank you," Kash hollered.

"Sir, this can't be right," a man at a console stated.

"Commander Pan, are you there?" a voice came over the comms. "Try again..."

Aja squeezed Kash's hand in hers and laid her head on his arm.

"We read you Flagship Lima," Pan replied.

"Thank the Gods," the voice replied. "We appear to have stopped moving."

"They traveled further than is possible," the man at the console stated. "Much further."

"Are these coordinates correct?" the Flagship officer replied.

"I'm afraid they are," the other man answered.

"What is it?" Pan asked.

"We're four days away from you, sir," the man on the comms stated. "How did we get this far?"

Everyone turned and stared at Kash again in disbelief.

"What?" Kash stated more than asked. "I told you they were powerful."

"Is the vessel intact, and everyone okay?" Aja asked.

"Yes," the man replied. "We are functional and intact. Nalla is just fine, Detective Aman."

"Thank the Gods," Aja whispered, stroking Kash's arm.

"I should go," Kash said quietly to Detective Aman. "I need to find Doctor Moss quickly, now."

"Wait," Aja replied. "I can help... come with me."

Detective Aman led him to her office. She sat at her desk and brought up a file on her computer. She spun the monitor, so Kash could see it and smiled at him.

"This is a transport vessel registered to Mr. Crigg," Kash stated as he read. "I don't..."

"The brother," Aja interrupted. "The Mr. Crigg in our morgue is Lemi Crigg."

"This is registered to a Festo Crigg," Kash stated.

"The older brother," Aja affirmed. "He's an arms dealer and mercenary. The Consortium military sends him and his army in when it's somewhere that we shouldn't be seen... doing things that we shouldn't do."

"Crigg did that to his own niece?" Kash asked, appalled. "I think I'm going to be sick."

"Kash, he has an army," Aja reiterated.

"And that won't save him if he has my Omia."

"You would fight an army for her?"

"I will defeat an army for her."

"Oh, my," Aja said as her body shuttered.

"Are you okay?" Kash asked the now flush Aja.

"I heard what you said in the holding cell," Aja said with a hint of lust in her voice. "Would you really do that to me? ... if I were naked?"

"Oh... uh... maybe if it was consensual," Kash stammered. "I was just trying to..."

"It would be consensual, but my ship is four days away, and my office has glass walls," Aja purred as she stroked Kash's leg. "You are such a powerful man... so strong... Can you get a room? The sooner, the better."

"I have a better idea," Kash stated. "Calynn, get down here right fucking now."

"On the way, Boss."

"How do you feel about a threesome with my gorgeous pilot?"

The Chase Continues

"Bringing her in now, Boss," Calynn chirped.

"Let's hope we don't have to bribe anyone this time," Kash replied. "The first two stops were fucking expensive."

"Yea," Calynn agreed happily.

"Why are you so happy?"

"We fucked a woman from Ooga," Calynn giggled.

"Are you still stuck on that?"

"She was sooo gorgeous. You have to admit that."

"She was gorgeous, but I still don't like how thin her people are."

"And so passionate."

"And her boobs were shaped funny... unnaturally round if you ask me."

"And the way she whimpered when you were pounding her..."

"Okay, stop!" Kash ordered as he adjusted himself. "I can't go walking up to some Merchant Marines with an erection. That'll get me dead... quickly."

"You could always pound me quick to take care of it," Calynn said with a devious smile.

"That's the opposite of stop it," Kash complained as he walked away shaking his head.

"Okay, but am I still the eye candy?" Calynn hollered from behind him.

"Did your tits fall off?"

"Nope... I'll be right behind you, smart ass."

"Another stupid little rock with no name that needs a damn bubble to hold an atmosphere," Kash mumbled to himself.

"Actually, it's just an electromagnetic field that creates gravity and holds..."

Kash stopped walking and turned to Calynn. The look on his face told her to stop talking. He didn't want to be mean to her, but she had been annoyingly too happy since they spent time with Aja. She gave him a cute little smile and swayed her hips back and forth. Her jeans hugged her hips perfectly, and the baby-doll top she was wearing showed off her flat stomach and her amazing breasts.

Kash sighed and grabbed her hand to pull her closer.

"I know you have this fascination with Aja being from Ooga and saying you are beautiful," Kash said softly. "But I need the walking, talking super-computer version of Calynn right now... not the giddy teenage girl after her first kiss version."

"Sorry, Boss," Calynn replied.

"Head in the game..."

"Not in the clouds," Calynn finished his statement for him.

"Good girl."

The base they were at was built on the remnants of a small moon or giant asteroid. At some point, it collided with something, sheering it in half near its equator. It looked like a spiked or jagged ball that had been cut in half. Some entrepreneurial criminals had built hideouts, bars, and brothels here because it doesn't fall under Consortium jurisdiction since it technically isn't a planet. Places like this became very popular with outlaws, mercenaries, gangs, or people who just didn't want to pay taxes.

This base was much bigger than the first two they had visited. It was nearly 1,000 kilometers across and boasted more than one settlement. Kash chose to visit the one with the spaceport big enough for Festo's transport vessel first.

The port was a busy place. All the goods and resources for the base needed to be imported. It's not like they could have a farm here. The atmosphere was fake, so it never rained, and the terrain was solid rock... no soil. Kash paid the Harbor Master the docking fee, and they made their way into the settlement. Most of the people here seemed to be dirt poor. They walked past some beggars on the street and a few vagrants lying on the ground who looked stoned out of their minds.

Most of the structures looked like they were thrown together by children out of whatever scrap they could find. Even the bars and the brothels looked ragged at best. The whole town seemed gloomy and reeked of despair, except for one building. It was three stories tall with actual glass windows and a stone and steel exterior. The building had fresh paint and was the only clean part of the settlement.

"Someone here has some credits," Calynn stated.

"And they don't care about the squaller surrounding them either," Kash added.

"Are we going in?"

"Yep."

"Do we have a plan?"

"Yep."

"Are you gonna share it with me?" Calynn asked as she stopped walking. "Before we walk into the bad guy's house... preferably."

"I'm tired of bribes, so let's make big fucking holes in their house if they act stupid."

"Oh... my favorite," Calynn said as she bounced by Kash. "I get to be a walking-talking super weapon."

Calynn was walking like she had a gun in each hand. Her arms were straight out, and she slowly spun in a circle as she walked. She looked utterly ridiculous... and mildly funny. Kash smiled and shook his head as he followed her.

"What?" Calynn asked as she lowered her gun hands.

"Nothing," Kash chuckled.

"But you're laughing."

"I was just thinking that if you walked in there like that," Kash giggled. "They would be stunned, to say the least."

"Are you mocking me?" Calynn asked sternly but then chuckled herself.

She grabbed Kash's arm as he approached and hugged it to her body. She laced her fingers through his and leaned her head against his arm. She caught him staring at her and smiled up at him. Kash smiled back as they continued to walk.

As they approached the large building, they could hear voices coming from around the side. Kash shrugged his shoulders and nodded in the direction of the noise. The duo walked hand in hand around the side of the building. There, they found some open roll-up doors, and the voices came from inside. Kash kept the same pace as they approached one of the opened doors. Inside, they could see many poker tables, and the room was decorated like a casino. It had plush carpet on the floors, posters on the walls, and lights angled at the tables. A group of men were talking at the far end of the room near the dimly lit stage.

"A stage?" Calynn questioned. "I wonder what kind of shows?"

"The shiny metal poles gave me a hint," Kash jested.

"Who the fuck are you?" one of the men shouted when he noticed them.

"Health Inspectors," Kash replied. "We're here to inspect your kitchen."

"What the fuck did you say?" the man said as he started to approach.

"Relax, fellas," Kash said as disarmingly as he could. "I just want to have a word with your C.O., and we'll be on our way. Is he here?"

"Nobody sees the boss, and you fuckers aren't invited," the man said as he started to rush at Kash and Calynn.

"That seems excessive," Kash said as the group ran towards them.

Calynn tugged at Kash's hand to get him to stop and stepped in front of him. Her hair and shirt were flowing upwards when she took her second step. Calynn was squaring off to fight the five men rushing towards them... alone. Kash saw a nearby chair and pulled up a seat to watch the show.

Three of the men were charging ahead while two stayed back from them just a bit. By the sound of his footsteps, the big man leading the way was a synth. He tried to hide the fact by moving at an average human pace, but his weight gave him away. The other two in the front were either synths or had implants that enhanced their movement. The two men in the back appeared to be fully human.

The big man suddenly accelerated at super-human speeds as he neared Calynn, but that didn't matter to her. Calynn shuffled her feet to close the distance and snapped a sidekick into the big man's chest. Her movements were so fast it was barely perceptible to the human eye. Two of the other four men got struck by their flying comrade, knocking them to the ground. The big man flew back to the stage and punched a hole in the far wall. The two men, still standing, looked at each other, then at Calynn, and raised their hands.

"Sooo, anyway," Kash said nonchalantly, "where... is your C.O. again?"

"Probably upstairs in his office," the closer man replied.

"How about you run and fetch him for me," Kash said, then pointed at the other man. "You... what are the odds you guys have some good bourbon?"

"I'll bring a bottle," the man said as he pointed toward a set of doors.

The two men left the room to complete their given tasks. The one man returned carrying a bottle of bourbon and a glass. Calynn took them from him and poured Kash a drink. Kash looked past Calynn and noticed that one of the men who had been knocked over by the big guy was slowly getting to his feet. He looked woozy.

"You alright, buddy?" Kash asked the man.

"Not that you care," the man replied sharply.

"Hey, I just wanted to talk. You rushed us."

"You shouldn't be in here!" the man barked.

"We walked in through the open door and were walking right up to you to talk," Kash explained. "It wasn't like we were hiding."

"Everyone knows to stay out of here," the man huffed.

"Well, we aren't from around here," Calynn rebutted. "In case you haven't noticed."

"You... I've never seen anyone move like that," the man said as he pointed at Calynn. "What the hell are you?"

"I'm just a woman," Calynn replied as she straightened her shirt. "Although my hormones have been a little crazy lately."

"You have been a bit moody," Kash jested.

"And my hair has had a mind of its own," Calynn added.

"Just pull it up... it's sexy up."

"Is it?" Calynn asked as she grabbed her hair. "Hey, you, military man, do you like my hair better up... or down?"

"Fuck you, bitch," the man replied as he went to check on the other man that was still on the ground.

"So much for second opinions," Calynn stated as she returned to where Kash was seated.

She stood behind him and put her hands on his shoulders. Kash could feel a slight tingle coming from her hands. He was about to say something when Calynn said something directly into his earpiece.

"Boss, there's a lot of movement coming our way. We are about to be surrounded."

Kash reached down and patted her leg to acknowledge he heard what she said.

"I don't know if I can protect you without... losing control again."

Kash stood up and turned to Calynn. She had a worried look on her face. He wrapped her in a hug and kissed the top of her head. He could hear the footsteps of the approaching men, so he said what needed to be said.

"Be a force of nature," Kash whispered to his friend. "Make them fear you, and they will never get the chance to threaten me."

Kash pulled back and looked into Calynn's eyes. She still looked worried, but there was determination there as well. Calynn grabbed a fistful of his shirt in one hand, popped up on her toes, and kissed him quickly. She closed her eyes as she lowered herself back down. Kash could see them glowing before she opened them again.

"Get down," Calynn ordered as she turned towards the approaching army.

Kash knelt down and held onto Calynn's hips. His forehead was now resting against her butt. He heard the men barking orders, their footsteps, and the sound of guns being readied... then everything was silent. Kash waited a few seconds and then peeked around Calynn's right hip. The men were all gone.

Calynn lowered her arms, and there was a massive flash of light. Kash quickly pulled his face back behind Calynn's body. He wasn't sure what she was doing, but she had a better chance of accomplishing it if he was where she wanted him to be. The next thing he heard, he couldn't decipher, but it sounded like their assailants were gasping for breath. Another flash of light came from in front of Calynn, accompanied by the eerie silence once again. This time, Kash stayed put and waited. A few seconds later, another flash of light and the sound of gasping and coughing returned.

"Stop," a voice begged.

"Drop your weapons," Calynn ordered in a demonic-sounding voice.

The clatter of weapons hitting the ground soon followed. Kash peeked out around Calynn again. The men were all on the ground, gasping for breath. Some were coughing, and others were vomiting. But they all looked like they had thin layers of ice on their clothes and bodies.

"By the Gods, Baby Girl," Kash exclaimed. "Should I just kiss your ass now... while I'm back here? I only wish to gain your favor, Goddess."

Calynn didn't reply, but she did tip her hips slightly to push out her butt. Kash smiled and pushed his face into her butt. He gave her a wildly exaggerated kiss and then slowly stood up. He wrapped one hand around her, placed it on her belly, and brought his mouth close to her ear.

"As you wish, Your Grace," Kash whispered in her ear.

"Please... no more," a man stated amongst the chorus of coughs.

"What did you do?" Kash whispered.

"I slipped them to the edge of the base's bubble," Calynn replied in his earpiece. "There's little to no air, and it's brutally cold... I didn't want to kill them if I didn't have to."

Kash actually shivered as he thought of how cold they must have been for those few seconds. And the low pressure would have made it nearly impossible for them to catch their breath.

"Good job, Baby Girl," Kash continued whispering. "Don't let your guard down yet."

Kash kissed Calynn's neck as he let her go. He walked out around some of the poker tables and stood in front of the downed soldiers. The men weren't wearing uniforms, but they were all dressed similarly. Most of them were wearing black utility pants and mock turtleneck shirts. There were some browns and tans mixed in also, as well as some polo shirts.

"I would like an audience with your C.O., please?" Kash asked cordially.

"Regarding?" one of the men close to him asked.

"Festo Crigg."

"What about him?" the man asked.

"He has something that belongs to me," Kash explained. "Well... she doesn't belong to him anyway. He is holding a doctor hostage. I mean to get her back... so my question to your commander would be where your allegiances lie? Would you take up arms for Festo? ... or would you fight against him?"

"I would answer by saying he owes me money," a man in the middle of the pack said as he stood. "But I don't think that makes me lean one way or the other as far as fighting."

"Okay... well, I know he came here in the last couple of days. Do you know who he stopped to see?"

"Me," the man replied. "To tell me he doesn't have my credits yet."

"That's a lie," Calynn stated. "He has just over sixty-two billion credits currently."

"Does Festo owe you more than Sixty-two billion?" Kash asked sarcastically.

"AAARRR..." a man near Kash shouted as he tried to mount an attack.

A flash of light ended his assault as the man was suddenly gone. The other men looked around with disbelief. They were waiting for their coworker to return.

"Yea... he's not coming back," Calynn stated. "Ever."

"Thanks, beautiful," Kash said and smiled at Calynn.

"Sure thing, Boss."

"How does she wield such power but still call you Boss?" the commander asked. "Do you also wield this power?"

"Not really," Kash replied.

"Yes, you do," Calynn corrected him. "It's yours... I just use it."

"But I have to be sitting in front of it to use it... you wield it like a weapon of the Gods."

"Okay, you maybe have a point there."

"Thank you, Your Grace."

"Keep that up, and you'll be doing more than kissing my ass, mister," Calynn giggled.

"You're obviously not military," the commander mumbled.

"Actually, I am," Kash replied. "I flew with the Legionnaires. From your comment, I assume you have a problem with my leadership style. Am I in charge? ... is she? ... what is this crazy dynamic they have?"

Kash paused and approached the man.

"I don't need you to approve of how I run my boat," Kash continued. "But ask yourself this question... did I get more from my singular soldier than you did from an entire battalion?"

"Only because of your superior technology," the man rebutted.

"The poorest of soldiers blames his gun for missing the target."

The commander scowled at Kash but didn't respond. He walked right into that insult and wasn't happy about it, but Kash decided to let him off the hook.

"So, would there be anyone on this rock who does hate Festo enough to take up arms?" Kash asked. "The enemy of my enemy is my friend."

"That's a death wish," the commander replied. "Festo has too much firepower. The Consortium will send him to occupy whole planets."

"Holy shit, how many men does he have?" Kash questioned.

"He has ten thousand unmanned aircraft and twenty thousand men that command another fifty thousand bots," the commander replied.

"Unmanned air," Kash stated and turned to Calynn. "They will be easy to defeat."

"Not these," one of the soldiers rebutted. "They have advanced sensors and swarm logic."

"Those are slightly harder to defeat," Kash relayed to Calynn. "Five extra minutes... maybe ten."

"You're fucking cocky," the soldier continued.

"What part of - flew with The Legionnaires, did you not get?" Kash asked in a forceful tone. "I've taken down whole planets with two hundred men in under four hourns. I have been the tip of the fucking spear. I was the gold standard... the one all other armies are judged by... but now I'm better than ever, and more importantly... I have her!"

Kash pointed at Calynn as he finished his rant. He was still staring at the soldier that had argued with him. Kash couldn't stand guys like that. He was ex-military but let himself go and still thought he knew everything.

"Just because your fat ass couldn't do it doesn't mean it can't be done!" Kash continued.

Kash turned his back as the man stood up. He knew the soldier would approach and try some fool hearty attack. Kash listened to his footsteps and timed his dodge perfectly. The soldier had thrown a wild punch that Kash easily evaded.

"Oops," Kash said as he faced the man. "You missed me."

The man started throwing sloppy punches from every angle, none of which landed on Kash. Kash easily sidestepped and dodged all the man's pathetic attacks.

"Okay... I've had enough," Kash exclaimed.

Kash's counterattack was quick and precise. He jabbed two fingers into the man's Adam's Apple. He hit him hard enough to stop him but not hard enough to kill him. The man fell into a heap on the ground, gasping for breath.

"Anyone else?" Kash asked as he stood calmly in front of the group.

"I think it's time for you to go," the commander stated.

"I think you're right," Kash said as he started to walk off. "You're too soft for this mission... pathetic excuse for a private army."

Calynn joined Kash as he walked, but they were both very aware of what was happening behind them. Once they turned the corner of the building, they both relaxed a little. Calynn grabbed his hand in hers as they walked.

"Any movement behind us?" Kash asked her.

"A little... but I'm on it," Calynn replied with a little giggle. "They have to wait for their guns to land before they can shoot at us."

"I love it when you're devious."

"I know," Calynn giggled. "Are we off to the next settlement?"

"Yea, I suppose. We need..."

"Incoming comm, Boss," Calynn interrupted. "Patching it through to you."

"Kash... Kash, are you there?" Triana's voice came through in his earpiece.

"Triana?"

"Oh, thank the Gods," Triana replied. "We need help. Poncia has just been occupied by some army."

Kash and Calynn paused and looked at each other in disbelief.

"They sent a comm saying that we had one day to tell them who sent the attack against them," Triana continued. "Nobody knows what they are talking about."

"Festo... it has to be him," Kash replied. "Calynn and I are the ones chasing him through the cosmos to get Omia back."

"They might have come looking for that politician you told us about," Triana stated. "Their big main ship is docked at Moilad."

"And they have four squadrons of swarm pilots," Guy added.

"Well, fuck," Kash exclaimed as he ran his fingers through his hair.

"What are we going to do, Boss?" Calynn asked.

"I don't know yet," Kash relented.

Calynn squeezed Kash's hand to bring his attention to her. When he looked at her, she nodded to his right. A military-grade synth was slowly approaching them. He was wearing surveillance gear and was purposely keeping his hands out and open.

"We gotta call you back," Kash said quickly, turning to the approaching man. "Can we help you?"

"That was some display back there," the man said as he continued to approach slowly.

"Thanks... who the fuck are you?"

"Actually, I am one of your competitors, Kash," the man said. "My name is Romox."

"Oh, I know your work," Kash said as he offered to shake the man's hand. "That royal you recovered last year was some good work."

"Prince Gommardabeichey," Romox confirmed.

"Goddamn mouthful, that one."

"I just called him Prince G," Romox said as he turned his attention to Calynn. "And this is?"

"My new pilot," Kash said as he motioned to Calynn, "Calynn."

"So you have the best reputation in acquisitions and a hot pilot?" Romox said as he smiled at Calynn. "Hi beautiful... it's a pleasure to meet you."

"Hi back," Calynn smiled at the man and offered her hand. "That's a big, powerful body you have there, Romox."

"If I told you that you had an amazing body yourself," Romox said as he approached Calynn. "Would you hold it against me?"

"No, she doesn't want to hold her body against yours," Kash said with a chuckle. "By the Gods, that's an old joke."

"Is it?" Romox asked. "I just heard it the other day."

"I studied Earth humor when I was in the orphanage. It kept me sane," Kash explained. "And humans have been recycling jokes like that for millennia. There's not a lot of original jokes anymore."

"Damn... I liked that one," Romox stated.

"So, what can we do for you, Romox?" Kash asked.

"I'm here on behalf of another militia that is having a feud with the one you just met," Romox explained. "They asked me to retrieve a deed to a mine in the Onno system. Which I did while you guys had them distracted."

"Watch yourself with property disputes," Kash advised. "Lots of forgeries floating around."

"Already sent a scan to the Trade Commission to verify it."

"Smart."

"So, what were you guys doing in there, and what the hell did you do that to those men?" Romox asked.

"We were looking for Festo Crigg," Kash explained. "And that's a trade secret."

"Festo? ... that fucking prick," Romox said with ire. "What do you want with him?"

"He has a woman we were sent to recover," Calynn stated. "A doctor from Poncia... and a friend."

"Festo is actually on Poncia now looking for who hired us to track her," Kash added.

"My client might be interested in taking down Festo... let me make a call," Romox said as he walked off briefly to gain some privacy.

Kash wasn't sure how he felt about having this new private army join his fight, but at the very least, he hoped they would be cannon fodder and distract Festo while he and Calynn made their move. They apparently didn't need long to decide, as Romox was already giving Kash a thumbs up.

"Boss, incoming comm," Calynn said with an odd look on her face. "Patching you in now."

"This is Kash."

"Kash, this is General Condor of the Carrier Group Oitias in his majesty's, King Khoi of Ooga, Royal Navy," the general stated. "Officially, we aren't here, but Princess Aja thought you could use our help."

"Princess Aja?" Kash and Calynn asked in unison.

"The princess doesn't usually reveal her true identity," Condor continued. "But when she explained it was about slave traders, well... let's just say the men and I couldn't volunteer fast enough."

"I'm stunned... and eternally grateful," Kash replied. "I almost can't believe you're here... unofficially."

"The Princess believed the situation to be dire," the general added. "What information can you share?"

"Princess Aja?" Calynn repeated, still in shock.

"We stumbled onto a large slave trade organization while tracking a missing doctor from Poncia, Doctor Omia Moss. We worked our way up through the food chain and landed on the doorstep of the Crigg brothers," Kash explained concisely. "Festo killed his brother, Lemi, and took our girl, Dr. Moss. We just received word that Festo is on Poncia looking for the people who put us on his trail. He means to hide his crimes by murdering those who could testify against him."

"Poncia is four days from here..." Condor started saying.

"I can get us there in thirteen hourns," Calynn interrupted. "Give or take."

"That's impossible," the general stated. "No ship is that fast."

"We are," Calynn replied.

"Nebula Vanguard is on board," Romox stated as he approached again. "They want to know when we're leaving."

"Now," Kash replied. "As fast as they can get ready."

"Did you hear that?" Romox asked the man on his comm.

Romox paused as he listened to the response.

"They can be ready in five hourns," Romox replied. "And I can be ready in twenty minutes."

"You?" Kash asked.

"I ain't gonna miss out on the chance to work with the infamous Kash," Romox announced. "I'm in."

"By the time we get there, Festo will be dug in and have every advantage," Condor stated. "We have two heavy artillery ships that can protect my carrier until we get the fighters launched. Once we have air superiority, we can work on ferreting Festo out of whatever hole he has dug."

"Did I hear you say he's on Poncia?" Romox asked. "He has a four-day head start."

"We can get there in thirteen hourns," Kash reiterated Calynn's point.

"There's no way my carrier can move that fast," Condor stated.

"Look," Calynn barked. "You are all going to give me command control of your vessels, and I will get us there in roughly thirteen hourns. In fact... does anyone want to place any large wagers on it? I've got five billion credits, and our ship that says it takes less than fourteen hourns to make the trip... any takers? ... no... then stop fucking arguing with me."

Calynn stormed off towards their ship without another word. Kash caught Romox staring at Calynn's ass as she walked away. He didn't say anything to the man. Instead... he joined him.

"She's got a lot of attitude to go with that ass," Kash said to Romox. "But she's the best fucking pilot you'll ever hear about."

"She better be," Romox conceded. "That's a hell of a trip in thirteen hourns."

"Trust me... between her, our nerve center, and the advanced tech we have. I can guarantee she makes that mark."

"I know your reputation, Kash," Romox relented. "If you say it's so... it's so."

"I, too, know of your reputation, Kash," General Condor said stoically. "You're not known as a man that tells untruths."

"Great... now that that is settled... let's get everyone loaded up and underway. We can work on a plan of attack while traveling," Kash explained. "I'll call my friends on Poncia and get us as much intel as I can... agreed?"

"Agreed," Condor and Romox said in unison.

"I'll get the Vanguard people read in while they load up," Romox stated as he walked off.

"I will assemble my senior tactical staff and await your call, Kash," Condor stated. "Condor, out."

Kash jogged to catch up to Calynn and wrapped his arm around her waist when he caught her. She barely acknowledged him as she kept walking.

"You're angry... about?"

"They believed you about my timetable but not me," Calynn growled. "They think I can't do it because I'm a girl, right?"

Kash sighed.

The Battle for Poncia

Kash eventually got Calynn to calm down. When the others gave her their command codes, it showed they trusted her and, more importantly, believed in her. That went a long way towards brightening her mood. She sucked down three Nutra-shakes while they waited for the Nebula Vanguard to join them in orbit. Once all the ships were in place, Calynn spun up the HLD and the Slip, and they were off. Kash had never seen Calynn so focused. She sat motionless at the helm, staring intensely at nothing. Kash couldn't imagine plotting the course and dodging random space debris for one ship, let alone seven. And she had to use the Slip to bring along six of them.

Kash helped monitor the ship's gauges for the first several hourns of the flight. Calynn was worried about the power consumption, but the increased mass they were moving increased the static produced. Their batteries seemed to be holding up under the stress. He also needed to make sure she was eating. Her brain was burning through calories at an exuberant rate. He fed her a Nutra-Shake nearly every hourn to replace the calories she was burning.

VRRRRVVVVATATAVVV

"That didn't sound good," Kash said about the unusual sound.

"I'm really stressing the Slip," Calynn replied almost robotically. "I've routed some more power to help offset the load."

"Don't worry, our little Alley Cat can do this," Kash said reassuringly. "And so can you, Baby Girl. Make the Gods fear you."

Calynn didn't respond. She just stayed focused on her task. Kash almost hugged her reassuringly but then chose not to distract her further and returned to his quarters.

"Key, Kash," Triana said over the comms. "Guy says they changed their deployment again."

"You're kidding me?"

"That's what he said."

"Shit... okay... when is he available again?"

"Seven minutes," Triana replied.

"I'll open a group comm again... thanks, Triana."

Kash sat at his desk and opened the comms. General Condor was the first to join.

"They changed their deployment again, didn't they?" the General asked.

"Indeed, they did."

"They intend to keep the battle fluid," Condor explained. "Having random deployments keeps us from making any plan of attack. It's standard tactical training."

"I'm beginning to think we should make last-second plans," Kash replied.

"Did they change things up again?" Romox asked as he joined the conversation.

"They did."

"Commander Wae here, Kash," a new voice said. "First, I'd like to say that it's a pleasure to work with you."

"Thanks for joining us, Wae."

"And then I would offer my insight on Festo Crigg," Wae continued. "We have crossed paths several times, and I can tell you that he relies heavily on the size of his army and the technology they possess. He possesses a rudimentary understanding of tactics at best. Watch for a pattern. I am willing to wager that the deployments repeat."

"I will do that," Guy shouted above some heavy background noise. "Also... I got a look at their swarm pilots... and I might have a suggestion."

"Wow, he's hard to understand through that noise," Romox commented.

"Sorry... the cockpit in these weren't built for comfort," Guy replied.

"What's the suggestion, Guy?" Kash asked.

"If I fly my colors," Guy stated loudly. "There's a chance the other swarm squadrons switch sides."

"That would be awesome," Romox said excitedly. "You should do that."

"There's also a chance," Guy continued. "That they leave the battle to hunt me down."

"Both outcomes would be advantageous towards our cause," Condor replied. "However, I'm uncomfortable with you making such a sacrifice."

"Agreed," Wae chimed in. "Do you have a history with these men?"

"Not exactly... but," Guy paused, sounding unsure of himself.

"What is it, Guy?" Kash prodded.

"I'm the most famous of them," Guy relented. "The Battle of Topor... that was me."

All the stories of that battle sprung to life in Kash's mind. The tiny planet of Topor was under siege. The largest planet in that system, Ghehia Prime, was after the resources located on Topor. The Toporians were outnumbered and outgunned until a lone squadron of swarm pilots disregarded their orders and launched a counterattack. They used precision and skill to outmaneuver their enemies and struck fear into the hearts of the Ghehia army. The small group of men and their drone swarms moved differently than any other swarm before them. The Ghehia army didn't have an answer for what they were doing. The squadron quickly killed the King of Ghehia and ended his offensive on Topor. The squadron was given a hero's welcome and then promptly disappeared. They were never seen again.

"You're Commander Liezdt," General Condor stated. "We teach your tactics from that battle in our military academies now. Swarms were never used like that before. That was brilliant."

"That was fifteen years ago," Guy sounded annoyed. "And the reason I went into hiding... I never wanted that kind of attention. I was just protecting my home. I was bombarded with people wanting to know everything about this young swarm pilot who saved Topor. We were hounded by the media night and day, but the worst were our superiors... they wanted to attack instead of just defend our home. They didn't care how many troops died... So, for my reward, I asked my squadron and me to be released from our service with our planes and swarms. We fled the area immediately. I changed my appearance, and when people ask my name, I tell them I'm just some guy. I haven't been home since."

"I've seen some things written about you on the militia blogs. You changed the survivability of that particular military occupation," Wae offered. "They used to be a blunt instrument that died in every conflict. Now, it's regarded as one of the best jobs to have. The other swarm pilots might join you out of respect."

"Or want to be known as the pilots that killed the great Liezdt," Condor added. "That is the risk."

"Exactly," Guy agreed. "And there's no way to tell until it's done."

"I would prefer keeping you in one piece," Triana said meekly. "Just my personal preference."

"Me too," Kash added.

"Just when it was starting to feel like a..." Guy's words fell off as he spoke.

"Like a home," Triana finished his thought.

"Not the place yet," Guy continued. "But the people... they feel like home... and I need to protect them."

"There is much honor in what you say," Wae stated. "But it comes with a cost too high to pay."

"But it gives us a chance," Guy argued. "Isn't that worth the risk?"

"That's a decision only you can make," Kash replied. "As none of us here would face the repercussions of your decision. That weight would fall solely on your shoulders."

"But you are also running out of time to make that decision," Condor added. "If Miss Calynn is correct, we will be there in six hourns."

"I know," Guy relented. "I'm going to make another pass... Guy, out."

"Wait, Guy," Triana begged.

Guy didn't answer. He was already disconnected from the comm link.

"He won't do anything stupid, will he, Kash?" Triana asked, full of emotion. "Tell me he will be alright."

"That man is in his element," General Condor responded before Kash could. "With the odds stacked against him, he found a way to victory. Self-sacrifice isn't his way. He didn't sacrifice a drone more than was needed to save his home planet. I believe we should allow him his due process. He will find a way."

"Where did you find such a great man?" Wae asked.

"In a brothel in the Joor system," Kash replied.

"Protecting us girls before we asked him to," Triana added.

"In a place where nobody asks too many questions," Kash continued. "Where nobody would ever look for him."

"Commander Liezdt increases our odds of success," Condor stated. "I eagerly await his next report... until then."

Condor and Wae disconnected from the comm link, leaving only Triana, Romox, and Kash.

"I still say my disruptor is the best play," Romox asserted.

"And I still say it's too risky," Kash replied. "You could ground Guy and his people or a civilian transport."

"Boss... new specs... for disrupt..." Calynn was struggling to make her point. "Shorten the... range."

"I don't think that's... wait a minute," Romox said, then paused. "She's sending me new code for... oh, that's amazing... Romox out."

"I miss you," Triana blurted out while alone on the comm. "You and Calynn... I didn't realize how much..."

"I can't do this now, Triana," Kash interrupted. "I need to stay on point."

"After?"

"I'm all yours... I promise," Kash lied.

If the mission was successful, he would be all Omia's, not Triana's. If they failed... he'd be dead, and she would never know he lied.

"See you soon... Boss," Triana said, trying to hide the sadness in her voice.

"Looking forward to it," Kash replied flirtatiously.

Kash rubbed his head in both hands as he contemplated their next move. His military training was screaming that they had to defeat the enemy, but his covert side said to sneak in and take Omia back. They didn't have to kill Festo... or wage a planetary war. He could tell Calynn to stop bringing the other ships with them, and they could slip in alone and take her. To hell with the rest of it... well, Seemo, and Omia's family... and that older couple that gave him those pies. He should maybe save them, too.

"Fuck," Kash relented as he walked over to his bed. "This is why you don't make friends, Kash. You can't save them all... it's impossible."

Kash didn't bother stripping down. He flopped down on his bed and tried to quiet his mind to get some last-minute rest, but then he remembered Calynn's shakes. He decided to sit up and meditate instead. It was time to push down all his emotions and stop being Kash. He would have to be someone he hasn't been in a very long time... Captain Kolby Smith... call sign... Dagger.

Kash had the fastest reflexes of any recruit ever tested in the Legionnaires. They immediately put him in the pilot training program. He set speed records for every obstacle course and training mission he flew. It didn't take him long to be better than his instructors. His first deployment put him and 115 other Legionnaire pilots against 232 space pirates. They were expected to each kill two... Kash took down seventeen enemies in his first combat engagement. He only got better from there.

When the HLD shut down, Kash was already in his flight suit.

"You're no Tec-Ace Mark-7, but you're certainly faster than one," Kash said to his ship. "I'll take care of you if you take care of me... time to earn the savant part of your name."

Kash marched to the cockpit with a purpose. He found Calynn slumped over in her chair. She was clearly exhausted. He lifted her from her chair and sat her in a jump seat.

"I have to fly The Cat," Calynn argued weakly.

"I'm a combat pilot, Baby Girl... I got this."

Calynn smiled a soft smile at him as he buckled her in.

Kash turned to the helm and sat in the chair. He plugged his suit into four ports of the helm and then started adjusting the ship's trim. He needed maximum maneuverability. Next, he brought the weapons online and engaged the magnetic shielding.

"Time to find out if that laser refracting coating was worth the money," Kash stated.

VVVZZZZSSSSSHHHHH

"What the hell was that?" Kash asked.

"The Slip," Calynn replied softly. "Melting."

"Melting?"

"I couldn't contain the heat anymore... I'm sorry."

"You just did the impossible," Kash replied proudly. "You have nothing to be sorry about."

"Deploy the artillery and lay down cover fire," General Condor ordered. "We must hold off those drones until we find their control centers."

Kash was glad that Condor was taking command of the battle. The man was accustomed to giving orders and engaging in planetary warfare. The Ooga forces and Nebula Vanguard would respond better to Condor than Kash. The general could manage the big picture, leaving Kash free to do the things that needed to be done.

"Sir," another voice said. "Three vessels launching from the surface."

"We have friendlies down there," Condor replied. "Commander Liezdt and his swarm squadron."

"Scanning... No, sir. It's heavy artillery. Moving at speed," the man replied.

"Deploy the fighters," Condor ordered.

"I'm on it, sir," Kash stated as he accelerated hard.

"Kash, wait for backup," Condor argued. "Gods, that ship is fast."

Kash was streaking towards the atmosphere at blinding speeds. Festo had deployed his drones at the edge of the atmosphere. The command module was cloaked and most likely protected by multiple shielding layers. Kash had better sensors than most and a better understanding of the drones, too. His sensors could detect the lack of air where the command module was. They could cloak the command modules' visual aspects, but they can't cloak physics. The cloaked vessels basically showed up as a low-pressure area in the atmosphere where there shouldn't be one. It was easy to miss if you didn't know where to look.

Kash set an implosion missile to implode just above the fake low-pressure area and fired the missile. He pulled back on the throttle to let the rocket do its thing and waited for his opening. When the implosion round went off, it sucked the command module out of its stationary orbit and tossed it into space. A few seconds later, all the drones in the area started to fall out of the sky. Kash was at full throttle instantly. He flew straight through the falling debris of the deactivated drones.

"How did you do that?" Condor asked.

"The command modules do not have propulsion that can operate without an atmosphere," Kash replied. "And the swarm logic can only operate a certain number of drones per module. If one module is destroyed or out of range, the drones attach to another module. But if all the other modules are at maximum capacity, they just fall out of the sky."

"How long until they cover the abandoned area?" Condor asked.

"Just a few seconds."

"Sir, I'm having trouble tracking his ship through the falling drones," another soldier commented.

"Absolutely brilliant tactic, Kash," the General praised him.

"Just get those gunships online to cover my return trip," Kash said as he banked hard. "A little help, Baby Girl."

"Whatcha need, Boss," Calynn sounded like her usual chipper self.

"Two implosion rounds on opposing arcs that impact on either side of the center ship."

"Calculating... and ready to fire."

Lasers and bullets were suddenly streaking through the sky toward Kash's ship. Kash banked hard, rolled the ship over, and dove straight down towards the ground. He pulled up hard at the last second, so they were skimming the surface of the desert below. Kash then accelerated dead vertically towards the hail of bullets and lasers.

"Boss?"

"Fire on my mark... and... Mark!"

Calynn launched the missile an instant before Kash spun the ship through a gap in the bullets.

TING TING TING

Three rounds landed on his ship as he rocketed through them.

"Port wing," Calynn announced. "Minimal damage."

"And ours?"

"On target... Shit, they got one," Calynn stated. "The other... impact... damn, it's shielded."

Kash rolled so he could see the implosion out of the cockpit windows. The ship on the port side of the center ship got sucked into the center one, so they collided. Their shields couldn't protect them from the collision. Both ships had massive damage to their hulls and engines. The two vessels peeled off and slowly headed back to their base. The third artillery ship was still in pursuit, rapidly approaching the drones in the upper atmosphere.

"Any time, General," Kash said urgently.

"They need more time," The General replied.

The drones broke formation and started to accelerate towards Kash's ship.

"Fuck me," Kash complained as he cut the throttle and rolled the ship over, so he was again pointed straight down.

Kash hit full throttle and flew directly at the artillery ship coming after them. Kash spiraled around a hail of munitions from the enemy ship and continued to close the gap between them rapidly. Kash tried to avoid another barrage but couldn't dodge them all. There were just too many.

TING TING... TING TING TING TING TING

"Boss?" Calynn asked, sounding uncertain of herself.

"DAMAGE?!" Kash barked.

"The lasers bounced off, but the hull took a beating from those mag-guns. Those rounds are huge."

"Any of them get through?"

"Yes."

"How bad?"

"Port wing is at eighty- five percent. The outer hull has multiple breaches at the cargo bay, but the inner hull is holding.... HOLY SHIIIIIT!"

Calynn shouted as Kash barely missed the enemy vessel as he raced past it. Kash cut the throttle and spun The Cat flat on the X-axis, so he flew backward for a split second. The one place where shielding was weak was where the thrust from the engines had to escape. Kash started to fire his mag-guns before his ship got hit by the turbulence from the larger vessel's thrust. He struggled with the controls to keep them pointed at the enemy ship's engines but got a few rounds to hit their target.

Kash turned so they were no longer drifting backward and hit the throttle again. A sudden burst of thrust from the enemy ship sent The Cat spinning out of control. Kash feathered the throttle and quickly regained control.

"One of the rounds hit the fuel supply," Calynn announced. "It's dumping fuel into the starboard engine... they're out of control."

"Where are the drones?" Kash asked as he leveled out.

"Being handled," Romox replied and laughed. "Wooooooo... I love this thing!"

Romox was flying his ship right through the middle of the drones. His disruptor, with Calynn's new programming, was knocking them out of the sky as he approached. Kash actually smiled for a second until he looked beyond Romox's ship.

"Oh, fuck," Kash relented. "Fighters."

The horizon was dotted with fighters racing towards their position. There had to be hundreds of them. Kash rubbed his face with his hand and sighed heavily. This was getting out of hand fast. Kash pushed his emotions back down and focused on the incoming craft.

"Perhaps we can help with that," a voice stated as several sleek silver fighters surrounded The Cat. "Captain Yaui, fifth division airborne, at your service."

"You're a sight for sore eyes, Captain," Kash replied.

"We'll handle these guys," Captain Yaui said confidently. "The Nebula Vanguard has already engaged the main ground forces outside the city to our South. You should..."

"Kash, help," Triana's voice interrupted the captain.

The sound of Triana being stuck followed her plea. Kash could hear her whimpering from the blow. Kash's entire body tensed with anger as he waited and listened.

"Who the fuck is Kash?" a voice asked.

A voice that sounded like a Crigg. That had to be Festo, and he had Triana... and Omia.

"Fuck around and find out, you piece of shit," Kash replied.

"Is that him?" the voice asked from a distance but then got closer. "Are you... Kash?"

"You must be Festo fucking Crigg," Kash replied. "How about we meet face to fucking face? So, I can properly introduce myself."

"Such filthy language," Festo said maliciously. "Why must he use such language?"

"You bring out the best in me," Kash bantered.

"Oh, so I deserve your foul tongue... is that it?"

"If the pedophile shoe fits..."

"HEY!" Festo barked. "That was my fucking brother, not me!"

"Such language."

Triana grunted as the sound of Festo hitting her again rang through the comms.

"It takes a big man to hit a little girl," Kash added sarcastically, trying to hold his anger in check. "Prove to me how dickless you are and hit her again... how weak are you that the only people you can beat on are tiny women? Is that why the little girl in the video had such old bruises on her body?"

"Listen here, Kash," Festo hissed. "I would never..."

"And yet the current situation begs to differ," Kash interrupted.

"I'll have the bruises tomorrow to prove otherwise," Triana added.

Another blow landed on Triana, and she grunted through it.

"Oh, Daddy," Triana said with a naughty tone. "You're so strong."

"No! ... don't you say that!" Festo barked.

"Do you want to spank me, Daddy?" Triana continued. "Spank me hard."

"NO! NO! NO!"

"What's wrong, big man?" Kash asked sarcastically. "Isn't she small and weak enough for you?"

"AAARGGGHHH!" Festo cried out.

Some loud crashing got further away, followed by a loud bang.

"He left the room," Triana said quickly and quietly. "I'm in the city. The politician's office."

"Why the hell are you there?" Kash asked.

"We were trying to help, okay?" Triana replied. "The people here don't deserve this."

"We're on the way."

Kash turned and accelerated towards the city. He was scanning the area as they approached. The ground battle was still raging in and around the city. Kash didn't see a good way in.

"Commander Wae?" Kash keyed his comms. "Are you there?"

"Go for Wae," the commander replied with gunfire in the background.

"Festo is in the Representative's Center. I need a way in."

"We're pinned down," We shouted over the background noise. "We could use some air support."

"On the way."

Kash skimmed the ground as he approached the city. He could see smoke rising from the town where they were fighting.

"Boss!" Calynn hollered at the same time Kash saw it.

Kash rolled the ship quickly to avoid a surface-to-air missile that had been fired at them.

"Two more inbound," Calynn alerted him.

Kash fired a missile at the ground in front of the approaching two missiles. He waited until the last second to turn away from the implosion round and the two other missiles. The shock wave from the explosion shook their ship.

"By the Gods, I'm barely eight meters off the ground," Kash complained. "How the fuck are they targeting us?"

"I don't know," Calynn replied. "I've got nothing on the scanners."

"Wae… Wae, they have Sams," Kash announced. "Air is out of the question."

"Understood," Wae replied.

Kash came to a complete stop and hovered two meters off the ground. He was scanning the city to try to find a way in. The smoke covered the missile sites, so he wasn't sure exactly where they were.

"General Condor?" Wae asked over comms. "Requesting an artillery strike, danger close."

"Strike package ready," the General replied. "Where's my target?"

"Sonic markers being deployed… now…now…now," Wae responded.

"Ordinance inbound," Cordon replied. "Impact in one-hundred and fourteen seconds."

"Kash," Triana whispered.

"Triana?"

"What does Omia look like?"

"Brunette, one-hundred sixty centimeters tall, epic tits."

"Does she have a mole under her left one?"

"Yes, she does. Why?"

"Festo and one of his thugs are coming this way," Triana replied. "And they're bringing her."

"Hide," Kash told her.

"Oh, Kash," Festo's voice came over Triana's comm from a distance. "Now, where did you go, little one? … come out now, or I will stab this one in the stomach."

"I'm here," Triana conceded.

"And is Kash still here?" Festo asked.

"I am," Kash replied.

"I have both of your women," Festo stated in a sinister tone. "We should meet… I wonder if you can get here before I beat the little brown one to death?"

"You do not want to anger me, Festo," Kash hissed back. "If you harm either one of them…"

"Enough words," Festo interrupted.

"Oh, no," Triana squeaked, then grunted as a blow landed on her.

"This is gonna be fun,' Festo said as another thud echoed through the comms.

Triana was coughing and whimpering. Kash turned to Calynn, who had a furious look on her face and a glow in her eyes.

"You fly… I'll shoot," Calynn growled.

Kash turned back and looked up through the windows. The artillery was due on target any second.

"Aaaahhhhffff," Triana cried out as she was struck again.

Kash didn't wait for the artillery. He hit the throttle and was soon rocketing towards the city. He was flying so low that he had to avoid the desert bushes. As they approached the buildings, Kash pulled up, and Calynn started spraying the Mag-guns into the smoke. The artillery from Condor struck the city just as Kash crested the top of a skyscraper. He inverted the ship and dove down the other side of the building towards the explosions. Calynn was once again spraying bullets everywhere.

"Where the fuck is it?" Kash asked as he looked for the building where Triana and Omia were.

"Two o'clock," Calynn replied.

Kash turned towards the Representative Center and accelerated directly at the front door. He let go of the controls and jogged back to the cargo hold. Calynn's footsteps were right on his heels. He grabbed two assault rifles and an armored vest. Calynn grabbed a pistol and an assault rifle, and they both jumped out the man door as Calynn remotely hovered the ship in the building plaza. The Cat then shot back up into the sky.

Calynn was just in front of Kash as they burst through the front door of the building. Bullets were whistling past them as the duo returned fire. Neither one of them broke stride as they sprinted up the stairs while still shooting. Calynn's accuracy was astonishing. Kash stopped shooting when he noticed he wasn't being as effective as she was. When her assault rifle was empty, he passed her the fully loaded one he was holding so she could keep shooting.

Six thugs were standing outside of the senator's old office. Kash and Calynn both fired at the group. Bullets were bouncing off of Calynn as the thugs fired back. Kash felt the searing heat of a bullet as it ripped through his left thigh. Three more rounds hit him in the vest, and one grazed his right bicep, but Kash never stopped moving. His military training had taught him how to block out the pain until the job was done.

BOOM

Calynn kicked the office door open violently but then slowly walked into the office. Kash surveyed the room as he turned through the door. Festo was behind Omia and Triana. Triana was bleeding from her mouth, nose, and a cut above her left eye. Omia was staring at the floor. She was beaten and bruised and dirty and too thin and looked broken... and stunning... by the Gods, she still looked gorgeous... even now.

BANG

Kash didn't even see Calynn's arm move as she shot the thug trying to flank them. Kash gathered his wits and approached Festo. Omia looked up and locked eyes with Kash for an instant before staring at the floor again. Kash's heart actually fluttered a bit when she looked at him, so he had to gather himself again.

"That's close enough," Festo barked.

"Why did you make me do this?" Kash uttered. "I really didn't want to do this."

"Why did you interfere with my business?" Festo barked.

"I didn't give a shit about you or your business!" Kash snapped back. "I really had no idea you or your operation even existed. I wasn't after you, nor do I care about anything you fucking do. I was after one girl. I only wanted the girl. Why couldn't you just give me THE FUCKING GIRL!"

"Perhaps an arrangement..."

"Oh, we're way past arrangements," Kash interrupted and pointed at Triana. "She's bleeding... and so am I. Someone... has to pay for that blood. And unfortunately... I know you exist now."

"My synth is military grade," Festo bragged. "You'll find it harder to get blood from me than my brother."

"A synth?" Triana scoffed. "If that's the case, you hit like a bitch."

"That wasn't full strength," Festo argued. "I needed you to bring him here. I can hit you at full strength now if you'd like?"

"Do we have time for more foreplay?" Triana bantered.

Kash raised his weapon in anticipation of Festo reacting to Triana's barbs, exposing himself.

"Smart girl," Festo stated as he stayed hidden behind the women. "Trying to give him an open shot, but I'm too smart for that."

"But not smart enough to give me what I'm after," Kash insisted. "You're still holding two women that don't belong to you. A wise man would give me the girls before I lose my temper."

By the time he finished speaking, Kash was hissing, and he took another step forward. Kash decided to force Festo to surrender. He motioned for Calynn to flank to the right and moved to the left. They both had their weapons trained in Festo's direction.

"Stop moving," Festo barked.

"Or what?" Kash asked. "Your options are surrender or die. If you hurt one of the women, you're cowering behind... you just die sooner."

"My men..."

"Are dying by the thousands," Calynn interrupted Festo. "Your drones are done, your ground troops are overwhelmed, and your swarm pilots are standing down out of respect for our swarm pilot... the day is lost, Festo."

"The day is never lost," Festo bickered. "Fuck the both of you!"

Kash didn't hear the report of Festo's gun. He was stunned by the little red dots appearing on Omia's body. Time was nearly at a standstill as he watched the bullets tear through his beloved. A red dot formed on Omia's leg, her pelvis, two in her abdomen, three in her chest... her head. Omia's body lurched forward in reaction to the bullets hitting her. Kash dove to catch her before she hit the ground.

"NNNNNOOOOOOOO!" Kash pleaded. "Gods no!"

Sanctuary

Time was moving agonizingly slowly. Kash couldn't seem to accelerate himself fast enough to get to Omia's falling body. A tortured scream pierced his stunned silence. A feral scream... and yet... it sounded very familiar.

Kash got to Omia just as she hit the ground. He wrapped himself around her to protect her from any more shots. When Kash looked back to Festo, he saw Triana diving to the ground as Festo... dissolved? Kash quickly turned to Calynn. Her eyes were ablaze with white light, and the screams were definitely hers. She was floating half a meter off the ground, and the colors around her seemed to be off. Like he was looking at her through a prism.

Kash returned his attention to Festo just in time to watch the man be pulled apart at a molecular level. The man tried to scream but couldn't. And then he ceased to exist. The only thing left of Festo Crigg was a pile of blood and dust.

Kash immediately returned his attention to Omia. He ripped off his vest and shirt and started tearing his shirt into strips and pressed them onto the bullet holes in her body to try and stop the bleeding. Omia's face was bloody from the bullet that grazed her head...

"It only grazed her head," Kash announced frantically. "It just grazed her. Calynn, get The Cat."

When Kash turned to Calynn, she was curled up in a ball on the floor, weeping quietly. Her whole body was shaking with each sob, even though she wasn't making a sound.

"Calynn! ... Baby Girl, get The Cat," Kash hollered. "We gotta get her to Meesha... HURRY!"

Calynn didn't reply. She was still curled up in the fetal position, crying... so Kash kicked her.

"HEY! Get the fucking Cat right goddamn NOW!" Kash barked and then turned back to Omia. "We're going to get you help... you're going to be okay... Calynn, NOW!"

Another pair of hands started to help apply pressure to Omia's wounds. So Kash let go for a second and grabbed hold of Calynn. He grabbed her face with his hand and made her look at him.

"She's still alive, but she won't be for much longer," Kash nearly hissed. "Snap the fuck out of it and get The Cat. We have to get her to Meesha. Meesha can save her."

Calynn's eyes changed from sorrow to determination. Kash let go of her and returned to Omia. He snatched the woman off the ground, cradled her in his arms, and started to run out of the office. The pain from his gunshot wound began to kick in, so he grimaced with each step, but the pain didn't slow his stride. He heard footsteps behind him and knew that Calynn was following him. He descended the staircase as quickly and safely as he could. He didn't want to go too fast, stumble, and hurt Omia more than she already was.

The Alley Cat Savant landed just outside the door when Kash reached the lobby. Calynn rushed past him and threw the doors open, so he didn't have to slow down. His ship was awaiting his arrival with the cargo doors wide open. He rushed up the ramp and headed straight toward the medical supplies he stored in a bin under his weapons racks.

"Grab all of this," Kash ordered as he kicked the lid off the bin. "All of it."

Kash rushed up the steps of the ship ladder to the catwalk and continued down the hall to his quarters. The ship was starting to move, but Calynn was being cautious at first. Kash laid Omia in his bed and knelt down to wrap an arm around her for support.

"Punch it!" Kash ordered as he heard the HLD spinning up.

Calynn executed the jump to faster-than-light travel while still in Poncia's atmosphere. Doing so was illegal because of the hole it punched in the outer layers of a planet's atmosphere. It allowed the frigid air from the atmosphere's edge to rush down to the planet's surface, causing a localized Icesurge Winter. It would take weeks for Poncia's atmosphere to recover.

The bin of medical supplies landed on the floor beside Kash. He grabbed several packets of clotting agent and started to tear them open to pour them onto Omia's wounds. Another pair of hands mimicked what he was doing, so Kash turned his attention to replacing Omia's lost blood. He quickly set up the stand and hung two bags of blood from it. He pulled the IV port device onto her arm and pressed the button. The little machine tightened the strap to secure itself, moved slightly, then beeped, and a green light lit up. Kash attached the hoses from the port to the bags and watched as the life-saving fluid started to move.

"She needs more than just blood," Triana said. "Push fluids, too."

Kash grabbed the bag of saline fluids and hooked it up to the port. Then he grabbed some gauze and started to gently pack the wound on Omia's skull. It was only then that he realized it was Triana helping him.

"Oh, shit," Kash exclaimed as he looked at Triana. "You can't be here."

"I wanted to help."

"You can't go where we're going. The people are very private. You can't know about them."

"I don't understand."

"Calynn... get Metra on comms," Kash ordered.

Kash sighed when he heard what came out of his mouth. The mental block that the Thracians had placed in his brain wouldn't allow him to say Meesha's name in front of someone new.

"I already did," Calynn replied as she knelt beside Kash.

"Kash?" Meesha asked over the ship's speakers.

"Hey... we have Omia, but she's been shot," Kash stated, still unable to say Meesha's name. "We're on the way to you as fast as possible."

"I will prepare a surgical team," Meesha replied. "Calynn, give me access to your ship's sensors so I can monitor her while in route."

"Sending access now," Calynn stated.

"Okay... let's see... Kash, do you have a cauterizing gun in your kit?" Meesha asked quickly.

"I do," Kash answered as he retrieved the device.

"Center hole in her chest, she has a nicked artery," Meesha explained. "You'll have to cauterize it, or she'll never survive the journey."

"How do I..."

"Give it to me," Calynn interrupted. "I can see it."

Kash didn't hesitate. He handed the cauterizing tool to Calynn and let her do it. Calynn paused and took a deep breath before putting the tool into Omia's chest.

"Slowly, Calynn... if you go too fast, you can damage the artery more," Meesha explained in a very calming tone. "Good... work it closed from both ends... like that, good job... you did really well."

"Thanks," Calynn replied and smiled at Kash.

"I'll monitor her from here and prepare for your arrival..."

"Wait," Kash interrupted. "We have another problem, too."

Kash smiled at Triana.

"I'm assuming that's the fourth body I see on the sensors?" Meesha asked.

"Her name is Triana, and she's a friend," Kash responded. "She was helping us with Omia, and I didn't realize she was here. There's no time to turn around and take her back."

"We will cross that bridge when you get here," Meesha replied. "For now, having an extra pair of hands is a good thing... and also explains why you haven't used my name."

"Your husband is going to be mad at me."

"For a moment, maybe, but then he will solve this problem like he solves so many others," Meesha said reassuringly. "Focus on your patient. I'll see you soon."

Calynn pushed the HLD to its limit. She managed to decrease the flight time to just over twelve hournrs, but when they arrived, the ship was making some strange noises.

Meesha and her medical team boarded the ship the moment they touched down. Kash, Calynn, and Triana all moved to the cargo hold to stay out of the way, as Meesha had instructed during their flight. Kash and Calynn hugged each other tight, and Triana tried to soothe them both. It seemed like it took forever before they brought Omia out on a stretcher. Meesha was barking orders in Thracian as they exited his ship.

Kash took a deep, cleansing breath, knowing he had done all he could to save Omia. It was in Meesha's skillful hands now. Kash allowed himself to relax and tried to find comfort in Calynn's arms. He started to feel dizzy.

"Hey... why is the room spinning?"

Kash fell to the ground, unconscious.

Beep......................Beep......................Beep......................Beep

Kash slowly opened his eyes to find himself in a hospital bed. When the world came into focus, Triana was smiling at him.

"Hey you," Triana said softly. "You gave us quite a scare."

"What..."

Kash had to stop and clear his throat.

"What happened?"

"You got shot in the leg, apparently," Triana replied. "And you forgot to tell us or take care of it yourself. You lost a lot of blood."

"Oh... yea... How's Omia?"

"Still in surgery."

"Where's Calynn?"

"With Omia... so you're stuck with me," Triana smiled as she spoke.

"Sorry... how are you?"

"A little freaked out," Triana confessed. "You gave us quite a scare when you passed out. Since you were here, Calynn went with Omia, leaving me alone on a strange planet of giant people. And your friend, Plekish, says I have to get a memory block thing. That sounds scary."

"Sorry about that. And It's okay, they did the block thing to me also... back when I first met them."

"But I thought you were their friend?"

"I am now," Kash explained. "But my first interaction with them was when they hired me to return Plekish after he was kidnapped."

"It's still scary."

Kash placed a reassuring hand on Triana's belly to comfort the girl. Triana sat on the edge of the bed to lower herself down and lay her head on Kash's chest. Kash wrapped his arm around her, so his hand was under her shirt in the middle of her back. He gently caressed her soft skin. His right arm had the IV port, and his bicep was wrapped in gauze. He carefully reached up for Triana's head but only got his hand to the nape of her neck.

"Am I hurting you?" Triana asked softly.

"My ribs are a little sore, but you're fine."

"I'm sorry. I wanted to go help my friends... I wish I had stayed with you two."

"You did what you needed to do. And we knew where to find you if we wanted to abuse you some more."

"Abuse me, huh?" Triana asked playfully.

"Just teasing you."

"If that was abuse," Triana said as she cuddled into his chest. "Please abuse me often."

Kash grimaced in pain as he tried to shift his body over to make room to pull Triana on the bed beside him. Triana felt it and quickly sat up.

"What's wrong?"

"That leg really hurts."

"Well, duh," Triana said sarcastically. "You were shot. Just lie still."

"Normally, I feel better faster than this."

"You've spent too much time in the regeneration pods lately," a Thracian man said from the doorway. "Your DNA is not the same as ours. Too much time in the pods can overstimulate your cells, causing permanent damage."

"Meesha never said anything about that."

"It has never been an issue with you before," the man said as he approached. "Some of your cells are still excited from your last visit, which led to our concerns."

"So, no miracle healing this time?"

"I'm afraid not, Kash."

"How's my friend doing?"

"Meesha and her team are still in surgery," the man replied. "Your friend was very weak when you got her here."

"Can I see her?"

"Not with your open wounds, no," the doctor replied. "Everyone in the surgical room must be stripped down and scrubbed clean to prevent contamination."

Kash knew better than to argue with the doctor. Thracians were very adamant about their protocols and procedures, and they didn't stray from their best practices.

"I understand," Kash relented. "Can you get me an update, though?"

"The last update I saw wasn't good," the doctor admitted. "Your friend was malnourished, dehydrated, and drugged before she was shot. Her organs aren't responding well... I'm sorry."

Kash pulled Triana into bed with him as the tears welled up in his eyes. He dragged the petite beauty up so he could bury his face in her chest and belly. Triana hugged his head to her body and tried to comfort him as best as she could. Kash pulled up her shirt to get his face directly onto her sweet-smelling skin. She wasn't the skin he wanted, but her soft skin was soothing, nonetheless.

"You should try to get some rest," the doctor stated. "I'm told you are familiar with these."

Kash had almost forgotten the doctor was there. He used Triana's belly to wipe the tears from his eyes and looked back to the doctor. The man was holding one of the pain-killing berries.

"Yes, please," Kash said as he reached out his hand.

"And you're aware of the side effects?"

"The whole room spins, inhibitions are lost, tongues are loosened, and I might wake up with a raging boner... yea I know. My friend here is well-equipped to handle all of those issues."

"I have cared for him when he was blackout drunk," Triana stated. "I should be able to handle this."

"Very well," the doctor agreed as he handed the berry to Kash. "My name is Vivush. Let me know if there's anything you need."

"Thanks, Vivush," Kash replied as he chewed the berry and buried his head in Triana's belly again.

Kash stared at nothing as his tears started falling on Triana's skin. He couldn't wait for the berry to kick in and knock him out. The pain in his leg was nothing compared to the hole in his heart right now.

"What can I do?" Triana asked softly. "I know I'm not who you want right now, but I can try to help."

Kash sighed and then looked up at his pretty friend. She was smiling softly and had concern in her eyes.

"I fell in love with Omia so quickly and completely. It was like a dream," Kash explained. "I've never felt that way about someone before... if I lose her... I don't think anyone can fill that void... but having you here is better than not having you here."

"I meant Calynn... I figured you would rather have her."

"I do have a lot of love for Calynn, but even she can't be Omia," Kash confessed. "I do really like you and value you as a friend. I also really enjoy fucking you. You're one of the best fucks I've ever had... easily top five..."

Kash paused and looked down at his growing erection.

"Oops," Kash said with a giggle. "Hey, if that doesn't go down, can you take care of that for me? Fuck, I'm so high... I love those berries."

"I know what it likes," Triana giggled also.

"I know what you like too... I'm just too fucked up to do it to you."

Triana said something else, but Kash couldn't understand what she said. When he tried to ask, his mouth didn't move. The darkness soon won, and Kash fell asleep.

Beep.....................Beep......................Beep.....................Beep

When Kash woke up, he felt warm. The sweet smell of Triana filled his nose, and he didn't have to open his eyes to see that she was still there. She did, however, reposition herself because they were now spooning. Kash pulled her closer and realized she was naked.

"Mmm," Triana moaned as she backed up into him. "Do you want seconds?"

"I wish I remembered the firsts."

"It's hard work to get a berry boner to pop," Triana said as she rolled into Kash's body. "I thought I was going to need help."

"Berry boner," Kash giggled. "That's funny."

"What's funny is a nurse walked in while I was... working on your problem, and she asked if I needed a drink or anything," Triana continued. "She brought me something to give me the energy boost I needed to finish you."

Kash grabbed Triana's left boob and pulled her tighter. He started to kiss her shoulder when she pulled away. Kash thought it was odd until he noticed she was looking toward the door. Kash followed her gaze and was shocked at what he saw. Calynn was standing naked in the doorway with her head down. Her arms crossed her body like she was trying to hug herself. When she looked up, and Kash saw her tears, he knew.

"Nnnnooooo," Kash cried out. "Please, no."

Calynn didn't reply. She stumbled into the room at first but then quickened her pace. She was sobbing uncontrollably when she climbed into his hospital bed and laid on top of him. Calynn wrapped one arm around his shoulders and the other around Triana's. Kash wanted to ask her questions but knew he wouldn't like the answers. The tears came quickly, and he was soon sobbing also.

Triana couldn't help but cry with them. The trio was trying to comfort each other while also seeking comfort themselves. Kash felt a weight on the bed and looked up to see a distraught Meesha sitting there.

"I'm sorry, Kash," Meesha said softly. "She was just too weak. I tried my best, but..."

Kash reached out to Meesha. He could tell she needed some comfort, too. Meesha placed his hand on her cheek and held it with both hands. She lingered for only a moment before returning to her duties. Kash, Calynn, and Triana continued to cry together. Kash lost all track of time.

3 weeks later...

"It's been a tough couple of weeks, to say the least," Kash told his therapist, Doctor Uva. "I know we weren't married or anything, and it really wasn't that long of a relationship... but I fell for her hard... I knew within the first day that I loved Omia. She was the perfect woman for me... And I never told her that... and now I never can. I have been trying to forgive myself for that... for not telling her that I loved her, but it's a work in progress. Umm... oh, the support we have received here on Thracia has been amazing. The service for Omia was beautiful. Plekish tells me that the cemetery is one of the most prestigious, and Omia will be cherished for generations. I did have the one outburst because Meesha was avoiding me. She felt guilty for not saving Omia for me since I saved Plekish for her. I had to tell her that I couldn't bear to lose her also... we hugged and cried a little bit, and then we were better. Being around Plekish, Meesha, and the kids has been great. Calynn was brushing Mala's hair last evening while I watched Plekish and Darjic play a game of chess. Having Triana here has also been a godsend. She bounces around tending to everyone's needs, and she's so happy and bubbly all the time... it's contagious... although... she does keep offering me her body, but I'm not... I'm just not ready for that yet."

"Can you elaborate on that?" Uva asked.

"Well... for me, having sex with multiple beautiful women is the norm," Kash explained. "Triana is not only gorgeous, but she's amazing at... several sexual acts. And I really enjoy being with her like that, but... I... I don't know why... but I'm just not interested in sex right now."

"Is it a sense of guilt?"

"Oh, Gods no," Kash replied. "Omia and I wanted to have a relationship that included other women. If Omia had gotten her way..."

Kash had to pause for a moment. It still hurts to talk about her sometimes. He swallowed his emotions and continued.

"If Omia had gotten her way, Calynn and Triana would be our girlfriends... had Omia and Triana met, of course."

"And how is your relationship with Calynn?" Uva asked.

"Stronger than ever... we cry a lot... probably because we remind each other how much we miss Omia. We don't talk about our therapy, but we both know that we are seeing a therapist. And it's been helpful to both of us."

"Her therapist and I have spoken," Uva explained. "And you are both doing well with your grief management. You both still need time to heal, but you do better when you support each other. The hard part will be ensuring you don't try to replace Omia with Calynn. And Calynn cannot replace Omia with you. I know how much you care for each other, but neither of you can ever be Omia... and it's unfair to ask her to try."

"I know... it's easy to try and have her fill that hole... even though I know she can't."

"Omia bored that hole in your heart," the doctor explained. "That's a hole that only she can fill. You must let that hole heal before Calynn can bore her own hole that only she can fill... if that's what you want."

"She deserves better than me."

"It's funny that she says the same of you."

"And poor Triana deserves more than we have given her. I should really thank her properly."

"But you're not ready for that. It would be an escape and not let you heal... you need to heal."

"I'm working on it," Kash said, a little harsher than he intended. "I know... don't get frustrated... I'm working on that too."

"Good job, Kash," Doctor Uva said with a kind smile. "You've done some excellent work here."

"Thanks, Doc," Kash smiled back. "You've been a big help. But if my friends ask, I'll deny it."

Kash chuckled at his joke, and Doctor Uva smiled. Meesha did a good job picking Uva to be Kash's therapist. Uva was an older woman who, in Kash's opinion, was the epitome of a grandma. She had kind eyes and the perfect temperament to handle Kash... and she could read him like a book.

"I think you should go talk to Miss Triana," the doctor said as she stood. "To clearly communicate your desires."

"Is that my homework for today?"

"It is indeed," Uva said with a smile.

"Same time tomorrow?"

"Same time tomorrow."

Kash stood and shook the doctor's hand before exiting the room. He looked for Uva's husband, Geentith, but he must have been busy somewhere else. Doctor Uva did her therapy sessions in her own house and lived only a few houses down from Plekish and Meesha. Kash took a deep breath when he exited the house and walked to Plekish's house. Triana was waiting for him outside. She was wearing leggings and a sports bra.

"You going for a run today?" Triana asked with a smile that lit up her whole face.

"Now, why would I do that?" Kash asked playfully.

"Because you go for a run after therapy every single time," Triana replied in a sassy tone, placing her hands on her hips.

"Was that sass? ... are you sassing me now?"

"I wouldn't have to sass you if you just answered my question."

"Which question was..."

"Are you going running or not?" Triana quipped. "I have this cute outfit..."

"Do you want to go for a run with me?" Kash interrupted her rant.

"Yes, please," Triana said, and the smile returned to her face.

Kash quickened his pace for the last two steps as he approached Triana. He lowered his stance and surprised her when he snatched her off the ground. Kash was now looking up at her. He put one arm around her waist, and the other was just below her butt when he lifted her. Triana squeaked in surprise and then giggled as she hugged his head into her chest.

"I'm so glad you're here," Kash said as he put the beauty down. "Your bubbly personality is so contagious. You make me smile."

"I'm glad I'm here too," Triana said with another smile. "I'm here for anything you and Calynn need, and this planet is just gorgeous. Oh, and the weather... it's always perfect."

"Yeah, I love it here. I think it's better than the Pleasure Planets," Kash agreed, then sighed before continuing. "So, my therapist says I need to address what you just said."

"Did I say something wrong?" Triana asked apologetically.

"No... no... it's what was implied," Kash replied, placing his hands on Triana's waist. "You have been beyond amazing in helping me through this, and I know Calynn appreciates you also... and I wish I could reward you by ravaging that hot little body of yours, but..."

"It will be right here when you are ready," Triana interrupted him. "But in the meantime... I'm not going anywhere... I'm still a willing ear to listen, a shoulder to cry on, or whatever you need me to be... including a running partner. I laid out your clothes and running shoes. Catch me if you can."

Triana dropped her leggings below her butt as she started to jog away.

"Did you just moon me?" Kash hollered.

"Go change." Triana hollered back.

Kash ran into the house and changed as quickly as he could. He passed Meesha in the hallway, kissed the back of her hand, and then ran out the door after Triana. Kash pushed his pace so he could catch up to her quickly. His leg still hurt when he ran, but at least he wasn't doing it to punish himself today. Today, he had a positive reason to run and make his leg sore.

Triana must have heard his footsteps behind her because she stopped running and looked back to see him. She was laughing and smiling, which also brought a smile to his face. Kash slowed his pace, grabbed Triana's hand, and gently pulled her along.

"Come on... I thought we were running?"

"Okay," Triana said as she started jogging again. "But just a quick run... I want to be back for Calynn."

"Me too... why do her therapy sessions always take so much longer than mine?"

"Because... girls are more complex... than you silly boys."

"Says the girl that mooned me and ran away."

"Can we... slow down?" Triana asked, half out of breath. "I can't... keep this pace."

"Sure thing," Kash replied with a smile.

The two friends chatted as they ran around the housing pod twice. It wasn't a very good workout for Kash, but it made him feel better, nonetheless. Triana was a good distraction and made life feel more... normal. They took turns showering and were ready for Calynn when she got to the house. Calynn had a quick cry, and then went back to her usual self. The trio were in the kitchen chatting with Meesha when Plekish got home.

"Good evening, my friends," Plekish said warmly. "I'm happy to report that your ship is fully functional once again, except for the Slip."

"I really broke it, didn't I?" Calynn asked meekly.

"The crystals have melted and cannot be replaced," Plekish replied.

"So, no more Slip?" Kash asked.

"Not until you find us more crystals."

"Why do I get the impression that's easier said than done?" Triana asked.

"The crystals have to be able to vibrate at two different frequencies simultaneously," Plekish explained. "They are exceedingly rare."

"That almost seems physically impossible," Kash stated.

"We have to excite them to do so," Plekish explained. "It is not a natural phenomenon."

"How will we know if the crystals can do that?" Calynn asked.

"I have a working theory on that, but nothing proven," Plekish replied. "We found the first deposit merely by accident and have since used up that stockpile. We have been looking for more to continue our work, but as you know... we don't venture off planet much."

"If you have the means to detect them, we will search the cosmos for them," Kash announced. "I'll do whatever it takes to help you, my friend."

"Thank you, my friend," Plekish said with a smile.

"Can we play stones?" Mala asked as she entered the room carrying the game.

"We have some time before dinner," Meesha replied. "We can play if our guests do not mind."

"You guys are too smart for me," Kash conceded. "Count me out."

"I'll be on your team, Kash," Mala said as she sat on his lap at the table.

"I'm afraid the game will have to wait," Calynn said as she looked at Kash. "Aja just sent me a message, Boss. She's been trying to get in touch with you."

"I haven't checked my messages since we arrived," Kash admitted. "What's so important it can't wait?"

"The son of a mining oligarch has gone missing."

"So."

"It's apparently her cousin."

"Oh... well that changes..."

"And the reward for his safe return is two billion credits," Calynn interrupted.

"Oh, my," Triana stuttered.

"And we're interested in doing this?" Kash asked.

"It's a lot of credits, and we kinda owe her for the support she sent us," Calynn replied.

"Getting you off planet and on a task could be good for you, too," Triana added. "I'm no doctor, but I think it would help."

"I agree," Meesha said with a kind smile. "But only if you stay in contact with Uva."

"Okay," Kash sighed. "Can we eat dinner first?"

"And play stones?" Mala whined.

"I will inform Rinktee of your impending departure," Plekish stated. "It will take two hourns or so to get everything on your ship put back together."

"I thought you said it was fully functional?" Calynn queried.

"It is," Plekish replied. "We had to gain access to every system to test them, and those components need to be put back into place."

The rest of the evening went by quickly. Darjic won the game of stones. Kash didn't quite understand the game, but it was a strategy game about putting rocks into little bowls. Triana helped Meesha with dinner and then served everyone with a big smile on her face. She was almost always on the move but still finished her meal before most. Calynn was a little fidgety, but Triana was the cure for that, too. It didn't take her long to have Calynn smiling again.

Kash soon found himself back on his ship. He hadn't been on his ship in three weeks, and it almost seemed foreign to him. He started to touch everything like he had to get reacquainted with his Alley Cat. The room where the nerve center is supposed to be has changed some. Kash took a moment to examine the additional equipment. Rinktee wanted to open the area up, but Kash told him the room still had to pass as a nerve center in case they were ever searched. It was safer for Calynn that way.

"If I pretend I'm a ship, will you touch me like that?" Triana asked playfully.

"He is being awful handsy," Calynn added.

"Do you think the metal turns him on?" Triana continued. "Do I need metal underwear?"

"Are you two done?" Kash laughed.

"Just waiting on you, Boss," Calynn stated.

"What's our destination?"

"Are we taking Triana home first?"

"I can stay," Triana replied quickly. "I mean... I'd like to stay. I can still be helpful."

"Then it's the Allio System," Calynn replied.

"ETA?" Kash asked.

"Four days, six hourns," Calynn answered.

"Let's get moving then."

The trio hung out in the cockpit as Calynn took them out. Once they were out of Thracia's atmosphere, Calynn engaged the HLD.

"My new interface feels... weird," Calynn stated as she checked her instruments.

"Did you break the old one?"

"No... but they upgraded it anyway."

"I can't believe we're going on a mission together," Triana said gleefully while clapping really fast.

"Easy, Thumper," Kash said mockingly. "Save your energy."

"Thumper?" Triana questioned.

"I think that was a remark based on your joyful clapping," Calynn stated.

"That's rude," Triana whined.

Kash didn't bother to respond. He turned and headed towards his quarters.

"Hey, mister," Triana said as she grabbed his hand. "Where are you going?"

"To bed... I like to be well rested for a mission."

"Can I come?"

"You're sweet-smelling skin is always..."

Triana didn't wait for him to finish. She rushed past him while pulling off her shirt and was working on undoing her pants as she turned the corner through the doorway.

"Do you think she knows I meant to actually get some rest?" Kash asked.

"Nope... I bet you find her naked with her ass in the air."

"My therapist is going be so pissed at me," Kash relented as he headed to his quarters.

Ting Ting Ting Ting

"What the hell was that?" Kash exclaimed as he looked around.

When his eyes fell on Calynn, she had a naughty look and a smirk on her face. She moved her hand over to the console and flicked it with her finger.

Ting

"Naughty girl."

Kash and Calynn will return.

Milton Keynes UK
Ingram Content Group UK Ltd.
UKHW042003281024
450365UK00003B/146